JN255857

Thoreau in the 21st Century
Perspectives from Japan

Edited by Masaki Horiuchi

The Thoreau Society of Japan

KINSEIDO
Tokyo
2017

This book was produced by the Thoreau Society of Japan.

Editor

Masaki Horiuchi

Associate Editors

Izumi Ogura
Michiko Ono
Yoshio Takanashi
Mikako Takeuchi
Mikayo Sakuma
Namie Ozawa

Thoreau in the 21st Century
Perspectives from Japan

Copyright 2017 The Thoreau Society of Japan

Kinseido Publishing Co., Ltd.
Tokyo, JAPAN

ISBN978-4-7647-1173-0

Introduction

The present volume, *Thoreau in the 21st Century: Perspectives from Japan*, was produced by the Thoreau Society of Japan to celebrate the bicentenary of Thoreau's birth. The Thoreau Society of Japan has a history of more than fifty years and has been actively functioning as a place of exchange between not only Japanese Thoreauvians but also many scholars interested in Emerson, Transcendentalism, and nineteenth-century American literature in general. It has already published several volumes of academic essays on Thoreau and his contemporaries. The question we faced in planning this book was, therefore, about its key concept—where would be the significance of producing yet another book on Thoreau, especially in English?

The title of this volume certainly embodies two concepts: the twenty-first century and sending messages from Japan. The former, I believe, does not sound very unusual because reading Thoreau or Emerson has always meant thinking about the present world and the ways of living in it. This collection of new essays is an attempt to confirm this meaning of reading Thoreau or Emerson. The world we live in has become increasingly confused and chaotic since 9/11, the symbolic starting point of the twenty-first century. Today our world is replete with many problems that could render us pessimistic about its future, such as environmental devastation, terrorism, international conflicts, refugee issues, and widening of income disparities. I hardly need to say that literary studies should not be restricted to a narrow network of specialists. In that case, what can we convey, through the reading of Thoreau or Emerson, to the contemporary world?—Answering this question is the first task of this volume.

The second concept—sending our messages from the perspectives of those who lead an intellectual life in Japan—does not naturally imply uniformity either in the content or the form of expression. The perspectives are not necessarily similar to those of American researchers. If the texts of Thoreau or Emerson hold remarkable universality and applicability, as they surely do, to express how we (living outside the United States) read them is itself an act of proving it. This is where our volume's second task lies. It does not necessarily require contexts of a direct comparison between Japan and the United States.

Our various remarks in this volume might occasionally show some traits unexpectedly revealed due to our lives in Japan. In writing the essays that follow, contributors were not required to explore both of these concepts; while some papers are rendered only by the viewpoint of the contemporary world where, undoubtedly, the United States is the main country of reference; some are written solely from a comparative perspective of Japanese context. It is clear, however, that all the essays are fruits whose nutrients come from the realities of life in Japan.

Dividing the contributed essays into coherent groups posed a difficult problem to the editor. After a troubling period of vacillation I decided on the simple construction that you see here—breaking the volume into two parts: one part on "political perspectives" and another on "philosophical perspectives." Nevertheless, I must hasten to add that the essays as a whole could not be clearly classified in terms of content or perspective: some discussed a political problem with a philosophical scope, and others addressed a philosophical theme urged by a political viewpoint. In fact, such a diversity of works could not be unambiguously divided into the two classifications. Therefore, the binary form of this volume merely reflects an expedient categorization, an almost fruitless attempt to classify a complicated assemblage of contributions.

It has been a long time since many Japanese researchers began to examine the meanings and significances of literary texts from a political perspective in American literary studies, with strong emphasis on history. This general trend, as far as I can ascertain, has reflected the trend of the American academic community and the papers included in the first part more or less show this tendency. Of course, this does not mean that they are mere followers. Rather, it is a clear result of their deep and sincere understanding of the discipline of American literary studies: The contributors have cultivated their perspectives on politics at the core of their thinking. They have each attempted to interpret text in their own way with original ideas.

Shoko Itoh discusses the contemporary significances of "Civil Disobedience," focusing on its correspondence to Solnit's writing on the ground of ecological thought and antinuclear attitude. Takao Yamaguchi employs the perspective of Hofstadter's criticism of "anti-intellectualism" and tries to reevaluate Thoreau by redefining the meaning of his "anti-anti-intellectualism" in the light of the present globalism. Namie Ozawa discerns the process of expanding one's subjectivity toward other nations and cultures in Thoreau's perspective on the Native Americans in *Maine Woods*, attempting to capture the creative way of attitude relevant to us in the present age. Mika Takiguchi, while taking the same topic as Ozawa as a starting point, draws a comparison with the representation of Native Americans by Washington Irving and, through this comparison, considers the problem of a subject's encounter with another race, paying attention to the standardized state of White identity in the nineteenth century. Junko Kanazawa tries to compare Emily Dickinson's attitude toward the fate of John Brown with that of Thoreau. This unusual approach reveals the poet's uniquely positive attitude toward facing the Civil War, which has previously been regarded as rather sluggish. Ayako Takahashi offers an exciting suggestion about how creative Thoreau's stimulation can be in the modern times, closely examining Anne Waldman's absorption of Thoreau's attitude toward political resistance into her poems. Yohei Yamamoto examines the validity of Thoreau's way of resistance in the actual situation of Okinawa, where the conflict with the US base is severely ongoing, and links it to an analysis of an Okinawan novelist and activist Medoruma Shun. Mikayo Sakuma addresses Emerson's choice of publishers, a new perspective in recent Emerson studies that clarifies the political stances of Emerson and others in his circle, thereby suggesting a new way of seeing literary writers. Asako Motooka discusses the starting point of Louisa May Alcott as a fiction writer by exploring the importance of the group network crossing the borders of individuals and, further, connects it to the problem of fandom in the modern world, such as in the Japanese "Otaku."

The papers included in the second part have varied contents addressing the problem of thought. They reflect differences in degree and direction, and many also contain political viewpoints. It would be no wonder that many of us wrote about philosophical topics, given that the texts of Thoreau or Emerson themselves include profoundly philosophical dimensions in the form of discourse-like prose, not fiction. But, at the same time, the second part of this book may possibly show a somewhat different tendency than that of American researchers, because, in Japan, researchers in the field of literary studies, or intellectuals in general who are interested in literature, have been drawn to the problems of Western thought especially after World War II—Marxism, existentialism, structuralism, and French post-modernism of Foucault, Derrida, and Deleuze, to name a few. (This somewhat reflects the compelling craving of Japanese intellectuals for what the Western culture offered us as a frame for viewing the world after World War II.) The introduction of these philosophical writers' works in Japan through translation was, in general, earlier and more detailed than in the United States. To be sure, many researchers who took doctoral degrees in the United States were equipped with the perspectives driving the academic trends there, but it was certainly a natural tendency for Japanese scholars to form their views in the local intellectual climate in Japan, independent of the internal perspectives in the United States. There is, certainly, a strong concern about how to evaluate our own situations with the help of the quintessential American thinkers such as Thoreau and Emerson. These tendencies, I believe, are to be congratulated because it is clear that American literature studies in the global era should not mean thinking like an American citizen. To borrow Emerson's phrase, every scholar across the world should be "a human being thinking."

Mikako Takeuchi critically surveys the impact and influence of Thoreau's political thought on African-Americans in American history and traces the line of Thoreauvian resistance up to the modern age in political philosophy. Maki Sadahiro presents a spirited attempt to render a new interpretation of the problem of friendship in *A Week on the Concord and Merrimack Rivers*, adopting insights from contemporary thinkers such as Derrida and Cavell. Kazuto Ono broadly explores how Thoreau views the universe and, in a comparison with the Japanese concept of heaven, praises it as a way of conceptualizing the world as an expanding whole. Michiko Ono closely examines the deep correspondence between Thoreau's thought and that of Kumagusu Minakata, a great Japanese thinker, focusing on their views of plants, thereby radically widening Thoreau's philosophical scope. Fumiko Takeno examines the problem of sound and music in *The Blithedale Romance* by Nathaniel Hawthorne, comparing it with the texts of John S. Dwight and Thoreau and reevaluating it from a modern perspective with the suggestions of Jaques Attali and John Cage. Atsuko Oda views the Emersonian fluxional use of symbols as something common to an aspect of Hawthorne's expression and emphasizes the importance of language, which generally evades institutional philosophy but is philosophically stimulating as suggested by Richard Poirier. Izumi Ogura also stresses the vital aspect of language in the use of paradox both in Emerson's and Thoreau's texts and focuses on its validity in the twenty-first century. Yoshiko Fujita explores the continuity and dissimilarity between the senses of nature in Thoreau and Muir and considers what kind of view should be essential for us in the modern age. Yoshio Takanashi concisely compares the philosophy of Emerson with the idea of Zen in Daisetsu Suzuki, a great Japanese thinker, and clarifies the similarities and differences between them. Masaki Horiuchi reevaluates the writings of the early Emerson as a whole, exploring the potential relevance of his thought as a usable tool in the twenty-first century.

I hope that this book, as a collection, will give the reader an impression of how diverse and fecund our studies are. At the same time, it might demonstrate how vital the old texts of Thoreau or Emerson are to Japanese researchers across the Pacific, acting as the daily sustenance of their thinking.

Many people were indispensable in producing this book. Especially, I deeply thank those who devotionally supported me as associate editors: Izumi Ogura, Michiko Ono, Yoshio Takanashi, Mikako Takeuchi, Mikayo Sakuma, and Namie Ozawa. Without their studious care and secure responsiveness, I could not have made this project possible at all. I also thank the Thoreau Society of Japan for its emotional and financial support.

Masaki Horiuchi

Contents

Part II Philosophical Perspectives

Part I

★★★

Political Perspectives

"Civil Disobedience" in the Nuclear Age: Thoreau and Solnit's "Journey into the Hidden Wars of the American West"

Shoko Itoh

> It is this new, horrible sublime that Richard Misrach pursued with such brilliance and dedication, and that made his pictures so important for my own journey into the wars of the American landscape. . . . Imagine that Thoreau wrote *Walden* and "Civil Disobedience" as one book, so you had to understand solitary rapture and political confrontation in practically the same breath. (Rebecca Solnit, *Savage Dreams: A Journey Into the Hidden Wars of the American West* 46)

Introduction

The epigraph above is a quote from Rebecca Solnit's *Savage Dreams: A Journey Into the Hidden Wars of the American West* published in 1994. "Savage" has a double significance. The first meaning relates to Major Jim Savage, the discoverer of Yosemite Valley who worked to help the natives on the land, and relates to a sympathetic attitude toward them. The second meaning of the word "savage" implies "being savage" to "the savage" people in order to realize the Anglo-American dream of creating a "pristine" National Park. The dualism of dreams is embodied in the contrast between the "Half Dome" by two photographers, its magnificence highlighting this picturesque photograph by Ansel Adams (picture 1), and the "Half Dome" featured in another famous photograph of Yosemite (picture 2) by Richard Misrach. Misrach's photo, with its dead trees in the foreground and phantom-like rendering of the Half Dome in the background, is awe-inspiring. This awe is noticeable with regard to the journey into the "hidden wars," as in the Solnit subtitle, that occurs in relation to typical American landscapes, such as Yosemite National Park and Nevada Test Site. A parallel reading of this experience is to be found in *Walden* and "Civil Disobedience," as remarked later in the sources of the book. In other words, the impact of Misrach's picture contains the dualism inherent in

Thoreau's two representative literary works, which are not simply in binary opposition to each other, but rather constitute the two sides of a coin that were written in historical sequence and were fused into one.

Ansel Adams, *Monolith, the Face of Half Dome at Yosemite Half Dome* (1927)
https://jp.pinterest.com/juanngospodarou/ansel-adams/

Richard Misrach, *Burnt Forest and Half Dome, Yosemite* (1988).
Collection of Art Institute of Chicago. http://www.artic.edu/aic/collections/artwork/191465

I "Civil Disobedience" and the Antinuclear Movement

Sharply tracing Thoreau's popularity in his transition through the decades from the 1920s through the 1960s, Michael Meyer, in his *Several More Lives to Live: Thoreau's Political Reputation in America*, describes this transition as follows:

After the conservative politics of the 1950s came the deluge. Nearly one

> hundred years after Appomattox, the United States was again at war with itself. For a number of Americans in the 1960s, a travesty of American Principles rather than a preservation of those principles, created an intellectual and social milieu geared for the writings of H. D. Thoreau. (Meyer 151)

According to Meyer, "Civil Disobedience," along with the original source of environmental thought in *Walden*, became a bible for the anti-Vietnam War movement during the 1960s; Robert Stowell too advocated in the protest movements against nuclear-related facilities in different state territories and has reemerged from the anti-Iraq War movement to regain popularity amongst the American public movement.

In her book, Solnit refers to the emergence of the Nevada Test Site, which lies at so short a distance as 150 miles from Yosemite National Park, as "the country's bipolar of Eden and Armageddon." She has repeatedly broken into the restricted area at the Test Site, thereby spreading the protest movement and advocating civil disobedience in order to succeed to Thoreau's thought. She says, "There is a nice symmetry between Thoreau's night in Concord jail in 1846 and the activity around the Nevada Test Site. By refusing to pay taxes, Thoreau was protesting the US's war on Mexico, which was a war for land" (Solnit 11). She has also written concerning how "Civil Disobedience" has supported her activity as in: "Ceremony is a conversation between the participants and their gods that can allow witnesses or shun them. Too, civil disobedience—c.d., in activist slang—asserts that we *are* the public, and that as the public we will be across in history, not an audience to it" (69).

Her point of view, which, as the subtitle indicates, is that hidden wars are taking place in the American West, has gained equal support from five different recent studies on the Atomic West and Nuclear Landscape.

Firstly, two books on Hanford studies by scholars of history from University of Washington: *The Atomic West: Region and Nation, 1942–1992* and *Atomic Frontier Days: Hanford and the American West* have given the revelation of nuclear contamination in western cities. Secondly, *Nuclear Landscapes* (1991), a photo collection of nuclear ruins such as Trinity and Nevada Test Site by Peter Goin who has established the term "Nuclear Landscape" as well as *American Ground Zero: The Secret Nuclear War* (1993), another photo collection by Carole Gallagher depicting the reality of health hazard due to fallout and soil contamination in Nevada Test Site have captured this place literally a place of secret nuclear war. Thirdly, a geographical research tracing the reality of nuclear contamination and land spoilage in southwestern uranium mines as well as in nuclear-related facilities, *The Tainted Desert: Environmental Ruin in the American West* (1998) by Valerie Kuletz is a necessary study in this field.

Thoreau considered the West to be a land of liberty entirely unconnected with slavery. It was in this region that a collection of hard pastoral masterworks by John Muir and Edward Abbey, among other successors to Thoreau, were authored in a scenic spot that is crowded with national parks. Mary Austin's *The Land of Little Rain*, a book for locating ecology in the desert, was also a product of this place, in addition to many others. The transformation of this region into an atomic frontier reflects national ignorance of environmental significance of the land and the harsh reality of the nation's nuclear policy and global nuclear proliferation, while "Civil Disobedience" is highlighted as a doctrine for the antinuclear movement, not only in this place but in the neighborhoods of various other nuclear plants. In this 72nd year of the post-war era, we should measure the impact of the paper written by Thoreau in 1848, in the middle of "manifest destiny."

II *Walden* as a Multicultural Text

Two major frameworks supporting Thoreau's *Walden* and "Civil Disobedience" have apparently contradictory characteristics, as Solnit remarks in the epigraph above. However, Solnit's theme also resides in the fact that the magnificent beauty of Yosemite, which John Muir, under the influence of Thoreau, had an affection for, is a multi-structural landscape that appears superficially in the amazing wild nature of the Half Dome, while also encompassing the history of exclusion by arms of native tribes who had occupied the land for a long time. Furthermore, in their fundamentals, these two works have common characteristics that are essential to Thoreau. Elise Lemire's *Black Walden: Slavery and Its Aftermath in Concord, Massachusetts* is an epoch-making study in *Walden* especially in the 21st century. Lemire has investigated the history of slavery around Concord during the age when "slavery was legal in Massachusetts," from the establishment of Concord village in 1635 to Independence of America, in order to carefully unlock pieces of data associated with the historical roots of major African-American former slaves and their lives after emancipation. The entrance to Walden Woods stood near a place that was populated by those who left their former masters after emancipation, seeking their independent lives. This was also a place that, since the 18th century, had been inhabited by town outsiders who settled there by squatting. In such circumstances, the word "squat" was used intentionally to reflect Thoreau's usage of the same word: he willingly identified himself as "a squatter" rather than a tenant on Emerson's land.

Lemire's book could be called a "slave story," covering as it does the pre-*Walden* history from 1635 through 1820, while Thoreau's *Walden* plays the role of a "post-slave-story." On the second page of Chapter 14 of *Walden*: "Former Inhabitants; and Winter Visitors," which Thoreau started with the lines "East of my bean-field, across the road, lived Cato Ingraham, slave of Duncan Ingraham" (Thoreau 257) is a story of an African-American at play in *Walden* before Thoreau's settlement there, which is, accordingly, an extension of pre-*Walden* history. Thus, we could construe Thoreau's settlement in Walden as bearing a significance in relaying the efforts of former slaves to make their own living in this place, in order to successfully accomplish independence as human beings. According to Randall Conrad's "Realizing Resistance: Thoreau and the First of August 1846," a meeting of thirty abolitionists was held on August 1, 1846 at the pond-side house. This meeting took place one week after Thoreau's imprisonment in Middlesex County Prison, and in one year and a month after the meeting he left the pond. Thoreau's three conducts, going to prison, the abolitionist meeting, and returning to town illuminate Thoreau's aim in leaving Walden. He really found another life to live.

What makes this assumption possible is the drawing in which the locations of the bean-field and former-slaves' residences are illustrated. The process of reaching this assumption was specifically described in my paper "The Black Walden and Thoreau's August 1st" and here I will simply rehearse the conclusion: in the first week of June 1845, prior to his settlement, Thoreau commenced heavy work to reclaim a bushy hill for cultivation as a bean-field. While exploring the woodland and turning up soil, he encountered some hollow caverns, seemingly habitation sites, including former kitchens and wells, which showed him the hidden history of the land. It was Thoreau's reclamation works that uncovered the real meaning of America, and his cultivation of beans there meant to him a subsistence on agriculture that had not been accomplished by native Americans, former-slaves, or Concord farmers.

III "Civil Disobedience," Mystery of the Text and the Title

Leaving Walden, Thoreau gave a lecture entitled "On the Relation of the Individual to the State" at Concord Lyceum on January 29, 1848, regarding his one-night experience inside the jail on July (24, though uncertain), 1846. This lecture was later published as the well-known "Resistance to Civil Government" in the May 14, 1849 issue of *Aesthetic Papers* (189–211), which was commenced by Elizabeth Peabody and ended after the No. 1 issue. Peabody had flourished as both a magazine editor and a critic, and created her long-cherished magazine that included Hawthorne's "Main Street," Emerson's "War," and others in Boston. Peabody was someone with an understanding of "Transcendentalism," according to Diane B. Jones. Furthermore, Lawrence Rosenwald, in his article in the *Historical Companion to Thoreau*, specifically discusses the importance of the emergence of the word "resistance" in Thoreau's paper title (195). When the paper was posthumously published in *A Yankee in Canada* in 1866 from Tickner & Fields, on pages 123–51, it was entitled "Civil Disobedience," though no editor's name for this edition nor any reference in the text of Harding's variorum edition can be found. However, Glick, who compiled the paper in the Princeton Edition of *Reform Papers* by using the text and title of the 1849 version, noted in his "Textual Introduction" that "the *Yankee* version found variants counting thirteen" and "an altered title could be possibly sought for by Thoreau before he was dying" (314, 318). The phrase "civil disobedience" is absent in the original text of the 1849 version nor is it found in any of Thoreau's texts, although "civil" and "disobedience" are used twice and three times respectively at significant points in the paper, and these two words create a paradoxical idiom that implies war and peace, which is a specific characteristic of Thoreau.

It is clear from these five points and the change of the title that Thoreau's focus was on the relationship between the civil and the government, and that the title of the version by Tickner & Fields, which was of great benefit in the acknowledgement and propagation of Thoreau's thought. "Civil Disobedience" became a legal term for "conscientious objection" and was often used later in the independence movements of colonies and civil rights movements of the 20th century. In Japan, Hiromi Ichikawa's *Heiekikyohi no Shiso* [*The Philosophy of Civil Disobedience*] briefly summarizes how, according to Thoreau, "Civil Disobedience" is one attempt to realize justice and a type of pronounced political participation act insofar as it is an act of protest against and accusation and rectification of existing "injustice" (21). "Civil" has four dictionary entries (which are "a citizen with a law-abiding spirit"; "not military"; "polite and morally right"; and "of public official"), wherein the meaning of "not military" is intensified in Thoreau's paper that deals with injustice. With the statement "If the injustice is part of the necessary friction of the machine of government, let it go . . . but if it is of such a nature that it requires you to be the agent of injustice to another, then, I say, break the law." (*Reform Papers* 73) Thoreau prompted an action when facing an unjust law by saying that, in the case of an unjust law, "if execution of the law would harm others, then the law should be broken," which has been modified as "nonviolent direct action" and used by Solnit and other environmental activists.

IV Two Major Frameworks of "Civil Disobedience"—Philosophy of Neighbor and Ecological Thought

"Civil Disobedience" has two significant ideological frameworks. First, it calls for the novel "Philosophy of Neighbor" in modern America, which supported the manifest destiny, based on the idea of politics, of selected people or white Americans. At night in July 1846, Thoreau viewed the town of Concord from his jail window. The town was divided from him by the wall and, as an outsider, outside of the institution, he realized the hypocritical essence of the Concord community. To them, a neighbor was a neighbor within the community they belonged to, a Concord resident, or an American, "his neighbor, your neighbor." Thoreau's distinctive use of the words "our neighbor," however, meant a neighbor of any kind, including minorities, such as immigrant Americans, black and native Americans, and Mexican victims of American invasion. As discussed in *Yomigaeru Soro* [*Sauntering to the Inner Wilderness*] by Shoko Itoh (236–41), the use of the word "neighbor(s)"—repeated twenty times in the text—pursued the concept of neighbor espoused in the "Parable of the Good Samaritan," a didactic story told by Jesus and depicted exclusively in Luke (10: 30–36). In this respect, it would be no exaggeration to say that "Civil Disobedience" was indeed an article about neighbors, in which Thoreau demonstrated that there were two kinds of neighbors, by means of his six repetitions of the word "neighbor(s)" in Section 7 and 8, all used in distinctive forms, that is to say some preceded with the pronouns "his" or "your," vs. others without.

Thoreau's concept of neighbor further appeared in the magnified and economic form of "world citizen" in the "Sounds" chapter of *Walden*. The "world citizen" therein is an indication of the epiphany that the formation of global consumers, owing to the distribution of goods made available by railways, could alter the quality of citizen beyond one town or one nation into the class of economic "world citizen," wherein people would profit from obtaining products from the backyard of the globe as commercial goods. Thoreau's cross-regional ethical norm was further related in "Civil Disobedience," and in fact forms the final section thereof.

> I please myself with imagining a State at least which can afford to be just to all men, and to treat the individual with respect as a neighbor; which even would not think it inconsistent with its own repose, if a few were to live aloof from it, not meddling with it, nor embraced by it, who fulfilled all the duties of neighbors and fellow-men. A State which bore this kind of fruit, and suffered it to drop off as fast as it ripened, would prepare the way for a still more perfect and glorious State, which also I have imagined, but not yet anywhere seen. (*Reform Papers* 89–90)

Shown here is the second framework, which is an ecological idea or idea that nature and society are fundamentally unified, by comparing justice to a seed that will bear fruit without fail. Thoreau once again repeats the word "neighbor(s)" without pronouns and ends with a botanical statement: "A State which bore this kind of fruit, and suffered it to drop off as fast as it ripened, would prepare the way for a still more perfect and glorious State." This is a sincere conclusion corresponding to a great faith in a seed in *Faith in a Seed.* A seed is, for Thoreau, a good beginning and, as such, faith in the seed overlaps with his expectation that the construction of a state composed of such neighbors will be accomplished. In addition, "If a plant cannot live according to its nature, it dies; and so a man" indicates an ecological view of a fundamentally unified society and nature.

This idea, which is extremely characteristic of Thoreau, is also expressed in "Succession of Forest Trees," an essay on natural history that forms part of *Faith in a Seed*, as follows:

> Convince me that you have a seed there, and I am prepared to expect wonders. I shall even believe that the millennium is at hand, and that the reign of justice is about to commence, when the Patent Office, or Government, begins to distribute, and the people to plant, the seeds of these

things." (*The Natural History Essays* 91).

The idea of the government as the Patent Office for seed distribution depicts the government as being set within the mechanism and not as the machine itself. Accordingly, for Thoreau, neighbors encompass nature, and human beings and all of society, including wild creatures, count as neighbors. This assertion by Thoreau is, as James Findley also comments in more detail, an ecological protest based on "Justice in the Land" (Findley 1–35).

V "Civil Disobedience" in the 20th Century

During the 20th century, the century of wars, "Civil Disobedience" was considered a universal idea that had once been present with mankind in ancient Greece; indeed, studies into the genealogy thereof flourished. Specifically, to give instances of well-known famous speeches by Mahatma Gandhi and Martin Luther King Jr., "An unjust law is itself a species of violence. Arrest for its breach is more so." (Gandhi) were dispatched from prison and their realization of just law, formed in prison, is attributable to Thoreau's thought. There are too many other works to enumerate but just to name a few: Tomoji Abe, *Ryōshin-teki Heieki Kyohi no Shisō* [*The Philosophy Behind Conscientious Objection to Military Service*]; George Woodcock, *Anarchism: A History of Libertarian Ideas and Movements* (1962); Hugo Adam Bedau, *Civil Disobedience in Focus*; and Mary Ellen Snodgrass, *Civil Disobedience: An Encyclopedic History of Dissidence in the United States*. Further, according to *Bloom's Literary Themes: Civil Disobedience* (2010) edited by Harold Bloom, "Civil Disobedience," as a motif in literature as well as a concept, has become a source for the literature of all times and places.

According to the web document of "CD Training," we have increasing nonviolent activities against the nuclear power plants such as the following:

> In the late 1970s mass civil disobedience actions took place at nuclear power plants from Seabrook, New Hampshire to the Diablo Canyon reactor in California and most states in between in this country and in other countries around the world. In 1982, 1,750 people were arrested at the U.N. missions of the five major nuclear powers. Mass actions took place at the Livermore Laboratories in California and SAC bases in the midwest. In the late 80s a series of actions took place at the Nevada test site. International

disarmament actions changed world opinion about nuclear weapons.
(http://www.actupny.org/documents/CDdocuments/HistoryNV.html)

In these circumstances, the most noticeable and historically prominent echo of Thoreau is the passage from Mario Savio's historical antiwar speech at Berkeley during the anti-Vietnam War movement, in which he said: "There's a time when the operation of the machine [government] becomes so odious, makes you so sick at heart, that you can't take part! You can't even passively take part! And you've got to put your bodies upon the gears and upon the wheels . . . upon the levers, upon all the apparatus, and you've got to make it stop!" The tradition of employing the image of "wicked machine" for government, as referred to by Thoreau, has been succeeded by such works as Edward Abbey's *The Monkey Wrench Gang* and women's environmental justice literature that describes their resistance, at the risk of their lives, by breaking into the restricted area in Nevada Test Site in the 21st century.

VI Women Environmental Literature and "Civil Disobedience"

The literature of the protest against the Nevada Test Site is represented by writers from California, Nevada, and Utah, including Terry T. Williams, Solnit as discussed in Itoh ("Literature" 97–98). The Nevada Test Site covers an area of 1,350 square miles, which is larger than Rhode Island, in the Great Basin zone. It is surrounded by mountains and was reserved for military use by the US Air Force in 1951. The author that took the initiative of coupling the Test Site literature with "Civil Disobedience" was, as well known, Williams, in the epilogue "The Clan of One-Breasted Women" in *Refuge: An Unnatural History of Family and Place* in 1991. The importance of the epilogue has been pointed out by virtue of the plenitude of previous studies. However, it should be particularly noted here that Williams expressed deep sympathy for Hibakusha (Atomic Bomb survivors) in "Downwinder in Hiroshima" in *The Nation* immediately after her return home from a visit to Hiroshima by saying "Other private details are shared and I think about how each individual story is carried like a wound, like a talisman, how much we need to hear the truth of one another's lives" (Williams 661).

In *Savage Dreams*, Solnit struggles together with Shoshone women who have claimed ownership of all the land around the test site and further discusses it in the context of American and world history. In Part One, regarding the protest activity in joint struggle with the local people, "Civil Disobedience" is replaced with "nonviolent direct action" from the outset of the book, and she describes the relationship between Thoreau and her as having "a nice symmetry" (9). She refers to the long history of "Civil Disobedience" as practiced by many religious communities and civil rights activists and also makes reference to some cases that have been driven to collapse or a huge number of arrests, as well as success cases in Eastern Europe. While regarding the government as opposed to "civil disobedience," she states the flexible opinion that "the government is not a finished work, and it must constantly be re-created" (10).

In the second half, Part Two, she discusses Thoreau's works further, including "Walking," and traces the landscape of Yosemite National Park and its establishment as well as the history of Miwok ostracism, thereby repeatedly pointing out that the uninhabited wild landscape of the national park and the nuclear landscape are virtually historically sequential. As such, racism, the landscape in the West, and nuclear history are discussed analytically and in a structure that employs a retrograde format from present to past with the words "I came to Test Site four springs in a row . . . , the place began to make sense to me" (20) used to describe the deepening intrusion into the restricted area and thus to trace the process of the struggle that led her to becoming a full-fledged female combatant.

Solnit, an eco-activist from California, thinks the meaning of the activity in that place should not be confined domestically and says, "However foolish and futile this antinuclear activism seemed close up, at a distance it commanded respect" (25). The influence of the movement worldwide is noted in connection with the action against the underground nuclear test in Kazakhstan by a local poet Olzahas Suleimenov on February 12, 1989, when he read aloud an anti-nuclear testing statement rather than a poem in order to call for a meeting. Furthermore, regarding "Walking," she considers the motion and emotion of the scientists at the Trinity test in 1945 in her statement: "Thoreau displays for us both ways of walking, for Utopia and for Arcadia. Majority of the physicists took the former forward to nuclear weapons, while Szilard, for example, going for the latter became after the war a biologist and a peace activist" (134). She shows us that Thoreau advises us Arcadian walking to some "Holy Land," and walking should be an art of sauntering: "If you are ready to leave father and mother, and brother and sister, and wife and child and friends, and never see them again—if you have paid your debts, and made your will, and settled all your affairs, and are a free man—then you are ready for a walk" (*The Natural History Essays* 94). Thus, walking for Thoreau is a kind of meditative pilgrimage for idealized land when he or she is absolutely free.

In her discussion of "global justice," Solnit in *A Paradise Built in Hell* is directed toward a community beyond the relationship between individuals and nation. The idea of Utopia invoked by victims in such an emergency situation as a nuclear power plant disaster could be construed as an appeal to build a community beyond a nation. This may be close to the concept of an ideal nation that Thoreau reached in "Civil Disobedience." *Savage Dreams* further states explicitly that the struggle described therein is a cross-border philosophical movement in order to survive nuclear power and disaster, and uniquely overviews the internal relationship between the national park and the nuclear test site, which are inherent to the landscape of the American West. *Savage Dreams* could be said to be unparalleled as environmental literature, as it focuses on reviving and magnifying the literary works of Thoreau from the nuclear age back in the 1940s, through the present days.

Works Cited

Bedau, Hugo Adam. *Civil Disobedience in Focus*. New York: Routledge, 1991. Print.

Conrad, Randall. "Realizing Resistance: Thoreau and the First of August 1846," *Concord Saunterer* 12/13 (2004/2005): 165–94. Print.

Findlay, John. *Atomic Frontier Days: Hanford and the American West*. Seattle: U of Washington P, 2011. Print.

——. ed. *The Atomic West: Region and Nation, 1942–1992*. Seattle: U of Washington P, 1998. Print.

Findley, James. "Justice in the Land: Ecological Protest in Henry David Thoreau's Antislavery Essays." *The Concord Saunterer* 21, 2013: 1–35. Print.

Ichikawa, Hiromi. *Heiekikyohi no Shiso*. [*Philosophy of Civil Disobedience*] Tokyo: Akashi-Shoten, 1969. Print.

Itoh, Shoko. "*Black Walden* to Soro no Hachigatu 1nichi" ["*Black Walden* and August 1st of Thoreau"]. *Henry David Thoreau to Amerika Seishin: Amerika Bungaku no Genryu wo Motomete* [*Henry David Thoreau and the American Spirit: In Search of the Origin of American Literature*] Ed. The Thoreau Society of Japan. (Tokyo: Kinseido, 2012): 185–202. Print.

——. "Kaku no Basho no Bungaku" ["Literature of Nuclear Places"]. *Kaku to Saigai no Hyoushou* [*Representing Natural and Nuclear Disasters*] eds. Sanae Kumamoto and Asako Nobuoka (Tokyo: Eihosha, 2015): 74–109. Print.

——. *Yomigaeru Soro* [*Sauntering to the Inner Wilderness*] Tokyo: Kashiwashobo, 1998. Print.

Lemire, Elise. *Black Walden: Slavery and Its Aftermath in Concord, Massachusetts*. Philadelphia: U of Pennsylvania P, 2009. Print.

Meyer, Michael. *Several More Lives to Live: Thoreau's Political Reputation in America*. Westport, CT: Greenwood, 1977. Print.

Rosenwald, Lawrence. "The Theory, Practice & Influence of Thoreau's *Civil Disobedience*." Ed. William Cain. *Historical Guide to Henry David Thoreau*. New York: Oxford UP, 2000. Print.

Ryan, Howard. "Critique of Nonviolent Politics: From Mahatma Gandhi to the Anti-Nuclear Movement." 1996. Web. http://www.hartford-hwp.com/archives/27d/002.html. 1 Aug. 2015.

Savio, Mario. "Sit-in Address on the Step of Sproal Hall." Web. http://www.americanrhetoric.com/speeches/mariosaviosproulhallsitin.htm. 1 May 2015.

Snodgrass, Mary Ellen. *Civil Disobedience: An Encyclopedic History of Dissidence in the United States*. New York: M E SHARPE, 2008. Print.

Solnit, Rebecca. *Savage Dreams: A Journey Into the Hidden Wars of the American West*. 1994. San Francisco: U of California P, 2014. Print.

——. *A Paradise Built in Hell: The Extraordinary Communities That Arise in Disaster.* New York: Penguin, 2010. Print.

Stowell, Robert. "Modern Civil Disobedience and Thoreau." *Thoreau Society Bulletin* (Fall 1959): 1. Print.

Thoreau, Henry David. *Reform Papers*. Ed. Wendell Glick. Princeton: Princeton UP, 1973. Print.

——. *The Variorum Civil Disobedience*. Ed. Walter Harding. New York: Irvington, 1967. Print.

——. *Walden*. Ed. J. Lyndon Shanley. Princeton: Princeton UP, 1971. Print.

——. *The Natural History Essays*. Ed. Robert Sattelmeyer. Salt Lake City: Peregrine Smith, 1980. Print.

Williams, Terry Tempest. "'A Downwinder in Hiroshima.'" *The Nation* 260.19 (1995): 661–66. Print.

——. *Refuge: An Unnatural History of Family and Place*. New York: Random House, 1991. Print.

Woodcock, George. *Anarchism: A History of Libertarian Ideas and Movements*. New York: U of Toronto P, 1962. Print.

Water Vein of Useful Ignorance:
Henry David Thoreau's Anti-Intellectualism

Takao Yamaguchi

Introduction

The presence of an anti-intellectualistic tendency has often been indicated in the works of Henry David Thoreau. First, Richard Hofstadter mentions Thoreau along with Ralph Waldo Emerson in his book, *Anti-Intellectualism in American Life*, which has determined the historical vein of anti-intellectualism in American life. F. O. Matthiessen, in his *American Renaissance: Art and Expression in the Age of Emerson and Whitman*, points out Thoreau's criticisms of the industrial capitalism and the superficial intellectualism that merely copied the Old World's culture, though he does not use the term "anti-intellectualism." In American literary studies in Japan, Reiko Maekawa summarizes Hofstadter's argument and considers the importance of anti-intellectualism today, in the context of the implications of his research in the modern world (Maekawa 45–68). Takayuki Tatsumi analyzes in detail a "homeopathy" that Michael Moor's *Stupid White Men* criticizes—the then President of the United States George W. Bush's anti-intellectualism—by using Moor's anti-intellectualistic technique. The book also analyzes anti-intellectualist attraction in the United States, tracing anti-intellectualism to Thoreau's writings (Tatsumi 19–57). We cannot talk about traditional anti-intellectualism in the United States without discussing Thoreau.

Hofstadter published his anti-intellectualism study in 1963 when the influence of McCarthyism had subsided. Although McCarthy carried out the anti-communist Red purge supported by religious fundamentalism and patriotism, and anti-elitism was doubtlessly the anti-intellectualism of the age, he did not declare his own view of anti-intellectualism in American life until religious fundamentalism with anti-reason gradually became destabilized. After the publication of his book, the academic concept of anti-intellectualism has rarely been dealt with in depth. Maekawa finds three reasons. First, the history of thought was not a part of mainstream science. Second, with the appearance of the New Left, the framework of intellect and anti-intellect made a radical reassessment of the problem, and a system of the modern intellect was relativized in the steam of multi-culturalism. Third, owing to the influence of growing mass media and expanding globalism, anti-intellectualism became a mental attitude not only of Americans but of all people all over the world. Even if Hofstadter's historical research of thought has not been reconsidered for the above reasons, it continues to be relevant, particularly to understand modern political climates in both the United States and Japan. In this sense, the analysis of the mind of the traditional American anti-intellectual is very relevant today. It is necessary to revisit the idea of anti-intellectualism in the twenty-first century.

In this paper, I examine Thoreau's intellectual legacy by considering how anti-intellectualism works in Thoreau's works. To begin with, Thoreau's "Walking" is analyzed with respect to anti-intellectualism, associated with a new form of thought in the New World in Ralph Waldo Emerson's *Nature* and "The American Scholar," which is known as the "Intellectual Declaration of Independence." And also, Thoreau bitterly criticizes functionalism and pragmatism based on the industrial capitalist economy of the mid-nineteenth century. Certainly, he blamed capitalism for opposing nature in the already civilized United States that promoted the Industrial Revolution, but denounced the dominant ideology of the pragmatist intellectual. Thus, when I consider Thoreau's anti-intellectualism, I will discuss what is "true" intellect rather than what attitudes object to intellect. In the final section of the paper, I explore Thoreau's "true" intellect in an illiterate lumberjack and a "poor weak-headed pauper," and also the water vein of intellect and the migratory shad.

1. Anti-intellectualism as Intellectual Democracy

American anti-intellectualism began with Anne Hutchinson's antinomianism in the seventeenth century, followed by Jonathan Edwards' "Great Awakening" during the eighteenth-century Enlightenment. In the nineteenth century of transcendentalism, anti-intellectualism became mainstream with Emerson's address, "The American Scholar."

> The odds are that the whole question is not worth the poorest thought which the scholar has lost in listening to the controversy. Let him not quit his belief that a popgun is a popgun, though the ancient and honorable of the earth affirm it to be the crack of doom. In silence, in steadiness, in

> severe abstraction, let him hold by himself; . . . . (Emerson 53)

This address, which has been called "Our Intellectual Declaration of Independence" by Oliver Wendell Holmes, holds on to a principle of a unique American culture, while denying the old European culture or intellect. The American Intellectual Declaration of Independence came into existence by defining an intellectual position that refuted that of Europe. At the end of the address, after explaining the importance of believing that "in yourself is the law of all nature, . . . in yourself slumbers the whole of Reason," Emerson continues:

> Mr. President and Gentlemen, this confidence in the unsearched might of man belongs, by all motives, by all prophecy, by all preparation, to the American Scholar. We have listened too long to the courtly muses of Europe. (Emerson 59)

Emerson had already clarified the importance of disassociation with Europe in his *Nature*, which had been published the previous year. In this introduction, which begins with the introspective words, "Our age is retrospective," he calls out to the readers to quit the intellectual subordination to the old culture of Europe and to create a new culture based on American nature:

> Why should not we also enjoy an original relation to the universe? Why should not we have a poetry and philosophy of insight and not of tradition, and a religion by revelation to us, and not the history of theirs? Embosomed for a season in nature, whose floods of life stream around and through us, and invite us, by the powers they supply, to action proportioned to nature, why should we grope among the dry bones of the past, or put the living generation into masquerade out of its faded wardrobe? (Emerson 3)

The Europeans created the "original relation" based on what they saw with their own eyes and their own culture. Emerson stated that Americans could also create a new culture with the power of the rich nature that the Europeans did not have. His *Nature* can be perceived as the Declaration of Anti-intellectualism insisting that anti-intellectualism against Europe makes America culturally independent.

What we must not miss is Emerson likening the power of nature to the stream because when Thoreau narrates intellect or anti-intellect, he always imagines rivers. "Walking," originally a lecture given in 1851 and posthumously published in 1862, clarifies Thoreau's anti-intellectualism. Walking from the East to the West, Thoreau identifies his walking steps with the transatlantic history.

> We go eastward to realize history and study the works of art and literature, retracing the steps of the race; we go westward as into the future, with a spirit of enterprise and adventure. The Atlantic is a Lethean stream, in our passage over which we have had an opportunity to forget the Old World and its institutions. If we do not succeed this time, there is perhaps one more chance for the race left before it arrives on the banks of the Styx; and that is in the Lethe of the Pacific, which is three times as wide. (*Essays* 254–55)

While Emerson wishes to free Americans themselves from their English ancestors' history and religion, and across the Atlantic, hopes to create new values in the new continent of America; Thoreau places the Atlantic as a turning point of intellect. The forgetting river, the Lethe, flows between the eastside of the Atlantic, which is rich in history and arts, and its west side. According to Greek mythology, the Lethe is in the land of the dead and those who drink its water forget everything that happened when they were alive. If we take Thoreau's words, Americans began a new intellect in the new world as an opposing intellect to the aristocratic old world's intellect. Hofstadter illustrates that Americans are disdainful of the past of the civilization on the basis of their anti-intellectualism, presenting America as a country whose people escaped from the past with most of its inhabitants having decided to delete their own past. He positively evaluates their mentality, instead of perceiving their escape from the historical burden as passivity:

> Among other things, the American attitude represented a republican and egalitarian protest against monarchy and aristocracy and the callous exploitation of the people; it represented a rationalistic protest against superstition; an energetic and forward-looking protest against the passivity and pessimism of the Old World; it revealed a dynamic, vital, and originative mentality. (Hofstadter 238)

Thoreau's optimistic viewpoint about obtaining a chance to remove the old world and its institutes from his memory is in contrast with the passivity and pessimism of the old world. According to him, if the Americans should fail in this American continent, they could go eastward to the Pacific and forget the past of the sluggish civilization.

In this part, Thoreau's positivity makes him intuitively identify the necessity of engendering a new culture in America. He sees the Rhine panorama, wherein he imagines the heroic age of the Middle Ages. Some historical remainders such as old cities or ruined castles attract him. Soon after, he goes to see the Mississippi panorama and organically relates the two mighty rivers that represent each continent:

> I saw that this was a Rhine stream of a different kind; that the foundations of castles were yet to be laid, and the famous bridges were yet to be thrown over the stream; and I felt that *this was the heroic age itself*, though we know it not, for the hero is commonly the simplest and obscurest of men. (*Essays* 260)

Immediately after seeing the two panoramas, Thoreau understands the resemblance between the rivers. He sees "the heroic age" of the Middle Ages in the Rhine panorama, and that of the present or future ages in the Mississippi. Thoreau, whose imagination covers the Atlantic and the continents, while reaching the Middle Ages, activates his creative intellect temporally and spatially. As the Atlantic lies as an ocean trench of the turning point of intellectual attitude between the old world and the new one, it appears that civilization and history are made by the rivers flowing through the continents. Thoreau supposes the rivers are the sources of new intellect like the seas.

Thoreau is positive about the potential of the American nature creating new intellect. According to him, if the moon in America is larger than in Europe, the sun too is bigger and the American stars are shinier, symbolizing the height to which American inhabitants' philosophy and poetry and religion grow up. He also closely associates the rich nature of soil with the intellectual activities of those who live there. For example, "our thoughts will be clearer, fresher and more ethereal, as our sky—our understanding more comprehensive and broader, like our plains—our intellect generally on a grander scale, like our thunder and lightning, our rivers and mountains and forests,—and our hearts shall even correspond in breadth and depth and grandeur to our inland seas" (*Essays* 258–59). Importantly, Thoreau supposes here that the anti-intellect against the old world's traditional intellect is guaranteed by the geological and meteorological condition of American vast nature. If European intellect tends to shut itself up in books, Thoreau's intellect is open and dynamic, backed by rich nature. As he says "why was America discovered?" (*Essays* 259), this difference between Europe and America is not geographical accidents but historical necessity ordained in America.

In Thoreau's imagination, nature, particularly the rivers, are sources of intellect and cultures of human beings. In fact, according to him, similar to how the great cultures have developed historically on the riverside, a great culture could be born along the rivers in the new American continent. Similar to how the many mythologies had developed by the global great rivers such as the Ganges, the Niles, and the Rhine, American mythologies could develop by the American great rivers such as the Amazon, the Plate, the Orinoco, the St. Lawrence, and the Mississippi. Thoreau says, "Perchance, when, in the course of ages, American liberty has become a fiction of the past—as it is to some extent a fiction of the present—the poets of the world will be inspired by American mythology" (*Essays* 267).

Thoreau insists that we free ourselves from the European old culture and create a new American culture from nature because Thoreau's "true" intellect is based on nature. As a result, Thoreau is compelled to adopt a pose of anti-intellect and to practice "true" intellect.

2. Anti-intellectualism as Industrial Capitalist Pragmatism

The anti-intellectualism against the traditional European intellect is not Thoreau's only intellectual attitude. His best achievement in his works is consistent criticism of the modern business. When the United States rapidly accomplished modernization and industrialization, the capitalists and scientific experts whose priority was economical profit pursued functionalist thought. This businesspeople's intellectual attitude is the anti-intellectualism of the modern industrial capitalistic economy. In fact, Hofstadter says in his book, "The main reason for stressing anti-intellectualism in business is . . . simply that business is the most powerful and pervasive interest in American life" (Hofstadter 237). Thoreau's criticism of business can be called "anti-anti-intellectualism." A trader is clearly described as an anti-intellectualist in the "Reading" chapter of *Walden*.

> When the illiterate and perhaps scornful trader has earned by enterprise and industry his coveted leisure and independence, and is admitted to the circles of wealth and fashion, he turns inevitably at last to those still higher but yet inaccessible circles of intellect and genius, and is sensible only of the imperfection of his culture and the vanity and insufficiency of all his riches, and further proves his good sense by the pains which he takes to secure for his children that intellectual culture whose want he so keenly feels; and thus it is that he becomes the founder of a family. (*Henry David Thoreau* 405; hereafter abbreviated as *HDT*)

Thoreau ridicules the trader sarcastically and criticizes the inconsistency in the act of the illiterate and scornful trader approaching a circle of intellects and focuses on the insincerity with which the pragmatic anti-intellectualist trader pursues intellect, based on a superficial motivation. However, this sarcasm makes us feel disappointed because the traditional intellect acquired by the success of his business is brought to his children, and the process reproduces superficial intellectualism. Hofstadter calls the intellectual succession "mugwump culture" (Hofstadter 400) and clarifies the intellectual and cultural character of the class of gentlemen. After the power of the aristocratic class who led the American democracy, such as the Puritan ministers and Founding Fathers, had weakened; the gentlemanly class who was wealthy in culture but poor in power and influence began to emerge:

> What was left was a gentlemanly class with considerable wealth, leisure, and culture, but with relatively little power or influence. This class was the public and the patron of serious writing and of cultural institutions. Its members read the books that were written by the standard American writers, subscribed to the old highbrow magazines, supported libraries and museums, and sent their sons to the old fashioned liberal-arts colleges to study the classical curriculum. (Hofstadter 400)

Although the mind of the mugwump inherits high will and austerity from the Puritans and intellectual involvement and civil interest from Founding Fathers, it is never associated with real-world experiences and gradually loses its power. The affected manner is a problem of the culture created by English intellectualist successors. Introducing George Santayana's comment that they "cared more that intellect be respectable than that it be creative" and Gilbert

Keith Chesterton's comment that "they showed more pride in the possession of intellect than joy in the use of it," Hofstadter says: "for them tradition was not so much a source of strength or a point of departure as a fetish" (Hofstadter 402). How then do we learn a "true" intellect? Saying: "Most men have learned to read to serve a paltry convenience, as they have learned to cipher in order to keep accounts and not be cheated in trade" (*HDT* 406), Thoreau rejects pragmatist intellectual skills necessary in marketplaces, and sees "reading as a noble intellectual exercise" (*HDT* 406). Interestingly, he offers a constructive suggestion that a whole society should practice "a noble intellectual exercise." The inhabitants in the village of Concord should think about how they should strengthen their culture than boast rapid progress there. Thoreau proposes to build an unusual school for adults:

> We have a comparatively decent system of common schools, schools for infants only; but excepting the half-starved Lyceum in the winter, and latterly the puny beginning of a library suggested by the state, no school for ourselves. We spend more on almost any article of bodily aliment or ailment than on our mental aliment. It is time that we had uncommon schools, that we did not leave off our education when we begin to be men and women. It is time that villages were universities, and their elder inhabitants the fellows of universities, with leisure—if they are indeed so well off—to pursue liberal studies the rest of their lives. (*HDT* 409)

Thoreau's opposing attitude to European aristocrats is apparent here. Although he evaluates the deeds once performed by European aristocrats, he differentiates it from his proposal. Thoreau's goal to reach is to have not an old type of school where intellect and knowledge is exclusively given to the privileged, but a new school for ordinary people who have been unable to access education. Although the proposal cannot be realized due to its utopian plan, what Thoreau would like to do is to engage in the democratic distribution of intellect that is peculiar to the United States and that which Tocqueville noted. According to Maekawa, Tocqueville's average Americans were exemplary citizens who wanted knowledge, participated in a volunteer activity, and learned a jurist mind through a jury system. As a result, equalization of intellect and knowledge became more advanced than Europe, though there were little prominent intellects in the United States (Maekawa 57). Thoreau's suggestion is part of the intellectual democracy in the United States.

Thoreau's passion to try to improve the educational environment was shared with those who had a different motivation at the time. This was the lyceum movement, in which Thoreau was involved. According to Jeffrey S. Cramer's annotations of Thoreau's *Essays*, the lyceum movement itself was originally launched to promote general adults' education through lectures in Millbury, Massachusetts, in 1826. In 1829, modelled after the Society for the Diffusion of Useful Knowledge in London, the Boston Society for Diffusion of Useful Knowledge was founded to support the lyceum movement (*Essays* 272). By 1834, the American lyceums had rapidly multiplied to reach 3,000. The foundational purpose of the Boston Society for Diffusion of Useful Knowledge oddly overlaps with Thoreau's purpose for school:

> From infancy to the age of seventeen, the means provided in this city by public munificence and private enterprise, are ample. From seventeen to the age when young men enter on the more active and responsible duties of their several stations, sufficient opportunity does not appear to be afforded for mental and moral cultivation. At this period of life, when the mind is active and the passions urgent, and when the invitations to profitless amusements are strongest and most numerous, it is desirable that means should be provided for furnishing at a cheap rate, and in an inviting form, such useful information as will not only add to the general intelligence of the young men referred to, but at the same time will prepare them to engage more understandingly, with a deeper interest, and with better prospect of success, in the pursuits to which their lives are to be devoted. (Russell 176)

The society's recognition that adults do not have opportunities to learn and need to be provided places where knowledge is offered is consentient with Thoreau's. However, Thoreau rejects the proposition because he knows the value of providing useful knowledge to society. In fact, the final part of the foundation purpose states, "It is proposed that the first courses of Lectures should be given to those who are engaged in Trade and Commerce; and that they should include the subjects of Universal Geography and Statistics, and of the Moral, Natural, Political, and Legal Sciences, so far as they may be connected with commercial transactions" (Russell 176). Thoreau bitterly criticizes society's anti-intellectualism in his "Walking":

> We have heard of a Society for the Diffusion of Useful Knowledge. It is

> said that Knowledge is power, and the like. Methinks there is equal need of a Society for the Diffusion of Useful Ignorance, what we will call Beautiful Knowledge, a knowledge useful in a higher sense: for what is most of our boasted so-called knowledge but a conceit that we know something, which robs us of the advantage of our actual ignorance? What we call knowledge is often our positive ignorance; ignorance our negative knowledge. (*Essays* 272)

Of Thoreau's numerous paradoxes, this one is the most ironical because useful knowledge is said to be less useful than useful ignorance. According to Thoreau, there is nothing more useful than to be self-conceited regarding knowing well enough (*Essays* 272). Knowing what one doesn't know is what Thoreau evaluates as positive usefulness of ignorance.

3. Thoreau's Anti-/Intellectualism: "Opening New Channel of Thought"

Thoreau has shown his anti-intellectual attitude toward European traditional intellect and his anti-anti-intellectualism toward modern industrialization and pragmatic anti-intellectualism. Although what he criticizes is clear, understanding what "true" intellect is in his view rather ambiguous. How does Thoreau think about "true" intellect? It is the lumberjack and the simple-minded pauper who Thoreau considers to be a genius.

Because the lumberjack has "a certain positive originality" and he is "thinking for himself and expressing his own opinion," Thoreau judges him to be a genius. And his genius makes Thoreau suggest that "there might be men of genius in the lowest grades of life" (*HDT* 442). Another visitor, "an inoffensive, simple-minded pauper" confesses that he was "deficient in intellect" (*HDT* 443). In addition to his honesty, he accepted his own unfortunate fate and didn't blame anyone. Therefore, when given "a metaphysical puzzle," Thoreau thinks as follows:

> I have rarely met a fellow-man on such promising ground,—it was so simple and sincere and so true all that he said. And, true enough, in proportion as he appeared to humble himself was he exalted. I did not know at first but it was the result of a wise policy. It seemed that from such a basis of truth and frankness as the poor weak-headed pauper had laid, our intercourse might

> go forward to something better than the intercourse of sages. (*HDT* 443)

Owing to the simple-minded pauper's virtues such as simplicity, humility, truth, and sincerity, he is treated the same as sages. It seemed to Thoreau that a genius or sage should have originality and be able to think for themselves with sincerity and boldness.

However, Thoreau, who has often elicited many principles from something natural that nobody pays attention to, finds genius in a kind of fish. He empathizes with the migratory fish of shad caught in the Concord River in his *A Week on the Concord and Merrimack Rivers*:

> Still patiently, almost pathetically, with instinct not to be discouraged, not to be reasoned with, revisiting their old haunts, as if their stern fates would relent, and still met by the Corporation with its dam. Poor shad! where is thy redress? When Nature gave thee instinct, gave she thee the heart to bear thy fate? Still wandering the sea in thy scaly armor to inquire humbly at the mouths of rivers if man has perchance left them free for thee to enter. By countless shoals loitering uncertain meanwhile, merely stemming the tide there, in danger from sea foes in spite of thy bright armor, awaiting new instructions, until the sands, until the water itself, tell thee if it be so or not. Thus by whole migrating nations, full of instinct, which is thy faith, in this backward spring, turned adrift, and perchance knowest not where men do *not* dwell, where there are *not* factories, in these days. Armed with no sword, no electric shock, but mere Shad, armed only with innocence and a just cause, with tender dumb mouth only forward, and scales easy to be detached. I for one am with thee, and who knows what may avail a crow-bar against that Billerica dam? (*HDT* 31)

Shad that go out to the sea go upstream to spawn, but may be obstructed by the Billerica dam at the middle of the river. What Thoreau witnesses here is the shad's admirableness; while locks and dams were constructed and nature was destroyed as a result of industrialization, this migratory fish will not make any complaint but try to go upstream only with instincts. In fact, Lowell, which has led American industrial revolution through a textile industry, was built, and the river was rapidly developed for canal improvement. As Thoreau observes, the migratory fish such as salmon, shad, and alewives were gradually decreasing. However, the shad continued going on their own way to fulfill their destiny against the destruction of nature by industrial capitalism. Thoreau regards the shad as "still brave, indifferent, on easy fin there, like shad reserved for higher destinies" in any difficult circumstances, and affirms "[t]hou shalt erelong have thy way up the rivers, up all the rivers of the globe." Then he also tells them: "Keep a stiff fin then, and stem all the tides thou mayst meet" (*HDT* 31). Criticism and resistance to modernization is understood in the context of the shad. These non-intellectual, rather than anti-intellectual, fish that innocently live with instincts and never make a complaint symbolize a great current of destruction of nature. It is commonly perceived that here is a gradual decrease in intellect from a physical laborer and a simple-minded pauper to a fish, in a general sense. However, Thoreau considers the shad struggling to cope with the rough and tumble of life to be the "true" intellect.

We must pay attention to the mention of "way up the rivers, up all the rivers of the globe." Thoreau allows the shad in a local river of Concord to swim in the global great river. The image of the shad struggling with the hardships of life is universal intellectualism for Thoreau. He often associates his local rivers with the global great rivers. In "The Pond in Winter" chapter of *Walden*, after Thoreau explains that the ice taken from Walden Pond is exported to the East Indies, he concludes as follows:

> Thus it appears that the sweltering inhabitants of Charleston and New Orleans, of Madras and Bombay and Calcutta, drink at my well. In the morning I bathe my intellect in the stupendous and cosmogonal philosophy of the Bhagvat-Geeta, since whose composition years of the gods have elapsed, and in comparison with which our modern world and its literature seem puny and trivial; and I doubt if that philosophy is not to be referred to a previous state of existence, so remote is its sublimity from our conceptions. I lay down the book and go to my well for water, and lo! there I meet the servant of the Bramin, priest of Brahma and Vishnu and Indra, who still sits in his temple on the Ganges reading the Vedas, or dwells at the root of a tree with his crust and water jug. I meet his servant come to draw water for his master, and our buckets as it were grate together in the same well. The pure Walden water is mingled with the sacred water of the Ganges. (*HDT* 559–60)

The fact that the ice exported from Walden Pond actually is transported and spent all over the world makes Thoreau have a visual hallucination of the mingling of Walden water with that of the Ganges. This occurs when he bathes his intellect “in the stupendous and cosmogonal philosophy of the Bhagvat-Geeta,” which is the holy scripture of Hinduism. Thus, when he relativizes his fixed ideas using a foreign scripture, which clarifies the truth of the universe, and keeps questioning critically; all the global rivers link together and unite with one true water vein. Although Thoreau is very impressed by the Bhagvat-Geeta, he does not accept it at face value. Thoreau’s “true” intellect appears to be an intellectual attitude that is accessible to the truth flowing out of the sources of the global rivers. Therefore, Thoreau calls for an intellectual attitude of exploring the internal source of our own, rather than conquering the lands for the sources of the real rivers:

> What does Africa,—what does the West stand for? Is not our own interior white on the chart? black though it may prove, like the coast, when discovered. Is it the source of the Nile, or the Niger, or the Mississippi, or a North-West Passage around this continent, that we would find? Are these the problems which most concern mankind? Is Franklin the only man who is lost, that his wife should be so earnest to find him? Does Mr. Grinnell know where he himself is? Be rather the Mungo Park, the Lewis and Clarke and Frobisher, of your own streams and oceans; explore your own higher latitudes,—with shiploads of preserved meats to support you, if they be necessary; and pile the empty cans sky-high for a sign. Were preserved meats invented to preserve meat merely? Nay, be a Columbus to whole new continents and worlds within you, opening new channels, not of trade, but of thought. (*HDT* 577–78)

According to Thoreau, the truth is placed at the sources of the rivers. To trace the water veins and channels innocently and sincerely is his intellectualism and anti-anti-intellectualism against the prevailing ideology of business and pragmatic anti-intellectualism.

Of course, Thoreau’s statement here may sound musty old universalism. It may represent the American spirit which continues to find out a new frontier and never stops expansion. In the present time when we have experienced post-colonialism, it may be not exempt from blame for the Americanism as America-centered globalism. However, when we face today’s political state of the world, his statement seems not to be mere anachronism. The political and social trend in the direction of denying multi-culturalism which have been acquired over time in the history of the United States and regarding immigrants with hostility becomes more visible and gets accelerating, along with placing a priority on economic growth. This kind of anti-intellectualism has flourished in the time when we cannot realize steady growth while capitalism is expanding globally. Just as Thoreau feels sympathy for the shad which struggle against industrial capitalism, we also should find true intellect in people placed into dire straits by globalization today. Thoreau's anti-anti-intellectualism is of great significance in the twenty-first century.

Works Cited

Emerson, Ralph Waldo. *The Essential Writings of Ralph Waldo Emerson*. Ed. Brooks Atkinson. New York: The Modern Library, 2000. Print.

Hofstadter, Richard. *Anti-Intellectualism in American Life*. New York: Vintage Books, 1963. Print.

Maekawa, Reiko. "America-shakai to Han-chiseishugi" ["American Society and Anti-Intellectualism"]. *America no Bunmei to Jigazou* [*American Civilization and Self-Portrait*]. Eds. Uesugi Shinobu and Tatsumi Takayuki. Kyoto: Minerva, 2006. Print.

Russell, William. *American Journal of Education* 4.2 (1829): 176–186. *Google Book Search*. Web. 30 Aug 2016.

Tatsumi, Takayuki. "America-bungaku to Han-chiseishugi no Dentou" ["American Literature and the Tradition of Anti-Intellectualism"]. *Han-chisei no Teikoku: America-Bungaku, Seishin-shi* [*Anti-intellectualism in American Literary History*]. Ed. Tatsumi Takayuki. Tokyo: Nan'un-do, 2008. Print.

Thoreau, Henry David. *Henry David Thoreau: A Week, Walden, The Maine Woods, Cape Cod*. Ed. Robert F. Sayre. New York: Library of America, 1985. Print.

——. *Essays: A Fully Annotated Edition*. Ed. Jeffrey S. Cramer. New Haven: Yale UP, 2013. Print.

The Maine Woods:
What Thoreau Learned about the Penobscot People

Namie Ozawa

This paper attempts to clarify what Henry David Thoreau learned and understood through his interactions with the Penobscot people. Thoreau did not seem to have any interest in their social and political conditions and the colonial influence on them; rather, he sought to attain their secret of living with nature. He searched for images of ancient extinct tribes. As Linda Frost states, Thoreau ignored the history of the wars between the native people and whites; when he realized that there were differences between his ideal image of the natives and the reality, he ignored the reality and apotheosized the ideal image outside the hierarchy of the American society (21–47). However, while encountering many real Penobscots in his journeys, Thoreau gradually opened his eyes to their struggle to survive under the dominant white society by transforming their traditional lifestyle. Moreover, he finally seemed to grasp parts of the wisdom for balancing between nature and civilization in the Penobscots' way of living.

Thoreau visited the Maine woods three times, in 1846, 1853, and 1857, during which time he met the Penobscot people such as Louis Neptune, Joseph Aitteon, John Neptune, and Joseph Polis. He also explored the vast amount of literature on Native Americans and filled 12 notebooks on them over his lifetime. Selected parts of his notebooks appear in *The Indians of Thoreau* edited by Richard E. Fleck. It is inferred that he had worked on a project to write a book on Indians (Sayre 101–22). His last words are said to have been "Indians" and "Moose" (Fussell 327), suggesting that his soul was wandering in the Maine woods even at the moment of his death.

The lakes and rivers of Maine functioned as canoe traffic routes for native tribes over thousands of years (Cook 51–113). Thoreau, who traveled the ancient routes three times and spent time with native guides in the woods, came closer to the indigenous people than any of his contemporary literary writers, although he was somehow influenced by the romanticized image of "vanishing noble savages." That is, he was fascinated by native people, but was sometimes apt to understand them from the standpoint of an American intellect and failed to grasp the whole picture.

This paper aims to illuminate what Thoreau learned about the Penobscots against his contemporary modernization trend and reveals what he did not pay attention to by complementing his view with the ideas of local female writers as well as the historical and social situation of the Penobscot community. Finally, this paper shows how Thoreau gradually expanded his view of native people and partially came to understand the symbiotic wisdom that integrates nature and civilization, which modernized societies were losing. The wisdom he valued against the trend of his time seems to be a vital philosophy that is worth being handed down to the 21st century.

1 History and Social Situation of the Penobscots

To understand what Thoreau learned about the Penobscots, it is first necessary to grasp the history of indigenous people in Maine and their social situation during the mid-19th century.

The Penobscot people in Maine belong to the Wabanaki, who dwell from northern Maine to Canada. "Wabanaki" means "People of the Dawn," and are presently divided into five tribes: Penobscot, Passamaquoddy, Maliseet, Mi'kmaq, and Abenaki. Maine's native people have a long history spanning over twelve thousand years. They kept contact with the population on the opposite shore of the Bering Strait before Columbus reached the New World, and the Norse visited the New World numerous times between the 11th and 14th centuries. The Wabanaki's serious contact with Europeans profoundly changed their life starting in the 17th century, when they were forced to gradually concede their lands to colonists as the number of settlers grew (Bourque 111–27).

Chiefs Madockawando and Edgeremet ceded the lands on both sides of St. George River to Massachusetts Governor William Phips in 1694 (Bourque 104–05; Shay 1). However, this land transaction caused trouble later. Madockawando was said to be "either a Machias Passamaquoddy or a St. John Maliseet with no ties to mid-coast Maine property" in the eyes of the Penobscots (Rolde 117). In the beginning of the 17th century, the French and the English started to settle in the northern areas of North America and the French tried to keep the indigenous tribes under their control through the Jesuit mission's propagation of Christianity among them. The Wabanaki people gained more benefits from

French Catholic missionaries than from English settlers because the French had more intimate relations with them through inter-marriage and trade, while the English mostly acquired their lands. For around 100 years, from the mid-17th century to the mid-18th century, Maine was the battlefield of British colonies' wars against native tribes and European powers' territorial wars that involved native tribes: King Philip's War (1675–78), King William's War (1688–99), Queen Anne's War (1702–14), Governor Dummer's War (1721–26), King George's War (1744–48), and the French and Indian War (1754–63). As Colin G. Calloway mentions, Maine was not only the arena where the French and the English sought to gain more territory but also the cultural junction of various activities such as missions by both French Catholics and English Protestants, trade, hostage exchanges, and miscegenation (17). After the French and Indian War was over, the Wabanaki tribes lost the French support and could not prevent the influx of English settlers any longer.

In 1775, during the War of Independence, Governor Joseph Orono and Lieutenant Governor John Neptune of the Penobscots, who is the father of John Neptune Thoreau met, signed the Watertown Convention (Bourque 212–15) with the Massachusetts government and allied with the Colonials against the British forces. The Massachusetts government strictly banned settlers' encroachment into their lands on both sides of the Penobscot River, extending six miles from its headwater, and the Penobscots were protected from settlers cutting timber and hunting game in the area. In return for the protection, they fought for the Colonials. After the war, however, this treaty's promise of the Penobscots' right to the lands was disregarded and whites were encouraged to settle there (Bourque 215). The U.S. government called on the Penobscots to sign a quitclaim deed to the area, but they resisted (Bourque 216). Meanwhile, as the population of settlers rose, game and fish grew scarce. In 1818, the weakened Penobscots transferred the lands except for the islands on the Penobscot River to the Massachusetts government in exchange for a payment of $400, annuity, and their right to four townships (Bourque 217).

Maine was separated from Massachusetts and became a state in 1820. The state government called upon the Penobscots to sell the upriver townships to the states and used the money from this sale as a trust fund for the tribe. The state divided their lands to lots and let native households possess them. The Penobscots did not previously have a concept of private land ownership, but were made to own their lands individually.

The native people's population was dwindling and the state of Maine had started to protect them when Thoreau visited Maine from the 1840s to 1850s. When Thoreau stopped at Indian Island, 95 families with a total of 362 residents lived there (Rolde 196). Since a Quaker named Jeremiah Hacker advocated the necessity of educating indigenous people, an English school was established for them at the Indian village in Oldtown, and this English education for native people expanded to the surrounding areas (Rolde 199–202). Game protection laws were passed to protect wild animals and fish, but this restriction was lifted for native tribes for consistency with the treaties the state had signed before (Rolde 208; Bourque 222). The Penobscots shifted their lifestyle from hunting and gathering to agriculture and continued the fur trade. Some of them became lumbermen and boatmen as the lumbering business was prospering. Therefore, the Penobscots were assimilating themselves to the American way of life for survival when Thoreau witnessed their situation.

2 Penobscot people in Thoreau's *The Maine Woods*

How were the Penobscot people in the historical and social contexts above depicted by Thoreau? By comparing the biographic studies of the native guides and other local writers' descriptions of them with Thoreau's, I analyze Thoreau's understanding of indigenous people and what he learned about them.

Before meeting the Penobscots, Thoreau received information about them from his cousin George Thatcher, who lived in Bangor, which was close to Indian Island possessed by the Penobscots. In addition, Thatcher had known Joseph Polis, the guide for Thoreau's third travel in the Maine woods, since his childhood, and provided Thoreau with some knowledge of the Penobscot community (Huber 9). Further, Thoreau read anthropological and historical writings on Indians, documents of explorers in the New World, journals written by Catholic missionaries who had lived among native tribes, and other texts (Sattelmeyer 99–100).

Sattelmeyer suggests that it was extremely difficult for Thoreau to attain realistic images of Native Americans since the sciences in his era endorsed native people's inferiority and justified the government's Indian policy, including the Indian Removal Act (99–100). Therefore, Thoreau was not fully aware of the fact that the European invasion into the New World had deprived native people of their lands and that this caused the poverty and decline of the Penobscots he encountered.

2-1 Louis Neptune

In 1846, when Thoreau visited Maine for the first time, he sought to employ Louis Neptune as a guide to summit Mt. Ktaadn. Neptune had successfully led geologist Charles Jackson on his journey and was credited with saving Jackson's life in a snowstorm (Huber 125). However, Neptune missed the meeting with Thoreau, and thus, was unable to guide him. Consequently, Thoreau asked a white guide and pilot, George McCausline, to accompany him, and even expressed his irritation toward Neptune. This emotion turned into contempt in due time. Thoreau made acrimonious comments about Neptune and his tribes when he happened to meet him again at the end of his journey:

> Met face to face, these Indians in their native woods looked like the sinister and slouching fellows whom you meet picking up strings and paper in the streets of a city. There is, in fact, a remarkable and unexpected resemblance between the degraded savage and the lowest classes in a great city. The one is no more a child of nature than the other. In the progress of degradation, the distinction of races is soon lost. (78)

Thoreau did not mention that native people's degradation is mainly attributed to the white men's settlement and the government's Indian policy; rather, he participated in a typical colonial discourse, failing to recognize that indigenous people had been degraded not because of their inferiority but because of land deprivation by white people.

In contrast with this image of indigenous people as degraded savages, Thoreau later pursued an ideal image of native people expressed in poetic terms:

> He glides up the Millinocket and is lost to my sight, as a more distant and misty cloud is seen flitting by behind a nearer, and is lost in space. So he goes about his destiny, the red face of man. (79)

This image of native people is visionary and fits the notion of "vanishing noble savages" under Manifest Destiny. It does not reflect the real native people who faced the loss of their lands, scarcity of game, and poverty. Thoreau's interest lay in the Maine woods as "the virgin forest of the New World," which was "unmapped and unexplored" (83), as well as in the noble savages who lived in that paradise.

2-2 Joseph Aitteon

Joe Aitteon, who worked as a guide for Thoreau's second journey, was the son of the Penobscot chief John Aitteon (1816–58 in office). Aitteon comes from the French *Eitenne*, equivalent to the English name Stephen (Rolde 213; Sherwood, *Thoreau's Penobscot Indians* 8; hereafter abbreviated as *TPI*). The Aitteons' genealogy is regarded as belonging to the squirrel clan, which inherits chieftainship. The family has been thought to practice magic since the historically famous Chief Madockawando, whose daughter was married to a Frenchman Jean Vincent, Baron de Saint Castine. Joe Aitteon, Thoreau's guide, was entitled to become a chief, but after the election system was introduced, he became the first elected chief, called "governor" in his time. He was elected a total of seven times because he was admired and loved by his tribe.

Thoreau's depiction of Aitteon is ambivalent in that it fluctuates between respect and disappointment. Aitteon met Thoreau as a 24-year-old "unmixed blood" native. He wore a red flannel shirt, woolen pants, and a black Kosuth hat like a typical lumberman of his age (90). He whistled white men's songs such as "O Susanna" and did not know how to live only on game, fish, and berries provided by the woods, unlike ancient wild men (107). He did not know his ancestors' history, either, and Thoreau had to tell him about it (135–36). His lost Indianness disillusioned Thoreau. On the other hand, Thoreau seemed enthralled by the noiseless and swift movements of Aitteon chasing a moose he had shot and wounded and his shrewd sense of spotting the body.

Thoreau was attracted by the perceived wild character of native people as hunters, but did not have any empathy toward it. He criticized hunters who killed wild animals for their own interests, remarking, "What a coarse and imperfect use Indians and hunters make of nature! No wonder that their race is so soon exterminated" (120). Thoreau seemed to believe in his contemporary mainstream ideology that agriculture is more civilized than hunting and did not mention the fact that it was white people who pressed native people to hunt and kill animals because of the commercial value of the fur trade and that native people had not endangered wildlife for thousands of years because they took care not to disturb the ecosystem of nature.

On the other hand, female writers in Maine, Fannie H. Eckstorm and Marion W. Smith, offered a different perspective on Aitteon's character. They wrote short stories about Aitteon's accidental death (Eckstorm, *The Penobscot Man* 27–38; Smith, *Thoreau's West Branch Guides* 25–29; hereafter abbreviated as *TWBG*). Aitteon was a boatman who worked under John Ross, the boss of the West Branch Drive, a company that transported lumber. Aitteon especially excelled in rowing. Since it was a holiday on July 4th, Independence Day, an inexperienced boatman took the place of a veteran. The overloaded boat was trying to run Grand Falls and became wrecked in the rapids. Six days later, Aitteon's body was found in Shad Pond. Since he was loved by his comrades and tribal people and died at the age of just 40 years, his death was so lamented that his boot was hung on the branch of the pine tree near the pond for a long time and a cross was engraved on the tree trunk.

Eckstorm showed deep respect for Aitteon by depicting his death with pathos. She criticized Thoreau in *The Penobscot Man* by pointing out that he paid attention only to the wild Indian character of Aitteon and did not recognize Aitteon's humanity:

> But Thoreau hired an Indian to be aboriginal. One who said "By George!" and made remarks with a Yankee flavor was contrary to his hypothesis of what a barbarian ought to be. It did not matter that this was the sort of man who gave up his inside seat and rode sixty miles on the top of the stage in the rain that a woman might be sheltered:—all the cardinal virtues without aboriginality would not have sufficed Mr. Thoreau for a text. (28)

Eckstorm, who was a genuine Maine woman raised in the backwoods, was not an observer like Thoreau but lived with Aitteon as one of her comrades, and Aitteon was a father-like leader to the boatmen who carried lumber.

Thoreau also held mixed feelings toward cannibalism as a symbol of savagery, which was used to prove indigenous people's uncivilized inferiority and to justify the European colonization of the new continent. Thoreau seems to have almost espoused the colonizers' stance. When he camped out with the three native people he met at the carry near Moosehead, he entertained ambivalent emotions vacillating between his pleasure to know the wild culture of the native people and his loathing of savagery. On the one hand, he narrated his joy of lying with indigenous people in the tent and learning the names of places in their native language as well as his comfort of listening to natives talking to each other in their own tongue: "the sounds that issued from the wigwams of this country before Columbus was born" (136–37). On the other hand, when he saw moose meat smoking on a crate, it reminded him of a crate in a copperplate print illustration made by "With [John White] in De Bry's '*Collectio Peregrinationum*,' published in 1592, and which the natives of Brazil called *boucan*, (whence buccaneer,) on which were frequently shown pieces of human flesh drying along with the rest" (134). In the illustration, Brazilian natives are roasting human flesh on the crates. The scene had become a source of the horrible fantasy of Europeans for cannibalism, who were attempting to colonize the New World. Thoreau also heard from Aitteon about the Mohawk's habit of eating human flesh. Thoreau seems to have had discomfort with such savagery, as well as hunting, just like the other European colonizers.

Theodore De Bry's illustrations were made to promote Protestants' colonization of the New World, Asia, and Africa. He was a goldsmith and copperplate engraver who was born to a Protestant family in Liège, Belgium, in 1528. He moved to Germany to escape the persecution of Protestants and published *Collectiones Peregrinationum in Indian Orientalem & Occidentalem* together with his two sons. The collection consisted of 25 folio volumes, which contained around 50 travel accounts of European explorations to the overseas countries (Van Groesen 2). The first 13 volumes were reports on the New World—which was called *America- or India Occidentalis-series*, while the remaining 12 volumes were on Africa and Asia, called the *India Orientalis-series*. These volumes were a guidebook regarding the topography, inhabitants, and cultures on the New Continent, Asia, and Africa, and established Europeans' racial images when they were colonizing the areas.

The painter Thoreau mentioned was John White, whose name was sometimes spelled "With" or "Wyth." The first volume of the collections is about a British explorer Thomas Harriot's expedition to the Virginia Colony where White accompanied Harriot. He painted only fish roasted on the crate in watercolors, but De Bry inserted two native persons in the painting that he took from the other paintings and embellished the scene with his imagination (Sloan 191–92). In this first volume, however, there is nothing to suggest cannibalism. Thoreau mentions that the book was published in 1592, but the volume published that year was the Latino version of the third volume, whose first account was of Hans Staden's travel to Brazil, where cannibalism was depicted in De Bry's sensational copperplate print illustration. The first edition of Hans Staden's account was illustrated by wood-block print to tell the story simply, but cannibalism was sensationalized from De Bry's Protestant viewpoint (Whitehead 748) to help ease the colonization and enslavement of the indigenous people. Thoreau remarked, "They were smoking moose-meat on just such a crate as is represented by With in De Bry's 'Collectio Peregrinationum'" (134), but the Brazilian *boucan* and cannibalism comes from Staden's narrative in the third volume. Thoreau might have confused the first volume with the third one, or might have unconsciously repressed his memory of the third volume, which contains shocking illustrations of cannibalism.

Van Grosen explains that De Bry's Protestant intension is strongly reflected in *Collectiones Peregrinationum* (11). Sloan also points out that the book may have served as propaganda promoting anti-Catholicism and pro-Protestantism in the colonization race (85–86). De Bry modified the original paintings and added some words of his own when translating the first versions.

Clearly, Thoreau was unable to relinquish the colonial discourse contained in De Bray's Protestant propaganda. Thoreau indicates in *Walden* that mankind conquered cannibalism in the process of evolution and that people were still evolving from carnivore to herbivore (216). In *The Maine Woods*, too, when he heard about 22 moose carcasses left on the ground, he sighed, murmuring, "Although it was about as savage a sight as was ever witnessed, and I was carried back at once three hundred years" (135). He seemed to have a strong repulsion to hunting and eating meat, to say nothing of cannibalism.

2-3 John Neptune

Thoreau stopped at Governor Neptune's house at the end of his second journey to Maine. John Neptune was actually the Lieutenant Governor, but was called "Governor" because of his popularity among the tribal people. His clan was eel related to water, as his family name "Neptune" suggests, and possessed shamanistic power (Rolde 213–14). He owned his territory in the area north of the Kenduskeag River, known as the habitat of eel (Sherwood *TPI* 8).

Neptune was a legendary leader among the Penobscots. Since he seduced Governor John Aitteon's wife at the age of 60, he broke off his relationship with Aitteon and receded to Brewer with half of his tribal members. Thoreau's guide Joe Aitteon was the son of the governor. Fannie Hardy Eckstorm wrote biographic works on numerous Penobscot people, and her father Manly Hardy, a fur trader, lived in Brewer. The Hardys closely associated with natives and hunters, one of whom was Neptune. Neptune had a mistress, Molly Molasses, who was an old woman. Thoreau met her in Bangor after he stepped down from the steamer. Thoreau commented, "As long as she lives the Penobscots may be considered extant as a tribe" (157). Thoreau might have mentioned her because he heard rumors about her from his cousin Thatcher, but he did not allude to her relation with Governor Neptune or her background. Molly was poor and old when Thoreau met her, but she was known as a beauty when young. She had witnessed her tribe decline and become poorer and poorer while settlers increased in number and the lumber business thrived (McBride 75–94).

Later, Neptune re-established his political relation with Aitteon, who became the Governor with Neptune as the Lieutenant Governor. The two led the Old Party, which promoted hereditary governorship and the introduction of modern education including English reading, writing, and arithmetic. Thoreau's third guide, Joseph Polis, also promoted this education movement. The Old Party was opposed to the New Party, which advocated the election system and traditional Catholic education. Neptune was a charismatic politician who was also renowned as an orator and narrator of tales. He represented his tribe, insisted on their tribal right on the lands, and negotiated on various political and legal issues. He petitioned Maine's governor about the violation of the tribe's hunting rights and participated in the Maine legislative assembly as a tribal representative (McBride 75–94).

When Thoreau visited Neptune three years before Neptune's death in 1860, Thoreau described him as an 89-year-old man, though he was actually 86 years old (Huber 142) and was fit enough to hunt moose in the fall. Yet, since he was old and hard of hearing, he needed to be attended by women—one of whom was his third wife, whom he had married recently.

Thoreau's depiction of Neptune was realistic, but he never mentioned Neptune's social or personal background, or the network he had with other tribal people like Thoreau's own guides Joe Aitteon and Joseph Polis. Thoreau was not interested in the fact that they were struggling to survive in his day.

2-4 Joseph Polis

Sattelmeyer, quoting Thoreau's letter addressed to H. G. O. Blake, remarked that Thoreau greatly expanded his world view through his interaction with Polis and was impressed by Polis's wild wisdom, which white men did not have (108–09). Polis was a native who maintained a balance between nature and the civilized world. He retained his ancient tribal wisdom, but at the same time, adopted many elements of Euro-American culture and lifestyle. Polis was likely a member of the bear clan (Sherwood, *Joseph Police* 1; Sherwood, *TPI*; Smith, *TWBG* 33), as Thoreau noted that he inscribed a drawing of a bear paddling a canoe on the trunk of a fir tree. The bear clan was thought to consist of aristocrats (Sherwood, *Joseph Police* 3), and Polis himself was known as a shaman (Eckstorm, *Old John Neptune* 185–86; Sherwood, *Joseph Police* 8).

Thoreau was amazed by Polis's wisdom to live on the blessings of nature: Polis was able to make a solid canoe that endured the weight of their baggage for their travel (164). When Polis's canoe leaked a little, he made pitch from the turpentine of the pine to mend the canoe (205). He was knowledgeable about how to use plants. For example, he made various products out of birch bark, such as a sugar bowl (203), a candle (282), and a pipe (206), and used the underside of the birch bark to write on (274). He also made thread out of the black spruce root (204) and tea from the creeping snowberry (206) and checkerberry (273). He knew how to make soup from lily bulbs (288). He was familiar with the medical use of each plant (235). For instance, he diagnosed the symptoms of his colic, saying "Me doctor—first study my case, find out what all'em—then I know what to take." Then he drank a dipper of water with a charge or two of powder he poured from his powder horn, and he actually recovered (290–91).

Thoreau was also amazed by Polis's mysterious capability to understand nature when he found a phosphorus light at midnight, remarking, "Nature must have made a thousand revelations to them which are still secrets to us" (181).

Moreover, Thoreau noted that Polis had a familiar relation with animals as if he could embody them: He not only imitated a noise a snake made but also made "a curious squeaking, wiry sound with his lips" (206) to imitate a muskrat call. Animals were not inferior to men in native people's world.

Polis knew how to live in the woods. He could handle a canoe and travel without a compass. He was aware of his inter-relation with all plants and wild animals in the woods and was well-versed in how to survive in the ecosystem. All these pieces of wisdom were what Thoreau had wanted to understand: the symbiosis between humans and nature.

On the other hand, Polis managed to be well-poised between his wild way of living and Western civilization. He fused Protestantism and Catholicism flexibly with his own tribal shamanism without any difficulty. Polis kept the Sabbath more strictly than white men (193–94) and sung a hymn that seemed to have been taught by Catholic missionaries (178–79). Thoreau did not mention that the Anglo-Protestant missionary activities among natives were deeply involved with the conquest of those people, and at the same time, they were a countermeasure the English took against French Catholic missionaries converting natives. He seemed unaware of any trace of Europeans' invasion into the natives' territory.

Polis had wisely benefitted from the Euro-American way of living. His business sense and financial power were far from what Thoreau had expected from native people. Polis owned 50 acres of land in Oldtown, where he employed white laborers to grow potatoes. He also owned a hundred acres somewhere up a long lake-like reach below the Five Islands (290). He had a hunting ground in the north west of Ktaadn and earned income from his skillful dressing of moose hides (267). He possessed 6,000 dollars in assets and lived in a two-story white house with blinds that looked "as good as an average one on a New England village street" (157–58). Sherwood remarked that Polis also owned a shop where he sold traditional handcrafts like baskets, though this was not mentioned in *The Maine Woods* (*Joseph Police* 8). Polis's strong business sense was not something that white people expected vanishing noble savages to have, but it enabled him and his tribal people to survive the age.

Thoreau's surprise went further than that. In the beginning, Thoreau had regarded native people only as objects of his observation, but native people also observed white people and criticized them from their own viewpoint, as Laura L. Mielke points out (114). The fact that native people criticized whites should have innovated Thoreau's view. For example, Polis described that the people of the United States were "very strong," but some were "too fast" (197). Polis asked for an interview with Daniel Webster at his boarding house in Boston, but was kept waiting for a long time, and when he finally met him, Webster treated him contemptuously, as if Polis were a worthless visitor. Polis gave a low estimation of Webster, saying he "was not worth talk about a musquash" (252–53), though Webster was highly admired as a great orator and lawyer by whites. Thus, Polis offered another angle for viewing the American society.

Polis's deep understanding of English and the American social system was also beyond Thoreau's expectation. He could read and write in English and subscribed to a Bangor newspaper. He visited Augusta, the capital of Maine, as a representative of his tribe and met some Western chiefs in Washington. He behaved like an educated activist.

From Thoreau's standpoint, Polis showed him an ideal way of balancing nature and civilization. Polis may have given Thoreau some wisdom on how human beings can lead a symbiotic life with nature. The gap between Thoreau and Polis seems to have decreased and Thoreau began to stop regarding Polis and his tribal people as mere objects of his own observation; instead, he started interacting with them and developed a recognition of their humanity. Polis also started to see Thoreau in a more positive light. Polis had never referred to Thoreau, his friend Hoar, and himself as "we" but "you and I" (167). However, he paid respect to Thoreau by giving him the name "great paddler" (295) at the end of his journey.

3 Conclusion

In the beginning of the journeys into the Maine woods, Thoreau regarded indigenous people as "the other" he was observing, partly because his purpose was to seek the secret of wildness and native people's symbiotic attitude with nature. He described Louis Neptune as a typically degraded native. Similarly, Joseph Aitteon was shown only as an object of Thoreau's observation—a wild man whose human character did not mean anything to Thoreau. Though the moment of Thoreau's encounter with John Neptune was described realistically, the depiction was fragmentary and did not convey Neptune's totality as a leader who was striving to improve his tribe's situation and had a close and rich network with other tribal people such as Molly Molasses, Joseph Aitteon, and Joseph Polis. Polis, however, disrupted Thoreau's preconception and helped him open his eyes to the Penobscot people's community, which was trying to survive the changing age. He also gave Thoreau satisfactory wild men's secrets that Thoreau had wanted to attain. Thus, in his last journey, Thoreau began to grow out of the colonial concept of "vanishing noble savages" and understand the Penobscot people's wisdom that copes with the age and seeks a balance between nature and civilization.

Thoreau's sincere desire to meet indigenous people and try to learn from their language, culture, and wisdom, even against his contemporary Zeitgeist, is a valuable attitude for us to learn and inherit in the 21st century.

Works Cited

Bourque, Bruce J. *Twelve Thousand Years: American Indians in Maine*. Lincoln: U of Nebraska P, 2001. Print.

Calloway, Colin G. *Dawnland Encounters: Indians and Europeans in Northern New England*. Hanover: UP of New England, 1991. Print.

Cook, David S. *Above the Gravel Bar: The Native Canoe Routes of Maine*. Solon, ME: Polar Bear & Company, 1985. Print.

Eckstorm, Fannie H. *Old John Neptune and Other Maine Indian Shamans*. Orono, Maine: U of Maine P, 1980. Print.

——. *The Penobscot Man*. 1904. Breinigsville, PA :General Books, 2009. Print.

Frost, Linda. "'The Red Face of Man,' the Penobscot Indian, and a Conflict of Interest in Thoreau's *Maine Woods*." *ESQ* 39.1 (1993): 21–47. Print.

Fussell, Edwin S. *Frontier in American Literature and the American West*. Princeton, NJ: Princeton UP, 1965. Print.

Huber, J. Parker. *The Wildest Country: Exploring Thoreau's Maine*. Boston, MA: Appalachian Mountain Club Books, 2008. Print.

McBride, Bunny. *Women of the Dawn*. Lincoln: U of Nebraska P, 1999. Print.

Mielke, Laura L. *Moving Encounters: Sympathy and the Indian Question in Antebellum Literature*. Amherst: U of Massachusetts P, 2008. Print.

Rolde, Neil. *Unsettled Past, Unsettled Future: The Story of Maine Indians*. Gardiner, ME: Tilbury House Publishers, 2004. Print.

Sattelmeyer, Robert. *Thoreau's Reading: A Study in Intellectual History with Bibliographical Catalogue*. Princeton, NJ: Princeton UP, 1988. Print.

Sayre, Robert F. *Thoreau and the American Indians*. Princeton, NJ: Princeton UP, 1977. Print.

Shay, Florence N. *History of the Penobscot Tribe of Indians*. Indian Island: Penobscot Nation Museum, 1998. Print.

Sherwood, Mary P. *Joseph Police: Thoreau's Maine Guide*. Berwick, Ontario, Canada: Stormont P, 1970. Print.

——. *Thoreau's Penobscot Indians*. 1969. Berwick, Ontario, Canada: Stormont P., 1970. Print.

Sloan, Kim. *A New World: England's First View of America*. Chapel Hill: U of North Carolina P, 2007. Print.

Smith, Marion W. *Thoreau's Moosehead & Chesuncook Guides*. Millinocket, ME: Ye Olde Print Shop, 1972. Print.

——. *Thoreau's West Branch Guides*. Millinocket, ME: Ye Olde Print Shop, 1971. Print.

Thoreau, Henry D. *The Indians of Thoreau: Selections from the Indian Notebooks*. Ed. Richard F. Fleck. Albuquerque, NM: Hummingbird P, 1974. Print.

——. *The Writings of Henry David Thoreau: Walden*. Ed. J. Lyndon Shanley. Princeton, NJ: Princeton UP, 1971. Print.

——. *The Writings of Henry David Thoreau: The Maine Woods*. Ed. Joseph J. Moldenhauer. Princeton, NJ: Princeton UP, 1972. Print.

Van Groesen, Michiel. *The Representations of the Overseas World in the De Bry Collection of Voyages (1590–1634)*. Leiden: Brill, 2008. Print.

Whitehead, Neil L. "Hans Staden and the Cultural Politics of Cannibalism." *Hispanic American Historical Review* 80.4 (2000): 721–51. Project Muse. Web. 8 Oct. 2013.

Native American Representations in the Works of Thoreau and Irving

Mika Takiguchi

Henry David Thoreau was known for expressing a strong interest in Native Americans during his lifetime. He first depicted the Native Americans living in Massachusetts and Maine in the accounts of his travels, *A Week on the Concord and Merrimack Rivers* (1849) and later in *The Maine Woods* (1864). Washington Irving offered the description of Native Americans, *A Tour on the Prairies* (1835), in the account of his 1832 journey to Fort Gibson with Henry Ellsworth, the commissioner in charge of Native American relocation. While more than a decade separates these descriptions of Native Americans in New England and those living in the frontier areas, each account is given by someone who actually traveled alongside the people they describe. This may be the reason these accounts depict different images of Native Americans than the distorted descriptions of them provided by historians and preceding authors.

This paper will focus on the descriptions of Native American guides by Thoreau and Irving in their works *The Maine Woods* and *A Tour on the Prairies*. The first section addresses three Native American guides portrayed by Thoreau in *The Maine Woods*, and discusses the process whereby Thoreau gradually came to trust the Native Americans. The second section looks at Pierre Beatte, a mixed-blooded Native American guide (half-Osage and half-French) who appears in *A Tour on the Prairies*. I will trace the process whereby a man, depicted as an untrustworthy character during the first half of the trip, came to be trusted as an excellent and reliable guide by demonstrating his abilities and skills acquired while living on the frontier. Finally, I will compare Thoreau's and Irving's portrayals of Native Americans and reassess whether their depictions differed from those of their contemporaries and whether Thoreau and Irving had an impartial view of Native Americans.

1. The Native Americans as Depicted in *The Maine Woods*

The Maine Woods is a travelogue that describes the three trips that Thoreau took to Maine. The first essay "Ktaadn" is about Thoreau's trip that spanned from the end of August through September of 1846. At that time, Thoreau lived in a log cabin near Walden Pond. Thoreau took this trip from Bangor, Maine to Mount Ktaadn with his cousin George Thatcher. Their guide was Louis Neptune, a member of the Penobscot tribe, who lived on Mattanawcook Island. The second essay "Chesuncook" is a record of Thoreau's travels with Thatcher in September 1853 to hunt moose in the woods of Maine, accompanied by Joe Aitteon, a very proficient moose-hunting guide. "The Allegash and East Branch" essay that comprises approximately half of *The Maine Woods* recounts Thoreau's travels with Edward Hoar from July through August of 1857. At this time, Thoreau was nearly 40 years old and suffered from chronic pulmonary tuberculosis. During this trip, Thoreau expressed more interest in Joe Polis's language and knowledge than in those things that had previously interested him, like the wilderness, the cruelty of nature, and the destruction of nature. His essay depicts Polis's actions, words, and personality in great detail. I will next analyze the traits and methods of these three Native American guides, and discuss the process by which Thoreau came to regard Polis as an excellent guide in the final essay.

Thoreau describes Neptune, his guide to Mount Ktaadn, as "a small, wiry man, with puckered and wrinkled face" (10) and states that he and Thatcher were "thinking ourselves lucky to have secured such guides and companions" (10). Despite their high initial expectations, they later had to travel without a guide because Neptune did not show up at the scheduled meeting place due to a drunken incident. This makes Thoreau angry, and he writes:

> We were lucky to have exchanged our Indians, whom we did not know, for these men, the canoe is smaller, more easily upset, and sooner worn out; and the Indian is said not to be so skillful in the management of the batteau. (32)

Thoreau had a favorable impression of Native Americans before he started his travels, so he is disgusted by Neptune's unacceptable actions and as a guide. He also became aware of Neptune's disdainful demeanor. Thoreau's positive impressions of Native Americans changed to the stereotypical contemporary view of Native Americans as depraved people.

> Met face to face, these Indians in their native woods looked like the sinister and slouching fellows whom you meet picking up strings and paper in the streets of a city. . . . The one is no more a child of a nature than the other. In the progress of degradation the distinction of races is soon lost. . . . We thought Indians had some honor before. (78)

In fact, because Thoreau had asked two woodsmen, George McCauslin and Thomas Fowler to accompany them, he was able to fulfill his objective of climbing Mount Ktaadn without much disruption, even without Neptune. However, at the same time, Thoreau had experienced the wilderness and the cruelty of nature. That very experience convinced him of the need for a native guide: "an Indian is still necessary to guide her scientific men to its headwaters in the Adirondack country" (82). Thus, he could not get rid of the regretful feeling that he could have had a more fulfilling adventure if a Native American guide, familiar with the woods, had accompanied him on his trip to Mount Ktaadn.

Learning from his mistakes Thoreau hired a native guide who had deep knowledge of the woods, and skills that would help him achieve his objective on his second journey. The guide on his trip to Lake Chesuncook was Joe Aitteon, "a son of the Governor, . . . [who] had conducted two white men a-moose-hunting in the same direction the year before" (85). Thoreau's primary purpose was to learn about the Native Americans' lives in the woods and their customs: "we had employed an Indian mainly that I might have the opportunity to study his ways" (95). Aitteon enters the story as a more progressive and competent character than Neptune. Thoreau even describes his appearance in positive terms: "He was a good-looking Indian, twenty-four years old, apparently of unmixed blood, short and stout, with a broad face, a reddish complexion, and eyes, methinks, narrower and more turned up at the outer corners than ours, answering to the description of his race" (90).

However, Aitteon also disappears "like Indians" when Thoreau and Thatcher try to go trout fishing and does not return for over an hour. The two men still had unpleasant memories of Neptune from their previous trip, but after Aitteon returns, he expresses no feelings of guilt, insisting that he just went to look for moose. After this, Thoreau starts to watch Aitteon even more closely: "We made no complaint, but concluded to look out for Joe the next time. . . . for we had no reason to complain of him afterwards" (107). Thoreau finds himself surprised and impressed by Aitteon's abilities as a guide in the woods, which were unlike those of lumberjacks or McCauslin, the whites, who were accustomed to living in the woods. Thoreau shows us a glimpse of their humanity by stating that the Native Americans, who were typically considered to be silent, "kept up a steady chatting in their own language" (135). It can be understood as part of the nature of the Native Americans that Aitteon disappears "like Indians" and he and his friends often engage themselves in talking with one another. For Thoreau, Aitteon is an ideal guide because he could teach Thoreau the habits of the Native Americans and their skills in the woods.

However, Aitteon falls somewhat short of Thoreau's expectation of an ideal Indian, as the influence of white culture completely permeates him. While Aitteon has the appearance of a full-blooded Native American, his clothes are those of a white lumberjack. He "wore a red flannel shirt, woolen pants, and a black Kossuth hat, the ordinary dress of lumberman" (90). When preparing to enter the woods, he says, "I sha'n't go into the woods without provision,—hard bread, pork, etc." (107). Moreover, Thoreau finds that Aitteon "knew but little of the history of their race" (135–36). Robert F. Sayre discusses Aitteon as follows:

> As the lumberman's dress indicates, Joe was himself a synthesis of white and Indian cultures. . . . He had Indian skills in handling and repairing his canoe, . . . but he readily admitted to Thoreau that he could not subsist in the woods entirely on the woods, like his ancestors. . . . Thus, we get the impression that he was an easy-going man who had made his adjustments between red and white traditions. (Sayre 167)

Thoreau is concerned about Aitteon's apathetic attitude toward the history of his own tribe. However, he acknowledges Aitteon's excellent abilities in the woods and praises his savageness. In this way, Thoreau's trust in the Native Americans that was lost due to Neptune's actions is gradually restored.

While his companion Thatcher succeeded in his goal of moose hunting, from Thoreau's perspective, the trip to Chesuncook was incomplete. Thoreau had anticipated analyzing the customs and habits of Native Americans, but he was unsuccessful in collecting enough information. Aitteon, the modern twenty-four-year-old Penobscot Indian, was too young to provide the desired information relating to Native Americans. Thus, four years later, Thoreau hopes that "the third time is the charm," and takes a trip to the Allegash river basin in the woods of Maine.

It was previously noted that "The Allegash and East Branch," an account of the journey Thoreau took in July of 1857, comprises nearly half of *The Maine Woods*. This essay is centrally focused on the interaction with Polis, a Native American who could be considered a resident of the woods as he had learned the ancient knowledge and customs of the Penobscot tribe from his elders. At that time, Joe Polis was forty-eight years old, and "he was stoutly built, perhaps a little above the middle height, with a broad face, and, as others said, perfect Indian features and complexion" (157). His abilities as a guide were also highly praised by the local people. The boatman on the ship to Indian island describes him as "one of the aristocracy" (158). Upon hiring Polis, the first-class guide, Thoreau is happy stating "we thought ourselves lucky to secure the services of this man, who was known to be particularly steady and reliable" (158). Here, I would again suggest that the purpose of Thoreau's journeys is to acquire knowledge of the Native Americans' culture and their skills in the woods; it is presumed that he sees the Native Americans from the perspectives whether they are skilled or not.

Although Polis was a Native American who respected traditions, he had also learned the skills necessary to adapt to the changing times. Thoreau writes about Polis's faith as follows:

> He appeared to be a very religious man, and said his prayers in a loud voice, in Indian, kneeling before the camp, morning and evening,—sometimes scrambling up again in haste when he had forgotten this, and saying them with great rapidity. (199)

Thoreau removed himself from the social system and the religion when he chose to live a life in the woods. Thus, the various aspects of Polis's zealous Protestant lifestyle and adoption of the white culture may have shaken his preconceptions about Native Americans, prompting him to feel both surprise and reverence. While Thoreau was skeptical of religions and religious faiths, Polis not only accepts the religion and civilization forced upon his people, but through them, he also develops into an intellectual Indian. Even though white culture might have been forced upon Polis, his positive acceptance of the culture and use of it for his own development may have made Thoreau respect him.

Polis lives in "a two-story white one [house], with blinds" (157) in the village of Oldtown, and he subscribes to the Bangor newspapers as he recognizes the importance of literacy. He enthusiastically gives the best education to his son who was "the best scholar in the school at Oldtown, to which he went with whites," and he also "had recommended it [school] to his tribe" (293). When Thoreau hears about a dispute regarding the school in Polis's village, he says of Polis: "we thought that it showed a good deal of tact in him, to seize this occasion and take his stand on it; proving how well he understood those with whom he had to deal" (294). In order for Polis to convince his people, he needs their full trust in him in addition to his intellect, sincerity, and patience.

After the completion of his third trip, Thoreau wrote a letter to Harrison Blake on August 18th, 1857.

> The Indian, who can find his way so wonderfully in the woods, possesses so much intelligence which the white man does not,—and it increases my own capacity, as well as faith, to observe it. I rejoice to find that intelligence flows in other channels than I knew. It redeems for me portions of what seemed brutish before. (Harding 504)

While Thoreau admires Polis for his personal development, and absorbing white foreign culture, we can observe his biased idea that Native Americans innately lack intelligence. In his trip to the Allegash river basin, Thoreau was able to observe the Native Americans' way of living in nature and listen to their words more intently than he could in his earlier travels to Ktaadn and Chesuncook. When Thoreau met Polis, he was "one of the aristocracy" who embodied the beliefs and abilities of the Native Americans. In the end, Thoreau was able to learn many things from Polis's words and actions. As noted above, Polis showed an interest in the Christian faith and education, yet he did not idolize white society nor assimilate into it. Rather, he attempted to coexist with the whites and adapt to the progress of modernization. Polis balanced his intelligence and savageness, Native American skills in the woods that Thoreau had been seeking; thus, he could be considered Thoreau's ideal image of a Native American. James R. Martel describes the two men's relationship as follows: "If Thoreau seeks wild men as friends, he seems to have found one in Joe Polis, a flesh-and-blood incarnation of 'Wawatam'" (Martel 179). The trust in Native Americans that Thoreau had lost in his 1842 trip to Mount Ktaadn because of Neptune is restored, and it evolves into feelings of friendship and respect through his interaction with Polis. Thoreau tries to recognize the existence and value of other ethnicities, and ultimately understands, respects, and values Polis's personality and skills in the woods. Such an attempt by Thoreau can be viewed as the kind of act necessary to combat today's ethnic conflicts.

2. The Native Americans as Depicted in *A Tour on the Prairies*

In the fall of 1832, after he returned to America from spending nearly seventeen years in Europe, Washington Irving traveled to Fort Gibson along with Commissioner Ellsworth, who was in charge of relocating Native Americans. Irving organizes his travelogue into thirty-five chapters narrated by Geoffrey Crayon, the same pseudonymous narrator used in *The Sketch Book of Geoffrey Crayon, Gent.* (1819). During this journey, Irving and Ellsworth were accompanied by Irving's friend Latrobe, a young Swiss youth named Pourtalès, a man named Pierre Beatte who was of mixed French and Osage descent (a "half-blood" or "half-breed" in the derogatory epithet of the time) and who served as both guide and interpreter, and Antoine, (also called "Tonish"), another person of mixed-blood who was "a kind of Jack-of-all-work" (11). In this section, I will address how the guide, Beatte, presented as an untrustworthy person in the first half of this journey, gained the trust of Irving and became highly valued through the demonstration of his abilities as a Native American on the frontier. I will also discuss the significance of the other mixed-race person, Antoine.

At the beginning of the travelogue, Beatte is introduced as follows: "he was acquainted with all parts of the country, having traversed it in all directions, both in hunting and war parties; that he would be of use both as a guide and interpreter, and that he was a first-rate hunter" (11). His appearance is described as "thirty six years of age, square and strongly built. His features were not bad, being shaped not unlike those of Napoleon, but sharpened up, with high Indian cheek bones" (12), reflecting the typical characterizations of Native Americans. In this passage, Irving objectifies Beatte and clings to the opinion of mixed-blooded individuals held by his own society at that time.

> I confess I did not like his looks when he was first presented to me. . . . Such was the appearance of the man, and his manners were equally unprepossessing. He was cold and laconic; . . . . He had altogether more of the red than the white man in his composition; and, as I had been taught to look upon all half-breeds with distrust, as an uncertain and faithless race, I would gladly have dispensed with the services of Pierre Beatte. (12)

In the early 19th century, when the "full-blooded" Native Americans were seen as hating white society and fighting to preserve their original savagism, an image arose of mixed-blooded people actively embracing Western culture and greedily pursuing their self-interest as a consequence. This may be one reason why Irving looked harshly upon them. We can see that Irving himself shared the prejudices against Native Americans commonly possessed by the people of his time.

Although Irving suspects that Beatte is disloyal or unfriendly, as the story unfolds, he finds that Beatte has immense knowledge of the woods, and gradually softens his attitude toward him. Beatte proves himself a competent guide who has enough experience to predict "all kinds of trouble" (20). When their party had to cross a river on foot near the Red Fork, Irving says, "It was now that our worthies, Beatte and Tonish, had an opportunity of displaying their Indian adroitness and resource" (44). The word "worthies" has some ironic overtones, but it was rare for the two (especially Antoine) to display their abilities as mixed-blooded Native Americans during the journey. Because they were able to cross the river safely, Irving is highly impressed by Beatte's ability and becomes more appreciative of him. Beatte feels satisfaction and says quietly, yet proudly, "Dey now see de Indian good for something, anyhow!"(46), conveying his disdain for the rangers who had underestimated him. By describing the contributions of Beatte and Antoine, Irving indicates that it would not be possible to carry out the journey in this frontier without them, stressing the importance of native guides.

As the journey goes on and they must hunt for their food, Beatte's talent as a hunter draws everyone's attention. Irving notes his pleasure when Beatte returns to camp with his prey.

> Beatte made his appearance with a fat doe across his horse. It was the first game he had brought in, and I was glad to see him with a trophy that might efface the memory of the polecat. . . . If Beatte, however, observed this Indian taciturnity about what he had done, Tonish made up for it by boasting of what he meant to do. (57)

This indicates that the distance between the two is slowly lessening, and Irving's distrust of Beatte is gradually diminishing. Irving not only mentions Beatte's hunting ability but also highlights his taciturnity. Unlike Antoine, who is described as "vaporing, chattering, bustling" (14), Beatte's taciturnity has something in common with the characterizations of Native Americans in those days. Thus, Irving begins to see in Beatte reflections of noble Native American nature and develops increasing interest in him.

Beatte's skills as a hunter are so excellent that he is able to bring down game and also catch wild horses. Irving describes Beatte returning to the camp leading a wild horse as follows: "Beatte had suddenly risen to great importance; he was the prime hunter, the hero of the day. . . . Beatte bore his honors in silence, . . . that he began to be considered an oracle" (85). Initially, Irving is dubious of Beatte, but upon seeing his great skill as a hunter and his ability to work smoothly as an interpreter and a guide, he comes to think more highly of him.

On another occasion, when Beatte returns to the camp after bringing down a bear, he casually starts a friendly conversation with Irving in front of the campfire discussing uneventful everyday matters such as "rheumatic pains in his limbs" (115). We do not read of distrustful feelings like those described in the first half of the journey, and we can even identify the sense of companionship between them.

Beatte says he thinks of himself as "little better than a mere wreck" (115), describing how he broke his right arm and left leg on two separate occasions by falling off a horse. This conversation shows both Beatte and Irving attempting to develop a better understanding of each other by talking about themselves. Indeed, Irving even comes to feel a certain intimacy towards the guide. At the same time, Irving, who was initially unable to trust or empathize with Beatte, and moves from imagining his mind as sly or devious to thinking that his own mind and thoughts are quite similar to the Native American's:

> Beatte had been brought up a Catholic, and was inflexible in his religious faith; . . . and he evinced a zeal for the good of his savage relations and neighbors, Indeed, though his father had been French, and he himself had been brought up in communion with the whites, he evidently was more of an Indian in his tastes, and his heart yearned toward his mother's nation. (116)

Subsequently, Irving's assessments of Beatte continue to improve and he frequently uses words like "noble," "useful," and "admirable," while praising his actions. From this attitude, we see that Irving comes to regard those of mixed-race in terms of the same stereotype applied to those of one race.

However, it is important to note that through his journey with Beatte, Irving comes to regard him as a noble individual.

On the other hand, Irving writes that Antoine, a "half-blood" like Beatte, "was without morals, without caste, without creed, without country, and even without language" (5). Of all the characters in the book, Antoine is the one described in the most comical terms as he fulfills his duties.

> Having made this mention of my comrades, I must not pass over unnoticed a personage of inferior rank: . . . the squire, the groom, the cook, the tent man, in a word, the factotum, and, I may add, the universal meddler and marplot of our party. (4)

Irving frequently compares him to Beatte in ways that imply Antoine's inferiority. For example, in contrast to Beatte who serves as an interpreter and guide, Antoine is described as speaking "his jargon of mingled French, English, and Osage, which not one of them could understand" (9), implying a neither-here-nor-there quality to his language that prevents him from adequately fulfilling his duties as an interpreter. Antoine joined the journey at its outset, and when Beatte joined later, he exhibits jealousy of his counterpart's superior skill. "The latter, too, seemed jealous of this new-comer. He whispered to us that these half-breeds were a touchy, capricious people, little to be depended upon" (14). Antoine's description, which sounds oblivious to the fact that he is also of mixed-race, is described with much humor.

Further, despite having Native American blood, like Beatte, Antoine loses his way in the woods. He later succeeds in rejoining the group, but nonetheless, Antoine's native intuition as a "half-blood" should have been enough to prevent such a mishap. The comedy of his getting lost can be seen as a moment of Irving's trademark wit. The descriptions of Antoine reflect Irving's negative attitude toward those of mixed-race, and contrast with Beatte, who is portrayed as a capable "mixed-blooded" individual.

Passages expressing an aversion to Antoine appear everywhere in the story. Irving states of Antoine's cheerfulness that: "if repressed in one way, [it] will break out in another" (43). He points out the extent of Antoine's vanity: "Nothing could equal the vain-glorious vaporing of little Tonish, as he strutted about the shore, and exulted in his superior skill and knowledge to the rangers" (46). Antoine is again represented negatively: "No one, however, was more unmanageable than Tonish" (55). Furthermore, concerning Antoine's playing of the fanfaron and his effervescence, Irving says that it was this attitude "which made me strongly suspect there was some little fright at bottom, to cause all this effervescence" (93), demonstrating his inability to understand Antoine. In Irving's depictions of Beatte, an image arises of a silent and dignified Native American, who displays his abilities quietly and "without saying a word" (81). Antoine, however, is depicted as displaying habits of those of mixed-blood who can become neither completely Native American nor completely white.

While Irving highly values Beatte, who was close to the natives, he demonstrates his ambivalence towards those of mixed-blood, occupying a place in between civilization and savagism, through depictions of Antoine's incomplete knowledge and skill as a woodsman. Irving has the astonishing gift of portraying witty and comical characters that are easily loved by readers. Indeed, his energetic depiction of Antoine recalls Rip in "Rip Van Winkle" or Ichabod in "The Legend of Sleepy Hollow." Apparently, however, it was difficult for him to eliminate his biased view of Native Americans, because his lively and comical depiction of Antoine stresses all the negative stereotypes common in his day. Taking this into account, his gifted ability as a writer must be reevaluated.

3. Reevaluation of *The Maine Woods* and *A Tour on the Prairies*

Before Thoreau and Irving wrote their works, the images of Native Americans described by white historians or writers such as Cooper were of two extremes. On one side was the noble savage, a man of high integrity, represented by Chingachgook and Uncas in *The Last of the Mohicans* (1826), while the opposite side featured the degenerate and evil Native American, epitomized by Magwa.

From this perspective, it can be said that Thoreau and Irving portrayed Native Americans not in the lopsided views of either civilization or savagism, but in their keen and fair observations that were balanced between the two extremes. In terms of his ability as a guide and woodsman, Polis was the "intelligent Indian" that Thoreau had been seeking. Although a full-blooded Native American, he was also an earnest Protestant who had adapted to the white community and civilization. Similarly, although Beatte was of mixed-blooded descent, he had the taciturnity expected of Native Americans. He not only displayed his ability as a guide and interpreter but also took pride in his lineage as a Native American and felt superstitious forebodings, even though he was a Catholic with the deep faith of his French father. Thoreau and Irving extolled the virtues of those who displayed what could be regarded as traditional Native American traits—a profound knowledge of the woods, taciturnity and self-esteem—while also understanding the necessity of language and religious faith to adapt to civilization.

In the end, Irving was an antiquary who cherished the pathos of good old qualities. He depicted the mixed-blooded or Native American guides as those who upheld their traditions while adapting to the rapidly developing civilization. Meanwhile, Thoreau sharply observed nature and people, and while he accepted the savagism of the Native American guides, he completely trusted the very civilized Polis and regarded him highly. Polis and Beatte stood out because they succeeded in embodying two cultures.

From today's perspective, Thoreau and Irving predicted that America's culture would be created not only by whites, but also by all ethnicities among the American citizenry, including Native Americans and immigrants who were gradually increasing in numbers. It is likely that they wrote celebratory and appealing accounts of Native Americans who embodied both white and Native American cultures as a way of warning against the government's high-handed policies for establishing a civilized society. *The Maine Woods* and *A Tour on the Prairies* deserve to be reevaluated in the modern era as detailed travelogues that reveal a fair depiction of the conditions of the Native Americans in the mid-19th century. These travelogues should also be reevaluated as works that understand the blending of cultures when different ethnic groups co-exist.

Works Cited

Harding, Walter and Carl Bode, eds. *The Correspondence of Henry David Thoreau*. New York: New York UP, 1958. Print.

Irving, Washington. *A Tour on the Prairies: Thirty Days in Deep Indian Country*. New York: Skyhorse Publishing, 2013. Print.

Martel, James, R. *Love is a Sweet Chain: Desire, Autonomy, and Friendship in Liberal Political Theory*. New York: Routledge Press, 2001. Print.

Sayre, Robert F. *Thoreau and the American Indians*. Princeton: Princeton UP, 1977. Print.

Thoreau, Henry D. *The Writing of Henry D. Thoreau: The Main Woods*. Ed. Joseph J. Moldenhauer. Princeton: Princeton UP, 1972. Print.

Dickinson, Thoreau, and John Brown:
The Voice of the Voiceless

Junko Kanazawa

Is it a necessary coincidence for poets or authors from the same era to use the same metaphor? The poets and authors contemporary with the "martyr" John Brown use "the meteor-metaphor," as David Reynolds calls it, in describing Brown's execution on December 2, 1859.[1] Reynolds explains, "On November 15, while Brown was awaiting execution, an unusual astronomical event took place over the skies of the Northeast" (383). Walt Whitman in "Year of Meteors" and Herman Melville in "The Portent," both describe the scene of Brown's execution using the image of a meteor as the portent of impending war.

H. D. Thoreau writes about Brown in his journal on December 5, 1859: "His late career—these six weeks, I mean—has been meteor-like, flashing through the darkness in which we live" (*The Journal of Henry D. Thoreau* 13: 6; hereafter abbreviated as *J*). The next day he elaborates on this image:

> What a transit that of his horizontal body alone, but just cut down from the gallows-tree! We read that at such a time it passed through Philadelphia, and by Saturday night had reached New York. Thus like a meteor it passed through the Union from the Southern regions toward the North. (*J* 13: 10)

Thoreau uses "the meteor-metaphor" to characterize both Brown's career and the transport of his body after execution, rather than as a portent of future national disasters, as in Whitman and Melville.[2] Although Emily Dickinson does not directly mention Brown in her poems or letters, she too uses the image of a "meteor" with the word "martyrs" in a poem written in 1861. This case is very unusual for Dickinson, because she scarcely uses the words elsewhere.[3] We cannot determine to what extent Dickinson was conscious of Brown, but she may have responded to the words "meteor" or "martyr" that were widely used at that time, as other writers picked them up in their own ways.

Adding Dickinson's poems to the list of works containing "the meteor-metaphor" will include her among contemporary authors who lived in an era of extreme tension of an impending war. Thoreau met Brown in person, and immediately after he knew of the attack on Harper's Ferry, he supported Brown publicly, whereas Dickinson privately wrote poems at home. Faith Barrett succinctly summarizes studies of Dickinson and the Civil War, and insists that Dickinson responded to events during the war and also to writings by her contemporaries (*Context* 214). This re-reading of "the meteor-metaphor" compares Dickinson's poem with Thoreau's use of the same metaphor and examines Dickinson's struggle to be "a poet" during the Civil War, or rather, the process through which the war made her a poet.

1. Thoreau and Brown

On October 16, 1859, the abolitionist John Brown attacked the United States Arsenal at Harper's Ferry with his followers. The *Springfield Republican* to which the Dickinson family subscribed, reported the attack as front-page news on October 18.[4] The exact details of the situation were not yet wholly clear; the perpetrators were referred to as a "mob," and the article did not mention Brown's name. Thoreau was at Emerson's house with Amos Bronson Alcott when the news of the raid arrived at Concord on October 19 (Harding 416).[5] He immediately began writing about Brown in his journal, and, less than 10 days later, he delivered "A Plea for Captain John Brown" in Concord's First Church. This was a lecture in support of Brown, who was generally criticized for actions widely regarded as insane. As Betty L. Mitchell explains the atmosphere in the North:

> [T]he majority of northerners condemned John Brown and his men as fanatics. Northern condemnation of Brown, however, turned to indignation against the South when it became apparent during the old man's trial that formal legal procedures would be hurried over or completely bypassed in order to render a guilty verdict as quickly as possible. (65)

Brown's representation in newspapers changed from a leader of "a mob" to "a martyr" when he was executed.

Thoreau's papers, "A Plea for Captain John Brown" and "The Last Days of John Brown," are based on the journal he kept during that time. However, in reading the journal, what can hardly fail to attract notice is a form of wavering of topics. In his journal, Thoreau seems to wander from his daily observation of natural surroundings into the Brown issue, clearly juxtaposing his external observations and his internal thoughts on Brown. For example, on the day that Thoreau learned of Brown's attack, his journal entry on Brown is interrupted by notes on a wholly different topic, "Find the seedling archangelica grown about two feet high and still quite green and growing, though the full grown plants are long since dead, root and stalk" (*J* 12: 402). Following this, his thoughts return to Brown: "the remarks of my neighbors upon Brown's death and supposed fate" (*J* 12: 403).[6]

Further investigation reveals interesting interactions between the two ideas; that is, Thoreau's observation of "the old routine" of the natural world (*J* 12:447) supports his thoughts of Brown, and vice versa. Thoreau himself suggests that he "commonly attend[s] more to nature than to man" (*Reform* 145), but "[a]ny affecting human event may blind our eyes to natural objects" (*J* 12:448). For instance, a day before Brown's attack, Thoreau writes down in his journal, a long list of autumn fruits, from "barberries" to "mallows." When Brown is caught, tried, and executed, Thoreau uses the description of the harvest of autumn crops to tell of the martyred Brown and his followers: "They were ripe for the gallows" (*J* 12: 420). The background scenery of the autumn harvest appears as a metaphor for the Brown issue. The expression that Brown's body is "just cut from the gallows-tree," already mentioned above, also suggests a kind of harvest.

The prominent feature in the journal entry for October 19, the day Thoreau learned of Brown's attack, is the use of the seed as a metaphor in foreseeing the execution of Brown.

> Such do not know that like the seed is the fruit, and that, in the moral world, when good seed is planted, good fruit is inevitable and does not depend on our watering and cultivating; that when you plant, or bury, a hero in this field, a crop of heroes is sure to spring up. This is a seed of such force and vitality that it does not ask our leave to germinate. (*J* 12:406)

In "A Plea for Captain John Brown," this passage is re-used but appears strange and abrupt.[7] Robert D. Richardson, Jr.'s explanation is instructive for us to understand this passage against the background of the late 1850s, when Thoreau listed "all phenomena in Concord and the order in which they appeared each year." In the context of the description in his journal, this passage can be considered to be based on his research. Richardson writes, "He made a list of which fruits ripened on what day during one month of one specific year" (5). In the course of this research, he "became caught up, for a time, in the John Brown affair" (4). It seems as though the Brown affair distracted him from his research, but from a different viewpoint, Thoreau seems to explain Brown's actions by using the metaphor of "dispersion of seeds," which preoccupied his mind in those days. Writing about Brown may also be a part of his observing death and birth of natural phenomena.

Thoreau also notices that the course of nature disregards human society.

> I have been so absorbed of late in Captain Brown's fate as to be surprised whenever I detected the old routine running still. . . . It appeared strange to me that the little dipper should be still diving in the river as of yore; and this suggested that this grebe might be diving here when Concord shall be no more. (*J* 12: 447–448)

The natural surroundings proceed at their own pace without interest in human society, as "the swallows fly low" over corpses on the battlefield in Melville's poem "Shiloh." Thoreau's interweaving of the topics of Brown and nature in his journal highlights the profound viewpoint of death and birth of the natural phenomena that held him. As the Brown issue diminished in the press by January 1860, Thoreau's journal ceased mention on Brown (Meyer 311), and he soon turned his attention to Charles Darwin's recently-published *On the Origin of Species* (Richardson 11).

2. Dickinson and Politics

The most important influences on Emily Dickinson's political views were her father Edward Dickinson, *Springfield Republican* editor Samuel Bowles, and the "Secret Six" (supporters of John Brown) member T. W. Higginson, who led black soldiers as a colonel. Edward Dickinson is particularly important in any consideration of both the social and family atmosphere in which Dickinson was raised and lived. As a member of the U.S. House of Representatives, Edward Dickinson was active in the Congress when tension increased between the North and South, and he voted against the Kansas-Nebraska Act in 1854. Although Edward Dickinson opposed slavery, he was skeptical of radical social change and opposed Brown as well. According to Reynolds, he sent a message of support to the anti-Brown meeting held in Boston after the execution of

Brown (450).

A letter Dickinson sent to Bowles around August 1860 shows that Bowles, who was against slavery, also influenced her consciousness of racial issues.

> I am much ashamed. I misbehaved tonight. I would like to sit in the dust. I fear I am your little friend no more, but Mrs Jim Crow. . . . I will never be giddy again. Pray forgive me now: Respect little Bob o' Lincoln again! (L223)

Although it is not clear what background she refers to here, she seems to have been conscious of the racial problems in her own way.[8]

Around the time Higginson was preparing for his departure with his regiment, Dickinson sent her first letter of introduction to him, and their exchange of letters continued until the month of her death in 1886. His service as a soldier must have created a significant impression on Dickinson.

In the era that regarded taking action as important, these three men around Dickinson, as well as Thoreau, were typical "men of action." In "The American Scholar," Emerson writes, "Action is with the scholar subordinate, but it is essential. Without it he is not yet man. Without it thought can never ripen into truth" (60). For Thoreau, Brown's "action and character" moved him "to correct the tone and the statements of the newspapers" (*J* 12:424). Edward Dickinson was active for the benefit of the church, college, military draft, and the introduction of the railroad into Amherst; Bowles spoke for the partisan movement through his *Springfield Republican*; and Higginson led a black regiment: Dickinson was in contact with these activists at a time when she sought meaning in her existence. In her letters to friends, she exudes a sense of being "nobody" compared with activists, and we can hear the cry of her soul, which contemplates what she should do in times of national crisis. In a letter to Higginson, she writes, "I had a terror – since September – I could tell to none – and so I sing, as the Boy does by the Burying Ground – because I am afraid" (L261, April 1862). The text that follows will discuss how the germ of her distress ripens into the subject of poems written in those days.

3. Reading Dickinson's F187

The poem "Through the Straight Pass of Suffering" (F187) was sent to Susan Dickinson in 1861, then to Samuel Bowles in 1861, and was finally transcribed to a fascicle, probably in 1863. This process of rewriting shows that Dickinson returned to the poem several times during the war.[9]

The poem deals with "martyrs" who gave themselves to their faith in a cause. Adrian Chastain discusses early puritan martyrdom and contends that the old sense of "martyr" meant a person who was killed for his or her faith, but the definition evolved over time so that a soldier who killed people to keep his faith also came to be categorized as a "martyr"(5). In this paper, I use "martyr" in this broad sense. Given this definition, the war turned many men into "martyrs." Of the 3,000 residents in the village of Amherst, "384 Amherst College men served in the war and 31 were killed" (Miller 49).

Dickinson's poem begins with the concept of martyrs who proceed steadily without taking their eyes off their destination, God.

> Through the Straight Pass of Suffering
> The Martyrs even trod –
> Their feet opon Temptation –
> Their foreheads – opon God –

As if to show their steadfast faith in their proceedings, the iambic meter is kept once the martyrs appear and extends to the reference in the first line of the next stanza to "A Stately – Shriven Company – ." Dickinson rhymes "trod" with "God," as if to intensify the sense of their unwavering faith. However, all of a sudden, in the second line of the second stanza, the course of the procession swerves into the open space of the sky:

> Convulsion playing round –
> Harmless as Streaks of Meteor –
> Opon a Planet's Bond –

At this point, the iambic meter is interrupted by a line of trochaic meter, but then returns to iambic: "Their faith the Everlasting Troth – / Their Expectation – sure –." Eventually, however, in the last line of the poem, readers are again taken into another space, to the "Polar Air," with the rhythm of trochaic: "Wades so – through Polar Air –." These two digressions seem to interrupt the "Stately" steps of "the Martyrs." The meter fluctuates repeatedly, as if to contradict the steadiness of martyrs.

In considering the connotations of "martyr" in those days, an article in the *Springfield Republican* published on March 29, 1862, provides a typical example. The article "Our Martyrs and Their Resurrection" mourns the death of Theodore Winthrop, who died "on June 10, 1861 at the Battle of Big Bethel, the first land battle of the war" (Fuller 27). This article conspicuously idealizes the importance of being active in service. A nameless youth, once he takes up a weapon and gives himself for the cause, becomes transformed into an object of admiration.

> The spirit of liberty is increasing in power and truth, and the volume of it, the purity of it, are swelled by the souls of these young martyrs, who give their dust to the dust whence it came, and their life to the country whose ideas were its sustenance and inspiration.

From a 21st century viewpoint, this touch of admiration for the martyrs of liberty seems too light, without a feeling of grimness toward the fact of death. The article goes on to compare martyrs to "seed":

> These deaths of noble young men in battle, which, on our first hearing of them, make us shudder so and ask why this dreadful waste of life, are the snapping open of so many brave caskets, and the dropping into the fruitful soil of humanity of the quick seeds of a new national and human life.

The unsettled development and meter of poem F187 calls attention to the importance of the two words, "martyr" and "meteor," which Dickinson uses sparingly. Thoreau and other Transcendentalists generally regarded Brown as a martyr, and this tendency spread according to the change of the public opinion about him. On the day of his execution, December 2, 1859, the *Hampshire and Franklin Express*, to which Dickinson's family subscribed, repeatedly used the word "martyr" to refer to Brown.

As for the word "meteor" as mentioned above, it could be related simply to the appearance of a large meteor observed in New York. However, the newspapers at the time frequently juxtaposed their reports on the meteor and their articles on Brown. Therefore, Dickinson's use of the two words "meteor" and "martyr" might occur not only for her favorite device of alliteration, but because she was borrowing words from the contemporary atmosphere.

While Thoreau explores in his journal his personal, subjective ideas about Brown and natural surroundings, Dickinson's poem narrates events impersonally, as if from somewhere far above. We cannot find any trace of the narrator on the surface. In the search for the existence of the narrator, two words in the final stanza, "needle" and "wades," are important.

> Their faith the Everlasting Troth –
> Their Expectation – sure –
> The Needle to the North Degree
> Wades so – through Polar Air –

Helen Vendler focuses on the tenses of verbs in this poem, which begins in the past tense and ends with the present tense "wades." Vendler considers that martyrs trod eternally, and the subject "needle" implies the "internal compass" of their steps.

> [T]he Martyrs "wade" through suffering as if through a deep current. God awaits them at the Pole; the Martyrs have a single aim, His presence. They always know the direction in which to go, no matter what suffering they must endure in making their way to Him. Their internal compass is always set to the Polar chill of sacrificial death, and their eyes are on their goal. (59)

Although it could be convincing that the steps of "Martyrs" are expressed in the image of the "needle" which looks to the north, it is strange that "needle" is singular noun without respect to the plural "Martyrs." "Martyrs" may be regarded as one group in perfect file, and could be counted as singular.

Based on Vendler's interpretation of "wades," "needle" can be considered as a metonymy of a person who does needlework, and also as the existence of the missing narrator of this poem. In other poems, Dickinson uses needlework as a figure for the work of writing poetry, as in F1163.

> A Spider sewed at Night
> Without a Light
> Opon an Ark of White –

This poem suggests the work of writing poetry in the figure of a spider that is an idealized image of a poet, without the metric hesitation or stammer seen with "Martyrs" in F187. Vendler writes, "The complete autonomy of the spider is envied by Dickinson—who did care (at least at first) what her sister-in-law Susan or her friend Thomas Wentworth Higginson or others thought of her work" (419). By the time this poem was transcribed into a fascicle in 1869, her way of writing must have been developed and the image of the spider must also have reflected her own image as a poet. In the poem F681, Dickinson describes needlework, gardening, and writing poetry as equivalents. They are works Dickinson equally depicts from a woman's point of view.

Dont put up my Thread & Needle –
I'll begin to Sow
When the Birds begin to whistle –
Better stiches – so –

To return to the "needle" in F187, if it is regarded as a metonymy of a person who works at sewing, that is, who writes poems, the verb "wades" could stand for the motion of a needle over cloth, and also the motion of a pen over a piece of paper. The work of writing poetry is hard, strictly lonesome work that makes one feel as if one is entering a desolate space with "Polar Air," as Dickinson puts it in her poems.

In F926, the narrator talks about "Experience" in a thrilling way.

I stepped from Plank to Plank
A slow and cautious way
The Stars about my Head I felt
About my Feet the Sea –

I knew not but the next
Would be my final inch –
This gave me that precarious Gait
Some call Experience –

Or in F570, "I tried to think a lonelier Thing / Than any I had seen – / Some Polar Expiation – An Omen in the Bone / Of Death's tremendous nearness –" In both poems, the practice of writing poetry leads a poet to a desolate space where he or she can find no one with whom to speak. At times, the poet must face perilous situations.

Although the work of writing poetry is actually done within a room closed in a house, interestingly Dickinson relates it to infinite open space, as in these two poems. Paul Crumbley, in discussing the political aspects of Dickinson's poetry, interprets as follows:

> The way her poems are structured suggests that her aim is not to pose quandaries that her poems and their speakers solve, but rather to stage dramas of sovereignty and consent that require her readers to think independently about the political significance of choices made in the domestic sphere. (34)

These poems mentioned above should also be considered as examples of the poems Crumbley interprets. In the case of F187, the act of dealing with a "needle" might relate to Dickinson's act of binding fascicles in this period. According to Franklin, during the war, she transcribed over 900 poems and bound them into fascicles (1533) using a needle and thread.

If we include the figure of Brown in the class of "martyrs," his action demands public attention, and his resort to violence contrasts well with that of women's needle-work in their private sphere. The etymology of the word "martyr" is "witness," defined by *Webster's Dictionary* as, "One who, by his death, bears witness to the truth of the gospel," whose actions or behavior are intended for public observation. Meanwhile, writing poems is a highly private work; it is rightly compared to an activity in a space enclosed by ice. There is no one who observes or encourages the act, and the poet must "wade" with a burden of fear and doubt about one's own ability.

Dickinson sent this poem in a letter (L251) to Bowles in early 1861, where she regards the steps as her own.[10]

> Dear friend
> If you
> doubted my Snow –
> for a moment – you
> never will – again –
> I know –
> Because I could not
> say it – I fixed it
> in the Verse – for
> you to read – when

your thought wavers,
for such a foot as
mine –
Through the strait pass
of suffering – [page break]
[blank space]
The Martyrs – even – trod.
Their feet – opon Temptation –
Their faces – opon God –
    A stately – shriven –
Company –
Convulsion – playing round –
Harmless – as streaks
of meteor –
Opon a Planet's Bond –
    Their faith –
the everlasting troth –
Their expectation – fair –
The Needle – to the North
Degree –
Wades – so – thro' Polar Air! (Mitchell 129–30)

In this form, the message of the letter flows into the lines of the poem without breaks. This poem itself shows the steadfast steps of "martyrs," but put into her letter to Bowles, the message is about the narrator's (Dickinson's) steps that "waver" as the form of the lines wavers.

As in the letter to Bowles, although F187 starts with the figure of "martyrs" who are not concerned even with the appearance of a meteor, the course of its development sees those figures replaced by the third person singular, an unwitnessed narrator. The "waver" in the development of the poem and the rhyme might reflect the "waver" of the person with the needle.[11]

4. "Martyr Poet"

Dickinson repeatedly explores the theme of an inward battle unknown to anyone else. "Success is counted sweetest" (F112), "To fight aloud, is very brave –" (F138), "The Battle fought between the Soul" (F629) are examples written shortly before or during the war. These inward battles differ from those of "martyrs" who publicly expose their agonies and even fight with weapons in their hands. In her poems, a lonely narrator who fights without anyone's regard feels a form of envy toward the people who fight in public. F524 is one of the examples.

It feels a shame to be Alive –
When Men so brave – are dead –
One envies the Distinguished Dust –
Permitted – such a Head –

The Stone – that tells defending Whom
This Spartan put away
What little of Him we – possessed
In Pawn for Liberty –

The price is great – Sublimely paid –
Do we deserve – a Thing –
That lives – like Dollars – must be piled
Before we may obtain?

Are we that wait – sufficient worth –
That such Enormous Pearl
As life – dissolved be – for Us –
In Battle's – horrid Bowl?

It may be – a Renown to live –
I think the Men who die –
Those unsustained – Saviors –
Present Divinity –

Faith Barrett relates this poem to the historical background of Lincoln's suspension of *habeas corpus* in March 1863 ("Drums off" 119). Cristanne Miller notes, "Life is measured in this poem as the pragmatic 'Dollars' paid to avoid conscription" (57). Dickinson's brother Austin himself paid money in May 1864 to avoid conscription. We also find the feeling of envy on the part of the narrator who might stay at home without going to the war, while the capitalized "Men" may suggest soldiers, whose lives are expressed as an "Enormous Pearl."[12]

"We" may refer to women who stayed at home feeling frustrated by being able to do nothing special for a national crisis. A feeling of guilt is conspicuous, rather than a glorification of fighting. The phrase "we that wait" in the fourth stanza reiterates this sense of guilt. The contrasts "Alive" and "dead" in the first stanza are echoed by "live" and "die" in the final stanza. Although, in the beginning, "Distinguished Dust" may be stressed by capitalization with the "D" sound of alliteration, this emphasizes not only the glory of "Distinguished" but also the hollowness of being "Dust." Further, this poem bears the voice of those voiceless martyrs who died nameless.

This poem highlights two radically opposite situations, namely, performing action and tantalizing oneself in doing nothing. The work of activists in her life makes Dickinson desperately grapple with her own sense of identity in writing poems in a time of upheaval. We can find this sense in F665 as the extension of F187.

> The Martyr Poets – did not tell –
> But wrought their Pang in syllable –
> That when their mortal name be numb –
> Their mortal fate – encourage Some –
> The Martyr Painters – never spoke –
> Bequeathing – rather – to their Work –
> That when their conscious fingers cease –
> Some seek in Art – the Art of Peace –

"Martyr Poets" entrust their feeling of agony to their works rather than speak aloud. In this poem, the words "Poets" and "Painters" bear almost the same meaning. Shira Wolosky observes that the poem contains binary oppositions, such as "public / private," "selfhood / self-denial," "declare / deny," "assertion / renunciation," "utterance / revocation," "assertion / denial," and "claim / disclaim" (125). Wolosky suggests that this oppositional dimension may be closely related to the question of Dickinson's publication, but that is not my concern in this paper.

The time scale of F665 is important, as it is in poem F187, which starts in the past tense and ends in the present tense. In this change of tense, we find a possible trace of the narrator, who does not appear in the poem. In F665, the past tense may show the perspective of the narrator who is in the "present" and looks back into the past. As past martyrs (F187) head for heaven, martyr poets (F665) head for readers in the future.

In contrast to the time scale in Dickinson's poems, Thoreau is conscious of and celebrates living in the same era as Brown: "I rejoice that I live in this age, that I was his contemporary." At the same time he "foresee[s] the time when the painter will paint that scene, the poet will sing it, the historians record it" (*J* 12: 421). Thoreau praises Brown's "unwavering purposes, not to be dissuaded but by an experience and wisdom greater than his own. Not yielding to a whim or transient impulse, but carrying out the purpose of a life" (*J* 12: 420), while in Dickinson's poem F665, the narrator is conscious of readers in the future, whom the narrator helps to find "peace" rather than war—"Each Age a Lens / Disseminating their / Circumference –" (F930). The "p" sound is repeated as alliteration in "Poets," "Pang," "Painters," and through the hands of poets and painters reaches "Peace."

Betsy Erkkila considers the voice of Dickinson as that of a woman from a privileged family, speaking to her friends, especially socially or culturally elite people (144). Geoffrey Sanborn suggests that the presence of women, such as Irish servant Margaret Maher who supported Dickinson in the household, may have enabled her to write poems although we are not sure to what extent Dickinson herself was conscious of their presence. However, what is undeniable is that she withheld some poems regarding war or agony from her contemporaries.[13] F665 is one of them, which is told from a future-oriented viewpoint.

F665 reiterates the existence of "Martyr Poets" in the past and implies the existence of readers in future. Therefore, the time scale ranging from past to the future, with the background of war rather than Dickinson's privileged social status, serves to present not only representations of "pang" in the time of war, but also the possibility of "peace." Moreover, the "Pang" experienced by "The Martyr Poets" is transformed into encouragement. Beyond "wavering" and beyond the place and time, what is sent to readers in the highly charged atmosphere of this century is the voice of the voiceless, or the voice of a poet created by war.

Notes

1 As for Whitman, "meteors" could be related to other incidents than that of November 15. See Kummings (ed.) *Routledge Encyclopedia of Walt Whitman*.

2 Kent Ljungquist minutely examines whether Thoreau derived the image of the meteor from newspaper reports (677).

3 According to *Emily Dickinson Lexicon* [http://edl.byu.edu], Dickinson uses "martyr" in F47, F187 and F665, and "meteor" in F187 and F1488. And also see S. P. Rosenbaum (ed.) *A Concordance to the Poems of Emily Dickinson*.

4 I am grateful to Margaret R. Daikin, Archives and Special Collections of Amherst College, for her great advice and invaluable help in researching newspapers.

5 According to Ljungquist, Thoreau "consulted" some papers including *Atlas and Daily Bee about Brown* (677).

6 Michael Meyer focuses on the similarities of Thoreau's comments about his observing natural surroundings and his approach to Brown in his journal. Meyer explains the feature by suggesting "his characteristic preference for poetic truth over experiential facts." Meyer's conclusion may explain why Thoreau observed Brown but made no mention of his brutal actions in Osawatomie (310–11).

7 The passage occurs in "Plea" in almost the same form as in the journal. There are two places where the comma is inserted: "good fruit is inevitable," and "This is a seed of such force and vitality".

8 For Dickinson's reaction to slavery, see Benjamin Friedlander's "Auctions of the Mind: Emily Dickinson and Abolition."

9 On Dickinson's sending this poem (F187) to people in 1861 without copying it into a fascicle until 1863, Cristanne Miller observed, "Perhaps the poem was initially written when Dickinson was thinking of martyrdom generally, or thinking of the early war deaths. It may then have become more important to her in 1863 as the deaths mounted and the war went on" (July 17, 2016). I am grateful to Cristanne Miller for her invaluable insight.

10 This form is transcribed by Domhnall Mitchell from the original letter.

11 Considering Ann Rose's suggestion that the time of war made the younger generation "lost hold of inherited insights" (20), the sways in rhyme and development might be related to the sway in the younger generation who "tried to replace religion's assurances with temporal rewards, striving to invest their work, leisure, families, politics, and particularly their war with enduring meaning" (20).

12 This metaphor reminds us of the big pearl Cleopatra dissolves in a cup and drinks in Shakespeare's *Anthony and Cleopatra* (Act.2 Scene 5).

13 Cristanne Miller mentions the fact in her book *Reading*, although she does not analyze specific poems. Other uncirculated poems related to war are, for example, F384, F465, F480, F518, F524, F527, F545, F616, F629, F704, and F764.

Works Cited

Barrett, Faith. "Slavery and the Civil War." *Emily Dickinson in Context*. Ed. Eliza Richards. Cambridge: Cambridge UP, 2013, 206–15. Print.

——. ""Drums off the Phantom Battlements": Dickinson's War Poems in Discursive Context." *A Companion to Emily Dickinson*. Ed. Martha Nell Smith and Mary Loeffelholz. Oxford: Blackwell, 2008, 107–32. Print.

Crumbley, Paul. *Winds of Will: Emily Dickinson and the Sovereignty of Democratic Thought*. Tuscaloosa: U of Alabama P, 2010. Print.

Dickinson, Emily. *The Letters of Emily Dickinson*. Ed. Thomas H. Johnson. 3 vols. Cambridge, MA. Harvard UP, 1958. Print.

——. *The Poems of Emily Dickinson: Variorum Edition*. Ed. R. W. Franklin. 3 vols. Cambridge: Harvard UP, 1998. Print.

——. *Emily Dickinson's Poems: As She Preserved Them*. Ed. Cristanne Miller. Cambridge, MA: Harvard UP, 2016. Print.

Emerson, Ralph Waldo. *Essays and Lectures*. New York: Library of America, 1983. Print.

Erkkila, Betsy. "Dickinson and the Art of Politics." *A Historical Guide to Emily Dickinson*. Ed. Vivian R. Pollak. Oxford: Oxford UP, 2004, 133–74. Print.

Friedlander, Benjamin. "Auctions of the Mind: Emily Dickinson and Abolition." *Arizona Quarterly* 54.1 (Spring 1998): 1–26. Web.28 Sep. 2016.

Frothingham, O. B. "Our Martyrs and Their Resurrection." *Springfield Republican* 29 March 1862: 2. Microform. American's Historical Newspaper.

Fuller, Randall. *From Battlefields Rising: How The Civil War Transformed American Literature*. Oxford: Oxford UP, 2011. Print.

Harding, Walter. *The Days of Henry Thoreau: A Biography*. New York: Dover, 1982. Print.

"Items by Telegraphs." *Springfield Daily Republican*. Wednesday 16 November 1859: 1. Microform. American's Historical Newspaper.

Kummings, Donald D. ed. *The Routledge Encyclopedia of Walt Whitman*. London: Routledge, 2011. Print.

Leyda, Jay. *The Years and Hours of Emily Dickinson*. 2 vols. New Haven: Yale UP, 1960. Print.

Ljungquist, Kent. ""Meteor of the War": Melville, Thoreau, and Whitman Respond to John Brown." *American Literature* 61.4 (Dec 1989): 674–80. Project Muse. Web. Oct. 2. 2015.

Longsworth, Polly. "Brave among the Bravest: Amherst in the Civil War." *Amherst College Quarterly* (Summer 1999): 25–31. Print.

Melville, Herman. *Battle-Pieces and Aspects of the War: Civil War Poems*. New York: Prometheus, 2001. Print.

Meyer, Michael. "Thoreau's Rescue of John Brown from History." *Studies in the American Renaissance*. 1980: 301–16. Print.

Miller, Cristanne. "Pondering 'Liberty': Emily Dickinson and the Civil War." *American Vistas and Beyond: A Festschrift for Roland Hagenbüchle*. Trier, Germany:

Wissenschaftlicher Verlag, 2002. Print.
——. *Reading in Time: Emily Dickinson in the Nineteenth Century*. Amherst: U of Massachusetts P., 2012. Print.
Mitchell, Betty L. "Massachusetts Reacts to John Brown's Raid." *Civil War History*. 19.1 (March 1973): 65–79. Print.
Mitchell, Domhnall. *Measure of Possibility: Emily Dickinson's Manuscripts*. Amherst: U of Amherst P, 2005. Print.
Reynolds, David S. *John Brown, Abolitionist: The Man Who Killed Slavery, Sparked the Civil War, and Seeded Civil Rights*. New York: Vintage, 2005. Print.
Rose, Anne C. *Victorian America and the Civil War*. Cambridge: Cambridge UP, 1992. Print.
Rosenbaum, S.P. ed., *A Concordance to the Poems of Emily Dickinson*. Ithaca: Cornel UP, 1964. Print.
"Serious Troubles at Harper's Ferry, Va. The U.S. Arsenal seized by the mob." *Springfield Republican*. 18 Oct. 1859: 1. Microform. American's Historical Newspaper.
Sanborn, Geoffrey. "Keeping Distance: Cisneros, Dickinson, and the Politics of Private Enjoyment." *PMLA*, 116.5 (Oct., 2001): 1334–48. Web. 17 Nov. 2015.
"Thanksgiving in Amherst." *Hampshire and Franklin Express* 2 Dec. 1859: 2. Print.
Thoreau, Henry David. *The Journal of Henry D. Thoreau*. Ed. Bradford Torry and F. H. Allen, vol. I-XIII, Boston: Houghton Mifflin, 1906. Print.
——. *Reform Papers*. Ed. Wendell Glick. Princeton: Princeton UP, 1973. Print.
——. *Faith in a Seed*. Ed. Bradley P. Dean. Washington D.C.: Island, 1993. Print.
Vendler, Helen. *Dickinson: Selected Poems and Commentaries*. Cambridge: Harvard UP, 2010. Print.
Weimer, Adrian Chastain. *Martyrs' Mirror: Persecution and Holiness in Early New England*. Oxford: Oxford UP, 2012. Print.
Whitman, Walt. *Leaves of Grass and Other Writings*. Ed. Michael Moon. New York: Norton, 2002. Print.
Wolosky, Shira. "Public and Private in Dickinson's War Poetry." *A Historical Guide to Emily Dickinson*. Ed. Vivian R. Pollak. Oxford: Oxford UP, 2004, 103–32. Print.

Anne Waldman and Thoreau's Civil Disobedience

Ayako Takahashi

Introduction

Anne Waldman is a post-Beat generation poet. With Allen Ginsberg, she founded the Jack Kerouac School of Disembodied Poetics at Naropa University, where, since 1974, leading poets and writers have come to present techniques of writing to students, to read their works, and to discuss how and why they write. The school aims at providing inspiration, insight, and motivation to young working writers. Two volumes of *Talking Poetics From Naropa Institute* edited by Waldman and Marilyn Webb can be found in the annals of the school. Waldman also edited *Civil Disobediences: Poetics and Politics in Action* and constructed the overall poetics of engagement based on Thoreau's "Civil Disobedience." By focusing on essays edited by Waldman, I will discuss what Thoreau's civil disobedience offered the Beat poets and especially Waldman, and the contemporary significance of the concept of civil disobedience. To examine the contemporary significance of Thoreau, based on the historical significance of his research, I will discuss how Thoreau's civil disobedience was received by, and transformed for, Waldman and the Beat poets.

1. Beat Poets and Thoreau

In this section, I will examine how Thoreau influenced the Beat poets. Ann Charters mentions that "The lives of certain Beat writers—most notably Kerouac, Ginsberg, Burroughs, Snyder, Welch—have also been taken by the readers to represent larger issues related to the exercise of personal freedom in American society." This view of Charters corresponds to Waldman's citation of Thoreau's "Men at all?" (*Early Essays and Miscellanies* 204), as it inquires about the relationship between a nation and an individual. It also corresponds to Thoreau's questioning of human behavior in American society. Charters mentions that the Beat writers were recognized as a vital part of American culture, and they are still identified as avant-garde literary figures. Further,

Charters mentions the following:

> [T]heir biographies extend beyond unique personal sagas to embody several important contemporary concerns: the search through an interest in Buddhism and primitive religions for an alternative life-style to that of prevailing American materialism; protest against institutional power, particularly against the production of nuclear weapons and the development of the American military-industrial complex; efforts to liberalize legal restrictions on homosexuality and drugs, specially marijuana; regard for ecological balance on the planet. (Charters xiii)

Charters acknowledges that the Beat writers fought for individual freedom and demonstrated literary, social, and cultural liberation and that this liberation provided the impetus for overcoming social issues. The biographies of the Beat writers embody individual freedom; they expressed themselves not only in their literature but also practiced the kind of lifestyles they described in their literature. For example, Gary Snyder's Zen poetry and his thoughts on bioregionalism are supposed to have been developed from his own life experiences in Sierra Nevada.

Diane di Prima, a female Beat poet, wrote a highly symbolic line, "THE ONLY WAR THAT MATTERS IS THE WAR AGAINST THE IMAGINATION" (Di Prima 160). This line highlighted the severe irony of the lack of imagination in society. Snyder also cited Di Prima's phrase in his book *A Place in Space*. The biggest protest for the Beat poets, including Di Prima, was the war against imagination. As Thoreau criticized soldiers for marching to wars "against their wills" and "their common sense and consciences," we can infer that envisioning has been important and has been taken over since Thoreau.

Consider the following quotation from Thoreau:

> [A] corporation of conscientious men is a corporation *with* a conscience. Law never made men a whit more just; and, by means of their respect for it, even the well-disposed are daily made the agents of injustice. A common and natural result of an undue respect for law is, that you may see a file of soldiers, colonel, captain, corporal, privates, powder-monkeys, and all, marching in admirable order over hill and dale to the wars, against their wills, ay, against their common sense and consciences, which makes it very steep marching indeed, and produces a palpitation of the heart. They have

> no doubt that it is a damnable business in which they are concerned; they are all peaceably inclined. Now, what are they? Men at all? or small movable forts and magazines, at the service of some unscrupulous man in power? (*Collected Essays and Poems* 204–05)

As Thoreau criticized soldiers for marching to wars "against their wills" and "their common sense and consciences," we can infer that envisioning has been important and has been taken over since Thoreau.

This quotation seems to have motivated Waldman to write *Civil Disobediences*. Waldman confirmed the view that in paying excessive respect to the law, soldiers misunderstood the concept of justice and thus could not help but march to the battlefield in misery. Waldman also blames soldiers for "marching in admirable order over hill and dale to the wars, against their wills, ay, against their common sense and consciences" and agrees that "it is a damnable business in which they are concerned." Waldman points out the supposed dangers of misunderstanding what justice stands for in a large society. She wonders if human beings are "small movable forts and magazines." The unjust cable man that Thoreau had drastically criticized seems to overlap with both Waldman's works and her life itself as a performance poet who lived through the Beat and the post-Beat movement's protests against society. Waldman seems to be trying to develop a contemporary version of civil disobedience from the point of view of biocentrism.

2. Civil Disobedience and "Wildness"

Waldman incorporates Thoreau's ecological imagination through Snyder. We should pay attention to the "ecological resistance" of John Rodman, George Sessions, and Bill Devall, cited in *The Rights of Nature* by Roderick Frazier Nash. Their approach extends citizen sense to the whole of biology, which they base in the concept of deep ecology. The leader of Earth First, Dave Foreman, is considered to be "a radical environmentalist" and the face of environmental citizen protests (eco-sabotages). Therefore, studies on civil disobedience have mainly focused on the relationship not only between the nation and individuals but also between the nation and non-humans.

The Beat poets never repeatedly mentioned civil disobedience. An antithetical example includes Gary Snyder. He was strongly influenced by Thoreau's notions of "wildness." Sessions states that "Thoreau's 1851 statement, 'In wilderness is the preservation of the world' provides the basis for modern ecocentric environmentalism" (Sessions 165). Tsutomu Takahashi stated that "It is clear that Snyder writes *The Practice of The Wild* based on Thoreau's 'Walking'." (Takahashi 34; my translation) and that "Snyder chases in the etymology wood and goes around and back to Thoreau. He finally tries to catch the meaning of 'wildness' that he would try to redefine." (Takahashi 35; my translation) Katsunori Yamazato points out that Snyder's essay, *Earth House Hold* (called the twentieth century's *Walden*) is inspired by Thoreau's national views and strong critical spirit and that is the reason that Snyder inherited Thoreau's wildness. (Yamazato 67–8; my translation)

In his book *The Practice of the Wild*, Snyder quotes from Thoreau as follows: "'give me a wildness no civilization can endure.' That is clearly not difficult to find. It is harder to imagine a civilization that wildness can endure, yet this is just what we must try to do. Wildness is not just the 'preservation of the world,' it is the world" (*The Practice of the Wild* 6). This argument implies that wildness does not just mean physical space and the "preservation of the world" but also preservation of its spirit. It is worth remembering Thoreau's words: "what I have been preparing to say is, that in Wildness is the preservation of the world" (*Collected Essays and Poems* 239) and "Life consists with wildness" (*Collected Essays and Poems* 240). Snyder combines Thoreau's wildness with bioregionalism to discuss the issues contemporary society is facing.

When considering wildness, it is necessary to think of pastoralism as well. Pastoralism is one of the most important subjects in American literature because of its disconnect with technology; it tends to involve symbolic images like the machine invading the landscape.[1] Thoreau made a remarkable contribution to the development of contemporary pastoralism literature by writing on topics such as wilderness and civilization, nature and culture, and homocentrism and biocentrism. Laurence Buell states that the concept of pastoralism plays an important role in bridging the gap between homocentrism and biocentrism. Nash mentions that "In providing a philosophic defense of the half-savage, Thoreau gave the American idealization of the pastoral a new foundation" (Nash 94). Leo Marx's thesis, titled "Pastoralism in America," starts with the question of "whether pastoralism might yet provide the basis for an effective ideology in the United States" and concludes with the observation that "adherents of pastoralism would have to form alliances with the hitherto disadvantaged carriers of emergent values—those for whom 'the recovery of the natural' as yet has, in itself, little or no appeal" (Marx 66). Pastoralism originally refers to "the ways of herdsmen" coming and going from civilization to nature or wilderness. Focusing on the political aspect of pastoralism, Marx mentions that pastoralism succeeds the radical dissidence derived from the works of Emerson, Thoreau, and Whitman by youth culture and The New Left in the 1960s and 1970s. Shoko Itoh states that the importance of wildness grew stronger and stronger for Thoreau after *Walden* and was transferred to another concept—the anti-concept of "civil." Both civil disobedience and anti-slavery movements motivate Thoreau's pastoral inclinations (Itoh 95).

So far, the concept of civil disobedience had directly influenced the representation of Beat Poets. This strong desire for pastoralism, including "wildness" and civil disobedience, consequently gave them a significant sense of purpose. Though the concept of civil disobedience resonated with the Beat poets, it was not enough to capture their spirit. However, "wildness" greatly influenced Gary Snyder and gave him significant motivation to solve social problems. "Wildness" and civil disobedience, substantiated by pastoralism, greatly affected the Beat poets. This is clear from Waldman's works.

3. Anne Waldman and Thoreau's Political Imagination

How does Waldman incorporate Thoreau's political imagination into her feminism through Ginsberg and subsume Thoreau's ecological imagination into her biocentrism through Snyder? In this section, I will discuss Waldman's political and ecological imagination.

Waldman constructs her civil disobedience on the forgotten voice of women. One of her achievements is the re-evaluation of female Beat poets. She writes in her foreword to Brenda Knight's excellent book, *Women of the Beat Generation: The Writers, Artists, and Muses at the Heart of a Revolution*, "This book is testament, primarily, to the lives of these women, lest they be ignored or forgotten" (Knight xi). She goes on to write that "It is time for cultural historians, critical theorists, feminist literary critics, other poets and writers to take heed of this rich compendium of lore, literary history, and serious creative endeavor. And to acknowledge, as well, the suffering, difficulty, and dignity of these lives" (Knight xii). Therefore, Waldman invokes the forgotten voice of these women again. Waldman considers herself to be a narrator of the grief of "forgotten and ignored" women. Waldman, as the mouthpiece of female Beat poets, speaks for women's restricted conditions. At first glance, she seems to vindicate female Beat poets from feminism. For Waldman, feminism is the prototype for her civil disobedience. The next quotation is from one of her representative works, *Fast Speaking Women*:

> I'm a fast speaking woman
> I'm a fast-rolling woman
> I'm a rolling-speech woman
> I'm a rolling-water woman
>
> I KNOW HOW TO SHOUT
> I KNOW HOW TO SING
> I KNOW HOW TO LIE DOWN (572–78)

In a quoted part of the poem, Waldman consistently shouts and speaks quickly and aims to read aloud. Her lines are made rhythmic through the use of effective repetition, as in the lines "fast" and "rolling." At the same time, Waldman repeats "I'm a [ing] woman" in a monologue that is strongly influenced by Allen Ginsberg's *Howl*. Waldman's style imitates mantras and oral languages. "Feminafesto" is the term that Waldman gives to her civil disobedience. It is a combination of the words "feminist" and "manifest." Waldman states, "I propose a utopian creative field where we are defined by our energy, not by gender. I propose a transsexual literature, a transgendered literature, a hermaphroditic literature, transvestite literature, and finally a poetics of transformation beyond gender" (*Vow to Poetry* 24). Waldman believes that she can transcend the border between genders by defining energy: "masculine and feminine energies [can] be comprehended in the Buddhist sense of *prajna* and *upaya*, wisdom and skillful means, which exist in all sentient beings. These energies coexist and are essential to one another" (*Vow to Poetry* 24). Her views on Buddhism, which she practices, are explained in the following interview: "It also suggested opening up the dynamic and the inclusiveness to consider these things." Her inclusive vision is similar to the notion of deep ecology as explored by Nash and Devall. It led to her poetry in *Outrider*. The poetry reflects Waldman's synthetic poetics, which goes beyond various boundaries. Waldman states that "Outrider is a line of demarcation." The "demarcation" indicates the realm between genders, between languages, between arts, and between body and mind. Waldman further says that the outrider is "a hybrid" (*Outrider* 55) and is comprised of "Rhizomic poetics" (*Outrider* 70). Waldman argues about "Rhizomes" in the theories of Felix Guattari and Gilles Deleuze, which construct the postmodern and derivative worldwide foundation to be connectable like moss. "Rhizomic poetics" reflects not only Waldman's compatibility with nature but also synthetic or inclusive tendencies.

Therefore, Waldman's "Outrider" poetics have both conceptual and biological realms. After completing *Outrider*, Waldman wrote the poem "Manatee." Waldman states that "The poem is an investigation into and an improvisation upon some of the ideas and concerns of the Kalahcakra[2] layered with a vow to take *all the animals with you in your life, your poetry*." "Manatee" seeks to teach the reader about "multiple hydra-headed universes, and all fractals in chaos," which will emerge with "formation, stabilization, disintegration, emptiness" and continues:

> some of your friends will be there, waiting
>
> the winds of karma provide the impulse for a particular universe to evolve that comes from the collective karma of the clear-light strife-gone-mind of other beings who remain present during empty magma eons in between universal autumnal epochs. . .
>
> & these karma-winds provide the impulse for a specific birth to occur. . .
>
> & speaking further, she went on, Manatee, fresh from her initiation into the mysteries of time: (1638–45)

From fractals and chaos to formation and stabilization, the changes in the universe are depicted in the poem. Karma appears as a wind and provides the impulse to evolve and give birth. The flow of energy in Waldman's imagination becomes clear from how she depicts not only a human heart but also an animal's heart. Waldman, like Thoreau, sees the universe through all sentient beings.

Interestingly, Waldman includes the "Wild mind: elegantly self-disciplined" (*Outrider* 16) in the concept of "Outrider." In an interview in the same book, Waldman comments that she agrees with Gary Snyder's definition of the wild mind being "elegantly self-disciplined, self-regulating" (*Outrider* 70). Snyder quotes Thoreau's *Walden* when he develops this concept of wildness, and Waldman agrees with the concept of Thoreau's wildness.

Waldman's poetry is inspired by wildness, transgender issues, poetic concepts based on Kali, the Hindu goddess of death and destruction, A Maker of Poetry, the poet Ted Berrigan,[3] and endangered species. "Outrider" refers not only to leading hypermetric poetics but also to her own practices. Waldman uses "Feminamist" as her civil disobedience technique by speaking on behalf of forgotten women. She compiles her poetic work into the poems of "Outrider."

Waldman comments in an interview conducted at Naropa University in 2008 that:

> We borrowed the terms from Henry David Thoreau, which suggested, civilized and uncivilized, we are citizen, we are civilians, we are pacific duties that play rather than a lot of worlds, civil, are polite, we are trying to be wise, making offering a view to suggest, have an activity, practice to do. So disobedience is to commodification to a kind of straighter and conservative view of poetry, other things, this disobedience is connected with the wild mind, you know a kind of a pattern of disobedience, not violent, neglect, negative, shooting down to be active, disobedience is that a creative person struggle to use their imagination, Dian di Prima said that "THE ONLY WAR THAT MATTERS IS THE WAR AGAINST THE IMAGINATION" (Di Prima 160). So I think the civil disobedience is active imagination as free imagination, because it's a part of our duty as civilians, I think Thoreau also uses. So we wanted to publish the Naropa doing and war books. (Personal interview)[4]

Her poetry is based on "Fast Thought, Best Thought," which was originally advocated by Trungpa Rinposhe[5] and which she had been practicing with Ginsberg. Ginsberg considers his poetics to be a "breakthrough" and traces its origins to Whitman. Ginsberg argues that Whitman "opened up Chinese poetry and he also opened up Russian poetry" and that "Whitman is behind Mayakovsky and some of Yesenin. And a lot of the turn-of-the-century, prerevolutionary poetry that led to the revolution—the Futurist, the Russian Futurists." Ginsberg mentions that Whitman also "opened up the San Francisco Renaissance and Beat Generation, which did have some kind of socio-political fallout" (*Civil Disobediences* 244). Ginsberg considers Whitman's accomplishments to be "the great breakthrough" and concedes that "Howl" is similar to "the breakthrough thing," which is said to be a revolutionary political form of poetics (*Civil Disobediences* 254). Waldman states that "Allen Ginsberg's readings—his whole oral presentation was inspiring, and his personal encouragement was a real gift. I always had a self-conscious humorous way of commenting on what I was doing in the works—they couldn't just be completely one thing—purely political" (*Talking Poetics From Naropa Institute* 306). Waldman also demonstrates her sympathy for Ginsberg's political attitude in one of her poems, "I Remember Being Arrested . . .": "I remember being with Allen Ginsberg in Chicago during the Chicago Seven trials, I remember thinking that I would demonstrate with him anywhere in the world" (*In the Room of Never Grieve* 378). Waldman has been strongly influenced by Ginsberg's poetical imagination and political actions. Waldman believes Ginsberg's "revolutional poetic" to have originated in Whitman.

4. Conclusion

Two Japanese researchers, Tokihiko Yamazaki and Masayoshi Higashiyama, have discussed Thoreau's civil disobedience. I will build on their arguments in this section. Higashiyama argues "While exploring the notion that civil disobedience had been considered to be equivalent to hippiedom, what limits of Thoreau's political interpretation of the term are revealed? The contemporary civil rights movements including African Americans, students, and hippies are basically equivalent to Thoreau's" (Higashiyama 55, 67; my translation). Yamazaki proposes "Thoreau's civil disobedience directly corresponds to hippiedom" ("Henry Thoreau Kenkyu" 490; my translation) and "Mohandos Karamchand Gandhi and Martin Luther King, Jr. regard Thoreau's ideas as a weapon for popular liberation" ("Doutokutekikaikaku" 124; my translation). Richard J. Schneider mentions that "The 1960s were watershed years for Thoreau's reputation. He first became radicalized as an antiwar protester and advocate of passive resistance because of his essay 'Civil Disobedience' (1848) and its pertinence to the Vietnam War" (Schneider 20). The protests against the Cold War and Vietnam War, and the protests during the civil rights movement, can be said to have been inspired by Thoreau's civil disobedience. For Waldman, civil disobedience means an "active imagination and free imagination," while for Thoreau it means "our duty as civilians." To maintain an active and free imagination, one needs to fight. Waldman expresses her active and free imagination in the form of not only her poetic practices but also her activism. Other examples of "civil disobediences" are, as in the case of Allen Ginsberg, his revolutionary poetry, as demonstrated in *Howl*, which represents the mind breaking through. For Snyder, it is his Buddhist poetry. Snyder mentions that

"Poetry itself . . . by the virtue of its intuitive and imaginative openness, is a Dharma exercise" (*Civil Disobediences* 203). Poetry is civil disobedience.

Therefore, civil disobedience was the prototype of the protests by Beat Poets. Ginsberg's revolutionary poetry was inspired by Thoreau's political imagination. Snyder's Dharma poetry was inspired by Thoreau's ecological imagination. Waldman's outrider poetry was inspired by her practices at Naropa University. Waldman incorporates Thoreau's political imagination through Ginsberg and ecological imagination through Snyder. These variations indicate the transformation engendered by various imaginations. They also indicate the reception and transformation of Thoreau's civil disobedience, which inspired the Beat poets to give it contemporary significance.

Finally, for Waldman, civil disobedience is the inclusive realm of her thoughts as expressed in *Fast Speaking Woman*, "Feminafesto," and *Outrider*, which transcends the gender dualism and the synthetic realms of gender and biology at the same time. "Wildness," as the impulse for pastoralism, is crucial to her outrider poetry. Thoreau's civil disobedience and "wildness" were substantiated by pastoralism, which become a freely active imaginative catalysis. Waldman's civil disobedience is not only a collective concept but also an imaginative activism.

Notes

1 Savio's Statement, "Let your life be a counter-friction to stop the machine." Lipset and Wolin, *Berkeley Student Revolt* (163).
2 The term means "time-circle" and is a part of the teachings of Tibetan Buddhism.
3 A contemporary American poet and one of the New York School of Poets.
4 Personal interview with Anne Waldman, in Boulder, Colorado, July 2, 2008.
5 Trungpa Rinposhe (1939–87) was a propagandist of Tibetan Buddhism to the West and founded Naropa Institute in 1974.

Works Cited

Charters, Ann. "Foreword." *The Beats, Literary Bohemians in Postwar America*. Ed. Ann Charters; Gale Research 1983. *Dictionary of Literary Biography*; v. 16. Print.
Di Prima, Diane. *Pieces of a Song*. San Francisco: City Lights, 1990. Print.
Higashiyama, Masayoshi. *Henry Thoreau no Seikatsu to Shisou* [*Henry Thoreau's Life and Thought*]. Tokyo: Nan'undo, 1972. Print.
Itoh, Shoko. *Yomigaeru Thoreau* [*Sauntering to the Inner Wilderness: Nature Writing and American Society*]. Tokyo: Laurus-Kashiwashobou, 1998. Print.
Knight, Brenda. *Women of the Beat Generation: The Writers, Artists and Muses at the*

Heart of a Revolution. Berkeley: Conari Press, 1996. Print.
Lipset, Seymour Martin and Sheldon S. Wolin, eds. *The Berkeley Student Revolt: Facts and Interpretations*. New York: Doubleday, 1965. Print.
List, Peter C. *Radical Environmentalism: Philosophy and Tactics*. Belmont: Wadsworth Publishing Company, 1993. Print.
Marx, Leo. "Pastoralism in America." *Ideology and Classic American Literature*. Ed. Sacvan Bercovitch and Myra Jehlen. Cambridge: Cambridge UP, 1986, 39–69. Print.
Nash, Roderick Frazier. *Wilderness & American Mind*. New Haven: Yale UP, 2001. Print.
Oelschlaeger, Max. *The Idea of Wilderness: From Prehistory to the Age of Ecology*. New Haven: Yale University Press, 1991. Print.
Schneider, Richard J. "Thoreau and American Environmentalism: A Study in Critical Reception." *Critical Insights: Nature & the Environment*. Ed. Scott Slovic. Ipswich: Salem Press, 2013, 19–41. Print.
Sessions, George. Ed. *Deep Ecology for the 21st Century: Reading on the Philosophy and Practice of the New Environmentalism*. Boston: Shambhala, 1995. Print.
Snyder, Gary. *The Practice of the Wild*. Washington, D. C.: Shoemaker & Hoard, 1990. Print.
——. *A Place in Space: Ethics, Aesthetics, and Watersheds New and Selected Pros*. New York: Counterpoint, 1995. Print.
Takahashi, Tsutomu. "Yasei no Shigaku no Keifugaku: Emerson kara Gary Snyder e" ["The Poetics of the Wild: From Emerson to Gary Snyder"]. *Studies in Henry David Thoreau* 34 (March 2008): 31–40. Print.
Thoreau, Henry David. *Henry David Thoreau: Collected Essays and Poems*. New York: Library of America, 2001. Print.
——. *Early Essays and Miscellanies: The Writings of Henry D. Thoreau*. Princeton: Princeton UP, 1975. Print.
Waldman, Anne. *Fast Speaking Woman*. San Francisco: City Lights, 1996. Print.
——. *In the Room of Never Grieve: New and Selected Poems 1985–2003 Companion audio CD enclosed*. Minneapolis: Coffee House Press, 2003. Print.
——. *Outrider*. New Mexico: La Alameda Press, 2006. Print.
——. *Vow to Poetry: Essays, Interviews, & Manifestos*. Minneapolis: Coffee House Press, 2001. Print.
——. Ed. *Talking Poetics From Naropa Institute: Annals of the Jack Kerouac School of Disembodied Poetics*, Vol. 2. Boulder: Shambhala, 1978. Print.
——. Ed. *Civil Disobediences: Poetics and Politics in Action*. Minneapolis: Coffee House Press, 2004. Print.
Walls, Laura Dassow. "Walden as Feminist Manifest." *Interdisciplinary Studies in Literature and Environment; ISLE* 1.1(Spring 1993): 137–44. Print.
Yamazaki, Tokihiko, "Henry Thoreau Kenkyu no Doukou: Sengo Amerika no Seiji no Nakade" ["The Tendency of Henry Thoreau's Studies"]. *The Law Society of Osaka City University* 24 (1978): 473–501. Print.

——. "Doutokutekikaikaku to Fukujyukyohi—Henry Thoreau wo Chushin ni" ["Ethical revolution and denial of obedience: focusing on Henry Thoreau"]. *Aichigakuen Law Review*, 26 (1983): 93–125. Print.

Yamazato, Katsunori. "Mori no Seikatsu: Thoreau kara Snyder e ["Living in the Woods: A Comparative Study of Thoreau and Snyder"]. *Studies in Henry David Thoreau* 34 (2008): 63–73. Print.

Civil Disobedience and the Postwar Okinawan Novelist Medoruma Shun

Yohei Yamamoto

My life has been the poem I would have writ
But I could not both live and utter it.
—Henry David Thoreau

Introduction

Henry David Thoreau's notion of civil disobedience has inspired many thinkers and activists around the world. As Michael Meyer suggests in *Several More Lives to Live*, the values expressed in Thoreau's political essays have been widely accepted as universally applicable, and his nonviolent activism has been adopted not only in America but also among Asian pacifists such as Gandhi. However, little attention has been paid to the legacy of Thoreau's "civil disobedience" in Japanese literary history. One of the most significant cases of nonviolent direct action in postwar Japan has been the ongoing protests in Okinawa—namely, a form of civil disobedience directed against the US bases and the Japanese government's political support for them.[1]

Okinawan intellectuals, however, have never directly cited Thoreau as an influence. It is only through the historian Howard Zinn that a connection has been made between Okinawan literature and Thoreau's civil disobedience. Zinn has noted Thoreau's contributions to criticisms of the local and national governments of his time for their role in slavery. In truth, the Civil War and the Emancipation Proclamation did not fully resolve the problem of racial segregation in America, and, more broadly, we still confront the history of persecution and racism throughout the contemporary world.

Even though the concept of civil disobedience has spread throughout the world, the nonviolent ideal remains incongruent with reality. Wars, conflicts, colonialism, racial discrimination, and all manner of violence prevail and continue to be legitimized through various rationalizations. Such problems cannot be solved without understanding the reasons behind the violence. Yet, the reasons for these problems have become increasingly complicated in the contemporary world. According to Zinn, invisibility is a major reason for instances of appalling violence, such as the dropping of atomic bombs on Hiroshima and Nagasaki: "The incineration and radiation of several hundred thousand Japanese could be accepted by Americans because they were not seen as human beings, not made visible as were the victims of Japan" (xx). Later, in the 1960s, this invisibility of the other also enabled Americans to attack the Vietnamese using napalm, because "their deaths were recorded as statistics, but they did not appear as human beings" (Zinn xx). Likewise, Okinawa has been an invisible other for US occupiers, as well as the residents of mainland Japan. Occupied by the United States after World War II until the reversion to Japan in 1972, Okinawa is still home to many US military bases.[2]

Against this background, this study explores the relationship between political activism and literary work with a focus on the postwar Okinawan writer Medoruma Shun. Medoruma has insisted that the war is not over in Okinawa, even though seventy-two years have passed since the end of WWII. How should we interpret such a statement, and, more broadly, how do we situate contemporary politics in relation to our memories of war? I explore these questions by juxtaposing Medoruma's novella *Mabuigumi* (1998) with Thoreau's "Resistance to Civil Government." While there seems to be no direct inter-textual relationship between the two texts, some commonalities may be found in their deeper layers. In what follows, I will first clarify the relationship between literature and politics in Okinawa and then show how Medoruma's novels play an important role in that relationship. Through this analysis of Medoruma's work, I will also consider how Thoreau's political views can be applied to our society. In this way, the link between nonviolent protest in Okinawa and Thoreau's notion of civil disobedience will be revealed.

1. Contextualizing Postwar Okinawan Literature

In 1960, the philosopher and peace campaigner Tsurumi Shunsuke launched a protest against the revised security treaty between Japan and the United States. Then, in 1965, he established the Japan "Peace for Vietnam!" Committee with the influential writer Makoto Oda. The following year, he invited Howard Zinn to Japan as part of a series of initiatives. Zinn came with Ralph Featherstone, an African American activist who visited Okinawa to lecture on protesting the Vietnam War. Regarding Featherstone's impression, Tsurumi noted, "The Japanese were separated into two: Okinawans, and people other than Okinawans."[3]

In light of the concerns raised by this civil rights activist, Tsurumi observed that while mainlanders felt relieved by the superficial peace under the Constitution in the postwar era, "Okinawans were keenly aware that Okinawa served as the American frontline base" (Tsurumi 1982, 246). By providing military bases, Japan became complicit in violence perpetrated by the US. Moreover, the burden of US military bases in Okinawa distracted public attention from the violence in Vietnam.

Between 1960 and 1972—the year Okinawa reverted to Japanese administration—Okinawa's regional literature grew in stature. One symbolic event was Ōshiro Tatsuhiro winning the Akutagawa Prize for his novel *The Cocktail Party* in 1967, when the region was still under US military rule. The major themes of Ōshiro's novels include the Battle of Okinawa and the presence of US military bases in postwar Okinawa.

The Cocktail Party examines the hypocrisy of such social gathering on a US military base. Superficially, the party is an international goodwill event in which the Okinawan-born narrator, the party's American host, a journalist from the mainland, and a Chinese lawyer gather to study Chinese. They speak to each other in English, Japanese, and Chinese. One day, however, an tragic incident occurs and upturns the internationally friendly discourse—namely, the narrator's daughter is assaulted by a US soldier. The narrator seeks to bring the suspect to trial but faces a backlash in Okinawa and is forced to understand the situation for what it really is. He begins to sense the hypocrisy behind the "goodwill" party but also notices the prejudices of mainland Japan. His resistance begins when he recognizes his own hypocritical thoughts. In this way, the narrator's internal conflicts express the features of civil disobedience in Okinawa.

The geographical distance between Okinawa and the mainland is reflected in the different mentalities of the two. Though the narrator of *The Cocktail Party* feels oppressed by America, he also has a sense, "as a Japanese," of being a perpetrator against China during the Pacific War. He dwells on this awareness of being both victim and perpetrator. This dual consciousness (which will figure into the discussion of Medoruma Shun) comes from a mixed sense of assimilation into Japan and independence from it. Such a double-bind situation is also replayed in the father-daughter relationship. The narrator gears up for the court fight, but it causes emotional duress for his daughter. In this way, the novel depicts the duplicity of a narrator who becomes insensitive to the wounds of the other.

This aspect of the story can be seen as representing a return to the traumatic memories of the Battle of Okinawa. By evoking the memory of violence, the narrator, in a sense, adds insult to injury for his daughter. The novel, therefore, raises the question of how to break these negative chains. Many critics have suggested that the transition from the first person in the first part of the novel to the second person in the second part provides clues for approaching the theme. The situation in Okinawa requires such a duality of perspective, which has been adopted by its postwar generation of writers.

2. Medoruma Shun and Representational Strategies

Since Ōshiro Tatsuhiro bolstered the reputation of Okinawan literature, many talented Okinawan writers—such as Matayoshi Eiki, Higashi Mineo, and Sakiyama Tami—have attained literary fame, captivating a wide readership. One such writer, Medoruma Shun, is unique in that he seems to regard literature in the same light as politics, and believes no lines should be drawn between literature and social criticism. Michael Molasky indicates "Medoruma stands out from other Okinawan writers of his generation who seek to avoid political commentary" (169).

In a political essay called *Okinawa Sengo Zero Nen* [*The War Is Not Over Yet in Okinawa*], Medoruma recalls stories he heard from his grandparents about the cruelties of the Battle of Okinawa. He criticizes not only the US military but also Japanese soldiers who perpetrated violence against Okinawan civilians during the war. Criticizing the imperial regime for its role in the war and for currently hosting US military bases, Medoruma suggests that logistical support violates the principles of neutrality under the Japanese Constitution.

Like Thoreau, Medoruma insists that ideas are useless without action. As an activist, he has upheld this view. For example, he was recently arrested in Henoko, Nago, for protesting the construction of a new US military base. *Ryukyu Shimpo* reports on April 4, 2016 as follows: "While Medoruma and his colleagues were engaging in their usual protest activities at sea," several U.S. security guards captured Medoruma. "Medoruma was held captive inside Camp Schwab for eight hours." This event served to remind the public of the US military bases in Okinawa and bring national attention to the opposition movement.

In a dialogue between Medoruma and the Okinawan author Sakiyama Tami, quoted by Molasky, Medoruma explains the relationship between his literary work and political journalistic work, noting that this is a question "Japanese authors always feel compelled to ask": "If I reach the point where journalistic writing occupied most of my energy and feel that I should stop writing fiction, then I'll stop writing fiction" (22–23). With his compulsion to make political statements, Medoruma appears to challenge the tendencies of postwar Japanese literature while struggling to escape the privileged hierarchy of tradition that holds fictional works in higher regard. To fully understand Medoruma's position, we need to consider the relationship between his fiction and his political views.

Medoruma's novella *Mabuigumi* was published in 1998 after his short story "Droplets" won the Akutagawa Prize in 1997. This novella explores how multilayered violence occurs through socially constructed discrimination and systematic corruption stemming from cozy relations among bureaucrats, politicians, and businesses. The story evokes memories of the war, expressing Medoruma's ongoing preoccupation.

The protagonist Kotaro often loses his *mabui* ("spirit"). To "lose mabui" means to become shocked, frightened, or depressed, and then to remain in a poor condition for some time. Though the cause is not clear, it seems that Kotaro became shell-shocked after losing his parents in the Battle of Okinawa, and his traumatic memory causes him to lose his spirit. Uta, an old friend of Kotaro's parents, lost her husband in the war and had cared for Kotaro. She is not only his surrogate mother but also a *Mabuigumi* healer, whose role is to push his spirit back into his body, using a ritual process rooted in local tradition.

One day, Kotaro again loses his *mabui*. However, something strange happens this time: an *āman*, a hermit crab, gets into Kotaro's mouth and dominates his body. His spirit, meanwhile, leaves his body and, assuming a human form, gazes at the sea with a disconsolate look. Uta struggles to push back his spirit but fails; this time, her accustomed manner of *Mabuigumi* has no effect on Kotaro. Uta then notices that Kotaro's spirit is at "the exact spot where she had seen a sea turtle lay its eggs on the night Omito died" (126). Uta flashes back to the Battle of Okinawa in 1945, when Kotaro's mother, Omito, was killed. She and Uta hunt for food at night to feed their starving families. They manage to find a sea turtle's eggs by the seashore. Though they understand the risk posed by Japanese soldiers concerned about Okinawan spying, Omito ventures down the shore to get eggs. In the next breath, she is shot. Uta scrambles back to the cave, only to find that all the male villagers had been taken away by

Japanese soldiers. Uta loses her husband and Omito, as well as Omito's husband and other old friends, all at once.

Though it is noteworthy that Japanese soldiers kill Kotaro's mother, this point has thus far received scant attention. For Medoruma, the tragedy of the Battle of Okinawa stemmed not only from the actions of the US military but also from brutalization by Japanese soldiers. This is clear evidence of the degree to which Medoruma's fiction complements his political thought: "The records and testimony of the Battle of Okinawa uncover that there were many cases of residents massacred by Japanese soldiers. Japanese military at the time, while inciting the Okinawan residents on the battlefield, regarded those who spoke the dialect as spies. They did not trust the Okinawan people at all" (*Sengo Zero Nen* 34). One reason for such internal strife is that there is discrimination against Okinawans among mainland Japanese. Another reason is mainlanders' deep resentment toward the marginalized mindset of Okinawans and their struggle between subconscious assimilation with the mainland and independence from it.

As Howard Zinn suggests, the Americans who dropped atomic bombs on Hiroshima and Nagasaki behaved as if they did not see the Japanese as human beings. Likewise, Medoruma argues that Okinawan civilians were not seen as human beings in the power struggles between the US and Japan. Okinawa was sacrificed as a kind of "invisible other." What demands our attention is the fact that Okinawa, even in the postwar period, has faced ongoing discrimination and violence in the form of the dominant US bases. Medoruma's stories, however, are not only motivated by anti-US sentiment, but also by distrust of the Japanese government's policies.

Noteworthy among Medoruma's strategies is that the assailant who shoots Omito is obscured in the scene: Uta "fretted as she watched, when suddenly a dry noise—like the crackling of bamboo in fire—reverberated across the beach and Omito toppled over sideways" (127). Though it is clear that Omito is shot by a Japanese soldier, we must ask why the scene is so implicitly depicted. One reason is that the scene is presented from the point of view of young Uta, who could not easily believe a Japanese soldier would kill civilians. Another possible reason is that the shooter could refer not only to a specific Japanese person but also an abstract, vague, and more powerful opponent. By making the depictions ambiguous in his fiction, Medoruma develops his personal experience, as well as the oral stories heard from his parents and grandparents, into various sublimations that have an effect on the accusations against ongoing structural violence.

Returning to reality after her flashback, Uta, who associates the sea turtle with Omito, has suddenly come up with an idea that "this sea turtle was the reincarnation of Omito" (129). As the turtle glides into the ocean, Kotaro follows it as if bewitched by it. In the next moment, he vanishes. At the same time, Kotaro's body, which had been sick in bed in another place, is injured beyond help because the *āman* inside his body is startled by camera flashes and becomes angry. Kotaro finally dies both physically and spiritually. In a fit of passion, Uta aims to avenge Kotaro's death and struggles to kill the *āman* with the help of several villagers. The elusive crab is stubborn, but Uta brings it to the brink of death. Just before a villager named Kinjō Hiroshi delivers the final blow to the creature, an idea strikes Uta: "This *āman* might be a reincarnation of Omito" (132).

> "Hiroshi, wait!" she yelled, but she was too late. Kinjō's shovel, already in mid-swing, struck the *āman*. The blow smashed the *āman*'s carapace, and a dark-green liquid gushed out. Even then, it was still alive. Uta realized that the creature's two eyes were still staring at her, and she was taken aback by a thought that suddenly flashed across her mind: This *āman* might be the reincarnation of Omito ---. In a frenzy, Kinjō swung the shovel once more, delivering the finishing blow.
>
> For a short while, nobody moved or uttered a word. (132)

We can read this scene on multiple levels. At one level, as Davinder Bhowmik suggests, the cameraman mainly caused Kotaro's death because the camera flash triggered the *āman*'s fury. On a different level, this scene contains an alternative layer of self-criticism. In a sense, Uta and the villagers symbolically reenact the violence of Japanese soldiers during the war. Though Uta issues the order to kill the *āman*, the person who deals the deathblow is another villager, Hiroshi. Thus, two questions arise: Why did Hiroshi, not Uta, kill the creature? and Why did Uta intuit a connection between the *āman* and Omito?

There is no clear basis for Uta's idea that the *āman* is the reincarnation of Omito. First, Uta gets the idea that a sea turtle is Omito's reincarnation. Compared to this idea, her second intuition that the *āman* is the reincarnation of Kotaro's mother seems quite irrational. Associating a sea turtle that has laid eggs with Kotaro's mother seems very natural, but the figurative meaning of the *āman* that kills Kotaro remains indeterminate. It is ironic that symbols of birth and death simultaneously emerge when Kotaro dies. Suzuki Tomoyuki suggests Medoruma's stories reveal not a closed system of symbols but more complicated allegories that go beyond the meaningful order and reproduce unsettled residuals of meanings.[4] Though the unsettled metaphors in the text confuse even the most careful readers, such a discursive style creates a more powerful openness to interpretation.

With this story, Medoruma refuses to accept conventional representations that romanticize the war. Rather, he constructs the history of Okinawa as an alternative literary history of disobedience. Medoruma's literary world does not stabilize the signifier in a closed symbolic mode. Instead, he preserves the other as a continuous unknown other. Medoruma's style unsettles meanings, and what remains is something unspeakable between the lines. As Yoko Murakami suggests, memories of the Battle of Okinawa are portrayed, Medoruma's work as the painful present survivors share in the postwar period rather than a past that represents a completed story (266). His literary mode is a refusal to be dominated and resolved by representation, which can turn out to be violent to others.

In summary, Medoruma's work is characterized by the following: re-enacting the traumatic memories of the Battle of Okinawa, ambiguous reactions to the hitherto existing U.S. base, and (self-)criticism directed against Japanese expedient politicians, authoritative media, and intellectuals. By perpetuating memories of the Battle of Okinawa, Medoruma Shun's work has become what might be called "meta resistance literature,"—a counter-text against the status quo of the U.S base, as well as resistance to the "mainland" of Japan. In this sense, this literature can be seen as containing a double consciousness, or metacognitive text characterized by self-criticism.

3. Self-Criticism in Thoreau's "Resistance to Civil Government"

Having sketched the aspect of (self-)criticism in Medoruma's fiction, let us now consider how his "activist text" might resonate with Thoreau's notion of civil disobedience. In the lines quoted at the beginning of this paper, Thoreau regards writing poetry and living his life as two sides of the same coin. Thus, for Thoreau, writing about living in nature, as in *Walden*, and writing political essays such as "Resistance to Civil Government" represent two facets of a particular problem that lies in the intersection of art and politics.

One similarity between Medoruma and Thoreau is that, for both, private narrative is inextricably linked to moral philosophy. Medoruma, as seen in the dialogue with Sakiyama, struggles to go beyond the privileged hierarchy of literary tradition, and juxtaposes writing fiction on an equal footing with political activism and private narrative, insisting that ideas are useless unless they were followed by actions. Likewise, Thoreau juxtaposes his narration of his private experience with his political philosophy. Thoreau had refused to pay the poll tax in jail to show his disagreement with the government, and for that reason was arrested and put in jail. Insofar as he struggled to match his writing with his life, Thoreau tried to be a politically descriptive writer. At the same time, he struggled with the discrepancy between a writer's complicated accumulation of political creeds in antebellum America and words that could empathize with New Englanders. In this regard, Medoruma and Thoreau face the same problem: accountability for their own actions based on a sense of self-criticism. Thoreau complains that abolitionists seem to regard the state, society, and the nation collectively as an abstract power. Such criticism does not have a strong effect. Thoreau must have been aware that critics should be simultaneously subject to criticism. For Thoreau, writing itself is necessarily self-criticism, inextricable from life.

In the late 1840s, Thoreau developed a self-critical tendency toward irony and skepticism in his political attitudes. In "Resistance to Civil Government," Thoreau strategically imbues the words "civil" and "citizen" with two different connotations, interweaving them through exaggerated discourse. He uses the terms "civil obligation" (67) and "civil neighbor" (75) in reference to the masses of men while using the term "citizen" as follows: "to speak practically and as a citizen, unlike those who call themselves no-government men, I ask for, not at once no government, but at once a better government" (64).

These two terms, "civil" and "citizen," basically refer to the general public in the same sense. On the one hand, "civil" refers to the masses, carrying connotations of the expedient majority. "Citizen," meanwhile, refers to people conscious of being the minority. Thoreau's distinction between the two appears to reflect his skepticism about a democracy that is largely based on a system of majority rule. His criticism of unfair laws and democratic governance stems from such skepticism: "After all, the practical reason why, when the power is once in the hands of the people, a majority are permitted, and for a long period continue, to rule, is not because they are most likely to be in the right, nor because this seems fairest to the minority, but because they are physically the strongest" (64).

To stand up to the physically strong majority, Thoreau uses ironic and skeptical rhetoric to highlight his disobedience, which is characterized by metaphors pertaining to mind and body. While individuals in a democratic society are incorporated as modern bodies with voting rights and tax obligations, Thoreau regards a body that lacks autonomy as a useless machine: "The mass of men serve the State thus, not as men mainly, but as machines, with their bodies" (*Higher Laws* 66). This phrase "the mass of men" echoes his famous statement in *Walden* that "the mass of men lead lives of quiet desperation" (8), which criticizes pressure from the group to conform. In "Slavery in Massachusetts," Thoreau also employs language that polarizes mind and body to criticize slavery. By juxtaposing making "mankind into sausages" with making a person "into a slave," Thoreau first activates the audience's moral conscience rather than its political conscience (*Higher Laws* 96). Such corporeal metaphors reflect Thoreau's skepticism about some of the foundations of democracy—the arbitrary system of voting, the "mass of man" without conscience, or the desperate, silent "majority of the men of the North" (*Higher Laws* 102). The important thing here is that Thoreau criticizes Northern people, including himself. In this way, Thoreau's rhetoric embodies his self-critical strategy for questioning the morality of a majority that accepts an unfair society characterized by slavery.[5]

As in Medoruma's *Mabuigumi*, Thoreau utilizes the rhetoric of mind and body to enact textual resistance. Medoruma depicts allegorical work of splitting up one person into soul and body. In addition, it is interesting to note that the opening scene of *Mabuigumi* describes the radio gymnastic exercises in the community. As Susan Bouterey suggests, this opening prefigures that literary theme of mind and body; the radio music for calisthenics "blasted through a large loudspeaker on the roof of the community center" (112) irritates Uta because it sounds totalitarian to her. So though "half of the elderly participants lived alone and therefore enjoyed the company," Uta "continued her boycott" of radio gymnastic exercises, which take control of people's bodies and standardize their minds (Bouterey 113). In this way, the metacognitive function of objectifying body and spirit is present in both Thoreau's and Medoruma's texts on roughly the same level, regardless of theme or literary genre. Medoruma and Thoreau both emphasize physicality to make their texts more vibrant and effective in their resistance against the power of the majority. Their nonviolent activist texts offer their own bodies as a self-sacrifice; this is because a body serves to embody conscientious ideas as opposed to representing the right to vote itself.

Thoreau's awareness of corporeality is important because it pertains specifically to the theme of life and death. There is critical agreement that "life" is a key term in Thoreau, but in this context, it is worth noting that he also highly valued death, or the resolution to die. He later modified his valuation of life and death, deepening his consideration of the dynamic relation between the seemingly antithetical concepts. Thoreau's awareness of life and death as two sides of the same coin enforces his self-critical resistance: he criticizes America and, at the same time, he is criticized as American. Such double vision offers resistance against objectifying self-justification. By employing self-criticism, Thoreau struggles to suppress modern self-justifications.

If we reread one of the most famous passages in *Walden*, we find that Thoreau is already considering the transgressive boundaries between life and death: "I went to the woods because I wished to live deliberately, to front only the essential facts of life, and see if I could not learn what it had to teach, and not, when I came to die, discover that I had not lived. I did not wish to live what was not life, living is so dear" (90). Here, while insisting on the importance of life by referring to "the essential facts of life" and how "living is so dear," he also reminds us about death with the phrase "when I came to die." In doing so, Thoreau reminds the audience that human beings should be resigned to their natural destiny to die, contrary to the claims of the doctrine of manifest destiny. Yet, he also declares emphatically in *Walden* that "living is so dear."

Alexis de Tocqueville said that an individual in the United States can feel helpless before the "tyranny of the majority" and was deeply concerned about finding a way to break the deadlock. Thoreau and Medoruma share Tocqueville's concern about the vulnerability of democracies: when a minority—such as an ethnic, religious, political, or racial group—"suffers an injustice" and may be targeted for oppression by the majority, "to whom can he turn?" (252) Thoreau and Medoruma are not typical left-wing thinkers who always criticize the establishment. Rather, both are radically liberal-minded in the sense that they can be self-critical in their writings.

Notes

1 For instance, the reversion movement by the Association for the Protection of Okinawa (Okinawa o Mamoru Kai) in the mid-1960s is one remarkable example. For details, see Rabson 176–78. *The Okinawan Diaspora in Japan.*

2 For further details on postwar Okinawan protests, see Tanji Miyume.

3 This civil movement is known by its Japanese acronym "Beheiren." In 2004, Tsurumi founded, with Nobel laureate Kenzaburo Oe and others, the Article 9 Association, a body aiming to defend the country's pacifist Constitution, which renounces war.

4 This feature reminds me of Barbara Johnson's critique of Thoreau's figurative style in *Walden*: the symbols in his work "clearly are symbols but that do not really symbolize anything outside themselves. They are figures for which no literal, proper term can be substituted. They are, in other words, catachresis—'figures of abuse,' figurative substitutes for a literal term that does not exist" (448).

5 Jack Turner highly evaluates Brown's action and Thoreau's plea, and attaches great importance to the "valuation of the ideal over the corporeal" (467).

Works Cited

Bhowmik, Davinder. *Writing Okinawa: Narrative Acts of Identity and Resistance*. London: Routledge, 2008. Print.

Bouterey, Susan. *Medoruma Shun no Sekai / Okinawa: Rekishi, Kioku, Monogatari* [*The World / Okinawa of Medoruma Shun: History, Memory, Narrative*]. Tokyo: Kageshobo, 2011. Print.

Ikeda, Kyle. *Okinawan War Memory: Transgenerational Trauma and the War Fiction of Medoruma Shun*. Abingdon: Routledge, 2014. Print.

Johnson, Barbara. "A Hound, a Bay Horse, and a Turtle Dove: Obscurity in Walden." 1987. *Walden and Resistance to Civil Government*. Ed. William Rossi. New York: Norton, 1992. 444–50. Print.

Meyer, Michael. *Several More Lives to Live: Thoreau's Political Reputation in America*. Westport: Greenwood, 1977. Print.

Medoruma, Shun. "Droplets." 1997. Trans. Michael Molasky. Ed. Molasky and Steve Rabson. *Southern Exposure: Modern Japanese Literature from Okinawa*. Honolulu: U of Hawai'i P, 2000. 255–86. Print.

——. "Mabuigumi." 1999. Trans. Kyle Ikeda. *Manoa* 23 (2011): 112–34.

——. *Okinawa "Sengo" Zero-nen* [*Zero Year "After the War" in Okinawa*]. Tokyo: Nihon Hōsō Shuppan Kyōkai, 2005. Print.

——, and Sakiyama Tami. "Shōsetsu no Genba Kara [A Dialogue from the Sceneof Writing Novels]." *Keeshi Kaji* 27 (2000): 22–33. Print.

"Medoruma's Arrest: Suppression of the Opposition Movement must not be Tolerated." *Ryukyu Shimpo* 11 April 2016. Web.20 Apr. 2016. < http://english. ryukyushimpo. jp / 2016/04/11/24819/>.

Molasky, Michael. "Medoruma Shun: The Writer as Public Intellectual in Okinawa Today." Ed. Hein, Laura and Mark Selden. *Islands of Discontent: Okinawan Responses to Japanese and American Power*. Lanham: Oxford: Rowman & Littlefield, 2003. 161–91. Print.

Murakami Yoko. *Dekigoto no Zankyo: Genbaku Bungaku to Okinawa Bungaku* [*The Echoes of an Event: Literature of Atomic Bomb and Okinawan Literature*]. Tokyo:

Impact Shuppan, 2015. Print.

Oe Kenzaburo and Medoruma Shun "Okinawa ga Kenpo o Tekishi Suru Toki [A Dialogue: When Okinawa Regards the Constitution with Hostility]" *Ronza* 62 (July 2000): 176–77. Print.

Ōshiro Tatsuhiro. "The Cocktail Party." Ed and trans. Steve Rabson. *Okinawa: Two Postwar Novellas*. Center for Japanese Studies, 1989. Print.

Rabson, Steve. *The Okinawan Diaspora in Japan: Crossing the Borders Within*. Honolulu: U of Hawai'I P, 2012. Print.

Stewart, Frank and Katsunori Yamazato, ed. *Living Spirit: Literature and Resurgence in Okinawa*. Honolulu: U of Hawai'i P, 2011. Print.

Suzuki Tomoyuki. *Me no Oku ni Tsukitaterareta Kotoba no Mori: Medoruma Shun no Bungaku to Okinawa Sen no Kioku* [*The Harpoon of the Words Stabbed in the Back of the Eye: Medoruma Shun's Literature and the Battle of Okinawa*]. Tokyo: Shobunsha, 2013. Print.

Tanji, Miyume. *Myth, Protest and Struggle in Okinawa*. Routledge, 2007. Print.

Thoreau, Henry D. *The Higher Law: Thoreau on Civil Disobedience and Reform*. Princeton: Princeton UP, 1973. Print.

——. *Walden*. Ed. Lyndon Shanley. Princeton: Princeton UP, 1971. Print.

de Tocqueville, Alexis. *Democracy in America*. Trans. George Lawrence. New York: Harper, 2006. Print.

Tsurumi Shunsuke. *Senjiki Nihon no Seishinshi: 1931–1945-nen* [*An Intellectual History of Wartime Japan, 1931–1945*]. Tokyo: Iwanami Shoten, 1982. Print.

Turner, Jack. "Performing Conscience: Thoreau, Political Action, and the Plea for John Brown." *Political Theory* 33 (2005): 448–71.

Zinn Howard. Introduction. *The Higher Law* by Henry D. Thoreau. ix–xxx.

Emerson's Circles and Publishing:
Character and Print Culture in Nineteenth-Century American National Literature

Mikayo Sakuma

1. Introduction

In the nineteenth century, American society had its local heroes, including literary authors who were later considered to have shaped the era of American Renaissance, as defined by F. O. Matthiessen. Looking back on the development of American literature, the rise of commercial print culture should be considered in terms of not only the expansion of the reading public but also the personalization of journalism. Edward Widmer notes that "the scope of journalism was expanding, bringing ideas about politics and culture into the same discourse, and dominated by brash editors who felt qualified to decant on both" (11). Print culture embraced edgy, individualized discourse with its growth of journalism. Printing also involved the act of copying, and the marketplace for the reading public involved various types of copying, as Deidre Lynch argues (6). Meredith McGill contends that, facing the growing marketplace for literary works, the act of copying (i.e. reprinting) brought about the issue of authorial ownership as copyright (11). Indeed, copyright issues influenced economic matters and international relations. The writers of American Renaissance were entangled in this flourishing journalism and needed to frame their literary place in this burgeoning mass society. Since the cogent analysis of Michael T. Gilmore, the relationship between the literary and the marketplace has been reexamined in the field of historical and literary analysis. However, the transformation of the idea of copying in relation to national literature has not received adequate attention. I assume that Ralph Waldo Emerson was able to recognize its importance and to enhance his ideas through an act of copying.

During a period of booming journalism, the character of American literature as part of national culture surfaced among American authors. A wave of foreign literature simultaneously supplied the American reading public with books at lower cost due to the lack of copyright agreements in transatlantic negotiations. Competing with famous British authors, American authors struggled to gain popularity among the reading public. As McGill argues, the kindling of a national literature was contingent on an awareness of literary property. The delay in copyright agreements created controversies among literary figures; in the process, American literature established itself as a literature of democracy. While American hegemony expanded toward the Pacific and across the Caribbean Sea, the fame of American literature as a literature of democracy spread as far as Japan.

Referring to the studies on the nature of authorship in relation to copyright and the literary marketplace, this paper attempts to reconsider the national literary movement and publishing in the nineteenth-century America as a process of disseminating American character in a global context. Ralph Waldo Emerson writes in "The American Scholar," "Character is higher than intellect" (*The Collected Works of Ralph Waldo Emerson* I: 61; hereafter abbreviated as *CW*). I consider his emphasis on character over intellect to reflect the problem of the decentralized print culture and the position of authors in the midst of social and cultural change. In addition, I would like to call attention to how American authors recognized the literary property of authorship and to investigate how Emerson's idea of character influenced the Japanese national literary movement during the Meiji Era (1868–1912).

2. Emerson and His Invisible Publishers

After gaining acclaim as an inspiring lecturer, Emerson published his first essay *Nature* with the James Munroe and Company. According to Wilson H. Kimnack, Kenneth Minkema and Douglas Sweeney, the eighteenth century was regarded as "the great age of the printed sermons in America" (xvi); thereafter, pastors and ministers had attempted to publish their sermons. Emerson, who resigned his first pastorship at the Second Church in Boston, did not publish his sermons as other pastors did. Instead, he published a new style of essay that was different from other published works. Books published in the same year "asserted the new conception of religion," but Emerson's book is "a wholly audacious inquiry" (Richardson 225). Emerson's *Nature* explores a personal relationship with the truth. James Munroe might have taken a risk in publishing this new type of essay. However, the history and nature of the James Munroe and Co. as a publishing house has not received sufficient attention. Even with the transformation of the print industry, which led to consociated print companies, Emerson seemed to be loyal to his first publisher, James Munroe.

Emerson's career was framed by his alma mater Harvard, which introduced him to ministry and later provided an avenue for his intellectual networking through the Transcendental Club. James Munroe was among his Harvard connections.

According to the George Nichols Papers, James Munroe and Nichols bought the Harvard University Bookstore in 1833. Nichols, who became a prominent citizen of Cambridge, graduated from Harvard Divinity School in 1828 and may have met Emerson when the latter entered Harvard Divinity School in 1825. Although there is no record of James Munroe in the *Harvard Year Book*, Nichols may have later told Emerson about his business partner. James Munroe had a printing office in Boston in an area where many printing houses were located, and Harvard University Bookstore was able to work as a liaison office in Cambridge. Unsurprisingly, when Emerson chose his publisher, he used his Harvard connections, asking James Munroe to publish his first essay. An author's choice of publisher could play a key role in his literary career in the age of an awakening national culture.

McGill attempts to explain print culture at the time, asserting "[n]ot only was the national market for books distributed across multiple, loosely affiliated regional publishing centers, each of the major cities—Philadelphia, New York, and Boston—claimed to be the center of national culture" (1). As McGill suggests, the development of American journalism triggered a characteristic turn, resulting in a process of decentralization and conflict with federal power. Literary figures also became constrained by the federal or market powers over their authorship.[1]

Emerson's first publisher, James Munroe, owned a Boston-based publishing company. In the Boston area, strong publishing companies with nationwide reach emerged as a result of consolidation. A typical case was Ticknor and Fields. According to Michel Winship, Ticknor and Fields began their business in 1832 when John Allen, Willian Davis Ticknor and Timothy Harrington Carter agreed to purchase the retail bookselling business of another Boston firm, Carter and Hendee (15). Winship provided a detailed history of Ticknor and Fields, mentioning "the preeminent publisher of belle letters, especially poetry, in the United States of the mid-nineteenth century" in the aim of "a fuller and richer understanding of how American literary culture emerged and functioned during the period" (7–8).

The purchase of the Harvard Bookstore by James Munroe was a similar merger in a small scale. Through networking and mergers, business partners often started publishing companies by purchasing the print house or bookselling shop. Emerson's networking was also a product of partnerships with various people. Emerson's alma mater and Boston-Cambridge human resources helped him publish his works.

Boston cultivated its literary character and developed into a noteworthy hub in American literary culture later in the nineteenth century, as shown in a description of a popular Boston bookstore called The Old Corner Book Store: "With the exception of the Athenaeum, no other surviving building in Boston was more frequented by New England literary figures of the nineteenth century."[2] Boston's literary figures gathered in and around Washington Street to buy books, and authors frequented the area for publishing and literary talks. The scene became a symbol of the flourishing of nineteenth-century American literature. Emerson's literary circle was nurtured in this regional atmosphere.

3. Waking the American Character

The *Edinburgh Review* of 1820 suggests the poor condition of American culture: "The Americans are a brave, industrious, and acute people; but they have hitherto given no indication of genius, and made no approaches to the heroic, either in their morality or *character*. They are but a recent offset indeed from England; and should make it their chief boast, for many generations to come, that they are sprung from the same race with Bacon and Shakespeare and Newton . . ." (emphasis added).[3] Winship uses this revealing excerpt to analyze the transformation of American culture in the nineteenth century. Through the likes of Washington Irving and James Fenimore Cooper, American authors developed their reputation in England, and Emerson followed in their footsteps in an effort to showcase the originality of American thought. Winship remarks that "[n]o matter how one chooses to define American literature or to evaluate it today, there can be no doubt that by the 1850s a thriving literary culture had been established in the United States" (11). American authors and the print industry endeavored to make the originality of American literature recognizable at least in the 1840s.

An increasingly popular publishing culture arose in New York. With a boom in cheap newspapers, New York became the center of American journalism. Born and educated in Boston, Emerson must have been anxious about this trend because he noted that New York journalism was too political (*The Journals and Miscellaneous Notebooks of Ralph Waldo Emerson* VIII 314; hereafter abbreviated as *JMN*). Benedict Anderson penetratingly observes that nationalism is the collateral of a mature print culture. The development of American culture was entangled with a nationalistic and politically oriented journalism as well as a regional print culture, whether or not the authors welcomed this shift. Emerson attempted to distance himself from New York journalism, although he helped his coterie publish their works in New York. In "The American Scholar," Emerson declares that "there are creative manners, there are creative actions, and creative words; manners, actions, words, that is, indicative of no custom or authority, but springing spontaneous from the mind's own sense of good and fair." Emerson stresses the importance of creativity, juxtaposing it with the barriers that he associates with the traditional means of intellectual engagements such as "the books, the college, the school of arts, the institution of any kind" (*CW* II: 57). The creativity that Emerson embraces should help American culture free itself from institutions. In "Character," he further explains what he means by character: "This is that which we call Character, —a reserved force which acts directly by presence, and without means. It is conceived of as a certain undemonstrable force, a Familiar or Genius, by whose impulses the man is guided, but whose counsels he cannot impart; which is company for him, so that such men are often solitary, or if they chance to be social, do not need society, but can entertain themselves very well alone" (*CW* III: 53). Emerson advocated the importance of "character," which nurtures "creativity": "The mind now thinks; now acts; and each fit reproduces the other. When the artist has exhausted his materials, when the fancy no longer paints, when thoughts are no longer apprehended, and books are a weariness, —he has always, the resource to live. Character is higher than intellect" (*CW* II: 61). When Emerson claims that character is more important than intellect, he suggests that American cultural identity should be rooted in ingenuity rather than in knowledge. This agenda can be easily deduced from his iconic essay "Self-Reliance," but we should also pay attention to the influence of the development and concerns surrounding journalism at the time. Emerson's approbation of character over intellect has often been erroneously cited as a form of anti-intellectualism; on the contrary, his regard for character reflects his philosophy of life and does not run counter to intellectualism.[4] For him, quasi-intellectualism is the product of institutions rather than of individual intellect, and New York journalism, which had a strong relation to politics, served as a bulwark of such metaphorical institutions.

American authors who wanted to distinguish themselves from their British counterparts urgently needed to flesh out characters on American soil in the nineteenth century. Emerson's essay regarding the necessity of character heralds the making of American culture. Observing the transformation of British print culture in the eighteenth century, Lynch argues that the creation of character in novels mirrors the reader's social recognition (40–41). Lynch further analyzes the relationship between character and print culture and notes the importance of copying: "Newton also bestowed the name on a copying machine of his own invention. Newton's equation of the copy machine and the divine principle suggests how central the systems of copying that underwrote the semiotic understanding of character were to the early modern mentality" (41). With the development of print culture, the characters in novels circulated rapidly among people who recognized and praised the particularities of such characters. In Britain, the differences that distinguished the island nation from continental Europe corresponded with the abundance of British culture (Lynch 60). The reverence for characters among readers should indicate their awareness of the inner self, which should reflect the abundance of British culture, but it may reveal not only laudatory aspects of personality but also their social reality. Emerson's praise of character should be reexamined in light of the transformation of print culture and social change of his day. As the *Edinburgh Review* indicates, American culture needed its original character to represent American social realities.

In *Nature*, Emerson creates a figure called the "transparent eyeball." Although Emerson did not write novels, his "transparent eyeball" became a memorable character in the work of a fellow Transcendentalist, Christopher Cranch. Lawrence Buell describes this image: "Fledgling Emersonians chuckle over the hyperbolic effusion in *Nature* where the writer imagines himself walking in the woods, buoyed up by force of his exhalation to 'become a transparent eye-ball' (*The Complete Works of Ralph Waldo Emerson* I: 10; hereafter abbreviated as *W*)—as well as the droll cartoon of this passage by Christopher Cranch, of a top-hatted eyeball on stilt-like legs, which anticipates later journalistic caricatures of Emerson the lecturer as angular ectomorph" (*Emerson* 92). A newspaper at the time describes, "Mr. Emerson is [as] a tall man, full six feet high, but slender and bony, and in his plain suit of ill-fitting black, looked not unlike a New England country schoolmaster. His face is thin and strongly marked, his nose large, and his eye-brows highly arched and meeting."[5] Thus, Cranch's caricature of Emerson's "transparent eyeball" epitomizes Emerson's character. According to Buell's interpretation of Emerson's role in popular culture, the American character that Emerson advocated ultimately prevailed nationwide (*New England Literary Culture* 63–64).

As a disciple of Emerson, Henry David Thoreau's character seemingly resembles that of his mentor. Emerson's eyeball is situated alone on the bare ground: "To go into solitude, a man needs as much from his chamber as from society. I am not solitary whilst I read and write, though nobody is with me. . . . Standing on the bare ground,—my head bathed by the blithe air, and uplifted into infinite space,—all mean egotism vanishes I become a transparent eyeball" (*CW* I: 8–10). In *Walden*, Thoreau's narrator begins his "simple and sincere account of his own life" by proclaiming that "[w]hen I wrote the following pages, or rather bulk of them, I lived alone, in the woods, a mile from any neighbor, in a house which I had built myself, on the shore of Walden Pond, in Concord, and earned my living by the labor of my hands only" (3). To establish American originality, both Thoreau and Emerson asserted the necessity of solitude in the midst of the social transformation of nineteenth-century America.[6]

New York journalism seemed to envision a "big" American literature. Edward Widmer explains this aspiration by analyzing Evert Duyckinck's notion of American literature at this time: "the new books they expected would be big, reckless, and thoroughly 'original,' to the most overworked adjective. A notebook fragment contains Duyckinck's hope that American culture would lead the country to 'the healthy tone of a true republic,' away from 'European vanities,' and toward 'the wisdom and democracy and sober self-government of our American ancestor'" (97). Duyckinck, however, was unable to present or represent memorable American characters, and his role in establishing original American literature was limited to an unremarkable reference book of his days.

Emerson advocated for the development of American originality in various ways, for instance, participating in lecture tours, founding *The Dial* magazine, and publishing his own works. When he worked on drafts of his lectures or books, he seemed to return to and borrow the sentences from his journals to elaborate his ideas. For Emerson, the process of crafting manuscripts was repetitive and perennial. Emerson's journals are the original source of his developmental thoughts, and his process of copying of his writing and reproducing his works speaks to the derivative nature of his lectures and essays. Once Emerson's fame was established, the singular character that Emerson advocated was reproduced and distributed through various media. The iterant message of solitude paradoxically created an American character who transcended his humdrum existence.

Emerson used various types of media. Bonnie Carr O'Neill argues that Emerson's lectures, which journalists covered in reports that included descriptions of his physical appearance, especially highlighted the aspect of quantifiable visual likeness and made him a cultural celebrity (740). Nonetheless, his attempts to advocate for the American character were entangled with the innovative dissemination of print culture and the influence of journalism. The rapid circulation of newspapers propelled Emerson's fame as a lecturer and increased his popularity across the country. To consider the process of Emerson's increasing fame, we could go back to Lynch's analysis of copying. As I mentioned before, Emerson's procedure of crafting his manuscripts followed the process of copying. The readers of Emerson's published lectures or essays reiterate the process of reproduction. The relationship between the original and the copy was a latent issue about the dissemination of Emerson's image and thoughts. While Emerson's lecture tours broke physical regional boundaries, his fame through reprinting reached as far places as possible. McGill argues that an investigation of the nineteenth-century culture of reprinting "uncover[s] a literature defined by its exuberant understanding of culture as iteration and not origination" (4).

Once created, the American character needed to be disseminated to the American people. Through his lectures, Emerson advocated for the American character and then Emerson's published essays and coverage endorsed his image and thoughts. His image of the American inspired a diverse audience. Similar to Emerson's way of producing his own image, his message of solitude was reproduced in the reading public, ultimately confirming the American character. The dissemination of the American character showed complex continuities with the production of copies through the mass market publishing. Thus, Emerson's praise of the singularity of the American character was in step with the development of print culture as iteration.

4. Marketplace and Authorship

McGill cogently explores the field of social influences in the literary market, both national and transatlantic and notes that the idea of authorship was recognized through copyright law. Referring to the case *Wheaton v. Pete*, McGill shows the complicated situation surrounding the American copyright law,[7] which involves "federal control over interstate commerce" (69). Returning to the antebellum period, we notice that various mutually opposing movements occurred simultaneously and that continuous tensions between the federal government and the state over the development of the nation culminated in the Civil War.

Situating himself within a social and cultural transformation, Emerson tactfully designed his project to ensure "a promise of a new era in intellectual life" (Gura 70). In *Nature*, he proclaims, "Let us demand our own works and laws and worship" (*CW* I: 7). His way of making his new philosophy public was multitasked. He used the burgeoning print culture and succeeded in publishing his books while traveling for lecture series on the East Coast and in the West.

Emerson advised Margaret Fuller and Thoreau about choosing publishing companies. He recommended that they explore the center of journalism in New York, which was outperforming Boston in terms of various newspaper publishing and networking at the time. In a letter dated on April 24, 1844, Emerson advised Fuller regarding her choice of publishers:

> Booksellers also are vanity & vexation. This morng [sic] I visited Little of L.&B. & learned that Brown had departed to Phila. Yesterday P.M.; that just previous to his departure Little had consulted him on the question whether "ten cents the copy" was our due, or "ten per cent"? (which is ten cents a copy if a copy costs a dollar, but only 7 1/2 cents if it cost 75 cents). And Brown had answered distinctly, "ten per cent." . . . The Pendulum swung back to Munroe & Co. . . . The only advantage the L & B have in my eyes is a greater power in N.Y. and of that I am not sure they were not able to hinder Past & Present from being published as they thought they could. (*The Letters of Ralph Waldo Emerson* VII: 248; Hereafter abbreviated as *L*)

Emerson compares two publishers in terms of cost and the market, analyzing the regional differences. Prior to this letter, Emerson sent Thoreau to New York to serve as a tutor in William Emerson's family. Emerson's aim was not only to provide Thoreau a stable job but also to give him "a chance to test the New York literary market" (Thoreau, *Correspondence* 73). However, Thoreau's exposure to New York journalism discouraged him out. After a conversation with the Harpers in New York, Thoreau seems to better understand the reality of the book market business:

> Some propose to me to do what an honest man cannot—Among others I conversed with the Harpers—to see if they might not find me useful to them—but they say that they are making fifty thousand dollars annually, and their motto is to let well alone. I find that I talk with these poor men as if I were over head and ears in business and a few thousands were no consideration with me—I almost reproach myself for bothering them thus to no purpose—but if it is very valuable experience—and the best introduction I could have. (Thoreau, *Correspondence* 135)

The print culture in New York was a bigger business than what Thoreau had imagined. Emerson encouraged Thoreau to become acquainted with the literary men in New York, and Thoreau reported back to Emerson about those with whom he met and gradually came to comprehend the world of journalism in the city. He apparently submitted his manuscripts detailing his observations of nature for publication and received a letter from John O'Sullivan, including the following lines:

> Articles of this nature are not in general published in the D[emocratic] R[eview] on the responsibility of the individual name of the author but under the general impersonality of the collective "we"—(the name of the author being usually indicated in pencil on the Index in the copies sent to the editors of newspapers). This system renders a certain pervading homogeneity necessary, inviting often the necessary of this process of editorial revision, or rather communication. (Thoreau, *Correspondence* 130)

O'Sullivan's letter reveals his politically oriented editorial principles, which demand national unity. He later justified the Texas annexation as "the dear and sacred designation of *Our Country*" ("Annexation," emphasis added), referring to the nation's "manifest destiny."[8] In a letter to Emerson, Thoreau expresses some anxiety about New York journalism:

> Literature comes to a poor market here, and even the little that I write is more than will sell. I have tried the Democratic Review, the New Mirror, and Brother Jonathan. The last two, as well as the New World, are overwhelmed with contributions which cost nothing, and are worth no more. The Knickerbocker is too poor, and only the Ladies' Companion pays. O'Sullivan is printing the manuscript I sent him some time ago, having

> objected only to my want of sympathy with the Communities. (Thoreau, *Correspondence* 139)

Thoreau continued corresponding with journalists such as Horace Greeley, who tried to help him publish his work (Thoreau, *Correspondence* 175), and Evert Duyckinck. Eventually, Thoreau's first book *A Week on the Concord and Merrimack Rivers* was published in 1849 by Boston-based publisher James Munroe. Thoreau owed a considerable debt to Munroe for the publishing of his book. Although *A Week* was a market failure, Thoreau continued in his efforts to get his second book *Walden* published, eventually succeeding in 1854.[9] Emerson comments on Thoreau's idea of publishing as follows: "Henry Thoreau has been showing me triumphantly how much cheaper & every way wiser it would be to publish the book ourselves paying the booksellers only a simple commission for vending it & conducting personally the correspondence with distant booksellers; —but such heroisms are not for me this spring" (*L* 250). Thoreau, who made pencils as part of his family business, believed that publishing should not be institutionalized. However, Thoreau's notion of connecting publishing houses and selling nationwide predicted the transformation of the print industry, which aimed to consolidate businesses to achieve broader access to the market in lieu of decentralization. Emerson was aware of the transformation of print culture, and he may have advised Thoreau on the best way to get his work published.

Len Gougeon argues that Emerson's writings about social problems shows his political activism (xxxv). Emerson describes New York journalism as "destructive, not constructive," or "politico-literary" (*JMN* VIII: 314), exhibiting his dislike or distrust of politics. However, his attitude regarding the New York publishing industry reveals his tactics, when navigated a multivariate print culture. Given Gougeon's discussion, Emerson's remarks about journalism, criticizing that in New York and endorsing that in Boston, reflect his political stance. Emerson encouraged his friends to use New York publishing companies, but he himself remained with Boston-based companies, first with James Munroe and later with Ticknor and Fields, and he may have enjoyed good terms with these publishers over the course of their long relationship. Considering the transformation of print culture and his role as the center of a new cultural movement (i.e. Transcendentalism), we should reconsider why Emerson criticized New York journalism while clearly recognizing its importance.

According to Widmer, New York journalism became the center of the national culture movement. Among others, Duyckinck compiled a guide to American literature and made the massive two-volume *Cyclopaedia of American Literature*, "the largest and most comprehensive book of its type then written, and still a useful reference work" (120). Witnessing the rise of New York-based journalism, which attempted to lead to an American literature, Emerson reexamined the politics of New York journalism, and he was inclined to defend Boston's aloofness based on its "self-reliance." Meanwhile, Boston-based Ticknor and Fields ultimately became an influential publisher. Following Ticknor's prosperity, Emerson remained with the Boston publishers while he encouraged Transcendentalists to publish their works with New York publishing companies, whose market reached all corners of the United States. Given the antebellum political upheaval, Emerson's strategy was bifocal, balancing marketplaces through decentralization.

James Kloppenberg analyzes Emerson's antislavery perspective as follows: "Emerson himself [was] notoriously wary of politics, including in his disdain the political party that called itself the Democracy because he believed the most people in politics never scratch beneath the surface of their lives. In 'Man the reformer,' Emerson minimized the significance of institutions because only the individual matters" (677). However, Emerson was aware of the importance of the print market and attempted to use it to disseminate his agenda. If his alliance with Boston publishers and criticism of politico-literary New York journalism exposed the problem of publishing in relation to market value, his balance between New York journalism and Boston publishers indicated his new awareness of authorship and character as individual rights. While New York journalism championed the collective "we" of national unity, Emerson valued the individual rights and regionalism of the American character.

Attempting to publish Thomas Carlyle's "Cromwell," Emerson wrote to Wiley and Putnam in 1846, mentioning "a very unfavorable aspect, when I first heard of your printings" (*L* 324). This type of communications with publishers probably increased Emerson's awareness of the copyright problem in the United States. The lack of international copyright protection was perceived as an obstacle for American literary authors in terms of authorship, and some called for an international copyright law. Among those in Young America movement, some thought that an international copyright law was necessary to develop a national culture. However, without such a law, the American print industry profited from the reproduction of British authors' works. After Charles Dickens visited the United States, he accused American pirate publishers in *American Notes* (1842). Protecting copyright presented the problem of centralization, which President Andrew Jackson opposed at the time (McGill 109). This problem of decentralization in politics and in the industry complicated the copyright issue for American authors. As McGill argues, given the lack of international copyright, the culture of reprinting ironically enabled the emergence of works with American content (203). Ultimately American content was to be the literature of democracy.

Despite internal problems related to literary property in the United States, the dissemination of Emerson's ideas to the world was allowed as an approachable avenue for overseas readers. The lack of international copyright law may have helped Japanese visitors introduce Emerson to Japanese readers.[10] As an exemplar of "self-reliance," Emerson and his message reached Japan; through him Japanese literati witnessed a flowering national culture in the United States. Japanese literary figures aspired to awaken a national literature in Japan. Although American authors did not receive international copyright protections,[11] Emerson was introduced to Japanese readers as a model of national literature. For Japanese readers, Emerson opened a window into Anglo-American thoughts on the value of the inner self and democracy. The delay of international copyright protections for American authors allowed a new kind of distribution of American national literature.

5. Toward Public Property

Edgar Allan Poe was among the first of the American authors to recognize the copyright problem as a lack of recognition of authorship, and he used and circumvented such authorship. McGill argues that "Poe actively resists both the literary nationalist call to civic authorship and Henry Wadsworth Longfellow's more gentlemanly cosmopolitanism, both models that make the author central to accounts of literary value" (170). Duyckinck supported the international copyright movement for American authors, but Duyckinck's "author" referred a unified voice for national culture. Poe resisted this idea of a unified American voice. We recall Thoreau, who was anxious about the insistence of New York journalism on a singular "we." Poe, extolling the originality of the author, valued individual character in line with Emerson's thought. Poe's rise to fame and authorship is remembered in tragic terms. His subsequent failed claim of originality and authorship also reveals the problematic dimension of authorship in nineteenth-century America.[12] Poe's struggle over copyright and originality in the face of New York journalism epitomizes Emerson's tactics in relation to New York's politics and print culture. McGill concludes that the "[a]ntebellum struggle over the right to reprint domestic and foreign texts demonstrates that literary property is never simply or only a matter of individual property rights, but rather of systems of circulation in which persons, corporate bodies, and the state have complicated and often conflicting interests" (276). In the antebellum era, solving the problem of authorship and copyright was an issue not only for literary figures but also for print industry politics. This problem delayed international copyright protection. However, under such conditions, *Uncle Tom's Cabin* received international popularity (McGill 272–75). Similarly, Emerson's national and international popularity was the result of various types of reproduction. Overcoming these legal and market issues, Emerson established himself as an American cultural icon for readers both in the United States and abroad. For example, in Japan, Emerson was acclaimed as a representative of the American individualism.

Emerson's position on journalism requires us to reconsider the meaning of authorship. For Emerson, the author should aim to publicize character and the American character would emphasize the values of individual rights. The process associated with Emerson's American character, which was shared both nationally and internationally, circumvented the copyright problem by simultaneously stressing distribution and recognizing authorship as character. Emerson subverted the idea of the author as a mediator and facilitator of character. When Emerson's approach illustrates the singularity of American national culture and copyright, it also indicates the importance of recognizing the public's interest in American character and the potential to break the boundaries of the original and the copy in distributing the iconic image of American character. Thus, the dissemination of American character promoted the value of democracy and reinforced the relationship between culture and politics for the next century.

Notes

1 We can refer to Lynch's analysis of eighteenth-century British print culture and personal identity: "Eighteenth-century ways of thinking about the relation of personal identity to the articulate surfaces and the verbal signs that made it public knowledge were not only bound up with the metropolitan culture market of bookselling and print selling. They were also bound up with the institutions that the state developed to increase wealth and expedite commerce by accelerating the

circulation and exchange of information and value" (41).
2 *Athenaeum Items*. November 1960.
3 *Edinburgh Reviews* 33 (January-May 1820): 79–80.
4 See Horiuchi's discussion of Emerson's character.
5 *Cincinnati Gazette*, January 28,1857.
6 Gilmore analyzes the antebellum writers' individuality as their alienation from the reading public.
7 The Wheaton v. Peters case indicates the singularity of the American idea of copyright, which values on public property rather than authorship. "Wheaton v. Peters (1834) self-consciously restates the British debates over literary property, reformulates its terms, and rejects both common-law copyright and the Lockean argument that undergirds it" (McGill 45).
8 John O'Sullivan, "Annexation," *United States Magazine and Democratic Review*, 17: 1 (July-August 1845): 5–10.
9 At that time, the average wage of Lowell Mills girls, who were thought to be elite female workers with an innovative work-dorm system was $ 1.75 a week (Thoreau, *Correspondence* 160). Thoreau's *Walden* was sold for $1.00 by Ticknor (Thoreau, *Correspondence* 315).
10 In 1870, Tanejiro Mekata met Emerson in the United States, and Masakazu Toyama, Professor of English at Tokyo Imperial University, delivered a lecture on Emerson's work in 1876 (Koizumi, 241).
11 In 1891, international copyright gained protection in the United States under the Berne Convention.
12 See McGill 214–17. Although McGill's emphasizes reprinting rather than authorship, I argue that authorship and its transformation are important when considering American character.

Works Cited

Buell, Lawrence. *Emerson*. Cambridge: Belknap-Harvard UP, 2003. Print.
——. *New England Literary Culture from Revolution through Renaissance*. Cambridge; New York: Cambridge UP, 1986. Print.
Emerson, Ralph Waldo. *The Collected Works of Ralph Waldo Emerson*. Eds. Robert Ernest Spiller, et al. Cambridge: Belknap-Harvard UP, 1971–2013, 1971. Print.
——. *The Complete Works of Ralph Waldo Emerson: With a Biographical Introduction and Notes*. Ed. Edward Waldo Emerson. Cambridge: Riverside P, 1903–. Print.
——. *Emerson's Antislavery Writings*. Ed. Len Gougeon and Joel Myerson. New Haven: Yale UP,1995. Print.
——. *Journals and Miscellaneous Notebooks of Ralph Waldo Emerson*. 16 Vols. Eds. William Gilman and others. Cambridge: Belknap-Harvard UP, 1960–. Print.
——. *The Letters of Ralph Waldo Emerson*. Vol 7. Ed. Eleanor M. Tilton. New York: Columbia UP: 1990. Print.
Gura, Philip F. *American Transcendentalism: A History*. New York: Hill and Wang,

2007. Print.

Hara, Hidenori. "Zasshi no Ho to Hakubunkan." ["The Law for the Magazines and Hakubunkan"]. *Bulletin of the International Japanese Culture Center*. 23 (2001): 143–78. Print.

Horiuchi, Masaki. "Jikono Bigaku to Shintai / Chikara / Fuhen." ["Self-Aesthetic and Body / Power / Universality"]. *Bulletin of the Graduate Division of Letters, Arts and Sciences of Waseda University* 61.2 (2016): 5–19. Print.

Kimnack, Wilson H., Kenneth P. Minkema and Douglas A. Sweeney. Editors' Introduction. *The Sermons of Jonathan Edwards*. Eds. Kimnack Wilson et al. New Haven: Yale UP, 1999. ix–xlvii. Print.

Kloppenberg, James T. *Toward Democracy: The Struggle for Self-Rule in European and American Thought*. New York: Oxford UP, 2016. Print.

Koizumi, Takashi. "R. W. Emerson' Idea of God and Its Reception of Masanao Nakamura, Kanzou Uchimura, and Toukoku." *Bulletin of Modern Japanese Studies* 29 (2012): 241–66. Print.

Lynch, Deidre. *The Economy of Character: Novels, Market Culture and the Business of Inner Meaning*. Chicago: U of Chicago P, 1998. Print.

McGill, Meredith L. *American Literature and Culture of Reprinting, 1834–1853*. Philadelphia: U of Pennsylvania P, 2007. Print.

O'Neill, Bonnie Carr. "'The Best of Me Is There': Emerson as Lecturer and Celebrity." *American Literature* 80.4 (2008): 739–67. Print.

Thoreau, Henry David. *The Correspondence of Henry David Thoreau*. Ed. Ed Walter Harding and Carol Bode. New York: New York UP, 1958. Print.

——. *Walden*. Ed J. Lindon Shanley. Princeton: Princeton UP, 2004. Print.

Widmer, Edward L. *Young America: The Flowering of Democracy in New York City*. New York: Oxford UP, 1999. Print.

Winship, Michael. *American Literary Publishing in the Mid-Nineteenth Century: The Business of Ticknor and Fields*. New York: Cambridge UP, 1995. Print.

This work was supported by JSPS KAKENHI Grant Number 17k02551.

Modernity of Louisa May Alcott's Unpublished Manuscript "Pogram's Lay-vice"[1]

Asako Motooka

Louisa May Alcott's literary career began with mimicking and rearranging Charles Dickens's works.[2] Being huge Dickens fans, she and her sisters created a family newspaper *The Pickwick Portfolio* inspired by *The Pickwick Papers* (1836–37) in their childhood. Alcott was captivated not only by penning fan fictions, such as family newspapers and poems, but also by producing novel-to-stage adaptations.

Such Dickens's influences on Alcott's works have been a focal point for critics (Crisler 29–35; Eiselein 24; Boyd 48–49; Lenahan 21–23).[3] Observing a striking resemblance between Oliver Twist and an orphan boy in *Little Women* (1868–69), Jan Susina identifies Alcott's obsessive attention to Dickens (164–65) but fails to demonstrate whether Alcott was swayed or not by other Dickens fans among her literary circle. Her fellow fans' presence cannot be overlooked by the fact that Dickens enthusiasts had almost always surrounded Alcott since her childhood. Certainly, her family and community members not only encouraged her for writing Dickens fan fiction pieces but also actively participated and helped in her creative activities. These derivative works were nothing other than result of—and helped to perpetuate—Alcott's social interactions with other Dickens fans.

This study clarifies the dynamism of fan activities by analyzing editorial practices in Alcott's unpublished manuscripts and by redefining them within a framework of "fandom." Of those scripts, the focus here is on the following unpublished, private manuscripts archived in Harvard's Houghton Library: a drama script titled "Pogram's Lay-vice" and two additional drafts that clearly refer to Dickens's *Martin Chuzzlewit* (1843–44). Alcott's documents allow us to think of Dickensian fandom as a site of cooperation in receiving and producing works, since after completing her drafts, Alcott had peers circulate them, express their opinions, and provide her with detailed feedback.

In this essay, I first investigate how Alcott enjoyed performing Dickens-inspired theatricals. Subsequently, I closely examine Alcott's editorial practices in her dramatic scripts. By analyzing differences between drafts, we ascertain that these manuscripts are products of participatory fan activity, going beyond the editor's direct control. Consequently, I attempt to reinterpret Alcott and her peers' fan-driven practices in the context of postmodern *otaku* culture in Japan and the United States by using literary critical terms such as Henry Jenkins's "fandom" and Hiroki Azuma's "database consumption." Revaluating Alcott and her friends' dramatics as a pioneering example of fan culture illuminates modernity of their theatrical practices in the mid-nineteenth century America.

1. Falling in Love with Dickens: Alcott and Her Literary Circle

Sales of Charles Dickens's works, as the British Anthony Trollope once said with mixed feelings of admiration and jealousy, were the equivalent of what one eats every day—mutton legs and loaves of bread (Trollope 372; John 3). Dickens's unprecedented popularity surged in both Britain and in America from the 1840s onward. An American librarian explained this in an interview with *Harper's New Monthly Magazine*: "Next to Harper['s papers] come Dickens's novels . . . . We have Scott's novels, but they are much less read than Dickens is" (Abbott 776). Dickens's works kept abreast with contemporary bestseller magazines and were much more popular than the works of the British bestselling novelist Sir Walter Scott.

The ever-growing Dickens boom triggered numerous adaptations and related merchandise, such as parodied stories, museum exhibits, and most importantly, feature plays. One example is Little Nell, the innocent girl in *The Old Curiosity Shop* (1840–41), who dies a tragic and early death; in an American play, however, she does not die, but lives on happily. As for *Oliver Twist* (1837–38), the eponymous starving Oliver says, "Please, sir, I want some more," naively asking for another serving in a poorhouse (12). In an American dramatic version, a greedy man asking for money declaims the well-known line (McParland 19).

Likewise, Alcott penned dramatic scripts based on his works and performed them with and for literary community members. A noteworthy feature of her theatrical practices is her dramatic experience as a member of The Concord Dramatic Union, founded by novice teacher Franklin B. Sanborn and constituted by Alcott and her sister Anna, local teenagers George Bartlett and Alfred Whitman, and Ralph Waldo Emerson's children Edith and Edward (Cameron 14; Emerson 1: 137; Whitman, "Letters" 101–02). For this company, Alcott composed dramatic scripts—*Scenes from Dickens* and "Mrs. Jarley's Waxworks"—acted her favorite characters and moved audiences to laughter (Alcott, *Letters* 87; Whitman, "Meg" 107–08; Porter 11).[4] Interestingly enough, George Bartlett, Alcott's co-star, later became popular with his home theatrical guide, titled *Mrs. Jarley's Far-Famed Collection of Waxworks* (1873) (D'Alessandro 2). Despite the time difference in these pieces' composition, it is a surprising coincidence that both Alcott and her colleague Bartlett wrote spin-off works featuring Dickens's Mrs. Jarley. Considering the multiple aspiring writers in the drama company, we can assert that although Alcott's strong affinities with Dickens certainly emerged from her reading experience, her activities within her family and community dramatic circle also affected Alcott's taste for literature.[5]

A certain episode underlines her group-oriented self-formation. In 1863, when Alcott published *Hospital Sketches*, publisher James Redpath offered her a position as a newspaper editor. At that time, she was jubilant that her prior experiences of writing and editing the family newspaper had finally translated into a career opportunity. She commented with joy that "[the] editorial plan was so like an old dream coming true, that my family shouted over it, as we have had several domestic newspapers" (Alcott, *Letters* 89). Notably, although Alcott herself had an opportunity to join the literary world, she was delighted as if the whole family had received the offer. Without her family interactions, Alcott could not have enjoyed consuming and producing works that were derivatives of Dickens's works; further, she also might not have learned how to excite her readers with her writings.

Indeed, Daniel Shealy partially illuminates Alcott's career advancement through family members.

> In the mid to late 1840s, . . . she [the young, stage-struck Louisa May Alcott] co-authored plays with her older sister Anna . . . . With the four Alcott sisters assuming the roles of the Dickens characters, Anna (Meg in *Little Women*) as the editor Samuel Pickwick, Louisa (Jo) as the literary Augustus Snodgrass, Lizzie (Beth) as the rosy Tracy Tupman, and May (Amy) as Nathaniel Winkle, the famous Pickwick Club was re-born—not in Victorian England but in rural Concord, Massachusetts. (Shealy, "Louisa" 15)

Shealy seems to clarify Alcott's career stages, from a young Dickens lover to a full-fledged writer, but he pays no attention to her family's influence on her writing endeavors; he ignores the contemporaneous significance of her participation in a Dickens fan group and its collaborative quality. Shealy narrates her success as if she could have achieved her career path only through her own literary potential. Considering that Alcott plugged away creating fan fictions, more focus should be on what Alcott "co-authored" with her sisters than what she "authored" individually: it is certain that her creativity is rooted in family-based collaboration. Alcott's engagement in the fan fiction writing circle raises the following question: What is the difference between being an individual fan and being a member of a fan community? To be more specific, how does the experience of literary works' collective reception not only differ from that of solitary reading but also generate impact on a writer's literary career?

To investigate the relation between fan activity and writers' creativity, in the next section, I examine the editorial process of "Pogram's Lay-vice" and two additional drafts.

2. Editorial Process of the Unpublished Drama Script "Pogram's Lay-vice"

A series of "Pogram's Lay-vice" drafts comprises Alcott's dramatic script based on Dickens's *Martin Chuzzlewit*. Although it is unclear exactly when she wrote the manuscripts, they were presumably written in the late 1850s, around the time when there occurred a drastic change in Alcott and her sisters' performance style. Since childhood, they had mainly played Shakespeare's tragedies, but they began to perform comical arrangements of Dickens's works after joining two local theatrical companies, that of Walpole in 1855 and of Concord in 1857 (Stern, "Trouper" 177–85). From 1860 onward, Alcott switched from composing dramatic scripts to writing novels. Consequently, in the late 1850s, Alcott supposedly scripted a series of "Pogram's Lay-vice" drafts.

Three manuscripts contain the main characters' names atop the first page: (A) "Pogram," (B) "Julius Washington Merryweather Bib," and (C) "Pogram, Bib & Chuzzlewit." Given that manuscript C's title combines key characters of manuscripts A and B, and adds the supporting Martin Chuzzlewit who appears in those drafts, we can hypothesize that Alcott revised former drafts and incorporated them into the third. The play's title is also critical for testing this hypothesis because Alcott bestowed a play title—"Pogram's Lay-vice"—only on manuscript C. Moreover, each dialogue in manuscripts A and B contains no character names; only manuscript C lists casting names as if to imply that Alcott finalized the script, prepared it for a stage performance, and was about to distribute it to the cast.

More evidence about the editing process lies in her handwritten memos. At the headers of manuscripts A and B, Alcott provided the same note "Please save & return to Miss Alcott"; it is certain that Alcott passed those drafts to multiple people around her. The return "to Miss Alcott," including her family name, indicates that Alcott circulated them beyond her family members. Needless to say, if she shared those drafts in her home, the return address would have been something like "To Louisa." On manuscript C, however, instead of leaving the instruction memo mentioned above, Alcott placed several "+" marks near corrected parts. They are most likely Alcott's memoranda to let her companions see and check where, after revising former versions, the editor incorporated their ideas into the rewritten version. Obviously then, manuscripts A and B should be early drafts of manuscript C that is the revised version or even the final script itself.

"Pogram's Lay-vice" depicts the story that Bib, as common acquaintance of a young British man, Martin Chuzzlewit, traveling in America and of a female Transcendentalist, Mrs. Hominy, introduces both to an American civil servant, Mr. Pogram. This plot was created by cutting and reassembling various elements from *Martin Chuzzlewit*: episodes in which Chuzzlewit fulfills his dream of visiting America (chapter 16); meets Mrs. Hominy at an anti-British rally (chapter 21); is troubled by Mrs. Hominy asking questions regarding his impressions of the United States (chapter 22). Chuzzlewit, on his way back to Britain, exchanges words with Mr. Pogram, who fiercely argues in favor of British people.

By way of gleaning these fragments for her spin-off, Alcott changed Mrs. Hominy's character into someone who acts and behaves differently from the character in the source material. The clearest example occurs when Bib introduces her to Mr. Pogram. In the original novel, Mrs. Hominy, a philosopher and writer who lectures on foreign affairs, appears at Mr. Pogram's reception party with other two female Transcendentalists. Since Mrs. Hominy and Mr. Pogram know one another, Bib does not need to introduce them. Instead, Mrs. Hominy presents her literary companions to the reception party participants

(507–08). In contrast, in the A version, Bib does not explain who Mrs. Hominy is, so that readers do not get any information about her, for example, whether she is a Transcendentalist and has previously known Mr. Pogram. Without Bib's introduction, Mrs. Hominy opens her mouth and then shuts it again due to the unseasonable interruption of Mr. Pogram's speech.[6] If the only words Mrs. Hominy is able to get in edgewise are "Epic, self-contained" (3), we can be sure that Alcott cynically depicted the scene in which Mr. Pogram forced the originally talkative woman to content herself with making, literally, a single comment.

The situation worsens in manuscript B because Mrs. Hominy cannot deliver every single word. When Bib is about to introduce her to Mr. Pogram, unfortunately enough, the tea bell rings. Immediately afterward, Bib asks the civil servant to take their leave and get something to eat with the tea; in doing so, they keep Mrs. Hominy out of their conversation. Thus, in scripts A and B, Alcott reduces Mrs. Hominy's didactic, effusive aspect and depicts her as a woman forced to remain silent.

In manuscript C, by contrast, Mrs. Hominy, who should have been frustrated of being unable to speak in previous versions, breaks her silence and returns as an eloquent speaker similar to the original character. Due to her initiatives in making public appearances and speaking on her own accord, Mrs. Hominy gains an influential voice. For Alcott does not have the literary women—Miss Codger and Miss Toppit—appear in this version, and instead introduces Mrs. Hominy as only one female Transcendentalist. On behalf of Miss Codger, who is absent from "Pogram's Lay-vice," Mrs. Hominy delivers her wordy speech beginning with "Toe [sic] be presented to a Pogram by a Bib, indeed a thrilling moment is it in its impressiveness on what we call our feelings" (4). Here, Mrs. Hominy's speech is a blatant rip-off of Miss Codger's: "To be presented to a Pogram . . . by a Hominy, indeed, a thrilling moment is it in its impressiveness on what we call our feelings" (Dickens, *Martin* 508).

While comparing the above quotations, we cannot overlook different personal characters both of Miss Codger in *Martin Chuzzlewit* and of Mrs. Hominy in "Pogram's Lay-vice." It is because, by switching the speakers from Miss Codger to Mrs. Hominy, Alcott clearly highlights the verbal battle between Mr. Pogram and Mrs. Hominy that has intensified. More specifically, according to the original text, Miss Codger is regarded as an intellectual who has much press coverage in Britain, but Americans attach little importance to her as "[t]he oldest inhabitant, as never remembers anything" (Dickens, *Martin*

508). Unlike Miss Codger, who is famous for her forgetfulness, Mrs. Hominy is a representative American female whose status is the same as Mr. Pogram's. Nevertheless, she treats the distinguished political figure on the same level as Bib, and reveals her slight interest in the former, contrary to her courteous speech. This being the case, Mr. Pogram interpreting her statement as criticism and flying into a rage seems reasonable.

Mrs. Hominy's voice is conflated not only with Miss Codger's but also with a youth dreaming of studying in Britain, and an American swindler deceiving Martin. By internalizing various characters' words and thoughts, Mrs. Hominy gets into deeper trouble with Mr. Pogram. In fact, just after meeting the public servant, Mrs. Hominy begins to express her primary concerns without so much as greeting him. By exemplifying an American hawk killing a British lion, she expresses a thinly veiled insult, warning that conflicting emotional attitudes trigger a major crisis. She continuously preaches the virtue of gentleness: "Yes, we are ardent, we are young, yet there is poetry in wildness, & every alligator basking in the sun is an Epic self-contained" (4). Once again, Mrs. Hominy appropriates lines originally delivered by an American youth eagerly wishing to study abroad in Britain: "I am young, and ardent. For there is a poetry in wildness, and every alligator basking in the slime is in himself an Epic, self-contained" (Dickens, *Martin* 341).

As with Mrs. Hominy, Mr. Pogram also borrows other characters' words from the original text. Mr. Pogram is a politician and foreign critic, whose belief is close to American exceptionalism and the Monroe Doctrine that warns Europe against interfering with the United States. Being dense about other characters' anti-British resentments, Mr. Pogram's xenophobia becomes more obvious in "Pogram's Lay-vice" (Dickens, *Martin* 498–99; Alcott, "Pogram's Lay-vice" 2). Mr. Pogram adopts words coming from the very lips of a young Columbian, an anti-British-meeting participant in *Martin Chuzzlewit*, with little modification, saying, "Ah, prejudice! But sir, I know the British Lion; alone I dare state Lion, alone I taunt him, & I tell him that Freedom's hand once twisted in his mane he rolls a corse before me & the Eagles of the great Republic laugh ha! ha!" (Alcott, "Pogram's Lay-vice" 3). Through such changes in character, to be certain, the politician's animosity grows stronger than in *Martin Chuzzlewit*.

A highlight of their relationship in Alcott's rewritten version is how they break up their public squabble: the more Mr. Pogram accentuates his anti-British feelings, the more Mrs. Hominy's words effectively soothe his anger.

For, depicted as a silent woman in manuscripts A and B, Mrs. Hominy does not possess any influence over Mr. Pogram's rage; in fact, nothing would bridle his temper, except, in manuscript B, a cup of tea that he is supposed to drink later. As contrasted with the previous two versions, Mrs. Hominy reappears at center stage in the revised one. Alcott revives Mrs. Hominy's presence as a peerless woman by removing the other two female Transcendentalists in the drafts of "Pogram's Lay-vice." Concentrating power in the words of Mrs. Hominy, Alcott enlivens her remarks so they go too far given Mr. Pogram's xenophobia.

In the light of both the drafts' drastic modifications and the fact that Alcott circulated manuscripts to other dramatic society members, it is quite unlikely that a series of "Pogram's Lay-vice" drafts originates solely from Alcott's creativity. Rather naturally, Alcott seems to have introduced plot changes to regain her peers' favor, that is, to let Mrs. Hominy speak as much as or more than the original figure. The strongest possible reason behind revision is that Alcott's colleagues asked her to shed light on women's empowerment. Either by giving Mrs. Hominy good chances to speak up or by shifting the plotline's emphasis from British-American rivalry to the internal, American debate between Mr. Pogram and Mrs. Hominy, the literary circle attempted to emphasize the importance of women's participation in society.

Considering Alcott's editing process, we cannot be completely satisfied with Shealy's paper, which ignores the influence of Alcott's comrades and focuses on her growth from an amateur scriptwriter to a professional writer. "Pogram's Lay-vice" is certainly the product of cooperative creativity among Dickens fans.

3. Modernity of "Pogram's Lay-vice"

Henry Jenkins, an American media "aca-fan"—an academic who self-identifies as a fan—analyzes a similar blurry boundary between writers and readers by introducing the concept of fandom (Duffett 267–69). According to Jenkins, fandom is a community whose members express and mutually share their enthusiasm, creativity, and intelligence, so that they enhance their appreciation of original works. The past two decades have witnessed scholarly research on fan cultures and fandom. By employing Pierre Bourdieu's concept of "taste," some researchers characterize fan cultures as nothing more than legitimization and reproduction of existing social strata, since those fans ingather according to their already owned and valued cultural capital (Duffett 129–34). Others pay attention to an individual fan, for instance, a "closet fan" who keeps her / his fannish life secret from friends and family in reaction to their potentially stigmatized social identity as fans (28–29, 244). Unlike these researchers, Jenkins offers different possibility of multiple fans that they can join their interests and produce a synergy effect regardless of their social rankings or inequalities (Jenkins 17–19).

> . . . [F]ans actively assert their mastery over the mass-produced texts which provide the raw materials for their own cultural productions and the basis for their social interactions. In the process, fans cease to be simply an audience for popular texts; instead, they become active participants in the construction and circulation of textual meanings. (23–24)

As Jenkins explains, fans share, change, or create something new from existing stories.[7] Through their peer-to-peer activities, fans fill in their gaps in knowledge and interpretation, expand on narratives of minor characters, and even sometimes correct cultural hegemonies established in the canon. From reflecting on the highly committed interaction of Alcott and her peers, fandom also applies to their literary group in mid-nineteenth-century America.[8]

Aside from members' positive engagement in the writing process, the condition of postmodernity can be traced in how Alcott and her peers design characters. Just as Jenkins mentions that fandom members regard the canon(s) as the collection of "the raw material(s)," Alcott's circle appreciated the elements of character and bits of anecdote in Dickens's fiction rather than the whole story organized by the author. This is illustrated by how versatile identities in the original are gleaned and compressed into the voices of Mrs. Hominy and Mr. Pogram.

Placing more stress on works' components than on narratives, Japanese cultural theorist Hiroki Azuma indicates that "[t]he database becomes the center of the creative process in the computer age" (227). By referring to Jean-François Lyotard's concept of the end of grand narratives, Azuma observes that those narratives displaying shared societal values or ideologies are replaced by a huge database in the postmodern age. According to Azuma, otaku create their derivative works by customizing small narratives and character attributes extracted from the repository approximately after 1995 (47–55).

Indeed, Alcott and her comrades regarded Dickens's literary works as scraps of characters, plots, or situations, not as unified, prestigious, or authoritative books. In the pre-computer era, it was impossible for the Dickens fan group to use computers and electronic databases. Instead, through their reading experiences and knowledge, Alcott and her comrades cut various elements of Dickens's text and then pasted them into "Pogram's Lay-vice." In their script-editing process, we can ascertain their creative engagements' premature postmodernity.

Conclusion

Thus, fandom and fan fiction practices are often regarded as a particular phenomenon of the networked and digital age, but, as clarified in this paper, even in the pre-computer era, otaku have created peer-to-peer network and socialized with each other within their communities. A prime example of those peer-based fan cultures in Japan is Comic Market, founded in the 1970s, which is the biannual distribution venue for self-published books, known as *doujinshi* (Tamagawa 110–12). In the communal marketplace, fans have facilitated the sharing and viewing of their and other dedicated fans' DIY products. Before 120 or more years, surprisingly enough, Alcott not only made her otaku community, but also created databases and produced their fan fictions. If they engaged in activities similar to Jenkins's "fandom" and Azuma's "database consumption" in an analogue age, that fact could provide a new perspective linking studies of nineteenth-century American literature and contemporary fan culture in Japan and the United States.

Moreover, this paper leads us to question the conventional concept of "romantic authorship" that celebrates the author's singularity and originality. When illustrating that Alcott, who later became a professional writer, developed her literary potential through peer-to-peer communications in a grassroots fan community, in studying her works, it becomes crucial to investigate not only intertextuality tracing inter-relations between texts but also interpersonal relations between authors.

Notes

1 This is a revised version of a paper presented at the 2014 Annual General Meeting of the Thoreau Society of Japan, held at Hokusei Gakuen University, Hokkaido, Japan (October 3, 2014). This research is supported by JSPS KAKENHI Grant Number JP26770112.

2 Many of Alcott's works express her excessive partiality to Dickens. For an account

of a Dickens-inspired literary tour of Europe, see "A Dickens Day" (1867, 1). For her "costume play," that is, dressing like her favorite nurse character Sarah Gamp in *Martin Chuzzlewit*, see *Hospital Sketches* (1863, 33). For Alcott's love for Mrs. Gamp, see also Cheever 139; Alcott and Alcott 9; LaPlante 258; Matteson 328.

3 For contemporary critics' comparisons between Dickens's and Alcott's texts, see Clark 215, 217, 232, 243; Tyler 15–16.

4 On December 14, 1863, at the request of Bartlett, then a stage manager, Alcott dramatized six *Scenes from Dickens*, reorganized the Concord Dramatic Company, and performed at the Tremont Theatre for the Sanitary Fair. Instead of endless disappointments, such as the want of experienced actors, the theatricals realized $2,500 for the fair (Alcott, *Letters* 99–100; Alcott, *Journals* 121–22; Stern, "Biography" 135–36).

5 For similar amateur collaborative activities, see Mary Louise Kete's *Sentimental Collaborations*, that introduces contemporary people's practices sympathy through writing funeral poems in mid-nineteenth-century America.

6 Manuscripts A, B, and C have no page numbers, so I assigned each page a number.

7 For the relationship between fandom and participatory culture, see Duffett 125–34, 297.

8 Daniel Cavicchi addresses music fandom in nineteenth-century America. He mainly focuses on music fans' collective behavior, such as collecting goods from their favorite artists and waiting for the star to appear, so that he pays little attention to fans in group(s), which I emphasize in this paper.

Works Cited

Abbott, Austin. "A Village Library." *Harper's New Monthly Magazine* May 1868: 774–77. *Making of America*. Web. 26 April 2014.

Alcott, Louisa May. "A Dickens Day." *The Independent* 26 Dec. 1867: 1. Print.

——. *Hospital Sketches*. 1863. Ed. Bessie Z. Jones. Cambridge: Belknap-Harvard UP, 1960. Print.

——. *The Journals of Louisa May Alcott*. Ed. Joel Myerson and Daniel Shealy. Athens: U of Georgia P, 1997. Print.

——. "Pogram's Lay-vice." N.d. MS Am 2745 (105), Houghton Lib, Harvard U.

——. Untitled manuscript with a character's name: "Julius Washington Merryweather Bib." N.d. MS Am 2745 (105), Houghton Lib, Harvard U.

——. Untitled manuscript with a character's name: "Pogram." N.d. MS Am 2745 (105), Houghton Lib, Harvard U.

——. *The Selected Letters of Louisa May Alcott*. Ed. Joel Myerson and Daniel Shealy. Athens: U of Georgia P, 1995. Print.

Alcott, Louisa May, and May Alcott. *Little Women Abroad: The Alcott Sisters' Letters from Europe, 1870–1871*. Ed. Daniel Shealy. Athens: U of Georgia P, 2008. Print.

Azuma, Hiroki. *Otaku: Japan's Database Animals*. Trans. Jonathan E. Abel and Shion Kono. Minneapolis: U of Minnesota P, 2009. Print.

Bartlett, G[eorge]. B. *Mrs. Jarley's Far-Famed Collection of Waxworks*. London:

Samuel French, 1873. Print.

Boyd, Anne E. *Writing for Immortality: Women and the Emergence of High Literary Culture in America*. Baltimore: Johns Hopkins UP, 2004. Print.

Cameron, Kenneth Walter, ed. *Young Reporter of Concord: A Checklist of F. B. Sanborn's Letters to Benjamin Smith Lyman, 1853–1867, with Extracts Emphasizing Life and Literary Events in the World of Emerson, Thoreau and Alcott*. Hartford: Transcendental Books, 1978. Print.

Cavicchi, Daniel. "Loving Music: Listeners, Entertainments, and the Origins of Music Fandom in Nineteenth-Century America." *Fandom: Identities and Communities in a Mediated World*. Ed. Jonathan Gray, Cornel Sandvoss, and C. Lee Harrington. New York: New York UP, 2007. 235–49. Print.

Cheever, Susan. *Louisa May Alcott: A Personal Biography*. New York: Simon and Schuster, 2010. Print.

Clark, Beverly Lyon, ed. *Louisa May Alcott: The Contemporary Reviews*. 2004. Cambridge: Cambridge UP, 2010. Print.

Crisler, Jesse S. "Alcott's Reading in *Little Women*: Shaping the Autobiographical Self." *Resources for American Literary Study* 20.1 (1994): 27–36. Print.

D'Alessandro, Michael. *Staged Readings: Sensationalism and Class in Popular American Literature and Theatre, 1835–1875*. Diss. Boston U, 2014. Print.

Dickens, Charles. *Martin Chuzzlewit*. 1843–44. Oxford: Oxford UP, 2009. Print.

——. *Oliver Twist*. 1837–39. Oxford: Oxford UP, 2008. Print.

Duffett, Mark. *Understanding Fandom: An Introduction to the Study of Media Fan Culture*. New York: Bloomsbury, 2013. Print.

Eiselein, Gregory. "Contradiction in Louisa May Alcott's *Little Men*." *New England Quarterly* 78.1 (2005): 3–25. Print.

Emerson, Ellen Tucker. *The Letters of Ellen Tucker Emerson*. Ed. Edith E. W. Gregg. 2 vols. Kent: Kent State UP, 1982. Print.

Jenkins, Henry. *Textual Poachers: Television Fans and Participatory Culture*. Updated Twentieth Anniversary ed. New York: Routledge, 2013. Print.

John, Juliet. *Dickens and Mass Culture*. 2010. Oxford: Oxford UP, 2013. Print.

Kete, Mary Louise. *Sentimental Collaborations: Mourning and Middle-Class Identity in Nineteenth-Century America*. Durham: Duke UP, 2000. Print.

LaPlante, Eve. *Marmee and Louisa: The Untold Story of Louisa May Alcott and Her Mother*. New York: Free Press, 2012. Print.

Lenahan, Hayley Miller. "Domestic and Subversive: The Roles of Women in the Children's Novels of Louisa May Alcott." *Honors Thesis Collection* 50 (2012): 1–85. Wellesley College Digital Scholarship and Archive. Web. 8 July 2013.

Matteson, John. *Eden's Outcasts: The Story of Louisa May Alcott and Her Father*. New York: Norton, 2007. Print.

McParland, Robert. *Charles Dickens's American Audience*. 2010. Lanham: Lexington, 2012. Print.

Porter, Maria S. "Recollections of Louisa May Alcott." *New England Magazine* Mar. 1892: 3–19. Print.

Shealy, Daniel, ed. *Alcott in Her Own Time: A Biographical Chronicle of Her Life, Drawn from Recollections, Interviews, and Memoirs by Family, Friends, and Associates*. Iowa City: U of Iowa P, 2005. Print.

——. "Louisa May Alcott's Juvenilia: Blueprints for the Future." *Children's Literature Association Quarterly* 17.4 (1992–93): 15–18. Print.

Stern, Madeleine B. "Louisa Alcott, Trouper: Experiences in Theatricals, 1848–1880." *The New England Quarterly* 16.2 (1943): 175–97. Print.

——. *Louisa May Alcott: A Biography*. 1950. Boston: Northeaster UP, 1999. Print.

Susina, Jan. "Men and *Little Women*: Notes of a Resisting (Male) Reader." *Little Women and the Feminist Imagination: Criticism, Controversy, Personal Essays*. Ed. Janice M. Alberghene and Beverly Lyon Clark. New York: Garland, 1999. 161–72. Print.

Tamagawa, Hiroaki. "Comic Market as Space for Self-Expression in Otaku Culture." *Fandom Unbound: Otaku Culture in a Connected World*. Ed. Mizuko Ito, Daisuke Okabe, and Izumi Tsuji. New Haven: Yale UP, 2012. 107–32. Print.

Trollope, Anthony. "Charles Dickens." *The Saint Paul's Magazine* July 1870: 370–75. Print.

Tyler, Moses Coit. "A Letter about Louisa May Alcott in London." 1866. Shealy, *Alcott* 15–16.

Whitman, Alfred. "Meg, Jo, Beth and Amy. Told by Laurie." 1902. Shealy, *Alcott* 102–09.

——. "Miss Alcott's Letters to Her 'Laurie.'" 1901. Shealy, *Alcott* 101–02.

Part II

★★★

Philosophical Perspectives

Thoreau's *Walden* and the Evolution of Resistance

Mikako Takeuchi

Thoreau's philosophy on civil disobedience and peaceful revolution has inspired human liberation over the centuries, from the abolition of slavery to the Civil Rights Movement. Thoreau made an everlasting contribution to politics by reviving the role of nature in social justice.

Critics have long portrayed Thoreau as either primarily a naturalist or a reformer. When the extinction of the frontier became evident around the turn of the twentieth century, Americans remembered Thoreau as an embodiment of regenerative nature. While Thoreau's image as a man of nature became widespread, criticism focusing on his political thought remained scarcely visible. A prominent exception was John Macy, who suggests that the neglect of Thoreau's essay on civil disobedience resulted from a fear of being "condemned as disloyally 'un-American'" (173). When the nation prospered as the greatest industrial power, Thoreau's criticism of American materialism was largely ignored. Against such conservatism, Vernon L. Parrington appraises Thoreau as "the severest critic of the lower economics that frustrate the dreams of human freedom" (406). Parrington's prerequisite for an understanding of Thoreau, however, is not nature but freedom, so that he "has little to say about Thoreau's use of nature" in *Walden* (Meyer 40–44).

Nature in *Walden* is highly political. Deep in the woods, Thoreau confronted the pro-slavery government with his acts of defiance to conformity, and explored the laws of nature through his writings. While the word "slavery" in *Walden* connotes the dehumanizing effects of industrialism, it also emphasizes the citizens' acquiescence or enslavement to unjust laws. Thus, in *Walden*, Thoreau reemerges as a distinctly integrated presence of a political thinker and a nature poet with the resonance of an African American mind.

I

Thoreau's political theory has often been portrayed as unrealistic or hyper-individualistic. Although Marxists found Thoreau's writings to be in affinity with proletarian ethics during the Great Depression, they considered his individualism incompatible with their ideology of collectivism and accordingly insignificant (Meyer 61–65). The post-World War II conservative social climate tended to "minimize Thoreau's politics in favor of formalistic and mythic readings of his prose" (114). Outright criticism of the nation and assertion of political subjectivity ran counter to the conformism of the Cold War era.

Thoreau's individualism continues to be a focus of criticism today. Hannah Arendt insists that a truly civil disobedient person can function in a collective manner. Thoreau's conscience is unpolitical because his primal concern is "the individual self and its integrity" (59–62). Harry V. Jaffa argues that "Thoreau wishes to have no decisions by society to which everyone has not consented—that is the essence of his anarchism" (202). Jonathan McKenzie maintains, "In Thoreau's personal accounting, political participation is not vital to him" (148).

Thoreau's principal purpose, however, is not to explain how civil disobedience works in a practical circumstance; rather, it is to rouse the reader into right action. Ralph Ellison holds that Emerson, Thoreau, and Whitman pursued justice not only as Americans seeking independence from Europe but also as members of a civilization: "These early writers enjoined us to experience nature and society to the hilt. They asked us to interrogate ourselves, to interrogate nature and the universe by way of realizing ourselves, by way of paying our debt to history" (312). For Ellison, Thoreau's involvement with nature and politics transfigures into an organic whole, in which both elements are inseparable.

The descriptions of nature in African American literature are apparently different from those of Thoreau's. Richard Wright, for example, illustrates the natural beauty of the South on one whole page in *12 Million Black Voices* (1941), but eventually discloses that the cycle of seasons remorselessly slips past the descendants of slaves:

> To paint the picture of how we live on the tobacco, cane, rice, and cotton plantations is to compete with mighty artists: the movies, the radio, the newspapers, the magazines, and even the Church. They have painted one picture: charming, idyllic, romantic; but we live another. (35)

Wright sees a landscape radically different from the paradisiacal one promulgated by the mainstream American culture. The nightmare is ascribed to the exploitative economy that has used the African American labor to multiply profits: "To plant vegetables for our tables was often forbidden, for raising a garden narrowed the area to be planted in cotton. The world demanded cotton, and the Lords of the Land ordered more acres to be planted—planted right up to our doorsteps!—and the ritual of Queen Cotton became brutal and bloody" (39). Sharecroppers were assigned plots of soil "already bled of its fertility through generations of abuse" (38). Alienated and severed from nature, the African American body eventually becomes one with the Southern landscape in Wright's metaphor of the bleeding earth.

Toni Morrison also describes alienation from nature in *Beloved* (1987). Natural elements often function as symbols of freedom; stars and blooming trees guided the fugitives northward to freedom. At the same time, nature is internalized in the African American body as a symbol of torture when Morrison compares the heroine's flogged and hardened back to "a chokecherry tree" (18, 93). Paul D, an ex-slave, recalls how he felt the Southern natural surroundings as a slave: "Listening to the doves in Alfred, Georgia, and having neither the right nor the permission to enjoy it because in that place mist, doves, sunlight, copper dirt, moon—everything belonged to the men who had the guns" (191). Therefore, he chose "the tiniest stars out of the sky to own" and saw it over the rim of the trench before falling asleep. Having attempted five escapes in vain, he drifted across the South. "And in all those escapes he could not help being astonished by the beauty of this land that was not his" (316). Both Wright and Morrison elucidate that unrestrained love for nature is the white people's privilege.

Notably, Wright reveals his strong empathy with Thoreau: "As an American Negro, I must admit that we American Negroes have no monopoly upon the concept of freedom or its various means of expression. Herman Melville, Thoreau, Whitman came before us, fired by the desire to express it" (Fabre 107). Thoreau's view of nature resonates with the polarized emotions expressed in African American literature. In fact, he experienced nature from an African American perspective. On October 1, 1851, after assisting a fugitive slave to escape for Canada, Thoreau wrote in his journal:

> The slave said he could guide himself by many other stars than the north star whose rising & setting he knew— . . . . The slaves bring many

> superstitions from Africa. The fugitives sometimes superstitiously carry a turf in their hats thinking that their success depends on it. (*Journal* 4: 113–14)

Through his direct contacts with fugitive slaves, Thoreau perceived their agony and aspiration reflected in the natural elements. Thoreau's political inspiration on the African American mind was derived from his philosophical standpoint in the natural environment.

In "Wild Apples," Thoreau envisages a true New World in the image of "the ground strewn with spirited fruit" (*Natural History* 197). What is eaten by creatures and is ripened with wild flavors unsuitable for the market is the fruit of supreme value for Thoreau. "Browsed on by fate," humans could also bear "the celestial fruit" of ideas. Thoreau aspires for a landscape filled with dynamic and novel fruits of thought: "Poets and philosophers and statesmen thus spring up in the country pastures, and outlast the hosts of unoriginal men" (195).

II

While Thoreau was writing *A Week on the Concord and Merrimack Rivers* in the cabin on Walden Pond, he made Sophocles' *Antigone* his companion. The Greek writer of the fifth century BC was aware that the higher law came from Zeus and other deities. The classic reasoning of an individual who dared to disobey the ruler's unjust decree is found in Antigone (Antieau 1–2).

Oedipus' daughter, Antigone, is determined to bury the dead body of her brother, Polynices, despite King Creon's prohibition of such a ritual. Creon has decreed that those who mourn and sprinkle sand on Polynices, whom he considers an enemy of his country, should be condemned to death by stoning. Antigone's sister, Ismene, declines to cooperate in the burial, by saying, "To act in opposition to the citizens I am by nature unable." In contrast, Antigone decisively prioritizes the divine law to the civil ruler's law. In *A Week on the Concord and Merrimack Rivers*, Thoreau cites Antigone's brave response to King Creon's interrogation as to why she transgressed his laws:

> "For it was not Zeus who proclaimed these to me, nor Justice who dwells with the gods below; it was not they who established these laws among men. Nor did I think that your proclamations were so strong, as,

> being a mortal, to be able to transcend the unwritten and immovable laws of the gods. For not something now and yesterday, but forever these live, and no one knows from what time they appeared." (135)

Thoreau integrates Antigone's remark with his criticism of the contemporary government. Wherever those called good citizens are "doing outrage to their proper natures" and lending themselves to the office of "some monster institution," war and slavery ensue (130–31).

The idea of natural law is traceable to *Antigone* as Ernest Barker defines: "This justice is conceived as being the higher or ultimate law, proceeding from the nature of the universe—from the Being of God and the reason of man." Lawmakers are subject to this immutable law, which is above law-making (312–13). The higher law gained a large-scale expression among the Stoic thinkers of the Hellenistic age, whose influence was adopted in Roman law. Justinian's law-books, *Corpus Juris Civilis*, founded a system of law of universal validity as the Emperor wrote, "The laws of nature, which are most equally observed by all nations, remain always stable and immutable, enacted as they are by some kind of divine providence" (d'Entrèves 32). The doctrine of natural law was grafted on the ethics of Christianity by Thomas Aquinas in the thirteenth century. Aquinas advocated in *Summa Theologiae* that, if rulers "command things to be done which are unjust, their subjects are not obliged to obey them" (d'Entrèves 46). To Aquinas, disobedience is not only a possibility but also a duty in certain cases, and a theory of resistance is built on this premise.

In the era of American and French Revolution, the idea of natural law evolved into a theory of natural rights. The ideologies of rationalism, individualism, and radicalism united to inspire human rights and equity. The Declaration of Independence drafted by Thomas Jefferson reflected the doctrine of human freedom explored in John Locke's *Two Treatises of Government*. "Man being born," Locke maintained, "with a Title to perfect Freedom, and an uncontrouled enjoyment of all the Rights and Privileges of the Law of Nature" (323). The radical principle held by the American *Declaration* of 1776 was to invalidate monarchy and aristocracy. Jefferson asserted that political bands with a government that is destructive of the "unalienable Rights" of man must be dissolved. The opening of the Declaration of Independence claims the people's right to assume "the separate and equal station to which the Laws of Nature and of Nature's God entitle them." As Alexander Tsesis indicates, the creation of a nation on the premise that persons had innate equal rights "meant that government had an obligation to exercise its power to preserve natural rights" (38).

In the nineteenth century, however, the age of science ushered in a science of law with the chief concern of creating order and coherence in the system of law. Accordingly, the conception of "law" was restricted to positive law, and principles abstracted from existing systems became the subject of general jurisprudence (d'Entrèves 98). The aim to be a positive science led modern jurisdiction to "steer clear of any criterion of validity of law—such as natural law—extraneous to the system" (100).

In keeping with the science of law, a counterrevolution had been developing since the mid-1790s. Once the Bill of Rights, the first ten Amendments to the Constitution, went into effect in 1791, conservatism accelerated in the next decades to replace higher law ideals of the Revolutionary era. Retreating from drastic social reforms such as abolition of slavery, the nation "reconceived the universal value of liberty as synonymous with freedom within an established social order" (Crane 33). Consequently, in the first half of the nineteenth century, when Thoreau emerged as a man of letters, the nation was undergoing the ebb of revolutionary egalitarianism and the higher law tradition. As Morton J. Horwitz suggests, "law was no longer conceived of as an eternal set of principles expressed in custom and derived from natural law" (30). The American legal environment in the early nineteenth century already had little resemblance to what existed in the Revolutionary era.

Against this historical background, literature emerged as the vanguard and resuscitator of the higher law tradition abandoned by the men of law. Thoreau became a distinctive presence with his broad and enduring influence on resistance movements. The government had continuously settled regional conflicts on slavery by means of compromise. The Missouri Compromise of 1820, which established a boundary between the free and slave states along the 36 degrees 30 minutes north latitude, was the earliest example of a political compromise since the nation's foundation. Thoreau's determination to revive natural law against legal positivism is evident in "Slavery in Massachusetts":

> If Nature can compound this fragrance still annually, I shall believe her still young and full of vigor, her integrity and genius unimpaired, and that there is virtue even in man, too, who is fitted to perceive and love it. It reminds me that Nature has been partner to no Missouri Compromise. I scent no

compromise in the fragrance of the water-lily. (*Higher Law* 108)

Thoreau metaphorizes the laws of nature with the purifying and uncompromising vitality of a water lily.

Confronting the neglect of the natural law, Thoreau satirizes in "Resistance to Civil Government" that you can rarely find one who has "a bone in his back" solid enough to call him a man: "Our statistics are at fault: the population has been returned too large. How many *men* are there to a square thousand miles in this country? Hardly one" (*Higher Law* 70). Thoreau's satire on the lack of noble character is also suggestive of a compromising provision in the Constitution. Article I, Section 2 gave the Southern states disproportionate political power by adding three-fifths of the number of slaves to the population in apportioning Representatives.

The major tension in the Constitutional Convention was the sectional conflict between the North and the South. The Three-Fifths Compromise was the greatest concession to the slave states of which the Convention made to secure the adoption of the Constitution (Lynd 153–62). With indirect phraseology, the Constitution legalized slavery in effect. Article I, Section 9 postponed prohibition of the slave trade until 1808. Article IV, Section 2 provided slaveholders with the right to retrieve fugitive slaves. These provisions burdened the democratic Constitution with grave self-contradiction. In "Life without Principle," Thoreau points out, "There is a part of us which is not represented" (*Higher Law* 174). His refusal to vote is not anarchism but a manifestation of logical judgment that the nation's representative government is devoid of democratic foundation and, therefore, invalid.

III

The serenity of Walden Pond is diametrically opposed to the corruption of politics. Thoreau calls the lake "earth's eye," or "God's Drop" (*Walden* 186, 194). Upon moving into the woods, Thoreau marvels at the height of Walden Pond: "For the first week, whenever I looked out on the pond it impressed me like a tarn high up on the side of a mountain, its bottom far above the surface of other lakes" (86). The poet finds himself elevated closer to the heavenly spheres:

> The winds which passed over my dwelling were such as sweep over the

> ridges of mountains, bearing the broken strains, or celestial parts only, of terrestrial music. The morning wind forever blows, the poem of creation is uninterrupted; but few are the ears that hear it. Olympus is but the outside of the earth every where. (85)

Walden Pond exemplifies to Thoreau a space of communion with the celestial words carried from the summit of Olympus where the gods dwell.

A "great crystal" distilled by nature (199), Walden Pond is an antithesis of the legislature with no purifying function. Thoreau considers that "we walk to lakes to see our serenity reflected in them." The remembrance of his country, however, spoils his walk (*Higher Law* 108). *Walden* abounds with criticism of the legislature, as Thoreau declares that he "was never molested by any person but those who represented the state" (172). He refused to pay tax to "the state which buys and sells men, women, and children, like cattle at the door of its senate-house" (171). Thoreau observes that wild creatures in the woods often represent nobler spirit than do the politicians in Congress. Finding a pile of stumps covered with two races of ants in warfare, Thoreau calls those combatants "the republicans" and "the imperialists," and emphasizes the superiority of their formidable spirit to the lawmakers' compromise. "The battle which I witnessed," Thoreau adds ironically, "took place in the Presidency of Polk, five years before the passage of Webster's Fugitive-Slave Bill" (232). The nation's loss of integrity in the fight for the democratic principle became evident in the Mexican War and its pro-slavery legislation.

Thoreau thinks that politicians have become "too old and dignified to go a-fishing" to the extent that they are completely ignorant about the pond: "If the legislature regards it, it is chiefly to regulate the number of hooks to be used there; but they know nothing about the hook of hooks with which to angle for the pond itself, impaling the legislature for a bait" (213). In Thoreau's imagination, the heavenly lake crystallizes higher laws, which lawmakers are entrusted to pursue.

Thoreau's moving into the cabin of his own make on July 4, 1845 embodies his declaration of independence. Thoreau recognizes from this vantage point that Americans established order on the surface, though "we know not where we are" (332). Speeches on social occasions sounded so shallow that they fell merely as noise to Thoreau's ear. "God is only the president of the day, and Webster is his orator" (330). The satire implies that the God's Laws of Nature are slighted by the contemporary legislation. Thoreau's question of

"What are men celebrating?" ultimately refers to the Independence Day, which became an illusory façade that deliberately excluded the equity of all races under the law.

While Thoreau was writing *Walden* in 1851, a fugitive slave named Thomas Simms was arrested in Boston, and was forcibly shipped back to Georgia nine days later on April 12 by federal marshals and city militia. April 19 commemorated the anniversary of the Battle of Concord, which erupted at the North Bridge and marked the outbreak of the Revolutionary War in 1775. Thoreau criticizes the participants, who celebrated the occasion despite the brutality of the Fugitive Slave Law they had witnessed:

> Just a week afterward those inhabitants of this town who especially sympathize with the authorities of Boston in this their deed caused the bells to be rung & the cannons to be fired to celebrate the courage & the love of liberty of those men who assembled at the bridge. As if *those* 3 millions had fought for the right to be free themselves—but to hold in slavery 3 million others. (*Journal* 3: 204)

Thoreau's cabin on Walden Pond functioned as a space to celebrate a different form of Independence Day. On August 1, 1846, a week after his imprisonment for his refusal to pay tax, the Concord Female Anti-Slavery Society held their annual commemoration of the emancipation of the West Indian slaves on Thoreau's doorsteps. Ralph Waldo Emerson, along with two reverends, addressed the assembly (Harding, *Days* 195). Lewis Hayden, who had escaped from slavery in Kentucky, was also invited as a speaker (Petrulionis 60). Thoreau alludes to the event in the "Visitors" chapter of *Walden*: "It is surprising how many great men and women a small house will contain. I have had twenty-five or thirty souls, with their bodies, at once under my roof" (140). Thoreau's cabin, in fact, became a station of the Underground Railroad. *Walden* reveals that among the visitors to his cabin were runaway slaves, whom Thoreau "helped to forward toward the northstar" (152).

Thoreau holds that an inward exploration of one's self demands far more energy than expeditions conducted by a government ship with innumerable men and boys in servitude. Empires in the world must embark on a truly rigorous exploration of humanity: "England and France, Spain and Portugal, Gold Coast and Slave Coast, all front on this private sea; but no bark from them has ventured out of sight of land, though it is without doubt the direct way to India" (322). The criticism of European imperialism is also directed to the United States, which operated domestic colonialism of slavery. "The way to India," that is, the westward passage to Asia explored since the era of Columbus, is redefined by Thoreau as an infinite expansion of the spiritual frontier. Thoreau's ubiquitous self on every distant shore of the world longs for a true dynasty of thought to emerge.

The story of an artist in the city of Kouroo narrated in *Walden* symbolizes a timeless dynasty of thought that is to be realized through the sincerest quest of truth. Thinking that "into a perfect work time does not enter," the artist devotes himself to the creation of a perfect staff (326). While he chooses the right wood in the forest, peels the material to give it a proper form, and polishes the staff into perfection, a "Kalpa" cycle—4.32 billion years—is repeated. The artist, however, transcends Time and acquires "perennial youth." His staff is completed to be the fairest creation of Brahma, the supreme god who rules the universe in India. Through the artist's uncompromising pursuit of truth, "a world with full and fair proportions" finally arises, replacing mortal cities and dynasties with more glorious ones of eternal value (327).

The artist of Kouroo who transcends Time is reminiscent of the "perennially young" Walden Pond (193). As Thoreau writes in "Life without Principle," the true resources of a country are not represented by the gold dug by miners or tobacco produced by slave labor. "The chief want, in every State that I have been into, was a high and earnest purpose in its inhabitants. This alone draws out 'the great resources' of Nature" (*Higher Law* 177). The artist of Kouroo draws out the greatest resources of Nature in the form of his time-transcendental perfect staff. The eternal truth pursued by the artist is symbolic of natural law, which originated in ancient civilization to be passed down forever.

IV

The criticism that portrays Thoreau as hyper-individualistic or anti-democratic is largely due to the poet's rhetoric of extravagance. As if anticipating such criticism, Thoreau remarks with irony that his expression "may not be *extravagant* enough." The original Latin connotation of the word "extravagant" is to wander beyond bounds. Thoreau's rhetorical style obviously aims at breaking through the boundaries of common sense: "I am convinced that I cannot exaggerate enough even to lay the foundation of a true expression" (*Walden* 324). Paradoxically, Thoreau's "extravagant" discourse derives its force from the simplest economy in the natural environment.

The minimal accounts of income and expenditure in the "Economy" chapter represent a powerful impact with regard to politicizing the entire text of *Walden*. Thoreau's financial accounts are counterevidence to slave economy, which accumulates undue profits through exploitation. By cultivating his bean field with the morning dew still fresh and making the soil express its seasonal thought in leaves and blossoms, Thoreau perceives that labor of the hands has "a constant and imperishable moral" (157). The mass of people live in unconscious despair because pure satisfaction "comes after work" (8). Thoreau's communion with the land is antithetical to speculative agriculture that regards the soil as a mere property to yield profits. His two-year experience in the woods proves that a self-sufficient life is possible "even in this latitude" (61). Thoreau implies that if you can support yourself by honest labor in frigid New England, so can you in the South.

The integrity of labor and fair distribution of wealth are central to *Walden*'s exploration. Thoreau's endeavor in the bean field symbolizes a form of resistance to the idleness of the privileged. Imagining how their sumptuous home economy is managed, Thoreau wonders that the floor does not give way under their feet and send them down "to some solid and honest though earthy foundation" (38). Thoreau declares to those who enjoy luxury at the expense of others, "The first question which I am tempted to put to the proprietor of such great impropriety is, Who bolsters you?" (38)

The question extends beyond the leisured to the government. Thoreau insists that "beautiful housekeeping and beautiful living be laid for a foundation" before adorning the house with beautiful objects (38). The analogy of housekeeping in *Walden* has a macroeconomic implication. The country thriving on slavery and war is a monstrous entity, "cluttered with furniture and tripped up by its own traps, ruined by luxury and heedless expense, by want of calculation and a worthy aim, as the million households in the land" (92). Thoreau's seemingly apolitical self-sufficiency confronts, in essence, the nation's outrageous economy of racial exploitation. In "Resistance to Civil Government," Thoreau indeed demands the nation with a direct imperative: "It must help itself; do as I do" (*Higher Law* 81).

Thoreau advises the leisured to "work till they pay for themselves, and get their free papers" (*Walden* 70). This rhetoric alludes to slaves purchasing their freedom from their masters in exchange for long years of extra toils. The metaphor of self-purchase is based on Thoreau's actual contacts with slaves.

His journal of October 1, 1851 begins: "5 Pm Just put a fugitive slave who has taken the name of Henry Williams into the cars for Canada" (*Journal* 4: 113). The slave had escaped from Virginia to Boston a year before and had been corresponding with his master, who was his father, through an agent about buying his freedom. He had collected five hundred dollars, but the master demanded six hundred. Tracked by the police, Williams fled to Concord on foot with a letter addressed to the Thoreaus by Abolitionist leaders, Rev. Joseph Lovejoy and William Lloyd Garrison. Thoreau lodged him until funds were collected, purchased his ticket, and led him to the depot. So grateful was Williams that, returning later from Canada to Boston, he bought with his last penny a statue of Uncle Tom holding little Eva and walked fifteen miles to present it to Thoreau in Concord (Harding, "Thoreau" 23).

On July 28, 1853, a Harvard Divinity School student from Virginia visited Thoreau and found him nursing a fugitive slave, who had come fainting to his door at daybreak. The guest was astounded at how Thoreau fed the fugitive and bathed his swollen feet: "Again and again this coolest and calmest of men drew near to the trembling negro, and soothed him and bade him feel at home, and have no fear that any power should again wrong him" (Harding, "Thoreau" 23). A renowned leader of Concord's Underground Railroad testified that almost every week some fugitive slaves heading northward were harbored overnight in town, and that "Thoreau more often than any other man in Concord looked after them" (Harding, *Days* 316). On November 1, 1853, the Thoreaus lodged a free black woman who was raising funds to buy her husband from his owner in Virginia lest he be sold further South. She had paid six hundred dollars, but the owner demanded eight hundred. Thoreau condemned the "despicable behavior all too characteristic of a slaveholder" (316).

Expressing his anti-slavery stand in financial terms, Thoreau counterattacks the slave economy that has degraded priceless life. In "Resistance to Civil Government" Thoreau maintains that disobedience to the government costs him less than obeying it: "I should feel as if I were worth less in that case" (*Higher Law* 79). In "Slavery in Massachusetts" Thoreau denounces the offense to his own humanity inflicted by the Fugitive Slave Law: "My investment in life here is worth many per cent less since Massachusetts last deliberately sent back an innocent man, Anthony Burns, to slavery" (106). In *Walden*, Thoreau warns that a student might run "his father in debt irretrievably" while reading Adam Smith, Ricardo, and Say because "that economy of living which is synonymous with philosophy" is not professed in colleges (52). If the "father" in this context were juxtaposed with the Founding Fathers, the household debts would be parallel to the nation's failure in fulfilling the ideals of democracy guaranteed by the Declaration of Independence.

Commanding the rhetoric of a business transaction, *Walden* confronts the nation's inhumane law and economy. Enterprise is essential to Thoreau's philosophy of life as he declares, "I have always endeavored to acquire strict business habits; they are indispensable to every man" (20). Walden Pond is "a good port and a good foundation" and accordingly would be "a good place for business" (21). Identifying his chores in the woods with the American business culture, Thoreau exhorts rigorous industry. Managing commodity, overseeing trade channels, conducting fair deals, and balancing accounts—all business logistics "task the faculties of a man" and "demand a universal knowledge" (21). The subversive connotation of the financial rhetoric becomes clearer when Thoreau asserts that "money is not required to buy one necessary of the soul" (329). By incorporating the resources of a business enterprise unto himself, Thoreau, as a political thinker, launches his spiritual trade—a true communion with the celestial empire of thought.

A century later, Thoreau's resistance inspired masses of people into action in the Civil Rights Movement. When Martin Luther King, Jr. started the bus boycott in Montgomery, Alabama to protest against segregation, he was convinced that the movement was closely related to the theory of resistance set forth by Thoreau (*Stride* 51). "No other person," King pronounces, "has been more eloquent and passionate in getting this idea across than Henry David Thoreau" (*Autobiography* 14).

Thoreau's rhetoric of business reverberates in the address that King delivered on August 28, 1963 at the March on Washington. King began this landmark speech with a declaration that they have come to the nation's capital to "cash a check." When the founders of the nation wrote the Declaration of Independence and the Constitution, they were signing "a promissory note" to proclaim that all men would be guaranteed "the unalienable rights of life, liberty, and the pursuit of happiness." However, the nation has defaulted on this promissory note: "Instead of honoring this sacred obligation, America has given the Negro people a bad check; a check which has come back marked 'insufficient funds.' But we refuse to believe that the bank of justice is bankrupt" ("I Have a Dream" 112). In King's imaginative economy, America's founding documents "promised a kind of prosperity on which no price could be put, the riches of freedom stored in the bank of justice" (Sundquist 68).

Using metaphors of a business transaction, King urged the nation to fulfill their covenant of natural rights.

Thoreau holds that, however lofty a primary design is, the posterity should complete the architecture: "If you have built castles in the air, your work need not be lost; that is where they should be. Now put the foundations under them" (*Walden* 324). Thoreau's principles loaded in the word "foundation" is succeeded by King's symbolism of the "funds" for universal opportunity. In "Economy" of *Walden*, Thoreau believes that individuals liberate themselves by learning the direction from nature:

> It is by a mathematical point only that we are wise, as the sailor or the fugitive slave keeps the polestar in his eye; but that is sufficient guidance for all our life. We may not arrive at our port within a calculable period, but we would preserve the true course. (71)

Thoreau's life on Walden Pond was intrinsically an act of political rebellion. Immersing himself in the natural environment, Thoreau aspired to restore the laws of nature from political neglect. *Walden* is Thoreau's testament of democracy as much as it is an account of rejuvenating encounters with nature. A century after the abolition of slavery, Thoreau's resistance inspired a massive movement into the establishment of the Civil Rights Act and the Twenty-Fourth Amendment to the Constitution for the equitable right to vote. Embarking upstream for the ancient source of natural law from his lakefront cabin, Thoreau initiated the passage to justice for future generations.

Works Cited

Antieau, Chester James. *The Higher Laws: Origins of Modern Constitutional Law.* Buffalo: William S. Hein, 1994. Print.

Arendt, Hannah. *Crises of the Republic.* New York: Harcourt Brace, 1972. Print.

Barker, Ernest. *Traditions of Civility: Eight Essays.* Cambridge: Cambridge UP, 1948. Print.

Crane, Gregg D. *Race, Citizenship, and Law in American Literature.* Cambridge: Cambridge UP, 2002. Print.

d'Entrèves, Alexander Passerin. *Natural Law: An Introduction to Legal Philosophy.* 1951. New Brunswick: Transaction Publishers, 2009. Print.

Ellison, Ralph. *Going to the Territory.* 1986. New York: Random House, 1995. Print.

Fabre, Michel. *Richard Wright: Books and Writers.* Jackson: UP of Mississippi, 1990. Print.

Harding, Walter. *The Days of Henry Thoreau: A Biography*. New York: Dover Publications, 1982. Print.

——. "Thoreau and the Negro." *The Negro History Bulletin*, Oct. 1946, pp. 12, 22–23. Print.

Horwitz, Morton J. *The Transformation of American Law, 1780–1860*. Cambridge, MA: Harvard UP, 1977. Print.

Jaffa, Harry V. "Thoreau and Lincoln." *A Political Companion to Henry David Thoreau*. Ed. Jack Turner. Lexington: UP of Kentucky, 2009. 178–204. Print.

King, Martin Luther, Jr. "I Have a Dream." *Great Speeches by African Americans*. Ed. James Daley. Mineola: Dover Publications, 2006. 111–14. Print.

——. *Stride Toward Freedom: The Montgomery Story*. New York: Harper and Row, 1958. Print.

——. *The Autobiography of Martin Luther King, Jr*. Ed. Clayborne Carson. New York: Warner Books, 2000. Print.

Locke, John. *Two Treatises of Government*. 1690. Ed. Peter Laslett. Cambridge: Cambridge UP, 1988. Print.

Lynd, Staughton. *Class Conflict, Slavery, and the United States Constitution*. Cambridge: Cambridge UP, 2009. Print.

Macy, John. *The Spirit of American Literature*. New York: Boni and Liveright, 1913. Print.

McKenzie, Jonathan. *The Political Thought of Henry David Thoreau: Privatism and the Practice of Philosophy*. Lexington: UP of Kentucky, 2016. Print.

Meyer, Michael. *Several More Lives to Live: Thoreau's Political Reputation in America*. Westport: Greenwood Press, 1977. Print.

Morrison, Toni. *Beloved*. 1987. London: Random House, 2010. Print.

Parrington, Vernon Louis. *Main Currents in American Thought, Volume Two, 1800–1860: The Romantic Revolution in America*. New York: Harcourt, Brace & World, 1927. Print.

Petrulionis, Sandra Harbert. *To Set This World Right: The Antislavery Movement in Thoreau's Concord*. Ithaca: Cornell UP, 2006. Print.

Sophocles. *Antigone*. Trans. Reginald Gibbons and Charles Segal. Oxford: Oxford UP, 2003. Print.

Sundquist, Eric J. *King's Dream*. New Haven: Yale UP, 2009. Print.

Thoreau, Henry David. *A Week on the Concord and Merrimack Rivers*. 1849. Ed. Carl F. Hovde, William L. Howarth, and Elizabeth Hall Witherell. Princeton: Princeton UP, 2004. Print.

——. *Journal, Volume 3: 1848–1851*. Ed. Robert Sattelmeyer, Mark R. Patterson, and William Rossi. Princeton: Princeton UP, 1990. Print.

——. *Journal, Volume 4: 1851–1852*. Ed. Leonard N. Neufeldt and Nancy Craig Simmons. Princeton: Princeton UP, 1992. Print.

——. *The Higher Law: Thoreau on Civil Disobedience and Reform*. Ed. Wendell Glick. Princeton: Princeton UP, 2004. Print.

——. *The Natural History Essays*. Salt Lake City: Peregrine Smith, 1980. Print.

——. *Walden*. 1854. Ed. J. Lyndon Shanley. Princeton: Princeton UP, 2004. Print.
Tsesis, Alexander. *For Liberty and Equality: The Life and Times of the Declaration of Independence*. Oxford: Oxford UP, 2012. Print.
Wright, Richard. *12 Million Black Voices*. 1941. New York: Thunder's Mouth Press, 1995. Print.

Thoreau's Ontology of "We": Friendship in *A Week on the Concord and Merrimack Rivers*[1]

Maki Sadahiro

Introduction: The Inescapable Relationality of Existence

What is the nature of community? As the globe is becoming increasingly interconnected through technologies, capital, and commodities, we are faced with questions as to the nature of "the common" and its relation to different notions of community. We take for granted that people in a given community have some traits in common, and that affiliations depend upon these shared traits, whether they are based upon history, heritage, or ideological goals. The idea of such a "communitarian" community associated with an organic world emerged and gained a certain cachet, in early twentieth century English literature especially, as a nostalgic response to modernity, and as an antidote to the fragmentation and alienation caused by industrialization and urbanization (Parmett 173). In this century, general interest in community has become even stronger. We can no longer presuppose that our identities are grounded within particular, bounded communities, but perhaps for this reason the possibilities of collective responsibility and other notions of collectivity have become increasingly important.

What does community actually mean? A number of philosophers have offered their analyses of the highly contested notion of "the common." Although their foci differ slightly—resting on notions of "friendship" (Jacques Derrida), "community" (Maurice Blanchot, Jean-Luc Nancy), or "multitude" (Michael Hardt and Antonio Negri) —their debates seem to stop conceptualizing community as a thing we can have or lose and instead imagine community / the common as a happening that is inextricably tied to our existence. To quote Jean-Luc Nancy, "community is given to us with being and as being, well in advance of all our projects, desires, and undertakings. At bottom, it is impossible for us to lose community" (35). According to this conception, community signifies one's inescapable relationality.

The collective possibilities of friendship were also explored by a thinker normally associated with extreme individualism: Henry David Thoreau. Born in Concord, Massachusetts, the same city where he died, Thoreau was anything but a communal person—if "communal" is taken to mean belonging to a given community in whose traditions and values one is immersed. All of Thoreau's writings show us a profound engagement with community, but, as I will demonstrate through an analysis of the Wednesday chapter of *A Week on the Concord and Merrimack Rivers*, with a particular focus on his essay on friendship, his community is not an immovable or monolithic entity. It is rather a state of becoming that continually dissolves and takes shape anew. Meredith McGill is quite right to observe that despite Thoreau's precise descriptions of local settings and their history, "the one thing Thoreau does not offer us is a clear sense of location in space and time, some stable ground beneath our feet" (371).

At first glance, the essay on friendship in the Wednesday chapter appears to have no intrinsic structural or thematic relationship to the travel narrative as a whole. But on closer inspection, the larger text of *A Week* makes sense as a context for Thoreau's philosophy of friendship. The traveler depicted there, who temporarily distances himself from the existing community to reflect on what the community really is, has a clear affinity with Thoreau's concept of the friend who needs distance both in time and space. In addition, and more significantly, Thoreau explores collective possibilities by employing the first person plural pronoun, "we." Without resorting to an essentialist understanding of community (while at the same time not abandoning the concept of being in common altogether), Thoreau sought to redefine one's constitutive relationality to others, elaborating on how collective potentialities can be actualized.

1. Away From Home: The Concord Community Deconstructed

When Thoreau was writing *A Week* in the 1840s, the concept of friendship, and the related notion of sympathy, was vital to a line of thought among intellectuals who saw this communitarian impulse as a potential political force and cultural idea. Sympathy, fraternity, brotherhood, friendship—these ideas helped to hold together the politically vulnerable and unstable nation whose populations were growing more diverse as a result of territorial expansion. According to Dana Nelson, the traditional agricultural community lost its practical power to unite people in the process of national expansion; as a result, people began to seek something in common with strangers to ameliorate a growing sense of anxiety (6, 11, 203). Nelson also observes that during this period people cultivated the idea of white brotherhood as a vehicle for fraternity. In a similar vein, Peter Coviello states that not only the idealization of whiteness, but also the ideal of "white manhood," with its codes of male sexual propriety, helped forge feelings of national belonging (17). Among these ideas that functioned to bridge the gap between strangers, romantic friendship was especially appealing to the transcendentalists because it was "more congenial to [the] republican ideology" of liberty and equality than the filial or marital relationships that were often associated with the colonists' bond to England (Crain 4–5).

Thoreau's exploration of friendship may have been driven by the same impulses that motivated some of his contemporaries, but his works tended to articulate the structure of community and communication rather than commenting on particular social relations. Thoreau's idea of friendship, I argue, resists completion and in fact seeks to establish a productive distance between friends both in time and space. As he puts it in *Walden*, "Individuals, like nations, must have suitable broad and natural boundaries, even a considerable neutral ground, between them" (141). What is this "neutral ground" that is not merely desirable but necessary for communication? What becomes possible within the neutral space that Thoreau places at the heart of friendship?

A possible answer to these questions begins with a look at how Thoreau postulates the individual's connection to the community in this travel narrative by using the defamiliarizing perspective of a traveler or stranger. The traveler who stands in contrast to the sedentary natives experiences community not as absorption into a cohesive whole, but rather as a disjunctive relationship in which boundaries are unfamiliar and in flux. In fact, although *A Week* is widely appreciated for its precise description of the locality in which it is set, that feature belies the unconventional understanding of community at the heart of the narrative and most conspicuously displays itself in the epigraph to the first chapter. There a quotation from Ovid's *Metamorphoses* is rendered in Thoreau's own translation: "He confined the rivers within their sloping banks, / Which in different places are part absorbed by the earth, / Part reach the sea, and being received within the plain / Of its freer waters, beat the shore for banks" (*A Week* 4). Ceaselessly a river flows, but the river's water and shape are never the same. Thoreau's intention in adding this epigraph to his narrative of the local Concord community seems to be to offer a critique of and an alternative to the idea of the bounded community that always assumes the same unchanging quality.

Thoreau's defamiliarization of community begins with the deconstructive treatment of host and stranger, by means of which he explores a seemingly irresolvable tension that arises in the experience of being with others. His interest in the arrival of a stranger resonates with Emerson's treatment of a "commended stranger" in "Friendship". In this essay, Emerson asserts that both despite and because of the host's uneasiness with fear, the tension "exalts the conversation with him": "How beautiful, on their approach to this beating heart, the steps and forms of the gifted and the true! The moment we indulge our affections, the earth is metamorphosed" (114). But such a "golden hour of friendship" does not last long. Once the stranger becomes a familiar acquaintance, he loses the power to excite and to inspire the host and instead terribly disappoints him. Though it may sound paradoxical, for Emerson the one deserving of friendship is the total stranger, not the familiar person. Because of this fleeting quality of the ideal friend (anticipated in Montaigne's address that he mistakenly attributed to Aristotle, "O my friends, there is no friend"), Emerson must admit, "I cannot deny it, O friend, that the vast shadow of the Phenomenal includes thee also" (116).

Despite sharing his mentor's interest in the stranger's capacity to call the familiar into question, Thoreau focuses equally on both sides of the encounter between stranger and host, depicting the event as more reciprocal than Emerson did. During the encounter, both stranger and host expose themselves to the unfamiliar in equal measure. For instance, during his boat trip, Thoreau sometimes goes ashore to visit a house to ask for water. The visitation of the stranger invokes episodes of biblical hospitality only to later undercut this association:

> The door is opened, perchance, by some Yankee-Hindoo women, whose small-voiced but sincere hospitality, out of the bottomless depths of a quiet nature, has traveled quite round to the opposite side, and fears only to obtrude its kindness. (*A Week* 242)

Contrary to Thoreau's (and the reader's) expectation, the host is no hospitable Christian open to outsiders; she appears to be a heathen. The transformation of a native New England woman into a Hindu woman, who has experience traveling "to the opposite side" of the world, should be understood figuratively. Thoreau uses the "heathen" metaphor frequently in his writing and associates it with his own withdrawal from society, the withdrawal to retain a critical distance from conventional ways of thinking. In other words, heathens are appreciated because they live on the "heath" to be "backward to adopt the doctrines which prevailed in towns" ("Huckleberries" 491). By depicting the stranger and the host as equally displaced people, Thoreau challenges the concept of community as a place of comfort and belonging. What is shared between them in the moment of hospitality is, then, if anything, shared senses of displacement. Importantly, the experience of making familiar things unfamiliar is not an event that occurs only once. Just as a week repeats itself over and over again, the arrival of strangers never ends and never allows the community to stay the same. The process of the community's repeated metamorphosis deconstructs the notion of a settled, "thingified" community, and instead presents it as a community of difference in a state of becoming.

2. Friend as Beautiful Enemy

In *Walden*, Thoreau emphasizes the necessity of a "sufficient distance" between individuals as well as between nations. He asserts: "If we would enjoy the most intimate society with that in each of us which is without, or above, being spoken to, we must not only be silent, but commonly so far apart bodily that we cannot possibly hear each other's voice in any case" (*Walden* 141). As in the encounter between the host and the stranger, spatial distance plays a fundamental role in preserving a disjunctive and productive relationship within the community. By introducing the travel narrative as a background, Thoreau further explores the possibility of temporal distance in the friend-enemy relationship in the Wednesday chapter of *A Week*.

The twisted logic of asking a friend to be an enemy has much in common with Emerson's so-called "transcendental friendship" ("Let [thy friend] be to thee for ever a sort of beautiful enemy") (124), and in Thoreau's case, too, the logic of the friend-enemy is not paradoxical but dialectical. "Sympathy," an elegy published in the *Dial* in 1839, is a clear showcase of this dialectical state that creates a temporal distance. The poem is about Thoreau's infatuation with the eleven-year-old Edmund Sewall (Harding 77–79). As one might easily expect, the friendship between Sewall and Thoreau was not associated with what we usually think of as mutual affection. He portrays the object of his affection as a "frenemy," whose capacity to attract him is perceived as an attack, albeit a passive one reminiscent of a landscape unfolding implacably before the viewer: "He forayed like the subtil haze of summer, / That stilly shows fresh landscapes to our eyes." Thoreau depicts his love for Sewall as a force so strong that it renders him unable to truly love his young friend: "Yet now am forced to know, though hard it is, / I might have loved him had I loved him less" (*A Week* 260). In a general sense, the loss of a friend whom one loves is deplorable, but it also prepares the way for another kind of friendship:

> Make haste and celebrate my tragedy;
> With fitting strain resound ye woods and fields;
> Sorrow is dearer in such case to me
> Than all the joys other occasion yields. (*A Week* 260–61)

As Thoreau's choice of the word "tragedy" indicates, the loss of the friend does not come about by chance. It is in fact a necessary, indispensable and constitutive element of friendship. The transcendental friendship is often associated with an unattainable ideal that reveals the discrepancy between the transcendental ideal and reality, but this understanding misses the fact that there is no such thing as successful friendship in an ordinary sense. Its failure is not merely painful, but also "dearer" or, to use Emerson's words, "a delicious torment" because it offers us the promise of a stronger pleasure. While Emerson warns that this torment should not be indulged ("these uneasy pleasures and fine pains are for curiosity, and not for life," 117), Thoreau appraises this failure as something to celebrate.

Stanley Cavell argues that "aversive thinking" is central to Emerson's perfectionism, in which one criticizes the current condition in favor of the not yet attained ideal self. Cavell calls it the capacity for self-criticism and gives an elaborate account of this double process: "his writing expresses his self-consciousness, his thinking as the imperative to an incessant conversion or refiguration of society's incessant demands for his consent—his conforming himself—to its doings, and at the same time to mean that his writing must accordingly be the object of aversion to society's consciousness, to what it might read in him" (145). This perfectionism is also applicable to Thoreau's idea of friendship that seeks the temporal realization of the ideal. A would-be friend appears as an enemy who arouses a more or less unpleasant dissatisfaction with one's present state, while at the same time, he is a real friend in that he inspires one to become what is good and ideal. Friends, Thoreau wrote, were those who "treated us not as we were, but as we aspired to be" (*A Week* 259).

3. The Paradox of Self-Sufficiency

The antagonistic relationship between friends that Thoreau envisions creates agency and freedom for growth, but at its heart lies an aporia concerning individuality and dependence. We usually think of the individual in terms of an absolutely free being-for-itself. Those who can aspire to preserve their freedom are considered to be good friends while friendship in which one individual blocks the transcendental freedom of the other is a common friendship that Thoreau despises. The paradox in this model of friendship is this: it relies on an idea of self-sufficiency that is undermined by its very definition of friend. Imagine: If I need a lofty friend to inspire me to reach my own ideal, free, and independent self, I actually exist by virtue of my reliance on my friend. In fact, at one point in the essay, Thoreau associates the temporal distance in friendship with debt; that is, to be what the friend expects us to be, we must "endeavor to wipe off these scores" (*A Week* 259). Indebtedness accompanied by high friendship belies the notion of freedom and agency: Why should I need a friend if I am a self-sufficient and a free being-for-itself?

James Crosswhite observes that Thoreau escapes this paradox that both Emerson and Aristotle are caught in. Correcting a general misunderstanding regarding Thoreau's concept of transcendental being, with the help of the theological concept of *perichoresis*, Crosswhite offers an elaboration of the relationships within the Christian Trinity. In a perichoretic or "indwelling" procession, each member of the Trinity is not taken as a being-for-itself but rather as a being who does not even exist prior to the relationship of giving to and receiving from others. Being is thus not a premise, but an effect of the relation on the other (Crosswhite 166–67). He writes:

> The most radical point about perichoresis relative to Thoreau is that from this perspective individuality and self-sufficiency are achievements of friendship, made possible by a befriending that is prior to whatever we call self-sufficiency—a befriending that generates self-sufficiency, and sustains it. (170–71)

On Crosswhite's reading, it is not fully articulated why this Christian concept resonates with Thoreau's idea of friendship, which in Thoreau's own words is an "essentially heathenish intercourse" (*A Week* 276). Still, the idea of a friend without being—that is, a friend who exists only in the relationship—recuperates an often overlooked facet of Thoreau's friendship: the impossibility of the friend's autonomy.

In part because critics generally focus on Thoreau's friendship in relation to individuality, scant attention has been paid to "Greeting," a prose poem that serves as a meditation on utility-based friendship. Thoreau must have been familiar with and have shared philosophy's disdain for utility-based friendship versus friendship predicated upon free agency. In fact, both Plato and Aristotle hold up lofty friendship between high-minded people as an ideal. In *Phaedrus*, utility-based friendship is ranked the lowest in the hierarchy of friendships and treated as something that should be overcome for the sake of eros, a forever unsatisfied desire. Similarly, in *The Nicomachean Ethics*, utility-based friendship is considered to be a different type of friendship from those relationships that strive for equality and independence (Crosswhite 159).

In spite of its lower status, in "Greeting," Thoreau discloses the utilitarian relationship as a very basic condition of the friendship that enables individualism. From the beginning of the address, the speaker accentuates their utility: "My most serene and irresponsible neighbors, let us see that we have the whole advantage of each other; we will be useful, at least, if not admirable, to one another" (*A Week* 286). The address goes out from Southern Italy to acquaintances in the Province area, over the mountains, so despite the use of the word "neighbors," these addressees are not neighbors in the usual sense but rather, to use Shannon Mariotti's words, those who "retain a certain distance, yet also evoke community and connection" (162). It is important to note that, as Mariotti fully elaborates, for Thoreau, neighborhood is the ideal democratic space where people exist together in relation to each other, without erasing their individuality (161). Nevertheless, beyond neighborhood as a static relationality, I argue, Thoreau seeks more radically to redefine one's individuated subjectivity in relation to others.

As the poem moves on, it dramatizes the way in which the neighbor's utility-based relationship is transformed and sublimated into the friend-enemy relationship. With curiously domestic metaphors, the speaker of the poem associates himself with "one of the old fashioned wooden trenchers," emphasizing an instrumental aspect of having a friend:

> Nothing can shock a brave man but dullness. Think how many rebuffs every man has experienced in his day; perhaps has fallen into a horse-pond, eaten fresh water clams, or worn one shirt for a week without washing. Indeed you cannot receive a shock unless you have an electric affinity for

> that which shocks you. Use me, then, for I am useful in my way, and stand as one of many petitioners, from toadstool and henbane up to dahlia and violet, supplicating to be put to my use, if by any means ye may find me serviceable. (*A Week* 287)

In his depiction of a utilitarian friendship between "neighbors," Thoreau is attentive to the danger of creating a comfortable but stultifying domestic environment. Dull daily life with thoughtless habits may damage a "brave man," and only a friend who has "an electric affinity" with him can shock him out of his dormant state. In short, it is the friend-enemy who protects one from being too much at home with dullness, and from being satisfied with one's present condition without critical reflections. In this sense, the friend turns out to be useful.

The sense of one's dependence on the friend is, therefore, a condition that creates an opportunity for self-reformation and even self-empowerment. The farewell to friends at the end of the poem appears to be a declaration of independence: "We have nothing to fear from our foes; God keeps a standing army for that service; but we have no ally against our Friends, those ruthless Vandals" (*A Week* 287). For Thoreau, one cannot stand alone without others; one's independence is achievable only through a relationship with another individual, even if it is the kind of low-ranking, utility-based friendship he disdains.

4. We Brothers + 1

If one's being depends inextricably on friends, how many friends can one have? As Jacques Derrida notes in *Politics of Friendship*, the question of the ideal quantity of friendships has been constantly posed as an inseparable part of meditations on what friendship really is (1–25). Regarding this fundamental issue, Thoreau's position seems to be ambivalent and brings to the fore another aporia between inclusive and exclusive friendships. On the one hand, he asserts an encompassing aspect of friendship that can serve as a model for the nation:

> A base Friendship is of a narrowing and exclusive tendency, but a noble one is not exclusive; its very superfluity and dispersed love is the humanity which sweetens society, and sympathizes with foreign nations; for though its foundations are private, it is in effect, a public affair and a public

> advantage, and the Friend, more than the father of a family, deserves well of the state. (*A Week* 277)

Ironizing and perhaps even criticizing America's paternalism in the 1840s,[2] he advocates encompassing friendship as a model for nation-building. However, the ideal of inclusiveness is more characteristic of Christian charity than the high friendship that is an "essentially heathenish intercourse" (*A Week* 276). Elsewhere in the same text, Thoreau writes, "Friendship is not so kind as is imagined; it has not much human blood in it, but consists with a certain disregard for men and their erections, the Christian duties, and humanities, while it purifies the air like electricity" (*A Week* 275–76). Christian philanthropy, which offers unconditional love to everyone, regardless of personal qualities, seems to run counter to the partiality and selectivity inherent to the ideal of transcendental friendship. Like Emerson, who notes that friends' conversations should follow the "law of one to one" (122), an inclusive friendship involving more than one person is not easily imaginable for Thoreau as well. In fact, he admits, "we cannot have too many friends":

> As for the number which this society admits, it is at any rate to be begun with one, the noblest and greatest that we know, and whether the world will ever carry it further, whether, as Chaucer affirms,
>
> "There be mo sterres in the skie than a pair,"
>
> remains to be proved; —
>
> "And certaine he is well begone
> Among a thousand that findeth one." (*A Week* 276)

Despite this creed, in another passage, Thoreau envisions a possibility of having "mo"(more) than a pair of friends: "I am ready to believe that as private and intimate a relation may exist by which three are embraced as between two" (*A Week* 277).[3] This apparent contradiction raises an obvious question: how does Thoreau envision the possibility of preserving the individuality that exists in a one-to-one relationship within a larger communal body?

To further explore the collective possibilities beyond friendship between two people, Thoreau uses the first person plural pronoun "we" throughout *A Week*, offering an insight into the communal being in its ontological dimension. At first glance, the "we" seems to have nothing to do with Thoreau's disjunctive understanding of the community because, as revealed through the narrative of a boat trip on the river with his brother John, it seems to be quite clear what this "we" indicates. Thoreau plainly calls himself and John "we two, brothers, and natives of Concord" (15), and the two rarely act separately, as if they were one person. With the Thoreau brothers in mind, it comes as no surprise that he associates intimate friendship with brotherhood in the following passage:

> My Friend is not of some other race or family of men, but flesh of my flesh, bone of my bone. He is my real brother. . . . we have never had a thought of different fibre the one from the other! (*A Week* 284–85)

Here, Thoreau makes an easily identifiable biblical passage about the origins of heterosexual love into a reflection upon an ideal model of male friendship.[4]

Philosophically, the "we" of this passage resembles Montaigne's concept of friendship *par excellence*, in which two persons "mingle and blend with each other so completely that they efface the seam that joined them, and cannot find it again" (Montaigne 139). This notion of friendship that allows for the dissolution of boundaries between self and other clearly stands in opposition to the transcendental notion of friendship we otherwise associate with Thoreau. Nevertheless, in *A Week*, while Thoreau absorbs himself deeply into this fraternal relationship, he still seeks to disrupt the complacency of this idealized community. The distance necessary for high friendship is not found between John and Thoreau, nor between "what I am now" and "what I aspire to be," either; rather, it exists between "we" and Thoreau's "I"—that is, the fraternal community and the one who takes a detached position to think beyond the community. Critics sometimes wonder why John is never mentioned in *A Week*, but it is perhaps stranger that the first person narrator rarely appears in the narrative. For example, instead of referring to himself in the first person, the narrator disappears behind the scene in the following passage:

> One sailor was visited in his dreams this night by the Evil Destinies, and all those powers that are hostile to human life. . . . But the other happily passed a serene and even ambrosial or immortal night, and his sleep was dreamless, or only the atmosphere of pleasant dreams remained, a happy natural sleep until the morning; and his cheerful spirit soothed and reassured his brother, for whenever they meet, the Good Genius is sure to prevail. (*A Week* 116)

Who is "he," and who is "his brother"? From the context, it is not so difficult to discover that "he" refers to Thoreau, but, at least formally and syntactically, whether "he" denotes Thoreau or John is not completely clear. Thoreau does not call himself "I," and John is not named "my" brother, either, because the speaker creates a distance not merely from John but also from himself. Instead of appealing to his own individuality and singularity by using the first person pronoun, Thoreau pulls John out of himself and also out of the "we," disrupting the self-satisfying space of fraternity.

Perhaps Thoreau is following Emerson's advice here: "Treat your friend as a spectacle" (123). Though indifferent, the gaze that positions itself outside the narrative is friendly, whether it is Thoreau's own autobiographical reflection or the reader's gaze. Thoreau's friendship-induced community disallows total communion and self-immersion, especially because his friend is dead.[5] It perhaps exposes the limit of our being that we cannot share death with others. After the death of John, Thoreau writes to his friend:

> I do not wish to see John ever again—I mean him who is dead—but that other, whom only he would have wished to see, or to be, of whom he was the imperfect representative. For we are not what we are, nor do we treat or esteem each other for such, but for what we are capable of being. (*Correspondence* 62)

The impossibility of sharing death marks the end of fraternity and the point at which Thoreau's conception of lofty friendship can begin. However tragic it may be, only through giving up fraternal presumptions can Thoreau initiate friendship once again, and herein lies an opening of a possibility for the dilation of the community between the two. In short, Thoreau's "we" opens the fraternal, bounded, and solitary community to the next world to come—that is, the future beyond what the "we" *is*.

Coda: Friendship to Come

Throughout *A Week*, Thoreau explores collective possibility beyond fraternity. Thoreau's friendship does not depend on the past commonality that familiar discourses of loss of community presupposes; rather, his friendship always requires distance both in space and time, presenting it as a potential opening for the future. "Atlantis," a poem often discussed as a representation of transcendental friendship, illuminates this potential—that is, friendship to come.

Although generally understood as being about the unattainableness of ideal friendship, it actually articulates its *attainability*. Associating the friend with "some fair floating isle of palms eluding the mariner in Pacific seas," the poem continues:

> Our fabled shores none ever reach,
> No mariner has found our beach,
> Only our mirage now is seen,
> And neighboring waves with floating green,
> Yet still the oldest charts contain
> Some dotted outline of our main. (*A Week* 262)

The island is presented as a utopia, and the communication between the islander and the seeker seems to have failed both in time and space: "There goes a rumor that the earth is inhabited, but the shipwrecked mariner has not seen a footprint on the shore. The hunter has found only fragments of pottery and the monuments of inhabitants" (*A Week* 263–64).

However, the crux of the poem has less to do with the explorer's unsatisfied and indefinitely deferred desire than with the reciprocity between explorer and islander, actualized by juxtaposition of different voices. In "Atlantis" the story is told not only by an explorer of the unreachable, but also by those who are sought, as suggested in the references to the island as "*our* fabled shore" and "*our* beach." The unknown Atlantis dweller, the same unreachable friend the seeker pursues, responds distantly but miraculously in the poem.

Significantly, this reciprocal *tele*-communication in "Atlantis" is also actualized in the experience of reading. The following image of the inland man thinking about books as well as human friends brings to the fore the literary communication across time and space, between text and reader:

> But he alone sits on the strand.
> Whether he ponders men or books,
> Always still he seaward looks,
> Marine news he ever reads,
> And the slightest glances heeds,
> Feels the sea breeze on his cheek
> At each word the landsmen speak,
> In every companion's eye

A sailing vessel doth descry. (*A Week* 263)

Thoreau seems to identify himself with this inland man and to practice his philosophy of friendship through his writing that is not friendly in the usual sense. He employs paradox, contradiction, and ambiguity to unsettle readers and even to rule out the possibility of empathy and intimacy with them. Like the lofty friend, the text's meaning is out of reach. This disruption of communication with Thoreau's text threatens to jeopardize our cherished values, conventional way of thinking, and self-assured interpretations; in spite of, or rather because of, the difficulty of communication, Thoreau's text, like the friend, enables continual reformation of our self.

Notes

1 Part of this paper has been published in Japanese. See Sadahiro.

2 Thoreau begins "Civil Disobedience" by saying that he agrees with the maxim "That government is best which governs least." Also he asserts, "I am as desirous of being a good neighbor as I am of being a bad subject" (84).

3 In *Walden*, Thoreau also writes, "I had three chairs in my house; one for solitude, two for friendship, three for society. When visitors came in larger and unexpected numbers there was but the third chair for them all, but they generally economized the room by standing up" (140).

4 Thoreau's ideal of same-sex friendship has been interpreted in terms of his homoeroticism and queer politics. For instance, Henry Abelove argues that Thoreau's anti-collectivist stance is resonant with the queer movement today. Milette Shamir also finds repressed same-sex love in Thoreau's ideas on friendship.

5 The epigraph of *A Week* clearly indicates that one of Thoreau's main concerns in the narrative is how to overcome the death of his brother John. It reads: "Where'er thou sail'st who sailed with me, / Though now thou climbest loftier mounts, / And fairer rivers dost ascend, / Be thou my Muse, my Brother—" (3). The sense of loss and elegiac tone is consistent throughout *A Week*. For discussions that focus on the elegiac aspects of the narrative, see Johnson 41–84, Peck 3–21, and Rossi 107–26.

Works Cited

Abelove, Henry. "From Thoreau to Queer Politics." *Yale Journal of Criticism* 6.2 (1993): 17–27. Print.

Cavell, Stanley. *Emerson's Transcendental Etudes*. Ed. David Justin Hodge. Stanford: Stanford UP, 2003. Print.

Coviello, Peter. *Intimacy in America: Dreams of Affiliation in Antebellum Literature*. Minneapolis: U of Minnesota P, 2005. Print.

Crain, Caleb. *American Sympathy: Men, Friendship, and Literature in the New Nation.* New Haven: Yale UP, 2001. Print.

Crosswhite, James. "Giving Friendship: The Perichoresis of an All-Embracing Service." *Emerson and Thoreau*. Ed. Lysaker and Rossi. 151–71. Print.

Derrida, Jacques. *The Politics of Friendship*. Trans. George Collins. London: Verso, 2005. Print.

Emerson, Ralph Waldo. "Friendship." *The Collected Works of Ralph Waldo Emerson.* Ed. Robert E. Spiller, Alfred R. Ferguson, et al. Vol. 2. Cambridge, MA: Harvard UP, 1971. 111–28. Print.

Harding, Walter. *The Days of Thoreau: A Biography*. New York: Dover Publications, 1982. Print.

Johnson, Linck. *Thoreau's Complex Weave: The Writing of A Week on the Concord and Merrimack Rivers, with the Text of the First Draft*. Charlottesville: UP of Virginia, 1986. Print.

Lysaker, John T and William Rossi, eds. *Emerson and Thoreau: Figures of Friendship.* Bloomington: Indiana UP, 2010. Print.

Mariotti, Shannon L. *Thoreau's Democratic Withdrawal: Alienation, Participation and Modernity*. Madison: U of Wisconsin P, 2010. Print.

McGill, Meredith L. "Common Places: Poetry, Illocality, and Temporal Dislocation in Thoreau's *A Week on the Concord and Merrimack Rivers*." *American Literary History* 19.2 (2007): 357–74. Print.

Montaigne, Michael de. "Of Friendship." *The Complete Essays of Montaigne*. Trans. Donald Frame. Stanford: Stanford UP, 1958. 135–44. Print.

Nancy, Jean-Luc. *The Inoperative Community*. Minneapolis: U of Minnesota P, 1990. Print.

Nelson, Dana. *National Manhood: Capitalist Citizenship and the Imagined Fraternity of White Men*. Durham: Duke UP, 1998. Print.

Parmett, Helen Morgan. "Community / Common: Jean-Luc Nancy and Antonio Negri on Collective Potentialities." *Communication, Culture & Critique* 5 (2012): 171–90. Print.

Peck, Daniel. *Thoreau's Morning Work: Memory and Perception in* A Week on the Concord and Merrimack Rivers, The Journal, *and* Walden. New Haven: Yale UP, 1990. Print.

Rossi, William. "'In Dreams Awake': Loss, Transcendental Friendship, and Elegy." *Emerson and Thoreau*. Ed. Lysaker and Rossi. 107–26. Print.

Sadahiro, Maki. "*A Week on the Concord and Merrimack Rivers* niokeru Yuai" ["Friendship in *A Week on the Concord and Merrimack Rivers*"]. *Strata* 24 (2010): 1–24. Print.

Shamir, Milette. *Inexpressible Privacy: The Interior Life of Antebellum American Literature*. Philadelphia: U of Pennsylvania P, 2006. Print.

Thoreau, Henry David. *A Week on the Concord and Merrimack Rivers*. Ed. Carl F. Hovde, et al. Princeton: Princeton UP, 1980. Print.

——. *The Correspondence of Henry David Thoreau*. Ed. Walter Harding and Carl

Bode. New York: New York UP, 1958. Print. Volume 1: 1834–1848.
——."Huckleberries." *Henry David Thoreau: Collected Essays and Poems*. Ed. Elizabeth Witherell. New York: Library of America, 2001. 468–501. Print.
——. "Resistance to Civil Government." *The Higher Law: Thoreau and Civil Disobedience and Reform*. Ed. Wendell Glick. Princeton: Princeton UP, 2004. 63–90. Print.
——. *Walden*. Ed. Lyndon Shanley. Princeton: Princeton UP, 2004. Print.

Thoreau's Expression of Heaven or the Universe in *Walden*

Kazuto Ono

1. A Lower Heaven

Henry Thoreau pays his supreme homage to Walden Pond in this way:

> It is no dream of mine,
> To ornament a line;
> I cannot come nearer to God and Heaven
> Than I live to Walden even. (*Walden* 193)

To Thoreau, Walden Pond is a perfect being with no need of adding any further ornament, and so is the nearest to "Heaven." But why? One of the reasons is the pond's high transparency, just as an oriental jewel has. It clearly reflects the blue sky. Thoreau compares the surface of the pond to "Sky water" (*Walden* 188). Generally, heaven owns blue sky as the surface of its territory. In other words, the blue sky symbolizes the whole heaven. So Thoreau likens Walden Pond to "a lower heaven" (86).

He also refers to a train dashing along the Fitchburg railroad by the pond. The train itself is compared by him with the train of steam clouds which are blown up from the smokestack and pipes of the locomotive engine.

> Their train of clouds stretching far behind and rising higher and higher, going to heaven while the cars are going to Boston, conceals the sun for a minute and casts my distant field into the shade, a celestial train beside which the petty train of cars which hugs the earth is but the barb of the spear. (116–17)

Thus Thoreau appears to be much more reverentially interested in heaven than the earth. His life at Walden Pond was apt to be directed toward heaven. He is in vain to touch the realm of heaven in person, so he relies on the pond because "it is intermediate in its nature between land and sky" (188–89). He touches the water of the pond which looks like the surface of heaven. He has to retain his body on the earth, but can raise his mind up toward heaven through the "Sky water."

Incidentally in Japan, *Shugendo*, a sort of mountain Buddhism (a mixture of Buddhism and Japanese traditional mountain worship in the primeval Shintoism) or mountaineering asceticism, has continued since about the 8th century or the beginning of the *Heian* Period, all the way to the present age. Believers in the religion, called *Yamabushi* or the mountain priests, sometimes go into a mountain area which is regarded as their natural temple or shrine. They usually remain there for a fixed period to train themselves in the ascetic practices needed to get the power of *dharma*, or the law, in the mountain Buddhism, and to experience a mysterious religious enlightenment (Wakamori 7). They believe that Buddhism or Shintoism deities exist in heaven. As mountains are generally higher and closer to the sky than ordinary flatlands, they appear as if they are in touch with heaven. Therefore, to the mountain priests, "their mountains serve as the point of medium between heaven and the earth" (26). They rely on the mountains to virtually approach the heaven and the deities. This is just like the role of Walden Pond to Thoreau for it is "intermediate in its nature between land and sky."

2. Thoreau on Mountains

Not only in the case of Japanese *Shugendo*, but also in a general world-wide view, mountains are apt to be regarded as isolated, pure, and sacred, and many religious houses or monasteries have been built at the foot of them or halfway up their slopes. Such a view is also true to Thoreau himself. In the chapter of "Tuesday" of *A Week on the Concord and Merrimack Rivers* (hereafter abbreviated as *A Week*), he tells of an episode of his climbing Mt. Saddleback, which rises in the western border of Massachusetts, in 1844. He stayed one night in a rude observatory on the mountain top.

The wooden observatory reminded him of its builders, some students of Williamstown College located at the northern foot of Mt. Saddleback. Then, he got the idea for an ideal university that should be set up in a mountainous area. It would be regarded as having a purifying effect on the students and the levels of scholarship there.

It would be no small advantage if every college were thus located at the

> base of a mountain, as good at least as one well-endowed professorship. . . . Some will remember, no doubt, not only that they went to the college, but that they went to the mountain. Every visit to its summit would, as it were, generalize the particular information gained below, and subject it to more catholic tests. (*A Week* 187)

According to him, the scholarship generally given to college students on a flatland for their own worldly objects could be purified into such a sacred and ideal one that may be given for the catholic bliss of all the people in the world, if it were exposed to the ethereal holy air of a mountain.

Early the next morning, Thoreau saw an ocean of mist cover the entire mountain just up to the base of the observatory. All around and beneath him was spread "an undulating country of clouds, answering in the varied swell of its surface to the terrestrial world it veiled." To him, it had "all the delights of paradise" (*A Week* 188). He was deeply impressed with the pure white country of the mist, appreciating, in a sense, a moment of eternity. Paradise is another name for heaven, or at least a midway point to it.

The destination of the Thoreau brothers' trip in *A Week* was Mt. Agiocochook (or Mt. Washington) which rises 6,288 feet above sea level in the northern backcountry of New Hampshire. It is the headspring area of the Merrimack River. Thoreau always called this mountain Mt. Agiocochook, the name which was given by the original inhabitants of the region. According to William Howarth, the name "Agiocochook" roughly translates to "the home of the Great Spirit" to them (Howarth 222). Thoreau must have been conscious of the meaning, and respected the holiness of the mountain.

3. Frequency of the Use of the Word "Heaven"

Getting back to *Walden*, Thoreau used the word "heaven" rather frequently. According to *Walden, A Concordance*, the word "heaven" is used 33 times, "heavens," 11 times, and "heavenly," 3 times (95). We can appropriately compare this frequency with that of the word "universe" in the same work, because the meaning of the universe is roughly close to heaven: both of them appear to be in an ethereal realm high up and far away from the earth. Thoreau used "universe," 17 times, "universal," 14 times, and "universally," 4 times (238). If we compare each merely in the singular noun form, "heaven" occurs almost twice as often as "universe." (Each frequency of the other related words is almost the same.) Thoreau's greater interest in heaven is fairly obvious.

Essentially heaven and the universe are roughly common in that they are different realms from the Earth and still widely cover its sphere. But their meaning and nuance are rather contrary to each other. Heaven seems to be an enormous sanctum we aspire to approach, but in vain. However, wide open sky is included in it as if it were the surface. The universe, on the other hand, is another territory, which is located across the upper atmosphere and cut off from the gravitational field of the earth.

According to a dictionary, "heaven" is "the expanse of space surrounding the earth like a great arch or dome", and also "the dwelling place of the Deity: a celestial abode of bliss: the place or state of the blessed dead" (*Webster's Third New International Dictionary* 1046–47). It covers the solid earth and has a relationship to it. As it is the place for the god and the spirits of saints, it also is a sacred place even for the living human beings who revere them. On the other hand, "universe" is "the whole body of things and phenomena: the totality of material entities" (2502). That means a world of matter itself, with scarce opportunity for the existence of human sense, mind and spirit, all of which are vital to our humanity. Thoreau's preference for the word "heaven" is sure to be based on this difference. Later, in the chapter of "Ktaadn" of *The Maine Woods*, he showed an excessive feeling of alienation from the scene of the limitless expanse of a burnt land in the primeval forest area in Maine: a vast space in the woodland once struck and burnt away by lightning. Thoreau was intimidated into saying, "Man was not to be associated with it. It was Matter, vast, terrific,—not his Mother Earth . . ." (70). Thus he had a phobia about overwhelming material domination.

Still, as mentioned above, heaven and the universe are roughly common in that they generally cover the sphere of the Earth. There are some cases when Thoreau himself does not distinguish between them clearly but tends to mix them. His hut by Walden Pond was far away from the busy streets of Concord and especially quiet in the night-time. His nearest neighbor became conscious of him from afar only by the flickering light of the hut at night (*Walden* 88). So Thoreau imagines his home as if located "in some remote and more celestial corner of the system, behind the constellation of Cassiopeia's Chair, far from noise and disturbance." The word "celestial" has almost the same meaning as "heavenly," having a connotation of being "sacred." So in this case, the universe can also be a sort of sanctum. Thoreau discovered that his house "actually had its site in such a withdrawn, but forever new and unprofaned, part of the universe" (*Walden* 88).

4. The Image of the Universe in Thoreau's Age

Generally, in the age of American Renaissance when Thoreau was alive, the ideas of heaven and the universe can be said to have been much closer to each other than today. To confirm this, we can look back at the astronomy of the early 19th century, referring to the conception and view of the universe then. It was mainly provided by the English astronomers, William Hershel (1738–1822) and his son, John (1792–1871). In their observation of the entire universe through an effective reflecting astronomical telescope which William invented, they found the form of the galaxy to be like a gigantic convex lens. The lens form of the galaxy was almost the same as what modern astronomy shows us, except that the galactic arms were considered in the older period to be pushed straight out of the circumference of the lens, while the modern shapes of them are of their being twined around the circumference (Robert Wilson 91–120).

According to Hershel and his son, the only galaxy whose existence could be confirmed in the whole universe was ours. In other words, our galaxy itself was the entire universe. Furthermore, our solar system was presumed to be located in the center of the galaxy. So our sun and the earth were able to occupy the central part of the universe: Galactocentrism. In a sense, it was as if the Ptolemaic theory of geocentricism had been extended into a scale of the whole universe (Sakurai 98–105).

The view that our human territory was thus located at the center of the universe was sure to have given confidence to such American literati as Ralph Waldo Emerson and Walt Whitman who were interested in the phenomena of the universe and astronomy at that time. Ordinarily, anything that occupies the central part of a locale seems to have a favorable chance of becoming the representative or the symbol of the situation. So it would have been natural for Emerson and Whitman to think that they might have the extraordinary qualification of becoming the representatives of the whole universe.

Whitman sings at the beginning of his poem "Song of Myself," "Walt Whitman, a kosmos" (Whitman 52). When he was conscious of such a self-centered location in the universe, he could have confidently considered himself to be representing the universe, and even regarded himself to be a sort of universe. Like Whitman, Thoreau was exceedingly confident with his life. To him, Walden Pond, where he stayed, was located virtually at the central point of the universe. He proudly demonstrates the situation, stating, "I cannot come nearer to God and Heaven than I live to Walden even."

This view that the Earth is located in the midst of the universe also means that it is wrapped up roundly by the celestial sphere of a galaxy that looks like a convex lens. It is roughly similar to an imagined form of heaven which covers the earth like a gigantic arch or dome. In Thoreau's age the scale of the universe was estimated to be much smaller than that of today. It was presumed to be about 6,000 light years in diameter and about 1,100 in thickness. This estimated smallness of the universe in size was also a reason for the plausible resemblance between heaven and the universe then.

On the other hand, the scale of heaven was imagined to roughly correspond to that of the solid earth, or maybe a bit larger because it was considered to cover the earth as an arch or a dome. Therefore, the universe and heaven at that period owned and covered the Earth jointly. And the universe could presumably be concluded to have been an enlarged heaven. Thus the existence of heaven was not so inconsistent with the universe. Furthermore, heaven is considered to have been endowed with a sense of reality by the substantial framework of the universe.

5. Thoreau's Idea of Living in Heaven or the Universe

Emerson's earliest essay *Nature* was treasured by Thoreau all through his life as his favorite rare book (Harding 60). The distinguished scene of a starry sky at the beginning of the work must have impressed him a lot. Emerson called the stars to be the "envoys of beauty" (*Nature* 7) and assigned them a sacred role to suggest the existence of a deity. Also he emphasized the solemn beauty of their scene by asking us, "If the stars should appear one night in the thousand years, how would men believe and adore; and preserve for many generations the remembrance of the city of God. . ." (7). No doubt Thoreau would have agreed with Emerson. Thoreau also admired the aesthetic sight of stars as follows.

> You lie on your back on a rock in a pasture (or the top of some bare hill) at midnight, and speculate on the height of the starry canopy. The stars are the jewels of the night, and perchance surpass anything which day has to show. (*The Moon* 3)

However, Emerson and Thoreau were fundamentally different. Emerson was a serene and ardent watcher of stars, whereas Thoreau tried to be more active, even in the realm of stars. While staying at the shore of Walden Pond, he imagined his hut, as mentioned above, as if it were located "in some remote and more celestial corner of the system, behind the Constellation of Cassiopeia's Chair" (*Walden* 88). Obviously this was imagined in his capricious hypothesis. But even so, Thoreau tried to make this description more valid and plausible, adding that his nearest neighbor became conscious of his existence "only by the flickering light of the hut" at night. In other words, he wanted to show his attitude of living freely, even in heaven or the universe, without being unilaterally bound to the solid earth.

While fishing in a boat on Walden Pond at night, Thoreau caught a horned pout. At that moment he imagined himself to be even able to cast his line high "upward into the air." Thus he "caught two fishes as it were with one hook" (175). One fish in the water was for nourishing his body and another one in midair might have been for his soul. So, the realm of "the air" was sure to lead his mind farther into that of heaven or the universe. Also he added: "I would . . . fish in the sky, whose bottom is pebbly with stars" (98). So he was not a passive observer of stars, but a positive activist, even in the realm of his imaginary extraterrestrial world.

At the same time, Thoreau directs his fancy to "cosmological themes in other spheres." Other spheres mean heaven or the universe, and cosmology is "a part of the science of astronomy that deals with the origin and development of the universe and its component" (*Webster* 514). Generally, the academic grappling with cosmology began with the question of how the solar system was created.

There are two theories set force by Buffon (Georges-Louis Leclerc, Comte de Buffon, 1707–88) and Immanuel Kant (1724–1804). Buffon insisted that once a comet collided with the primitive sun, and by the impulse many lumps and pieces were wrenched away and thrown out of the sun and became the planets and minor planets. Whereas Kant, and later Laplace (1749–1827), explained that there had been many primitive clouds of dust in the universe and once they began to revolve, gravity was created by the movement. From this effect the dust was collected and fixed into such solid forms as the suns and planets (Sullivan Ch. 5).

But which theory of the two Thoreau accepted has not been clarified yet, since he did not dare to explain at that time what the content of his cosmological fancy was. Still the cosmological inquiry itself must have had a beneficial effect upon his mind because it pulled him away from the routine and trivial view of his real daily life, even if for a while, and motivated him "to front only the essential fact of life" (*Walden* 90) by way of making this fundamental inquiry into the birth of the universe.

Thoreau was much interested in comets. Describing the vigorous passing of the Fitchburg railroad train along the shore of Walden, he compares it to that of a comet.

> When I meet the engine with its train of cars moving off with planetary motion,—or, rather, like a comet, for the beholder knows not if with that velocity and with that direction it will ever revisit this system, since its orbit does not look like a returning curve, ... (116)

In his Walden life, Thoreau was sometimes annoyed by the clamorous sound and sudden shaking of the ground caused by an approaching train. Also he was distressed by the economic confusion in his home town of Concord which was brought about by the change of the people's life style from one of sedate agriculture into restless commerce. Obviously the main cause of this confusion was the frequent operation of this train.

The rapid velocity and vigorous force of the train were compared to those of a flying comet by Thoreau, but also the economic confusion of his area might have been compared to the probable disorder of the solar system which could be caused by the seemingly abnormal orbit of a comet, such as the supposed collision of a comet with the primitive sun, the theory of which was advocated by Buffon.

Thoreau confesses, "I too would fain be a track-repairer somewhere in the orbit of the earth" (*Walden* 115). His true intention should have been to save the town people of Concord, who were on the verge of dropping out of their right path of life because many of them were busy in their frantic pursuit of financial profit, missing the true worth and significance of their lives. Still, it would be fun to accept Thoreau's expression of this as it is. Then we could see him standing confidently somewhere in the space of the solar system, watching the passage of the Earth to make sure if it is on its right orbit. This scene also reflects his ardent wish for active, aggressive behavior, even in the realm of the universe.

Thoreau's mental attitude toward a comet was actually ambivalent. He was sure to be concerned with the probable disorder of the solar system that would be brought by it. However, the dignified figure of a flying comet also attracted his mind. In his poem "To the Comet," which was made in his 20th year (in 1837), he suggests such traditional superstitious concerns about a comet as giving omens of war or famine, and arousing the fear of its probable collision with the Earth. But the next four lines show his candid admiration.

> Sculling thy way without a sail,
> Mid the stars and constellations,
> The pioneer*er* of a tail,
> Through the starry nations. (*Collected Poem of Henry D. Thoreau* 88)

The image of a boat, sculling in the dark night sky appears to be realistic and convincing for illustrating a flying comet. And the word "pioneer*er*" emphasizes Thoreau's admiration for it. Actually he had kept a yearning for living in the American West as a pioneer throughout his life. So he adores the comet's role as a pioneer in the universe by adding the suffix "er" in italics to signify "the pioneer of pioneers."

Actually Thoreau lived in the epoch of the American Manifest Destiny. During his Harvard days he planned to migrate to the West with his brother John. Also his mother Cynthia helped them prepare for the long-distance travel (Harding 58). But the plan collapsed because his brother contracted tuberculosis. Still later in his Walden life days, Thoreau entertained an imaginary trip to the West: from Walden Pond to the Great Plains, to the Pacific, and even farther and farther up into the universe. Thus, Thoreau's idea of his own Manifest Destiny is ultimately headed for the realm of the universe.

John Aldrich Christie referred to Thoreau as a "World Traveler," in spite of the fact that he remained in the United State—mainly in his hometown of Concord, Massachusetts—throughout his life except for his one short trip to Eastern Canada. Christie called him so, referring to his ardent interest in world geography and his enormous reading of travel books from around the world (Christie 3–20, 313–33). In such a sense, Thoreau can also be called a kind of space traveler.

> Start now on that farthest western way, which does not pause at the Mississippi or the Pacific, nor conduct toward a worn-out China or Japan, but leads on direct a tangent to this sphere, summer and winter, day and

night, sun down, moon down, and at last earth down too. (*Walden* 322)

No doubt, throughout his lifetime, Thoreau was fairly influenced by the popular trend of the actual development of the American West. But also this imaginative trip into outer space illumines Thoreau's own sincere process of seeking the true essence of life at Walden: "to front only the essential fact of life" (90). In order to reach this very marrow of life, one must transcend the showy trivial aspects of its surface. Thus Thoreau's concept of leaving the farthest edge of the West and plunging into the new frontier of outer space indicates this transcendental jump and search for the genuine core of life.

But still his metaphor of this space trip carries a solid sense. After leaving the Earth, the space traveler may proceed and go high up into the space of the solar system and farther into the realm of the boundless galaxy. The sun, the moon, and the Earth are disappearing on the way. Also the words "that farthest western way which . . . leads on direct a tangent to this sphere" are convincing. Thoreau's own experience as a land surveyor in his real life is effectively displayed here by using the word "tangent."

In "Walking" he declares his ardent admiration for the West: "Eastward I go only by force; but westward I go free" (*Excursion* 196). However, he also predicts the coming end and disappearance of the western frontier in *A Week*: "But we found that the frontiers were not this way any longer . . . . Go where we will on the surface of things, men have been there before us" (303). Therefore he tries to set up a new imaginary outer space frontier for a potential extension of the development of the American West.

Some literati in the American Renaissance period, such as Emerson, Edgar Allan Poe, and Whitman, were extremely interested in the universe and astronomy then. They often picked up the topics of astronomy into their works. But none of them had the idea of combining the American West with outer space to have a new space frontier. Thoreau was so unique for imagining such an original frontier as this even in those early days. Incidentally, Poe published an early scientific story of a space trip, "The Unparalleled Adventure of One Hans Pfaall" in 1835. He intended to make free use of his abundant scientific knowledge in this work, and successfully described the imaginary but plausible scenes of a space trip to the moon (42–108). But even then Poe did not regard the brand new space located on the way from the Earth to the moon as a new kind of frontier. So Thoreau was quite original in this trial.

6. Conclusion: Toward Modern Idea of the Universe

The modern view of the universe began with the two astronomers, Huber Curtis and Edwin Hubble. Curtis claimed that there should be many galaxies in the whole universe just like many islands in an ocean. Hubble observed many variable stars which changed their strength of light periodically. Using the period of the change of light as a kind of scale, he succeeded in measuring the distances of the variable stars between 1923 and 24. Some of the stars seemed to be located far more distant than the extent of our galaxy, which was supposed to be the only one in the universe then. This result proved Curtis's hypothesis: the theory of an island universe (Struve and Zebergs Ch. 19 and 20).

Actually about 170 billion galaxies are estimated to exist in the whole universe now. So the known size of the universe has extended to be about 170 billion times larger than the one claimed by William and John Hershel. Therefore, our galaxy is not at all the only one in the universe, but one of some 170 billions. In the latter period of the 20th century the existence of black holes was confirmed. Those black holes are considered to occupy the central part of each galaxy. So obviously we are not located in the center of the universe, and are not at all the representative of it as the people in Thoreau's age assumed. Rather, Isaac Asimov regarded us modern human beings as "the lonely orphans in the universe" (*Frontier* 299–302).

Also the upper part of the atmosphere of the Earth and the outer space area near the Earth have been closely investigated and directly observed by many space ships and the International Space Station. Thus, in our present age heaven has lost its actual substance, and its existence has been clearly denied. Merely its name and concept remain.

Again getting back to Thoreau's life in the American Renaissance period, he lived by Walden Pond for two years and two months. The pure transparency of the pond water attracted and led his mind toward sky and heaven, because the lake water was "intermediate in its nature between land and sky" (*Walden* 188–89). In Thoreau's age, heaven and the universe were regarded to coexist and jointly wrap up the Earth. Heaven was given its substance by the mystical holy image of the universe. In other words, the universe could have been the enlarged heaven. Our solar system was considered to be located at the center of the galaxy which was assumed as only one in the universe. Thoreau too believed in this geocentric view of the universe. To him Walden Pond was virtually situated at the center of the universe. So, just like Whitman, he could consider himself as one of the glorious representatives of the universe. He utters such a blissful moment of his mind as this:

> In eternity there is indeed something true and sublime. But all these times and places and occasions are now and here. God himself culminates in the present moment, and will never be more divine in the lapse of all the ages. . . . The universe constantly and obediently answers to our conceptions. (*Walden* 97)

In this situation, Thoreau himself can also be regarded to have culminated with God. He was sure to be both bodily and mentally at his peak.

But still he could not remain satisfactorily in a fixed static life style. He was vigorously active in his endeavor for the investigation of a true life as a life pioneer. So, he wanted to live and act even in a new imaginary frontier located in the realm of outer space. In the end, he entertained the unique idea of connecting the American West to the extraterrestrial world to create a pure original frontier.

At the end of *Walden*, Thoreau compares the human light of spiritual awakening to a true life with the natural physical light of the dawning sun, and declares: "The sun is but a morning star" (333). His actual intention here must have been to emphasize the vital importance of human enlightenment. Still, his expression of the sun being trivialized in size to be a point of light in the morning has a sense of reality because, in his mind, the new imaginary frontier lies boundlessly in heaven or the universe. So, if he moves steadily along it as a space pioneer and looks back from afar in the galaxy, the sun is sure to look like a minute point of light, losing the width of its disk.

Today, in spite of Thoreau's intension, the actual space frontier has begun to be realized in the outer space of our vicinity, and the word of frontier has lost its *naiveté* to be a cliché. This tendency seems to be in unison with the fact that we have lost the substance of heaven because of modern scientific investigations of the upper atmospheric zone on the Earth. In other words, the development of this new space frontier in our age is progressing without anyone making the necessary efforts to seek its inner mental worth and significance. We cannot connect directly with our sincere wish for seeking a true life while this development of the new frontier is taking place. However, Thoreau wanted to be a true life pioneer in his imaginative space frontier. To remember his aim and attitude again will surely heighten the inner value of the present practical development of the frontier which is being done beyond the realm of the Earth.

Works Cited

Asimov, Isaac. *Frontier*. London: Mandarin, 1991. Print.

Christie, John Aldrich. *Thoreau As World Traveler*. New York: Columbia UP, 1965. Print.

Emerson, Ralph Waldo. *Nature. The Complete Works of Ralph Waldo Emerson*, Vol. 2. Boston and New York: Houghton Mifflin, 1903, AMS, 1968. Print.

Harding, Walter. *The Days of Henry Thoreau*. Princeton: Princeton UP, 1982, 1992. Print.

Howarth, William L. *Thoreau in the Mountains*. New York: Farrar Straus Giroux, 1982. Print.

Ogden, Marlene A. & Keller, Clifton. *Walden A Concordance*. New York: Garland Publishing Inc., 1985. Print.

Poe, Edgar Allan. "The Unparalleled Adventures of One Hans Pfaall." *Edgar Allan Poe's Works*, Vol. 2. New York: AMS, 1973. Print.

Sakurai, Kunitomo. *Tenmongaku-shi* [*History of Astronomy*]. Tokyo: Asakura Shoten, 1990. Print.

Struve, Otto & Zebergs, Velta. *Astronomy of the 20th Century*. New York: Macmillan, 1965. Print.

Sullivan, Walter. *We Are Not Alone: The Search for Intelligent Life on Other World*. New York: Mcgraw-Hill, 1966. Print.

Thoreau, Henry David. *A Week on the Concord and Merrimack Rivers. The Writings of Henry D. Thoreau*. Eds. Carl Hovde, William L. Howarth, Elizabeth H. Witherell, Princeton: Princeton UP, 1980. Print.

——. *Collected Poems of Henry D. Thoreau*. Ed. Carl Bode. Baltimore: The Johns Hopkins UP, 1964. Print.

——. *The Maine Woods. The Writings of Henry D. Thoreau*. Ed. Joseph J. Moldenhauer. Princeton: Princeton UP, 1972. Print.

——. *The Moon*. Ed. F. H. M. New York: AMS, 1985. Print.

——. *Walden. The Writings of Henry D. Thoreau*. Ed. J. Lyndon Shanley. Princeton: Princeton UP, 1971. Print.

——. *Walden: An Annotated Edition*. Ed. Walter Harding. Boston: Houghton Mifflin, 1995. Print.

——."Walking." *Excursions*. Ed. Joseph J. Moldenhauer. Princeton: Princeton UP, 2007. Print.

Wakamori, Taro. *Yamabushi* [*The Mountain Priests*]. Tokyo: Chuo Kouron Sha, 1964. Print.

Wilson, Robert. *Astronomy through the Ages*. London: Taylor & Francis, 1997. Print.

Whitman, Walt. *Leaves of Grass*. Eds. Sculley Bradley & Harold W. Blodgett. New York: Norton, 1973. Print.

This paper is partially based on my book, *Ikiteiru Michi: Thoreau no Hinichijo Kukan to Uchu* [*A Living Way: Through Thoreau's Unusual places to the Universe*] Tokyo: Kinseido, 2015.

Thoreau's Views on Growth in Relation to Flora:

With Comparative Reference to Kumagusu Minakata

Michiko Ono

Thoreau had an abiding interest in education, which he considered as the "process of growth." While in his later years Thoreau concentrated on nature study and his essays centered on the natural history of Concord, some of his *Journal* entries in his last few years are on the subject of education (Miller 68). His record of nature—the lists and charts of flora and fauna—amounted to over 750 pages (Richardson 381), and with this voluminous record, it may look as if "the thinker" and the "poet" in Thoreau were conquered by "the observer," as Odell Shepard commented (Nabhan xiii). Nevertheless, if we take into account what Walter Harding once said about Thoreau: "His basic concern was not with nature itself but with man's place in nature" (*Handbook* 136), it is possible to suppose that Thoreau did not devote himself to the mere detailed facts of nature in his last years but was conscious of the relation between nature and "phases" of human life. He believed in the correspondence between nature and human experience (Lebeaux 65), and as I will point out below, his essays on nature were more than descriptions of what he observed. My purpose in this study is to try to shed light on Thoreau's principal significance of his views on "growth" found in his *Journal*, nature essays, and *Walden*. Also, I shall make a comparative study between Thoreau and Kumagusu Minakata, a Japanese naturalist and ecologist, who was born in 1867, five years after Thoreau's death.

Significantly, Thoreau writes in his *Journal* for October 26, 1857: "These similar phenomena of the seasons get at last to be—they were at first, of course—simply and plainly phenomena or phases of my life. The seasons and all their changes are in me. . . . My moods are thus periodical, not two days in my year alike. The perfect correspondence of Nature to man, so that he is at home in her!" (X: 137) This excerpt evidently shows Thoreau's belief in the correspondence between natural phenomena and his internal life. Anton M. Huffert explains this statement as "the assumption that the phenomena of nature parallel those of the mind" (309).

Also, Thoreau writes in his *Journal* for March 7, 1859: "The mystery of the life of plants is kindred with that of our own lives, and the physiologist must not presume to explain their growth according to mechanical laws, or as he might explain some machinery of his own making" (XII: 23). This observation suggests Thoreau's "mystical identification with Nature," as Huffert says (309). It also implies that Thoreau was convinced that the growth of plants should not be seen from the point of view of mechanism, or "necessitarianism" that was dominant in nineteenth-century science.

I

In the nineteenth century, the focus of science was "the law of causation," which explains two things. First: "There is a cause for every effect without exception"; second: "The same cause inevitably leads to the same effect" (Tsurumi 125; my translation). Nevertheless, although until the end of the nineteenth century "the doctrine of necessity" based on Newtonian mechanics had flourished in various fields of science; after 1925, when quantum physics was established, and during 1930s, the importance of "chance" came to be clearly identified by such physicists as Niels Bohr, Werner Karl Heisenberg, Paul Adrian M. Dirac, John von Neumann, and Eugene Paul Wigner (Tsurumi 127–28).

It is noteworthy that Jacques Monod, a French biochemist and the winner of the Nobel Prize in Physiology or Medicine for 1965, published *Le Hasard et la Nécessité* [*Chance and Necessity*] in 1970. The following is the first part of Chapter VII entitled "Evolution," where we need to pay particular attention to the penultimate sentence:

> The initial elementary events which open the way to evolution in the intensely conservative systems called living beings are microscopic, fortuitous, and utterly without relation to whatever may be their effects upon teleonomic functioning.
>
> But once incorporated in the DNA structure, the accident—essentially unpredictable because always singular—will be mechanically and faithfully replicated and translated: that is to say, both multiplied and transposed into

> millions or billions of copies. Drawn out of the realm of pure chance, the accident enters into that of necessity, of the most implacable certainties. For natural selection operates at the microscopic level, the level of organisms. (Monod 118)

However, as early as 1892, Charles Sanders Peirce, an American scientist and philosopher, published a paper titled "The Doctrine of Necessity Examined" in *The Monist*. Discussing his idea of "chance" in a persuasive manner, Peirce stated in the paper: "I propose here to examine the common belief that every single fact in the universe is precisely determined by law" (174). He argued that in the natural world there exists "real chance" to which the law of necessity does not apply, and that "there is an element of irregularity in nature." He further wrote: "Try to verify any law of nature, and you will find that the more precise your observations, the more certain they will be to show irregular departures from the law. We are accustomed to ascribe these . . . to errors of observation; yet we cannot usually account for such errors in any antecedently probable way. Trace their causes back far enough, and you will be forced to admit they are always due to arbitrary determination, or chance" (182).

Interestingly, Thoreau writes about "cause and effect" in his *Journal* for March 7, 1859 as follows: "The cause and the effect are equally evanescent and intangible, and the former must be investigated in the same spirit and with the same reverence with which the latter is perceived" (XII: 23). This excerpt seems to indicate that Thoreau was not affected by the law of causation, which was predominant in nineteenth-century science. Also notable is Thoreau's comment in "The Succession of Forest Trees": "Convince me that you have a seed there, and I am prepared to accept wonders" (743). According to Robert Sattelmeyer, Thoreau's implication of this comment is that "the seed is not only related to the mature fruit by material cause and effect but is perhaps an organic principle in itself of yet another order" (Sattelmeyer xxv).

In this connection, it may be worth referring to Kumagusu Minakata, a Japanese naturalist and ecologist. He had a profound interest in fungi, especially in mycetozoa, or myxomycetes[1] and collected numerous samples of them and published in a Japanese botanical magazine 196 varieties, ninety-nine of which were new varieties of his own finding. Actually, one of them has the nomenclature of "Minakatella longifila," which was termed by Gulielma Lister, a mycetozoologist, who published it in 1921 in *Journal of Botany*, a British botanical journal (Tsurumi 132).

While studying mycetozoa, Minakata came to hold the conviction that "chance" is important as well as "necessity," and came up with a geometric figure, or a model for a methodology. Although he fully understood the law of causation in nineteenth-century science, he maintained that "chance" should also be studied and sought for. Coincidently, Ilya Prigogine, the winner of the Nobel Prize in Chemistry for 1977, also came to gain a clear comprehension of the issues of "chaos" and "chance" while studying mycetozoa (Tsurumi 117, 136).

This reminds us that Thoreau likewise took a great interest in fungi, lichens, and other cryptogamous plants (XIII: 184). He writes in his *Journal* for October 10, 1858 as follows: "The simplest and most lumpish fungus has a peculiar interest to us, compared with a mere mass of earth, because it is so obviously organic and related to ourselves, however mute. It is the expression of an idea; growth according to a law; matter not dormant, not raw, but inspired, appropriated by spirit. . . . the humblest fungus betrays a life akin to my own. It is a successful poem in its kind" (XI: 204). Incidentally, this quotation serves as another example of Thoreau's belief in the correspondence between nature and his own life.

II

There are three notable similarities between Thoreau and Minakata besides the two being naturalists and ecologists. First, they lived out their beliefs, and acted upon their convictions. Second, they led a life of solitude in nature for a certain period of time—Thoreau, for two years and two months; Minakata, for two and a half years. And third, they stayed in jail for a short while because of their principles. Thoreau stayed in jail overnight because he was against slavery and did not pay the poll tax that supported slavery; Minakata was put into jail for eighteen days because he acted, on his ecological beliefs, against the government policy to cut down trees on a large scale. His struggle lasted for ten years, though this is not widely known even in Japan. Although they were not political figures, they both achieved an exceptional political result that gives a lasting impression upon later generations. Nevertheless, neither of them received the recognition that was their due in their lifetime (Tsurumi 52–56, 72–79).

It is noteworthy that, like Peirce, Minakata expressed his idea of "chance" in 1903, not in the form of a paper or a thesis but in his twenty-page letter to his friend, Horyu Toki, who was a learned Buddhist priest.[2] When Minakata wrote it, he had not read Peirce's "The Doctrine of Necessity Examined," but the essential part of his idea was the same as Peirce's. (Tsurumi 125–26). Paying attention to the relation between chance and necessity, Minakata predicted a paradigm shift in the twentieth century. Kazuko Tsurumi maintains that both Peirce and Minakata were pioneers who, at the turn of the century, groped for a paradigm shift in science methodology (Tsurumi 129–30).

Regarding Minakata's geometric figure mentioned earlier, it consists of numerous straight lines and curved lines that cross one another and create one intersection. He shows "necessity" by straight lines, and "chance" by curved lines. This figure is called "Minakata Mandala." Minakata, who had studied such Western sciences as anthropology, theology, and sociology, not to mention botany which was his specialty, clearly understood the limitation of natural science along with its possibility. Although Minakata Mandala was not a finished model, it was an ingenious attempt to formulate a methodology of future scholarship for grasping reality by integrating the logic of modern Western science with the philosophy of the East, especially that of ancient Buddhism.[3] He reinterpreted "mandala" as a model for the methodology of science to find the correlation of every possible phenomenon with other phenomena, whether material or spiritual (Tsurumi 87, 126; Nakazawa 14–15).

With regard to "mandala," it is originally a Sanskrit word meaning "a circle," which is a geometric figure representing the universe in Hindu and Buddhist symbolism. Carl Jung, a Swiss psychologist and psychoanalyst, began to use it in 1928 in his treatment in psychoanalysis and published a paper entitled "Mandala Symbolism" in 1950.[4] Parenthetically, according to Minakata's interpretation, in one of the four mandalas in esoteric Buddhism, the central deity called Mahavairocana subsumes the whole universe, larger than the universe itself, his inner power letting himself expand, representing the movement of pure wisdom, wherefrom spirit and matter are generated (Nakazawa 32–35).

Equally important, observing nature with profound interest, Thoreau made a significant finding in 1852 that "the year is a circle" and entered in his *Journal* as follows:

> For the first time I perceive this spring that the year is a circle. . . .
> Why should just these sights and sounds accompany our life? Why should I hear the chattering of blackbirds, why smell the skunk each year?

> I would fain explore the mysterious relation between myself and these things. I would at least know what these things unavoidably are, make a chart of our life, know how its shores trend, that butterflies reappear and when, know why just this circle of creatures completes the world. Can I not by expectation affect the revolutions of nature, make a day to bring forth something new?
>
> As Cowley loved a garden, so I a forest.
>
> Observe all kinds of coincidences, as what kinds of birds come with what flowers. (III: 438)

In this passage, the phrase "the year is a circle" is important in understanding Thoreau's views on the seasons. Also notable are the phrases: "this circle of creatures," "the revolutions of nature," and "all kinds of coincidences," the first two of which are almost identical in meaning, closely related to the words "the year is a circle." As to the first sentence in the passage, it sounds as if he had not looked on the year as a circle before, but this is inconceivable if we consider his experience as a poet and naturalist. It would be more appropriate to suppose that he visualized the cycle of the seasons, or "the revolutions of nature," as a geometric "circle" for the first time that spring. When he asked himself: "why just this circle of creatures completes the world?" he may have had the image of the world as a circle, a geometric form. Coincidentally, as previously mentioned, mandala, too, has the form of a circle, representing the universe or the truth of the universe. In Thoreau's writings we find numerous images of circles, such as tree rings, the ripples on the pond, or the circular movements of not only flying birds but also planets in the universe. He even refers to "all straight lines" made "in the midst of an unknown and infinite sea," in his *Journal*, suggesting that, if "their two ends" meet, they ultimately become circles (I: 54). With such profound interest in a "circle," it is conceivable that Thoreau had an image of something like mandala in his mind when he wrote the above passage, as suggested by the word "chart."

On the subject of the "circle," people in Concord in the early nineteenth century considered God "as a circle where centre was everywhere and its circumference nowhere," as Emerson cites in "Circles" as St. Augustine's description of the nature of God (216). Similarly, in Minakata Mandala, the focal point of numerous lines of "chance" and "necessity" could be anywhere, and there is no definite circumference depicted. In passing, Daisetsu Suzuki coincidentally explains a comparable idea in his lecture titled "Zen Opens Our

Eyes to the Self which is Altogether Unattainably Attainable": "Nalakubara'[5] who left his body that had sensibility and reason, can be compared to a circle without a boundary—that is, a circle whose center can be anywhere. This kind of circle has an infinite number of centers. The center is nowhere and everywhere; it is anywhere and at the same time it is nowhere. The body of Nalakubara' is, metaphysically speaking, 'here, now,' where all the past is absorbed and all the future is produced" (28; my translation).

III

Suppose the center of the circle moves continually upward, vertically; then we get the image of a spiral. Concerning the spiral, Goethe refers to the "spiral tendency" of the plant which "must first appear in the development from the seed" (Goethe 105–06). Goethe comments: ". . . we have actually discovered that spiral organs extend throughout the plant in the most minute form, and we are equally sure there is a spiral tendency whereby the plant lives out its life, finally reaching full development" (105). He also calls attention to the plant's "*vertical* tendency": "The vertical tendency expresses itself from the moment of sprouting; it is how the plant takes root in the earth and grows upward at the same time" (107). He further expounds on the close relationship between the two tendencies:

> The spiral system is the element that develops, expands, nourishes; as such it is short-lived and different from the vertical. Where its effect predominates, it soon grows weak and begins to decay; where it joins the vertical system, the two grow together to form a lasting unity as wood or some other solid part.
>
> Neither of the two systems can be considered as working alone; they are always and forever together. In complete balance they produce the most perfect development of vegetation. (106)

Regarding Thoreau's phrase "all kinds of coincidences," in the passage cited earlier, it should be noted that the word "coincidence" is a synonym of "chance," "accident," or "fortuity." It is most probable that Thoreau was conscious of "chance" in nature, like Peirce and Minakata. It took Thoreau several years to confirm how the plants and animals regularly reappear each season. Even if the same plants and animals reappear around the same time of the year, there must be some changes each time, no matter how minute they may be, and those changes can lead to diversification. Peirce says that "the diversification, specificalness, and irregularity of things" is "chance" (185). Referring to "the phenomenon of growth and developing complexity," Peirce further comments: "there is probably in nature some agency by which the complexity and diversity of things can be increased; and that consequently the rule of mechanical necessity meets in some way with interference" (186). When Thoreau entered in his *Journal*: "Observe all kinds of coincidences, as what kinds of birds come with what flowers," he may have had a similar idea as Peirce expresses.

In the "Economy" chapter of *Walden*, describing how the seed sends its radicle downward and its shoot upward, Thoreau writes: "Why has man rooted himself thus firmly in the earth, but that he may rise in the same proportion into the heavens above?" (15) This suggests Thoreau's belief that "rise" or "growth" entails "descending" or "difficulties." This brings to mind Goethe's words about "the spiral system" cited earlier.

In like manner, in the "Spring" chapter of *Walden*, Thoreau describes the growth of grass year after year, and draws from this a particular lesson about mankind. He calls the blade of grass "the symbol of perpetual youth" because of the way it pushes up through the soil, and though checked by the frost, it soon pushes on again, "lifting its spear of last year's hay with the fresh life below." Then he observes: "So our human life but dies down to its root, and still puts forth its green blade to eternity" (311). We find a similar view in his *Journal* for July 14, 1852:

> Trees have commonly two growths in the year, a spring and a fall growth, the latter sometimes equaling the former, and you can see where the first was checked whether by cold or drouth, and wonder what there was in the summer to produce this check, this blight. So is it with man; most have a spring growth only, and never get over this first check to their youthful hopes; but plants of hardier constitution, or perchance planted in a more genial soil, speedily recover themselves, and, though they bear the scar or knot in remembrance of their disappointment, they push forward again and have a vigorous fall growth which is equivalent to a new spring. (IV: 227–28)

This extract, in a similar fashion, shows that Thoreau sees the correspondence between the growth of trees and that of people. It implies his conviction that people should overcome difficulties and grow afresh, just as plants get over "cold" or "drouth," or even natural selection, which is suggested by the words "plants of hardier constitution," though at that time Thoreau had not yet read Darwin's *The Origin of Species*, which was published in 1859.

Furthermore, later in his life, Thoreau wrote about the wild apple in his *Journal* for October 28, 1857:

> Suppose I see a single green apple, brought to perfection on some thorny shrub, far in a wild pasture where no cow has plucked it. . . . I see some shrubs which cattle have browsed for twenty years, keeping them down and compelling them to spread, until at last they are so broad they become their own fence and some interior shoot darts upward and bears its fruit! What a lesson to man! So are human beings, referred to the highest standard, the celestial fruit which they suggest and aspire to bear, browsed on by fate, and only the most persistent and strongest genius prevails, defends itself, sends a tender scion upward at last, and drops its perfect fruit on the ungrateful earth; and that fruit, though somewhat smaller, perchance, is essentially the same in flavor and quality as if it had grown in a garden. That fruit seems all the sweeter and more palatable even for the very difficulties it has contended with. (X: 137–38)

This passage again represents Thoreau's idea of "growth" and also Darwinian theory of natural selection,[6] which is implied by such words as: "only the most persistent and strongest genius prevails." This excerpt also shows the correspondence between nature and human life. We may infer from this passage that Thoreau believed that human beings grow through "difficulties" they contend with, just as the wild apple gets "sweeter" and "more palatable" through them. We can see that the above excerpts are the examples of the same notion, and he was consistent in his idea from the time when he wrote *Walden* through the later years of his life. Even though growth may entail difficulties, difficulties are not "necessity"; rather, they can be taken as "chance" because of their unpredictability.

Peirce and Minakata both perceived the limitation of the doctrine of necessity and paid attention to "chance," long before it was made known by quantum physicists and Monod in the twentieth century. Thoreau, who was prescient and ahead of his time in his thoughts, must have been acutely aware of "chance" through his study of nature, even before Peirce and Minakata, at the time when the goal of natural science was to pursue the law of causation as "necessity." If so, with his scientific mind, it was quite natural for Thoreau to have a critical view about necessitarianism of his day.

IV

Thoreau asserts in "Dispersion of Seeds": "The development theory implies a greater vital force in Nature, because it is more flexible and accommodating, and equivalent to a sort of constant new creation" (*Faith in a Seed* 102). Taking Darwin's "theory of perception," Thoreau followed his meticulous way of observing nature. Robert D. Richardson, Jr. remarks that undoubtedly Thoreau "found Darwin's mind and writing congenial and suggestive" (244). Nevertheless, Harding states: "despite the fact that Thoreau was impressed with Darwin's theories, they had appeared too late to have any significant influence on his own thinking" (*Days* 429). Joan Burbick also comments: "Thoreau does not share Darwin's agnosticism and increasing skepticism about the correlation between law and intelligence" (128). Furthermore, Michael Berger claims that while Thoreau's empiricism supports "the positivistic Darwinian argument," there is also a great deal of "Transcendentalized natural theology in his late naturalistic writings" (117). Like Asa Gray, who wrote "Evolutionary Teleology" and "Review of Darwin's Theory on the Origin of Species by Means of Natural Selection," Thoreau did not seem to find anything objectionable to "the claims of both religion and science" in some particular issues (Burbick 152, 128). Significantly, David M. Robinson affirms: for Thoreau "nature study was an inherently philosophical activity, an investigation of the order and meaning of reality. The laws that structured the natural world, Thoreau believed, also structured human consciousness and defined human action. The inner life was therefore inextricably tied to the life of nature" (17).

In "Autumnal Tints," observing the scarlet oak each year, Thoreau writes as follows: "Lifted higher and higher, and sublimated more and more, putting off some earthiness and cultivating more intimacy with the light each year, they have at length the least possible amount of earthy matter, and the greatest spread and grasp of skyey influences" (*Selected Works* 704–05). The leaves reappear higher on the tree each year, and this vertical, upward linearity suggests "growth" or "the symbolic pattern of growth." According to Richardson, "Thoreau gradually came to accept a view . . . that any ordering force in the universe must be sought in the developmental principle . . . .

This new view holds that the laws of nature are the laws governing growth, maturation, reproduction, decay, death, and growth again" (384).

In his "Wild Apples" Thoreau expressed "the triumph over adversity" about which Robinson expounds: "The survival and growth of the wild apple illustrates the survival and growth of the creative mind struggling to prevail in a hostile world" (196). Further, Thoreau writes in his *Journal* for November 5, 1860: "I am struck by the fact that the more slowly trees grow at first, the sounder they are at the core, and I think that the same is true of human beings," and he wishes to see children, like trees, "expand slowly at first, as if contending with difficulties, and so are solidified and perfected" (XIV: 217). Of even greater appeal is his remark: "I do not state the facts exactly in the order in which they were observed, but select out of very numerous observations extended over a series of years the most important ones, and describe them in their natural order" (XIV: 199).

From these excerpts we can see Thoreau's point of view as an educator as well as a naturalist. As he wrote in *Walden*: "It is not important that he [a man] should mature as soon as an apple-tree or an oak" (326), so he entered in his *Journal* for January 14, 1861: "Nature is slow but sure; she works no faster than need be; she is the tortoise that wins the race by her perseverance; she knows that seeds have many other uses than to reproduce their kind. In raising oaks and pines, she works with a leisureliness and security answering to the age and strength of the trees" (XIV: 312). If Thoreau's purpose of writing *Walden* was to encourage a multitude of "discontented" people to improve their lives or find their own way of living, as he states in *Walden* (16); then we may conclude that among Thoreau's purposes in his late nature study was to inspire people who are despondent, by showing the results of his extensive observations of flora, to live their lives like plants and grow despite the difficulties they have to confront or contend with in the course of their lives.

In conclusion, Thoreau carried out meticulous observations of nature in his later years, perhaps because he hoped to have those with despondent hearts learn from the way of nature. Indeed, judging from the previously cited quotations from his *Journal* for October 28, 1857 and "Wild Apples," it may be safely said that this was Thoreau's principal aim in his study of flora in the last years of his life. As he believed in the correspondence between nature and human life, studying nature was, for him, a way to know himself. He repeatedly wrote in his writings that children are better educated in nature than under a rigid school system (Ono 155, 43). It may be worth noting that, coincidentally, Minakata displays quite a similar opinion: "If you stay in nature even for a while, or half a day, or a whole day, appreciating the scenery, it will have a good effect on your mind. This is a great education far superior to school education. . . . Indeed, we must know that there are few things in the world that are more valuable than natural scenery" (cited in Tsurumi 78–79; my translation). Thus, Thoreau and Minakata both valued nature as a source of inspiration and wisdom that would help people grow in the unpredictable sphere of human life.

Notes

1 According to *The New Oxford American Dictionary*, the mycetozoan, or the myxomycete, is "a simple mold, esp. an acellular one whose vegetable stage is a multinucleate plasmodium," which is now distinguished from fungi. Against the general belief, Minakata categorized the mycetozoan as "animal," not "vegetable." (Tsurumi 109). According to *The Oxford English Dictionary*, the words "myxomycetes" and "mycetozoa" first appeared in 1880, and in 1885 E. R. Lankester wrote: "It indeed seems not at all improbable that . . . the Mycetozoa represent more closely than any other living forms the original ancestors of the whole organic world" (*OED*, *VI*: 807).

2 Minakata started to express his idea of "chance" in 1893 in his letter to Toki, though in a less accurate way (Tsurumi 128).

3 A devout believer in esoteric Buddhism, Minakata claimed that the worldview of Mahayama Buddhism is superior to that of modern science of those days in the sense that Buddhism explains "chance" as well as "cause." Minakata tried to make a thorough investigation of the relation between necessity and chance (Tsurumi 126).

4 When the doctrine of necessity was dominant in science, it must have been highly improbable that the theory of "chance" would be accepted. Perhaps it was why Jung kept the idea of "mandala symbolism" to himself until 1950, and Minakata did not make known his idea of mandala except in his private letter to his friend Toki.

5 Nalakubara' is a son of Kubera, a Hindu god of wealth or guardian deity who guards the north. According to Chinese *Jing-de zhuandeng-lu*, Nalakubara' is said to give back his bones to his father and his flesh to his mother. (Suzuki 59)

6 Kinji Imanishi, a Japanese ecologist and anthropologist, claims that Darwin did not believe that he could explain every phenomenon related to evolution by his theory of natural selection. (Imanishi 4).

Works Cited

Berger, Michael Benjamin. *Thoreau's Late Career and "The Dispersion of Seeds": The Saunterer's Synoptic Vision*. Rochester, NY: Camden House, 2000. Print.

Burbick, Joan. *Thoreau's Alternative History: Changing Perspectives on Nature,*

Culture, and Language. Philadelphia: U of Pennsylvania P, 1987. Print.

Emerson, Ralph Waldo. *The Complete Writings of Ralph Waldo Emerson*, Volume I. New York: WM. H. Wise & Co., 1929. Print.

Goethe, Johann Wolfgang von. *Goethe: Scientific Studies*. Ed. and trans. Douglas Miller. Princeton, NJ: Princeton UP, 1988. Print.

Harding, Walter. *The Days of Henry Thoreau: A Biography*. Princeton, NJ: Princeton UP, 1982. Print.

——. *A Thoreau Handbook*. New York UP, 1959. Print.

Huffert, Anton M. "Thoreau as a Teacher, Lecturer, and Educational Thinker." UMI, 2005.

Imanishi, Kinji. *Shinka towa Nanika* [*What is Evolution?*]. Tokyo: Kodansha Gakujutsu-Bunko, 2008. Print.

Lebeaux, Richard. "The Many Paths to and from Walden." *Approaches to Teaching Thoreau's Walden and Other Works*. Ed. Richard J. Schneider. New York: The Modern Language Association of America, 1996. 63–69. Print.

Miller, John P. *Transcendental Learning: The Educational Legacy of Alcott, Emerson, Fuller, Peabody and Thoreau*. Charlotte, North Carolina: Information Age Publishing, Inc., 2011. Print.

Monod, Jacques. *Chance and Necessity: An Essay on the Natural Philosophy of Modern Biology*. Trans. Austryn Wainhouse. New York: Vintage Books, 1972. Print.

Nabhan, Gary Paul. "Foreword." *Henry D. Thoreau: Faith in a Seed*. Ed. Bradley P. Dean. Washington, D.C.: Island Press, 1993. Print.

Nakazawa, Shinichi. *Minakata Mandara* [*Minakata Mandala*]. Tokyo: Kawade-Shobo Shinsha, 2015. Print.

Ono, Michiko. *Henry D. Thoreau: His Educational Philosophy and Observation of Nature*. Tokyo: Otowa-Shobo Tsurumi-Shoten, 2013. Print.

Peirce, Charles Sanders. "The Doctrine of Necessity Examined." *Charles S. Peirce: The Essential Writings*. Ed. Edward C. Moore. Amherst, New York: Prometheus Books, 1998. Print.

Richardson, Robert D., Jr. *Henry Thoreau: A Life of the Mind*. Berkeley: U of California P, 1986. Print.

Robinson, David M. *Natural Life: Thoreau's Worldly Transcendentalism*. Ithaka: Cornell UP, 2004. Print.

Sattelmeyer, Robert. "Introduction." *Henry David Thoreau: Natural History Essays*. Salt Lake City: Peregrine Smith, Inc., 1980. Print.

Suzuki, Daisetsu. *Zen Hakko* [*Eight Lectures on Zen*]. Tokyo: Kadokawa Gakugei Shuppan, 2013. Print.

Thoreau, Henry David. "Autumnal Tints." *The Selected Works of Thoreau*. Ed. Walter Harding. Boston: Houghton Mifflin Company, 1975. 686–711. Print.

——. *Henry D. Thoreau: Faith in a Seed*. Ed. Bradley P. Dean. Washington, D.C.: Island P, 1993. Print.

——. *The Journal of Henry David Thoreau: In Fourteen Volumes Bound as Two, Vols. I-VII*. Ed. Bradford Torrey and Francis H. Allen. New York; Dover Publications,

Inc., 1962. Print; *Ditto, Vols. VIII–XIV*, 1962. Print.
——. "The Succession of Forest Trees." *The Selected Works of Thoreau*. Ed. Walter Harding. Boston: Houghton Mifflin Company, 1975. 732–744. Print.
——. *Walden*. Ed. J. Lyndon Shanley. Princeton, NJ: Princeton UP, 1971. Print.
——. "Wild Apples." *The Selected Works of Thoreau*. Ed. Walter Harding. Boston: Houghton Mifflin, 1975. 711–731. Print.
Tsurumi, Kazuko. *Minakata Kumagusu: Suiten no Shiso* [*Kumagusu Minakata: The Idea of the Convergence*]. Tokyo: Fujiwara-Shoten, 2009. Print.

This essay is a revised version of my paper "Thoreau's Views on Growth in Relation to His Observation of Nature," read at the 2015 Thoreau Society Annual Gathering in Concord, Massachusetts, on July 10, 2015.

"Silence Was Audible": Views on Music in the Works of Dwight, Thoreau and *The Blithedale Romance*

Fumiko Takeno

In Nathaniel Hawthorne's *The Blithedale Romance* (1852), there are many allusions to music. This is partly because the Transcendentalists, on whom the fiction was modeled, were devoted to music. Deeply influenced by Romanticism, they began to look to music as a cultural device to promote national unity. This paper explores the views of music amongst the nineteenth-century Boston literati, examining how three writers, Nathaniel Hawthorne, Henry David Thoreau, and John S. Dwight describe music in their works. Dwight, the future music critic, played an important role in the Brook Farm commune as a music teacher, where *The Blithedale Romance* is staged. Thoreau, as one of the transcendentalists and a disciple of Emerson, knew Dwight, often met Hawthorne, and admired music. They all shared the same point of view on music, which they found to be a universal language that helps people unite through its resonance. For them, music is "motion" and a vibration of one's feeling which "travels on until it becomes a vibration" in the other's feeling (Dwight, *Dwight's Journal of Music* 3: 156; hereafter abbreviated as *DJM*). In this sense, their concept of music is closely related to transmission, mobility, and space. However, there are differences in them respecting the idea of "universal harmony" that music was supposed to aim for. Centering on the works of Dwight, Thoreau, and *The Blithedale Romance*, I will discuss how they share and differ in the concept of music in their writings.[1]

I

When we read *The Blithedale Romance*, we may notice that it has numerous musical metaphors. The main character and narrator of the story, Coverdale, claims that in his life he has nothing to do but to "make pretty verses" and "to play a part . . . in our pastoral" (3: 43). Here, "a pastoral" or "a pastorale" refers to an "opera, cantata, or other vocal work, the subject of which is pastoral," other than a "poem, play or the like, in which the life of shepherds is portrayed" (*Oxford Dictionary of English*). It signifies a madrigal, the ancestor of operas in the history of music. Other characters in the story surely join his pastoral. Priscilla, a seamstress, is described as a "delicate" "instrument," and "fragile harp-strings" (3: 75); her father, Moodie, is an "instrument long out of tune, the strings of which have ceased to vibrate smartly and sharply" (3: 87); and philanthropist Hollingsworth persists in "such prolonged fiddling upon one string" (3: 56). Voices from the woods sound like "airs of merriment" "solemn organ-pipes should pour out" (3: 209). Adding to those voices, Coverdale pays attention to Zenobia's voice, describing it as "a fine, frank, mellow voice," "clear and melodious, but, just then, with something unnatural in its chord" with "musical, yet haughty accents" (3: 14, 212, 190). D. H. Lawrence rightly notices this musical air in the story and points out that the transcendentalists "met to till the soil," "tingling in tune with the Oversoul, like so many strings of a super-celestial harp," but that "all the music they made was the music of their quarrelling" (112).

This musical atmosphere in *The Blithedale Romance* partly owes to the transcendentalists' acute interests in music. The guru of the transcendentalists, Ralph Waldo Emerson, loved music and, if we follow Mark N. Grant's words, "set the tone for the group's exaltation of music" (38). Grant explains that the transcendentalists published eight literary magazines between 1835 and 1850, seven of which devoted at least one issue exclusively to classical music; in all, 183 articles on Euterpean art were published. Chief among these magazines were *the Dial* edited by Emerson and *the Harbinger* edited by George Ripley, the founder of Brook Farm. Charles Anderson Dana and Dwight among them, whom Hawthorne mentions in the preface of *The Blithedale Romance*, were prolific contributors of articles about music to *The Dial* and *The Harbinger* (Grant 37; Delano 125).[2]

The transcendentalists were deeply influenced by German and British Romanticism, which prioritized music among the arts. According to Alison Byerly, in poems by Wordsworth, Coleridge, Shelley, and Keats we see the same figures repeatedly: the bird's song representing the poet's ideal; the music of nature, whose winds and waters create a universal harmony in which the poet hopes to participate; and the Aeolian harp, the classic Romantic figure for the poetic imagination (37). In the world of *The Blithedale Romance*, Coverdale plays such a Romantic poet. He hopes to "make verses, tuning the rhythm to the breezy symphony," "something that shall have the notes of wild-birds twittering through it, or a strain like the wind-anthem in the woods," and enjoys watching the swallows twitter "a cheery anthem" (3: 99, 14, 118, respectively). He observes girls in the community to be wilder and more untamable than boys, "yet with a harmonious propriety through all" (3: 73). He also notices that "their steps and "their voices" "keep consonance with a strain of music, inaudible to us" (3: 73). We could trace Coverdale's phrase, "a strain of music, inaudible to us," back to the "sphere music" of the Greek philosophy. Milton writes likewise in his *Arcades* that "after the heavenly tune, which none can hear / of human mould with gross unpurged ear" (lines 72–73), following Pythagoras' idea of the celestial harmony.

The music that creates universal harmony is what the Romantic poet would want to participate in; for the transcendentalists, it was what the United States should have aimed for. Scott Gac argues that the transcendentalists believed culture could be a means to demonstrate a national spirit and could unify the people (157). It was also believed that music reigned supreme among other arts (Gac 156; McClendon 25). One of the transcendentalists, Christopher Cranch, held that listening to music delivers us "through chaos and through night, and seeming dissonance to concord and light" (qtd. in Gac 156; 524). Dwight also thinks much of the role of music in "the joining of individuality with universality" (Saloman 124). In the age of heated dispute over slavery, or the Native American removal, which consequently divided the nation, the transcendentalists were far more interested in the unifying characteristics of music.

II

Dwight and Hawthorne might have had some similarities between them, although they clearly differed in their views regarding things. In the then popular sonnet, *Fables for Critics* (1848), James Russell Lowell wrote of their proximity in nature: "When Nature was shaping him [Hawthorne] in clay," Lowell sings, she used "some finer-grained stuff for a woman" to make him fully and perfectly a man. And Nature, delighted at her success, "tried it again" in Dwight. She sang to her work during her operations, and "the music had somehow got mixed with the whole" (Lowell 65). As Lowell rightly observes, Dwight, who was widely known as the "transcendental pope of music" (qtd. in Gac 153; Lowens 71), was one of the most ardent advocates of music. In his articles, he repeatedly stated that "music is a universal language"; according to him, it is "the natural language of enthusiasm," which tends to "unite and blend and harmonize all who may come within its sphere" (*DJM* 3: 156, 30: 314). Dwight even seriously considered that music could be a practical instrument of international communication. In another article, he mentions his dreams of a world where one can communicate using this universal language:

> Because Music is the natural language of Sentiments . . . . For it would speak a universal language, which Asia and America alike may comprehend, with no interpreter and no dictionary but the heart, out of which and to which proccedeth [sic] all music. (*DJM* 3:74)

It should be noted that Dwight's vision encompassed the whole world. The Eurasian continent and the United States would communicate with each other through music.

Thoreau shares Dwight's idea. He dreams a harmonious world, which he thought was occasionally expressed through the music by Beethoven, the transcendentalists' favorite composer:

> In a world of peace and love music would be the universal language, and men greet each other in the fields in such accents, as a Beethoven now utters at rare intervals from a distance. (qtd. in Rhodes 327)[3]

Even though both Thoreau and Dwight were transcendentalists, their viewpoints differed in many aspects. In the so-called transcendentalist club meetings, Thoreau affirmed Emerson's appreciation of the independence of the solitary individual, while Dwight favored Ripley's vision of communal harmony (Saloman 10). Dwight supported the Brook Farm and played a significant role in the commune's development, while Thoreau questioned its very concept. Nonetheless, they had a similar utopian view of music.

As exemplified by the above quotations, their idea of music includes a concept of space and resonance among people. Further, Dwight concludes that music is a type of motion that gives power to people. He suggests that "[s]ound is generated by motion" and music is the direct "product of Motion" ("Music" 28; "The Age of Music" 156). In other words, "[i]t does not rest," and it "hurries us away with it" ("Music" 28). Furthermore, the power of music can move your body. "You listen" to music and "are transported" ("Academy of Music" 56) to another world. Undoubtedly, music can be defined as "a sound that is produced by vibrating strings, reeds, the human vocal chords, and other instruments" (Sally Driscoll, n.pag.); however, according to Dwight, the functions of music are not limited to the vibration of strings alone:

> If I sing, a vibration of my soul, my feeling, imparts itself to the atmospheric medium, and travels on until it becomes a vibration in your soul, your feeling.
>
> The spiritual fact of Music corresponds precisely with this physical fact. Its business is wholly with the moving part of human life. (*DJM* 3: 156)

Music travels by "penetrating all the walls of time and space" ("Music" 28). Therefore, Dwight sees that music has the power to move people, unite them, and resonate with their feelings.

The descriptions by Thoreau are full of vibration and mobility, as well; in fact, Kenneth W. Rhoads admits that Thoreau "frequently speaks of the music of nature in terms of vibration, or hum" (322). Thoreau feels that music "lifts" him "up above all the dust and mire of the universe," and when you are "attuned to the universe," you are "fitted to hear" and your being "moves in a sphere of melody" (*The Writings of Henry David Thoreau: Journal* 5: 271–72; hereafter abbreviated as *WHD*). He thinks that "[t]he human soul is a silent harp in God's quire whose strings need only to be swept by the divine breath" (*WHD* 1:50). In his work, he describes listening to the distant sound of a bell and appreciating the vibration:

> Heard at a distance, the sound of a bell acquires a certain vibratory hum, as it were from the air through which it passes, like a harp. All music is a harp music at length, as if the atmosphere were full of strings vibrating to this music. It is not the mere sound of the bell, but the humming in the air, that enchants me, ... All sound heard at a great distance thus tends to produce the same music, vibrating the strings of the universal lyre. (*WHD* 4: 142–43)

Thoreau joins with Dwight's belief in the empathetic power of music, although we could clearly see their difference. A vibration of one's soul is transmitted into another's for Dwight, while Thoreau "feels his blood flow in his veins" when he "hears a strain of music" (*WHD* 1:186), "because there must something in me [him] as lofty that hears" (*WHD* 1: 362). Thoreau is more interested in his personal experiences.

III

Theoretically, music is a system of human construction that arranges sounds in a melody and combines them in harmony, classifying pitches into modes and keys, rhythms into meters, and sounds into timbres (Lack 43, Wolfe n. pag.). While admiring music as the natural language of religious sentiment, "which seeks only universal harmony and order" ("Music" 31), and considering that music "delivers you from . . . all too individual aim or consciousness" and "bids your being melt and blend with its all-permeating sentiment" ("Academy of Music" 56); Dwight is fully aware of this musical feature.

However, Hawthorne expresses his concerns about the negative aspects of resonance and unification in music in his romance. In Chapter 14, "Eliot's Pulpit," we read how Coverdale's utopian idea of music is shattered by Hollingsworth. When Zenobia insists that she lifts up her "own voice, in behalf of woman's wider liberty" (3: 120), Hollingsworth rejects her idea. He claims that a woman's office is "that of the Sympathizer; the unreserved, unquestioning Believer" and considers women to be "the Echo of God's own voice, pronouncing—'It is well done!'" (122). In other words, while Zenobia expresses her hope to use her "living voice" to "compel the world to recognize the light of her [women's] intellect and the depth of her heart" (120), Hollingsworth urges women to be the echo of God's own voice. This assertion reflects the ancient Greek philosophy of the "music of the spheres," according to which string instruments echo the sound sent by gods to reveal a harmonious universe to humans.

Hollingsworth's assertion reminds us of Jacques Attali's discussion on a musical metaphor in Shakespeare's *Troilus and Cressida*. Attali analyzes the frequently quoted monologue of Ulysses and specifies that it clearly defines order as a system of vibrating chords separated by intangible differential intervals. Ulysses says: "Take but degree away, untune that string / And hark what discord follows!" (Attali 62; act I, scene iii, lines 109–110) Attali concludes that without exception, the strong prevail, while the weak are crushed. Harmony is the hierarchical system that protects the weak; however, it keeps intact the fixed differences between the rich and the poor.

Hollingsworth claims that women, who are "poor, miserable, abortive creatures," should be in their "own sphere." He would call upon his own sex "to use its physical force, that unmistakeable [sic] evidence of sovereignty, to scourge them back within their proper bounds" if women seek to "stray beyond it" (Hawthorne 3: 123). Hence, Hollingsworth's assertion resonates with Attali's hierarchical system in terms of maintaining fixed differences, thereby preserving a dog-eat-dog world. In the world of *The Blithedal Romance*, Dwight's ideal could turn out to be a dystopia.

In 1841, Hawthorne left Brook Farm after staying for a few months. In Concord, he became acquainted with Thoreau, who occasionally visited the Hawthornes to listen "to the music of the sphere," which Hawthorne "packed into the musical box" for his "private convenience" (Hawthorne 8: 316). In the same year, Thoreau sketched the repressive power of music in his journal:

> . . . when he speaks, too, does man assert his superiority. He conquers the spaces with his voice, as well as the lion. . . . A strong musical voice imposes a new order and harmony upon nature; from it as a centre the law is promulgated to the universe. . . . The brute growls to secure obedience; he threatens. The man speaks as though obedience were already secured. (*WHD* 1: 248)

Thoreau simply expresses the natural order of beasts snarling to hold its power through this statement; however, this passage echoes the scene portrayed in "Eliot's Pulpit," indicating the Hawthonesque dystopia.

IV

As Jannika Bock has argued, Thoreau had a high regard for Greek myth, and repeatedly alluded to the Aeolian harp (109–110). Thoreau's journals show that he considers nearly every sound in nature as music, especially the celestial one. He listens to the telegraph wire vibrating in the wind and calls it "the telegraph harp" (*WHD* 4: 238) and perceives that "[a]ll sound heard at a great distance thus tends to produce the same music, vibrating the strings of the universal lyre" (*WHD* 4: 142–43). The term "universal lyre" indicates that his view of music originates from the ancient Greeks' "music of the spheres," which comprises celestial sounds from the universe that are imperceptible to human ears. As mentioned earlier, according to Greek mythology, the lyre is the instrument of Apollo, a god of music, who is considered to send the external sound as music to remind us of universal harmony.

Coverdale also tries to listen to this imperceptible music in *the Blithedale Romance*:

> Girls are incomparably wilder and more effervescent than boys, more untameable, . . . breaking continually into new modes of fun, yet with harmonious propriety through all. Their steps, their voices, appear free as the wind, but keep consonance with a strain of music, inaudible to us. (Hawthorne 3: 73)

Furthermore, he mentions Priscilla's peculiarities and imagines that "[h]idden things were visible to her" and "silence was audible" (3: 187). For Coverdale, like Milton's *Arcades*, celestial music is inaudible and the one that we aspire to hear.

On the contrary, Thoreau was certain that he could hear the ideal music of the spheres:

> To ears that are expanded what a harp this world is! The occupied ear thinks that beyond the cricket no sound can be heard, but there is an immortal melody that may be heard morning, noon, and night, by ears that can attend, and from time to time this man or that hears it, having ears that were made for music. (*WHD* 3: 323)

Ample examples illustrate that Thoreau believed he could hear the ideal music. According to him, every morning, he wakes up to music that no one but him can hear and feels his "Maker blessing" him. Thoreau was convinced that "to the sane man the world is a musical instrument" (*WHD* 3: 275). Further, he insisted that the "prophane [sic] never hear music," whereas "the holy ever hear it." For him, music "is God's voice, the divine breath audible" (*WHD* 1: 144). Moreover, Thoreau's preference for sounds "[h]eard at a distance" (*WHD* 4: 142–43) reminds us of the heavenly message from the universe. Hence, we can imagine him standing alone in the forest listening intently to the sounds of music, which offers us a stark contrast to Coverdale who tries to catch the harmony through social relations in the Blithedale commune. Thoreau's concern is the relationship between the self and the universe, to the exclusion of the society.

Dwight's interest is limited to instrumental music. In his article, he recommends listening avidly to Handel, Haydn, Mozart, and Beethoven, yet he shares Thoreau's view of the Greek myth in that he believes that music "is God's alphabet, and not man's" ("Music" 31). Sill his argument mainly focuses on the impact of music on the society. As late as 1870, he insisted on the role of music in the integration of the United States, saying that "a great mixed people of all races, overrunning a vast continent" need music to "tone down our 'fierce democracy'" (*DJM* 30: 313). His idea of music which integrates a vast continent reflects the sense of space quite different from the one we find in Thoreau's sound "heard at a distance." As Sterling F. Delano puts it, Dwight was, after all, an individual committed to a specific social and economic program for the improvement of humanity (127). He was "the conscience of music criticism in nineteenth-century America" (Grant 52), struggling to pave the way to embody the lofty ideal of the transcendentalists through music. Although *Dwight's Journal of Music* ceased publication by the end of the nineteenth century, Dwight is still recognized as the first major music critic to have established the classical music tradition in New England.

Even though these three literates hold the same utopian views of music, derived from Romanticism and Greek philosophy, their focus varies when we look at the details. Dwight sought the way to link all human beings to achieve universal harmony. Music is surely the art form to make one feel united in concord for Dwight, but not for Hawthorne who found the idealism of Brook Farm dubious. Hawthorne believed that this harmony is necessarily accompanied by the oppression of the weak and women. At the end of the *Blithedale Romance*, Hollingsworth who tried to oppress the weak for the purpose of social reformation turns out to be confined in his planned correctional institution, while Coverdale, at his middle age, confesses his suppressed emotions of love for Priscilla in vain.

Hawthorne once wrote that Nature seemed to adopt Thoreau as her special child, and showed him secrets which few others were allowed to witness (8: 354). Certainly, Thoreau himself believed that he could hear divine music inaudible to others. He even mentions in his essay that silence is audible (*WHD* 1: 60–61; *The Writings of Henry David Thoreau: A Week on the Concord and Merrimack Rivers* 391). His confidence to catch the music of the spheres, which Coverdale aspired to acquire as well as Priscilla's love without success, stemmed partly from his quest for a stronger individuality, and also from his rejection of "a hierarchic governmental rule" (Bock 234), and his acceptance of all sounds as music. Thus, John Cage, a composer and one of the most celebrated cultural figures of the twentieth century praises Thoreau who "paid attention to each sound, whether it was 'musical' or not" (qtd. in Bock 66), and wrote 4'33", the so-called silent piece, sharing Thoreau's idea of silence (Shultis 52, Ono 137). If we follow Ryuta Imafuku's words, Cage could be taken as a "spiritual brother" of Thoreau (68). Thoreau's ears, his attentiveness to every sound, opened up his self to the world, which resonates with Cage's view of the modern music; Cage's words testify that Thoreau's thoughts on music have been transmitted to the present transcending time and space.

Note

1 Nathaniel Hawthorne's view on music has been partly discussed in my previous paper in 2006.

2 In the preface, Hawthorne mentions several transcendentalists who were involved in the functions of the Brook Farm, including Ripley, Dwight, and Dana:

> The Author cannot close his reference to this subject, without expressing a most earnest wish that some one of the many cultivated and philosophic minds, which took an interest in that enterprise, might now give the world its history. Ripley, with whom rests the honorable paternity of the Institution, Dana, Dwight, Channing, Burton, Parker, for instance. . . . (3: 3)

3 Thoreau also writes the similar observation in his journal:

> There is as much music in the world as virtue—at length music will be the universal language, and men greet each other in the fields in such accents as a Beethoven now utters but rarely and indistinctly. (*WHD* 1: 165)

Works Cited

Attali, Jaques. *Noise: The Political Economy of Music*. Trans. Brian Massumi. Minneapolis: The U of Minnesota P, 1985. Print.

Bock, Jannika. *Concord in Massachusetts, Discord in the World: The Writings of Henry Thoreau and John Cage*. Frankfurt am Main: Peter Lang, 2008. Print.

Byerly, Alison. *Realism, Representation, and the Arts in Nineteenth-Century Literature*. Cambridge: Cambridge UP, 1997. Print.

Delano, Sterling F. *The Harbinger and New England Transcendentalism: A Portrait of Associationism in America*. Cranbury, NJ: Associated UP, 1983. Print.

Driscoll, Sally. "Music." *Salem Press Encyclopedia*. 2016. Web. 24 August 2016.

Dwight, John S. "Academy of Music—Beethoven's Symphonies." *The Pioneer: A Literary and Critical Magazine*. Vol.1. Boston: Leland and Whiting, 1843. 56–60. Internet Archive, Web. 3 March 2016.

——. *Dwight's Journal of Music: A Paper of Art and Literature*. Vols. 3–4. Boston: Edward L. Balch, 1854. Internet Archive, Web. 3 March 2016.

——. *Dwight's Journal of Music: A Paper of Art and Literature*. Vols. 29–30. Boston:

Oliver Pitson and Company, 1871. *Internet Archive*. Web. 3 March 2016.
——. "Music." *Aesthetic Papers*. Ed. Elizabeth Peabody. NY: G. P. Putnam, 1849. 28–36. *Internet Archive*. Web. 3 March 2016.
Gac, Scott. "The Eternal Symphony Afloat: The Transcendentalists' Quest for a National Culture." *ATQ* 16(2002): 151–64. Print.
Grant, Mark N. *Maestros of the Pen: A History of Classical Music Criticism in America*. Boston: Northern UP, 1998. Print.
Hawthorne, Nathaniel. *The Centenary Edition of the Works of Nathaniel Hawthorne*. Eds. William Charvat et al. 23 vols. Columbus: Ohio State UP, 1962–97. Print.
Imafuku, Ryuta. "Mushin no Āchisuto." ["An Artist of Emptiness: Henry David Thoreau and John Cage."] *Studies in Henry David Thoreau* 40 (2014): 68–74. Print.
Lack, Tony. "Sounds of Silence." *Interdisciplinary Humanities* 32 (2015): 33–47. Print.
Lawrence, D. H. *Studies in Classic American Literature*. 1923. London: Penguin Books, 1977. Print.
Lowell, James Russell. *Fables for Critics by James Russell Lowell with Vignette Portraits of the Autors de Quibus Fabula Narratur*. London: Gay and Bird, n.d. Internet Archive, Web. 24 August 2016.
Lowens, Irving. "Writings about Music in the Periodicals of American Transcendentalism (1835–50)." *Journal of the American Musicological Society* 10.2 (1957): 71–85. Print.
McClendon, Aaron. "'for not in words can it be spoken': John Sullivan Dwight's Transcendental Music Theory and Herman Melville's *Pierre; or, The Ambiguities*." *ATQ* 19 (2005): 23–36. Print.
Milton, John. *Arcades with Introduction, Notes and Indexes*. Ed. A.W. Verity. London: Cambridge UP, 1908. *Internet Archive*. Web. 3 March 2016.
Ono, Michiko. *Henry David Thoreau: His Educational Philosophy and Observation of Nature*. Tokyo: Otowa-Shobo Tsurumi-Shoten, 2013. Print.
"Pastoral." Def. B I 3a. *The Oxford Dictionary of English*. 2nd ed. 2003. CD-ROM.
"Pastorale." Def. 1b. *The Oxford Dictionary of English*. 2nd ed. 2003. CD-ROM.
Rhoads, Kenneth W. "Thoreau: The Ear and the Music." *American Literature* 46 (1974): 313–328. Print.
Saloman, Ora Frishberg. *Beethoven's Symphonies and J. S. Dwight: The Birth of American Criticism*. Boston: Northeastern UP, 1995. Print.
Shultis, Christopher. *Silencing the Sounded Self: John Cage and the American Experimental Tradition*. Hanover: UP of New England, 1998. Print.
Takeno, Fumiko. "Buraizudēru Romansu no Oto to Ongaku." ["The Silence Was Audible: Sound and Music in *The Blithedale Romance*."] *Studies in American Literature* 42 (2006): 1–14.
Thoreau, Henry D. *The Writings of Henry David Thoreau: Journal*. 8 vols. to date. Elizabeth Hall Witherell, gen. ed. Princeton: Princeton UP, 1981–. Print.
——. *The Writings of Henry David Thoreau: A Week on the Concord and Merrimack Rivers*. Eds. Carl F. Hovde et al. Princeton: Princeton UP, 2004. Print.
Wolfe, George. "Henry Thoreau: 'True Musician and Harmonist.'" *Ball State University Libraries* (2009): n. pag. Web. 24 August 2016.

This paper was presented at a symposium organized by the Nagoya University American Literature / Culture Society and the Chukyo University Postcolonial / Tourism Research Group in Nagoya in 2016.

This work was supported by JSPS KAKENHI Grant Number JP16K02515.

Emerson and Thoreau as Writers in Hawthorne's Autobiographical Sketch, "The Old Manse"

Atsuko Oda

In July 1842—when Hawthorne and his wife, having accepted Emerson's invitation, moved to Concord to live their honeymoon life in the Emerson family's estate, which Hawthorne was to call "the old Manse"—Emerson had established himself as a major literary figure with his controversial lectures and the publication of his second book, *Essays: First Series*. During Hawthorne's residence in the old Manse, Emerson published his third book, *Essays: Second Series*, including his masterpieces, "The Poet" and "Experience." As Larry Reynolds aptly pointed out, Hawthorne entered "an Emerson world" and lived for three years within "the subtle influence" (1: 25)[1] of Emerson (61). It can be easily imagined that Hawthorne might have experienced rivalry or an inferiority complex as a result of his sustained encounter with Emerson. My argument, however, is that Hawthorne learned a precious lesson from his reluctant intercourse with Emerson: "The Old Manse" is a writer's autobiography of growth, or a private record of an allegorist's metamorphosis into an Emersonian symbolist. So we can understand the honest tribute to Emerson by Hawthorne, one of the best contemporary critics of Emerson's works, and enjoy a vivid description of the characteristics of Emerson's and Thoreau's writings.

Hawthorne was one of the intellectuals whom Emerson expected to support his project to build "a good neighborhood" (*The Journals and Miscellaneous Notebooks of Ralph Waldo Emerson* 8: 172; hereafter abbreviated as *JMN*), that is, a stimulating literary community. Since 1836 when Emerson lost his younger brother, Charles, who had been a good literary companion, Emerson must have been seeking a substitute for him. In 1838 Emerson met Thoreau who came back to his native village, Concord, graduated from Harvard College and then, in 1841, moved to Emerson's house as an assistant to both him and his family. One of Thoreau's biographers, Robert Richardson Jr. observed that Thoreau learned a great deal from Emerson but that he differed from his mentor in the very high value he assigned to the written word whereas, in a sense, Emerson distrusted language (*Henry Thoreau: A Life of the Mind* 95; hereafter abbreviated as *HT*). And Hawthorne responded to this "distrust" of the stability of language which characterizes Emerson's symbolism. Emerson's community worked well for Hawthorne, which is shown by his stories and sketches collected in *Mosses from an Old Manse*. Apparently most of his stories, including "The Celestial Railroad" and "Rappaccini's Daughter," drew on materials from his society in Concord. In these stories Hawthorne gives a satirical description of transcendentalists as unrealistic dreamers and the introductory sketch "The Old Manse" seems to be a typical sketch of the place and people of Concord, a miniature *Walden*, in which Hawthorne distilled his three years.[2] Neither Emerson nor Thoreau were good writers of fiction. But their work in the nonfiction prose genres of autobiography and essay stimulated Hawthorne so much in their styles and contents that he ventured to write two "autobiographical" sketches, "The Old Manse" and "The Custom House," to record his epoch-making days with Emerson and Thoreau. These sketches, read in succession, tell how his masterpiece, *The Scarlet Letter*, was conceived and refined by his close observations of Concord literati.

At the Emerson's Centenary in 1903 Henry James visited Concord. The village then was associated with Emerson's genius, followed by Hawthorne's, and James paid "Thoreau tribute in a hasty parenthetical phrase" (Buell 321). Now Thoreau is the most representative man of Concord of the three. Henry James's ranking is reversed. This situation might have been predicted by Hawthorne. At first Hawthorne favored Thoreau over Emerson. His well-known description of Emerson in his journal written just after he moved to Concord—"Mr. Emerson is a great searcher for facts; but they seem to melt away and become unsubstantial in his grasp" (8: 336)—helped establish Emerson as a mystic in contrast to Hawthorne as a realist and obscured their common interest in the relation between facts and ideas. Facts were definitely attributed to Thoreau who was later to declare that "I went to the woods . . . to front only the essential facts of life" in *Walden* (88). Hawthorne was impressed with Thoreau's "Natural History of Massachusetts" whereas Emerson, who had advised him to write it, did not think much of it (Richardson, *HT* 116).

Hawthorne's own interest at this time was manifested as follows:

> In the humblest event, I resolved to achieve a novel, that should evolve

> some deep lesson, and should possess physical substance enough to stand alone. (10: 5)

To become a mature novelist instead of an allegorist, Hawthorne thought he needed to give "physical substance" to an idea. Indeed, as he became more familiar with these Concord literati, both Thoreau and Emerson raised Hawthorne's awareness as a writer and a critic. Especially in Thoreau he found the congenial spirit of a realist. But at the end of "The Old Manse" he abstracted the sketch as "pages about a moss-grown country parsonage, and his life within its walls, and on the river, and in the woods, and the influence that wrought upon him, from all these sources" (10: 32). Facts of nature and their influence on humanity are two fundamentals of which Emerson's perception consists. So Hawthorne's mockery of Emersonian language is ambiguous and implies his approval of Emerson's views.

Later, in "The Custom-House," Hawthorne repeatedly refers to the Old Manse and, especially, to the happy days when he enjoyed "the invigorating charm of Nature" (1: 35) in Concord at the very meaningful phase in his autobiographical narrative, that is, just before and after the elaborate description of "a neutral territory" (1: 36). For the first time since he left Maine in his boyhood, Hawthorne enjoyed physical nature (Reynolds 62) and his observations written down in his journal show how he liked it. The Nature of Concord was a kind of "neutral territory . . . where the Actual and the Imaginary may meet" in Hawthorne's life. So a "mystic symbol, subtly communicating itself to my sensibilities, but evading the analysis of my mind" (1: 31), could be used as a comprehensible language in Concord. Hawthorne could locate himself somewhere between Thoreau's imagination into physical nature and Emerson's into intellectual power. In what follows, I explore how Hawthorne learned from both these writers as he developed his own views on nature and originality, symbolist methods, and double-consciousness.

1. The Old Parsonage

As Emerson underestimated fiction in general, even Hawthorne's works were not spared. He thought throughout his life that they did not deserve Hawthorne's genius. In September 1842 Emerson wrote in his journal as follows:

> N. Hawthorne's reputation as a writer is very pleasing fact, because his

> writing is not good for anything, and this is a tribute to the man. (*JMN* 7: 465)

Emerson respects Hawthorne's intellectual power which he thinks cannot find its own expression in his writings. Even *The Scarlet Letter* could not change his judgment.[3] He read major novelists like Scott and Dickens and complained of the superficialities of their works. Richard Poirier discusses Emerson's impatience with the premeditations required of the novelist to contrive the plot, and quotes an interesting passage Emerson wrote after he was "caught in the foolish trap & read & read to the end of the novel [Scott's *Quentin Durward*]" in 1841 (*The Renewal of Literature* 167–68):

> Then as often before I feel indignant to have been duped and dragged after a foolish boy & girl, to see them at last married & portioned & I instantly turned out of doors like a beggar that has followed a gay procession into the castle. . . . These novels will give way by & by to diaries or autobiographies;—captivating books if only a man knew how to choose among what he calls his experiences that which is really his experience, and how to record truth truly! (*JMN* 7: 418)

Emerson contrasts novels with diaries and autobiographies. He believes that human life is based on and confused by so much artificiality and fiction, which distances people from the law of nature, making all things worse. Hawthorne's own complaint against the "scribbling women" (17: 304) was thrown on the same ground as Emerson. Hawthorne was thinking about something different from such novels by calling his works Romance. Emerson told Thoreau to write journals at the very beginning of their intercourse (Richardson, *HT* 7). It was a habit of the educated and professional men. This advice came from a long tradition of Puritan self-reflection. In this cultural context Hawthorne talks about his ancestors' dissatisfaction with the descendant's profession of "a writer of story books" (1: 10) in "The Custom-House." Likewise the Old Manse oppresses and challenges him with the piles of old documents, including sermons and diaries.

Hawthorne introduced his new home, the Old Manse, first as a Puritan heritage and then as a place where Emerson wrote his first book *Nature*, entertaining the reader with a stereotype of Emerson as a strange megalomaniac who superimposes the magnificent images of "the Assyrian dawn and the

Paphian sunset and moonrise" on the horizon of New England (10: 5). But, put side by side with those grim pictures and writings of Puritan ministers, Emerson's work sounds like something of a breakthrough—a dawn for the dark heritage of Puritans. Browsing "a vast folio Body of Divinity; too corpulent a body, it might be feared, to comprehend the spiritual element of religion" (10: 18) and other venerable books in the garret, he concludes that they lack "any living thought, which should burn like a coal of fire, or glow like an inextinguishable gem" (10: 19). Hawthorne enlarges his attack to include the worse conditions of "the frigidity of the modern productions" (10: 20). Those metaphors of fire and gem for living thought seem to be very common and they are, especially, Hawthorne's pet metaphors used in his works from "The Great Carbuncle" to *The Blithedale Romance*, and they are also Emerson's as his main image of the mind which creates living thought are derived from "a volcano" (24) and its variation is seen in the opening paragraph of "Experience" which laments the present conditions of life, where nature has been too "sparing of her fire" (471). Hawthorne comprehends Emerson's view of nature and spirit better than any of their contemporaries.

Emerson wrote in the journal of 1846 that "Hawthorne invites his readers too much into his study, opens the process before them. As if the confectioner should say to his customers Now let us make the cake" (*JMN* 9: 405). This comment is true of "The Old Manse," too, where Hawthorne features the refreshing vigor of Emerson's words and validates his idea of a symbol, that nature is the vehicle of thought, which he had expressed in the "Language" chapter of *Nature* and then elaborated in "The Poet."

The symbol of spiritual facts or living thought is essential to the romance-novelist as well as the poet and philosopher. So in "The Old Manse" Hawthorne recalled that he studied Emerson's "master-word" which can move a lot of people, whatever "hobgoblins of flesh and blood" they may be. The relevant passage in "The Old Manse" would be the one in which Hawthorne ironically describes Emerson and his followers. But it can be read as a defense of Emerson from misunderstanding rather than criticism against him:

> These hobgoblins of flesh and blood were attracted thither by the wide-spreading influence of a great original Thinker. . . . For myself, there had been epochs of my life, when I, too, might have asked of this prophet the master-word, that should solve me the riddle of the universe; but now, being happy, I felt as if there were no question to be put, and therefore admired

> Emerson as a poet of deep beauty and austere tenderness, but sought nothing from him as a philosopher. . . . But it was impossible to dwell in his vicinity, without inhaling, more or less, the mountain atmosphere of his lofty thought, which, in the brains of some people, wrought a singular giddiness—new truth being as heady as new wine. (10: 30–31)

In the opening sentences Hawthorne playfully implies his wife's admiration for Emerson. She was fascinated with Emerson before Hawthorne. Though he confines his admiration to the poet-aspect of Emerson with reservations about his "original" thought, he shows that he is a better reader of Emerson as a philosopher than other followers afflicted with their "triteness of novelty" (10: 32). Emerson's "original relation to the universe" (7) and reliance on "genius" presuppose the universal, public, moral law of nature which relates them to reality. But the people mocked by Hawthorne are all lonesome hobgoblins who, afflicted with unsubstantial selfhood, abuse Emerson's idea of originality.

The latter part of the quotation recalls the passage in the essay "Experience" in which Emerson compares his "vicinity" to a profound mind to the discovery of inland mountains emerging from the clouds. Hawthorne's reference to "his vicinity" (10: 31) suggests his reading of "Experience" and his consciousness of the similarity between his own sense of the intangible and Emerson's sense of "vicinity." Both "Experience" and "The Poet" explain Emerson's interest in "the flowing or metamorphosis" (456) of thought or the force of life. This is also shared with Hawthorne who represents the flitting moment in which the reality of life reveals itself ranging from the actual to the imaginary. To conclude "The Old Manse," Hawthorne presents the same kind of symbolic river of consciousness as Emerson:

> How narrow—how shallow and scanty too—is the stream of thought that has been flowing from my pen, compared with the broad tide of dim emotions, ideas, and associations, which swell around me from that portion of my existence! (10: 32)

This passage is originally derived from his journal of 1844 (8: 250). Hawthorne found the idea of a symbol of this "broad tide of dim emotions" which is intangible, including what we call sub-consciousness, or life in its existential sense, during his Old Manse period. Hawthorne's "stream of thought" is a linear succession of words he wrote and different from the "floods of life" which stream through humanity and nature in Emerson's *Nature*. The latter is, as it were, a latent and unconscious part of Hawthorne's "broad tide of dim emotions." They both pursue the substantiality of internal life.

2. The Procession as an Emersonian Symbol

The most definite indication of Emerson and Thoreau's influence on Hawthorne is his recognition of the procession as a symbol of the stream of consciousness. Hawthorne presented an impressive procession scene in one of his earliest stories, "My Kinsman, Major Molineux." But this story was not collected in *Mosses from an Old Manse* and was to be finally chosen for *The Snow-Image* (1852). The former contained his recent work, "The Procession of Life." When he turned to writing novels, he preferred symbolizing an actual procession on the street like the one in "My Kinsman, Major Molineux," rather than resorting to his favorite allegorical procession. Historically America at this time witnessed many processions which had come into fashion after the presidential campaigns of Andrew Jackson. "The Procession of Life" is based on such a political procession but is still a sort of Spenserian, allegorical one. Emerson in "The Poet" defines the poet as a perceiver and user of symbols which can express the force of life in concrete forms and says:

> The schools of poets, and philosophers, are not more intoxicated with their symbols, than the populace with theirs. In our political parties, compute the power of badges and emblems. See the great ball which they roll from Baltimore to Bunker hill! In the political procession, Lowell goes in a loom, and Lynn in a shoe, and Salem in a ship. . . . The people fancy they hate poetry, and they are all poets and mystics! (454)

People symbolize their bond of union in a matter which they think represents their life and boast of their force of life in the stream of the procession. Emerson's use of the word "mystics" may imply his criticism of these processions as I discuss below. Hawthorne believes these political processions are a false symbol of life as is evident in "The Procession of Life." All his procession scenes, from "My Kinsman" to *The Marble Faun*, are ambiguous or ominous. This doubt is shared with Emerson and Thoreau. Emerson's comment on Scott quoted above implied the dubious nature of the procession in the disappointment of "a beggar that has followed a gay procession into the castle" (*JMN* 7: 418). Thoreau compares his contemporaries' snobbish interest in costume and manners to the procession in *Walden*:

> I delight to come to my bearings,—not walk in procession with pomp and parade, in a conspicuous place, but to walk even with the Builder of the universe, if I may,—not to live in this restless, nervous, bustling, trivial Nineteenth Century, but stand or sit thoughtfully while it goes by. (320)

They are all individualists who try to resist conformity to the mighty mainstream culture.

Thoreau determinedly detached himself from the procession of "transient and fleeing phenomena" (320) and turned to nature where he found home among flora and fauna. Thoreau's appealing charm lies in his description of this kingdom of nature, a substitute for the human world. For example, he describes fishes at moonlit night as if they were human beings:

> . . . he surveys the midnight economy of the fishes. There they lie in every variety of posture, some on their backs, with their white bellies uppermost, some suspended in mid water, some sculling gently along with a dreamy motion of the fins, and others quite active and wide awake,—a scene not unlike what the human city would present. ("Natural History of Massachusetts" 33)

Compare this passage with Hawthorne's description of the "pond-lily" after which he renamed the boat he had got from Thoreau in "The Old Manse":

> It is a marvel whence this perfect flower derives its loveliness and perfume, springing, as it does, from the black mud over which the river sleeps, and where lurk the slimy eel, and speckled frog, and the mud turtle, whom continual washing cannot cleanse. (10: 7)

Thoreau's description is less allegorical and more physical, symbolical, as well as denser and richer with living animals. Hawthorne was fascinated with his "wild original nature" (8: 353) and enjoyed holding intercourse because it was "like hearing the wind among the boughs of a forest-tree and with all this wild freedom," there was "high and classic cultivation in him too" (8: 369).

And at the same time Hawthorne understood Emerson's complaint about living with Thoreau as he thought that "such a sturdy and uncompromising person is fitter to meet occasionally in the open air" (8: 371). Against the human world, Thoreau could create that novelistic world of nature "which possesses physical substance" Hawthorne longed for. In "The Old Manse," Thoreau told Hawthorne that the ground between the Manse and the battlefield was once an Indian village. Thoreau's convincing tales of Indians illustrated with their relics made Hawthorne vividly imagine the Indian lives in which "the little windrocked papoose swings from the branch of a tree" in the middle of "the broad daylight of reality" (10: 11). Hawthorne, later supported by H. James, complained that all this was antagonistic to the novelist who needs a sophisticated, closely-organized society. Nonetheless, Thoreau's natural history showed Hawthorne that there had been a society worthy of representation in America.

In contrast, Emerson, who himself wished that his words sounded like forest trees as clearly told in his poems like "Woodnotes II," was not content with Thoreau's devotion to nature. Thoreau inherited from Emerson the significance of physical nature to humanity because it had symbolized his own unconscious belief. Emerson gave him a frame of spiritual reference in which he could find the meanings of his actions. So facts he presented became a fable of life, beating and breathing the creativity of nature. But Emerson tried to take one step further to translate the creativity into that of human mind. Emerson illustrated human creativity making its own days by the procession of "the lords of life," a motto to the essay "Experience." In this motto "the lords of life," such as "Use and Surprise, / Surface and Dream," progress in their own guise. It looks like a Spenserian allegory, but "Little man," who is involved in the procession, is not assigned a fixed allegorical meaning and is puzzled:

> Him by the hand dear nature took;
> Dearest nature, strong and kind,
> Whispered, 'Darling, never mind!
> Tomorrow they will wear another face,
> The founder thou! these are thy race!' (469)

This procession expresses the flow of consciousness and successive moods in the essay. Emerson and Thoreau are of the same party which, in the scientific frame of mind, believes in the correspondence between natural and moral laws, and Thoreau could know himself or his own nature, simply relying on the law of nature alone. Emerson thinks it more difficult to know the relation of nature to human life. Hawthorne had never thought much of nature before he moved to Concord but had been devoted to the mystery of human nature. So Emerson and Hawthorne could be of the same party which, in the spiritual frame of mind, seeks to express the genuine life in the complexity of consciousness.

3. The Concord River

Hawthorne's approval of Emersonian symbolism is best expressed in the description of the Concord and Assabeth Rivers. First Hawthorne as well as Thoreau in *A Week on the Concord and Merrimack Rivers* introduces the Concord River in reference to Emerson's poem "Concord Hymn." He parodies Emerson and reverses his heroic tone in "the dark stream which seaward creeps," calling it "the most unexcitable and sluggish stream" (10: 6) and then insists on a humbler token of the fight which is a good contrast to the granite obelisk. Referring to the river which Thoreau called "a huge volume of matter" (*Week* 11) as an idealized stream of time or consciousness and emphasizing its sluggishness to offset Emerson's belief that nature exists for use or that the poet possesses "the power of subordinating nature for the purposes of expression" (34)—all this implies that Hawthorne understands Emersonian symbolism well. So he suggests that the dark river with beautiful reflections should be "a symbol that the earthliest human soul has an infinite spiritual capacity" (10: 8). And then he proceeds to another novelistic episode of the Revolutionary War in his rivalry with Emerson.

What Hawthorne wanted to write most of all about Concord must be the symbolic potential of its rivers because the expansive mirror-image of nature reflected in this dull dark river was a perpetual source of fascination to him. In *The American Notebooks* he records a number of occasions when he found the sky and the earth reflected in the water. He meditates on the difference between the actual scene and its reflection. The following is one example, from the journal of September 18, 1842:

> But, on gazing downward, there they were, the same even to the minutest particular, yet arrayed in ideal beauty, which satisfied the spirit incomparably more than the actual scene. I am half convinced that the reflection is indeed the reality—the real thing which Nature imperfectly images to our grosser sense. At all events, the disembodied shadow is nearest to the soul. (8: 360)

The mirror-image of nature strikes Hawthorne as the embodiment of what Emerson calls that thought which is conveyed by the vehicle of nature. The mirror-image figuratively represents the symbolic language in which matter and mind are entwined. Hawthorne is excited to find himself in the middle of a spiritualized world, or what he later calls "a neutral territory." This experience illuminates Emerson's beliefs that "the whole of nature is a metaphor of the human mind" and that "The laws of moral nature answer to those of matter as fact to face in a glass" (24). To see the actual scene and its reflection in the enticing depth of the river is to see things symbolically in the relation between the material and the ideal, consciousness and sub-consciousness, and the signifier and the signified. Hawthorne recognizes Emerson's fluxional symbols in the mirror-images passing along his boat. So he converts his experience into that of Ellery Channing even though he enjoyed boating by himself and his pleasure of boating was strongly associated with Thoreau.

Indeed Channing wrote a poem titled "Boat-Song" which also deals with the reflection in the stream and Emerson made favorable comments on it in *The Dial* of October 1840. Emerson introduced it as a boat-song in which "the harmony proceeds so manifestly from the poet's mind" (224). Again Hawthorne gives a mock-Emersonian description of the river and the boating with Channing:

> Which, after all, was the most real—the picture, or the original?—the objects palpable to our grosser senses, or their apotheosis in the stream beneath? Surely, the disembodied images stand in closer relation to the soul. But, both the original and the reflection had here an ideal charm; and, had it been a thought more wild, I could have fancied that this river had strayed forth out of the rich scenery of my companion's inner world;—only the vegetation along its banks should then have had an Oriental character. (10: 22)

Reference to "an Oriental character" may be a recollection of or homage to Thoreau as well. But Hawthorne presented "so beautiful a river-scene" he "never could have conceived that there was" (8: 359), a succession of mirror-images, as symbols which could match Emerson's procession of the momentary moods in "Experience." Hiding his alliance with Emerson, Hawthorne makes fun of his idealism by explaining this river as straying forth out of the inner world and by calling such a symbolic interpretation "a thought more wild."

But it was Hawthorne himself who had had regarded the procession in "My Kinsman, Major Molineux" "as if a dream had broken forth from some feverish brain" (11: 228). By the phrase "thought more wild," Hawthorne confesses his tendency to go beyond the actual world to the spiritual realm, which is closer to Emerson's thought than Thoreau's wildness.

Hawthorne once called Emerson a "mystic" and his thought "unsubstantial" in his journal of 1842. But as Richardson says in *Emerson*, Emerson's mysticism, including the exhilaration he felt in crossing a bare common, is mysticism of a commonly occurring and easily accepted sort. And Emerson describes his life in nature as delightful and wild, using "the language of vision and rupture" (228–29). It is similar to Hawthorne's sensitivity to transient feelings which momentarily estrange his protagonists from the ordinary life. Hawthorne's description of boating with Channing goes on like this:

> The painted Indian, who paddled his canoe along the Assabeth, three hundred years ago, could hardly have seen a wilder gentleness, displayed upon its banks and reflected in its bosom, than we did. (10: 23–24)

Notice the identification of Hawthorne with Channing, the recurrence of the combination of physical nature with its reflection and the reference to Indians. As Thoreau wrote that "the Concord is remarkable for the gentleness of its current" (*Week* 9), "a wilder gentleness" also indicates the movement of the river and Thoreau's excellent skill at rowing which he learned by observing Indians (8: 356). This boating tells how happy Hawthorne, who might have had some reservation as usual, had been in Concord, grateful for his companionship with Emerson and Thoreau. Hawthorne refined his idea of language by perceiving the slippery relation between nature and thought and "the freedom which we [they] thereby won from all custom and conventionalism, and fettering influence of man on man" (10: 25). The river appears like an ideal world or "a neutral territory." So "a wilder gentleness," first of all, could be a most beautiful homage to Emerson.

Back at the Old Manse, leaving his sympathy with Emerson behind, Hawthorne presents a common usage of a "symbol" in the foreground, that is, an allegorical interpretation of a hound-shaped cloud crouching over the old Manse as if keeping guard (10: 25–26). But, at the same time, his subtler use of symbolism is working: at the end of the boat trip Hawthorne contrasts the old Manse with the river, saying "how gently did its gray, homely aspect rebuke the speculative extravagance of the day!" (10: 25). He uses the word "extravagance" in the same sense as the word "wild" or "stray." Richard Poirier deals with Emerson's superfluity in his book *Poetry and Pragmatism* and explains it in terms of "human desire to go beyond these usual stopping places in sentences, these nouns, abstractions, concepts that serve the function of homes or still points, making us their dependents" (40). Like Poirier, Hawthorne defends Emerson's view of language as vehicular and transitive, like ferries and horses, not stable like houses. Emerson had differentiated himself, "the poet," from Swedenborg, the mystic, and criticized the mystic for nailing a symbol to one sense though all symbols are fluxional (463). In spite of Hawthorne's ostentatious attachment to the old Manse, he finds new enjoyment in writing about the Concord River which made him aware of the importance of nature and that "extravagance" which Emerson and Thoreau expressed in their works.[4]

4. "Wilder Gentleness": Double Consciousness of Nature and Civilization

Despite the title "The Old Manse," this sketch featured the River. The house by the river is a fundamental form of human civilization. Hawthorne's favorable description of the house can be explained by the personal reason that he and his wife had difficulties finding a place to settle. On the other hand, Emerson's early lecture "Home" suggests that family tragedy might have taught him the ephemerality of personal relations and detachment from materialism (Patterson 26). Hawthorne wrote that "The old Manse is better than a thousand wigwams" (10: 11), or that the hearth of the household-fire was the most sacred place (10: 25). But those words should be read as fluxional symbols. Under the shallow thought, the deep joy of boating which he called "a wilder gentleness" would have come and gone in his mind. He wrote "The Old Manse" while Thoreau was living on Walden Pond. "The Old Manse" can also be said to be a very symbolic record of the mind which wavers between nature and civilization and "wilder gentleness" was the spiritual value shared among Emerson, Hawthorne, and Thoreau. Concord was the place where they could have benefits of both Indians and railroads without concerns about the air pollution which disgusted Emerson when he visited the industrial cities in England. And Concord is not Yosemite. It has an easily approachable nature. So Concord literati can provide good hints on the art of living in nature for the 21st-century urbanites who cannot do without comfortable and convenient lives of consumerism. It was the people in the age of materialism that Emerson in his lecture "The Transcendentalist" spoke to in favor of idealism (193) and mentioned the "double consciousness," or those two states of thought which diverge every moment (205). Hawthorne's phrase "wilder gentleness," which is a kind of oxymoron, touches this "double consciousness."

In *The American Evasion of Philosophy*, Cornel West presents a description of Emerson by Henry James, Sr. as an epigraph, to reveal the source of Emerson's authority as a cultural critic who exerted intellectual and moral leadership, and conveys that Emerson kept lecturing on nature for the cultivation of humanity: "Mr. Emerson's authority to the imagination consists, not in his culture, not in his science, but all simply in himself, in the form of his natural personality" (9–10). Emerson thought that it would take a long time for his contemporaries to accept his scientific view of nature based on the new idea of evolution. Such intellectuals as James Sr. and Hawthorne were not exceptional. But they could respond to his "natural personality," or his "wilder gentleness" as his thoughts crossed borders of civilization for the sake of more genuine human culture.

The Emersonian contrast between house and river is a perpetual symbol of human power to create and recreate life. His disgust of artificiality and reliance on the law of nature can have a new meaning in the present-day world where even the Japanese who have been accustomed to worship nature prefer the artificial, and where it is getting more difficult to locate the border between the natural and the artificial. So far Emerson's emphasis on nature has been obscured by his own symbolic language which allows such remarks as "The pine tree, the river, the bank of flowers before him does not seem to be nature. Nature is still elsewhere" (553). That is how he was replaced by Thoreau as an advocate of nature for our age. Thoreau's language is more physical and focuses on facts of nature which can be palpable. His writings on life in the woods are appealing to more people because they certainly take readers from home to another home in nature where they can imagine that gentleness which is in tune with the law of nature. Thoreau, in a sense, provides a positive view of the flowing of nature and life in the form of a house. But if you hope to sustain gentleness among civilized human beings, Emerson's belief in the power of ideas to change things and his attempt to combine natural history with the moral history of gentleness or kindness will be enduring because of his sane, rational, fluxional language of double consciousness.

Notes

1 All references to Hawthorne's works come from the *Centenary Edition* and appear parenthetically with volume and page number.
2 Lawrence Buell traced the process of sacralization of Thoreau's Walden and noticed that "The Old Manse" had started the tradition of urbanite self-consciousness about entering an oasis of pastoral felicity (323–24).
3 Emerson wrote after the funeral of Hawthorne that "I thought him a greater man than any of his works betray, that there was still a great deal of work in him" (*JMN* 15:59–60). Richard Poirier pointed out Emerson's reference to *The Scarlet Letter* as "ghastly" as well as "powerful." He explains that Emerson thought it "ghastly" to let the accumulations of artificial systems tyrannize your work, as if your own methods cannot modify the systems, including allegorizations and typologies (*The Renewal of Literature* 169).
4 I limit Thoreau's "extravagance" to his novelistic density in describing nature. Richard Poirier notes the development of Emersonian symbols in Thoreau's use of the word "extravagance" in his conclusion to *Walden* (44–47).

Works Cited

Buell, Lawrence. *The Environmental Imagination: Thoreau, Nature Writing, and the Formation of American Culture*. Cambridge: Harvard UP, 1995. Print.

Emerson, Ralph Waldo. *The Journals and Miscellaneous Notebooks of Ralph Waldo Emerson*. 16 vols. Ed. William H. Gilman, Alfred R. Ferguson, George P. Clark, et al. Cambridge: Harvard UP, 1960–82. Print.

——. "New Poetry." *The Dial: A Magazine for Literature, Philosophy, and Religion*, vol. 1. 1840. Reprint. Tokyo: Hon-no-Tomosha, 1999. 220–32. Print.

——. *Ralph Waldo Emerson: Essays and Lectures*. Ed. Joel Porte. New York: Library of America, 1983. Print.

——. *Ralph Waldo Emerson: Collected Poems and Translations*. Ed. Harold Bloom and Paul Kane. New York: Library of America, 1994. Print.

Hawthorne, Nathaniel. *The Centenary Edition of the Works of Nathaniel Hawthorne*. 23 vols. Ed. William Charvat et al. Columbus: Ohio State UP, 1962–97. Print.

Patterson, Anita. *From Emerson to King: Democracy, Race, and the Politics of Protest*. New York: Oxford UP, 1997. Print.

Poirier, Richard. *Poetry and Pragmatism*. Cambridge: Harvard UP, 1992. Print.

——. *The Renewal of Literature: Emersonian Reflections*. New York: Random House, 1987. Print.

Reynolds, Larry J. "Hawthorne and Emerson in 'The Old Manse'." *Studies in the Novel*, 23. 1 (1991): 60–81. Print.

Richardson, Robert D. *Emerson: The Mind on Fire: A Biography*. Berkeley: U of California P, 1995. Print.

——. *Henry Thoreau: A Life of the Mind*. Berkeley: U of California P, 1986. Print.

Thoreau, Henry David. "Natural History of Massachusetts." *Collected Essays and*

Poems. Ed. Elizabeth Hall Witherell. New York: Library of America, 2001. 20–41. Print.

——. *Walden: A Fully Annotated Edition*. Ed. Jeffrey S. Cramer. New Haven: Yale UP, 2004. Print.

——. *The Writings of Henry D. Thoreau: A Week on the Concord and Merrimack Rivers*. Ed. Carl F. Hovde et al. Princeton: Princeton UP, 1980. Print.

West, Cornel. *The American Evasion of Philosophy: A Genealogy of Pragmatism*. Madison: U of Wisconsin P, 1989. Print.

Paradoxical Truth in Emerson and Thoreau

Izumi Ogura

For scholars of American literature, Ralph Waldo Emerson and Henry David Thoreau are considered equivalent in their treatment of the concept of "nature." As one incarnation of the American mind, Emerson presents many features that people commonly share. Although his philosophy has an eclectic quality, it is strikingly original in its unprecedented idealism and concept of people's coexistence with nature. His belief in the harmonious blending of society and solitude is an ideal that many American writers have dreamed of and striven to achieve. Thoreau, Emerson's disciple and experimental follower, lived in a small cabin at Walden Pond for two years, two months, and two days—from July 4, 1845 to September 6, 1847. By "confronting" nature, Thoreau hoped to achieve self-realization and to understand his own existence from within. Focusing on the seemingly paradoxical concept of nature and its relationship with man, this paper explores the inner workings of Thoreau's philosophy of "wisdom" and Emerson's distinction between a poet and a mystic. By enumerating various aspects of these ideas, through an exploration of the paradoxes and paradoxical expressions of Emerson and Thoreau, this paper seeks to show how they believed the revelation of the self could be achieved.

I. Paradoxical Expressions by Emerson

In *Literary Transcendentalism*, Lawrence Buell compares Emerson with William Ellery Channing, arguing that while Channing tends to explain concepts in detail, Emerson speaks directly to the point, using paradox and contrast in his lectures to convince audiences of his essential message (113). For example, Emerson says, "I like the silent church before the service begins, better than any preaching" ("Self-Reliance" *The Collected Works of Ralph Waldo Emerson* 2: 41; hereafter abbreviated as *CW*). This reveals Emerson's attitude toward his own religious piety, which is not imposed by others but springs from the mind. The following quotation is another example of a paradoxical expression:

> A man in view of absolute goodness, adores, with total humility. Every step so downward, is a step upward. The man who renounces himself, comes to himself by so doing. ("The Divinity School Address" *CW* 1: 78)

Emerson describes Thoreau's paradoxical tendencies in his eulogy, "Thoreau": "The habit of a realist [Thoreau] to find things the reverse of their appearance inclined him to put every statement in a paradox" (*CW* 10: 428). Modern readers may find Emerson and Thoreau difficult to understand because of their frequent use of paradoxes in writing and ideas. Reading a text word by word does not necessarily enable us to easily understand what these writers meant, particularly as our understanding of a single sentence is often reversed by the following sentences.

Any discussion of Emerson's theory of writing immediately recalls the passage on expression in "The Poet," in which Emerson asserts, "The man is only half himself, the other is his expression" (*CW* 3: 4). In discussing Emerson's theory of writing, Albert Gelpi and Joel Porte interpret this sentence positively, arguing that poets find meaning only in expression (Gelpi 71–84; Porte, *Representative Man* 135–60; 285–99). Given that Emerson writes in his chapter on "Language" in *Nature*, "Particular natural facts are symbols of particular spiritual facts" (*CW* 1: 17) and "Nature is the symbol of spirit" (*CW* 1: 17), Gelpi and Porte's interpretation seems very reasonable. Emerson's proposition is that there is a correspondence between nature and spirit, and that the poet's role is to be a mediator, seer, and bard. In *Modern Criticism*, Walter Sutton points out that Emerson strongly influenced T. S. Eliot and other 20th century poets because he emphasized "the symbolic power of a concrete and sensuous poetic language" (4).

Emerson, however, casts doubt on his own concept of "expression." Does an expression represent the spirit? Does a word embody an idea? Emerson also considers silence, the opposite of expression. In fact, the sentence made famous by "The Poet" first appeared in his *Journal*, in a completely different context. In his *Journal* entry of October 9, 1841, Emerson follows this sentence with a relatively skeptical additional statement:

> The man is only half himself. Let me see the other half, namely his Expression. Strange, strange we value this half the most. We worship expressors

> [sic]; we forgive every crime to them. Full expression is very rare. (*JMN* 8: 104–05)

These quotations show that we tend to overlook the dual aspects of the paradox of silence and expression, focusing solely on expression.

When we read Emerson, we quickly notice that the "virtue of renunciation" is an imperative aspect of his philosophy. Emerson believes that as we grow up we lose freshness and purity, saying, "Infancy is the perpetual Messiah" (*Nature CW* 1: 42). Since we in our daily life do not have insight into a marrow, we can only do what Emerson calls "a very superficial seeing" (*Nature CW* 1: 9). Yet the innocent eyes of children, who have not yet been conquered by the laws of perspective or structural composition, look at all elements from an equal distance with a fresh perspective, sometimes recognizing an aspect that adults would not notice (Tanner 19–45).

Yet this virtue of renunciation is only the first step, a prologue to the second stage, which involves "the recognition of the self," as well as the third stage, "the return to society." What Emerson aims to achieve in "Self-Reliance" does not stop with the dialogue with nature, but continues on to the third stage, where the philosopher returns to society with new insights: "the great man is he who in the midst of the crowd keeps with perfect sweetness the independence of solitude" (*CW* 2: 31). A reader could easily be misled by Emerson's abstract terms, such as "nature" and "self-reliance"; in fact, the core of his ideas lies in the power to balance conflicting elements. Emerson's idea is not a one-way addiction to nature, like that of Jean-Jacques Rousseau, but a "cyclical" return to society.

II. Henry David Thoreau and the "wise" Visitor

In saying "I have always been regretting that I was not as wise as the day I was born" (98) in *Walden*'s "Where I Lived, and What I Lived For," Thoreau invites us to become as innocent as the day of our birth and introduces Alek Therien, the man in the woods, "a Canadian, a wood-chopper" (*Walden* 144), in "Visitors."[1] Exemplifying Thoreau's idea that man's intuition can only be restored in the woods, this Canadian woodchopper is "wise" enough to perceive the secrets in what Emerson defines as the "open book of nature." Thoreau finds in him an ideal type: the wild man, and says in "Higher Laws": "Fishermen, hunters, woodchoppers . . . are often in a more favorable mood for observing her [Nature] . . . than philosophers or poets" (*Walden* 210).

Thoreau describes living in a wood as being caged in nature rather than caged like a bird in a house: "Such was not my abode, for I found myself suddenly neighbor to the birds; not by having imprisoned one, but having caged myself near them" (*Walden* 85). Emerson says in his eulogy, "Thoreau," that for Thoreau "to detach the description from its connection" (*CW* 10: 421) makes it no longer true or valuable. This woodchopper is exactly the sort of man of the woods Thoreau wanted to present: he works in Walden woods, but does not work quickly or in earnest. Since his life is completely in harmony with nature, even after clearing 50 trees, Therien says, "I never was tired in my life" (*Walden* 147). He lacks a sense of "busy-ness" and "business" and "In him the animal man chiefly was developed" (*Walden* 146). This "great consumer of meat" (*Walden* 145) likes eating woodchuck, and when his dog catches one, spends half an hour thinking about whether he can sink it in the pond, and then take it home to dress (*Walden* 145). Thoreau asked him if he ever wanted to write down his thoughts, but he had never tried that—first, because he did not know what to write, and second because having to think and spell at the same time would kill him (*Walden* 148).

The woodchopper seems foolish, but Thoreau is impressed with his argument about the usefulness of money. The woodchopper says that if he owned an ox and wanted to get needles and thread at the store, "it would be inconvenient and impossible to go on mortgaging some portion of the creature [ox] each time to that amount" (*Walden* 149). Thoreau admires this wild man's insight: "He could defend many institutions better than any philosopher, because . . . he gave the true reason for their prevalence . . ." (*Walden* 149). The woodchopper embodies the sort of intuition that can only be acquired by living together with nature. As Thoreau writes, "I occasionally observed that he was thinking for himself and expressing his own opinion . . ." and "There was a certain positive originality . . ." (*Walden* 150). In short, Thoreau calls him "a prince in disguise" (*Walden* 148).

In his essay, "Walking," Thoreau proposes there should be a "Society for the Diffusion of Useful Ignorance" in addition to the "Society for the Diffusion of Useful Knowledge" (*Excursions* 214–15). The woodchopper is a precise embodiment of useful ignorance. Not until we enter the arena of the wild man do we attain true originality. Being primitive, the woodchopper is able to reveal his own ideas and intuition:

> He suggested that there might be men of genius in the lowest grades of life, however permanently humble and illiterate, who take their own view always, or do not pretend to see at all; who are as bottomless even as Walden Pond was thought to be, though they may be dark and muddy. (*Walden* 150)

Although Thoreau admires the wild man's renunciation of civilization and immersion in aboriginal life untouched by civilization, he observes that the wild man lacks an intellectual and spiritual side: "But the intellectual and what is called spiritual man in him was slumbering as in an infant" (*Walden* 147). Thoreau attempts to introduce these elements, but fails, "Yet I never, by any manoeuvring [sic], could get him to take the spiritual view of things . . ." (*Walden* 150).

Thoreau's theme is not only the return to ignorance, but the revelation this return enables. To Thoreau, this process integrates the "innocent eye" of children with adult "intelligence." Thoreau invites us to go back to a state of ignorance or "nothing," in which one can experience a revelation or insight, and then to bring this new insight back to society. Thoreau describes how we can experience the state of "nothing" in "The Village":

> Often in a snow storm, even by day, one will come out upon a well-known road, and yet find it impossible to tell which way leads to the village. Though he knows that he has travelled it a thousand times, he cannot recognize a feature in it, but it is as strange to him as if it were a road in Siberia. (*Walden* 170–71)

Although he loses his way and his eyes cannot see anything in woods, Thoreau has become one with nature, and is therefore able to lead the way to his cabin door:

> until I was aroused by having to raise my hand to lift the latch, I have not been able to recall a single step of my walk, and I have thought that perhaps my body would find its way home . . . . (*Walden* 170)

Only through such absorption and immersion can a man experience revelation:

> Not till we are lost, in other words, not till we have lost the world, do we

> begin to find ourselves, and realize where we are and the infinite extent of our relations. (*Walden* 171)

The woodchopper is a good example of the "virtue of renunciation" and the splendor of childhood, but once he has recovered his lost innocence through nature, he must be ready for the higher "recognition of the self." We can know the perfection of nature only through the combination of intuition and knowledge. Without both, we will never know the whole. Just as we can hear the sound of two hands clapping, but cannot hear the sound of one hand alone, so the woodchopper's originality and Thoreau's knowledge must be integrated.[2]

III. A Poet and a Mystic in Ralph Waldo Emerson

The paradoxical theme of the return from nature with recovered wisdom is also exemplified in Emerson's distinction between a poet and a mystic. Both poet and mystic share the characteristic of absorption in nature, achieved by renouncing social prejudices. The difference between them emerges at the point when a poet becomes capable of recognizing that all things change with time and that change is the source of vitality and beauty. Let us examine the invitation to nature in the famous transparent eyeball passage:

> Standing on the bare ground,—my head bathed by the blithe air, and uplifted into infinite space,—all mean egotism vanishes. I become a transparent eye-ball. I am nothing. I see all. The currents of the Universal Being circulate through me; I am part or particle of God. (*Nature CW* 1: 10)

The state in which we become a transparent eyeball and "nothing"—complete immersion in nature—is what Emerson calls in *Nature* the state in which, "inward and outward senses are still truly adjusted to each other" (*CW* 1: 9). This state of osmosis is also exemplified in his essay, "The Poet," by a man on a horse who has lost his way and throws his reins onto the horse:

> As the traveler who has lost his way, throws his reins on his horse's neck, and trusts to the instinct of the animal to find his road, so must we do with the divine animal who carries us through this world. (*CW* 3: 16)

By renouncing the reins and trusting to the instinct of the animal, he unites with the animal and conspires with the rhythm of nature. Travelling by relying on the instinct of a horse is a state of absorption into nature in which there is "no obstruction" ("Natural History of Intellect" *The Complete Works of Ralph Waldo Emerson* 12:63; hereafter abbreviated as *W*) to the angle of sight. By renouncing knowledge and trusting the sixth sense—intuition—something we are born with that becomes obscured and obliterated by *a posteriori* experience, a man can recover his innate ability to be at one with nature—he reaches what Emerson calls "an ecstatical state" in which "heaven flows to earth" ("The Method of Nature" *CW* 1: 130).

At the next stage, we move from "seeing" and "observing" nature to "entering" an object. Emerson says in "History" that this process of absorption is indispensable for an artist:

> A painter told me that nobody could draw a tree without in some sort becoming a tree; or draw a child by studying the outlines of its form merely, —but, by watching for a time his motions and plays the painter enters into his nature and can then draw him at will in every attitude. (*CW* 2: 10)

When an artist draws a picture, some part of his consciousness enters into a tree or becomes part of a child's movement. In other words, it is not a process of observing a form from the outside, but of understanding a child's movements from within; this is the exact process of "seeing-in" or insight.

Absorption is the process of becoming something else. Emerson's vision is not how he looks at the "tree" or the "child"—the vision of his eyes—but a "union with the things known" ("Intellect" *CW* 2: 193). Emerson writes about this absorption in his *Journal*: "All my hope of insight & of successful reporting lies in my consciousness of fidelity & the abdication of all will in the matter" (*The Journals and Miscellaneous Notebooks of Ralph Waldo Emerson* 7: 300; hereafter abbreviated as *JMN*). By renouncing and purifying the senses, a man is able to become an "Aeolian harp" at rest ("Nature" *CW* 3: 102), awaiting feeble and delicate touches of inspiration (Cavanaugh 25–35).

After experiencing the first stage in nature and the second stage of self-realization, the Emersonian self must move on to the third stage: disengaging from the experience and returning to society with a renewed revelation. This is the stage at which Thoreau becomes critical of the woodchopper's lack of knowledge and Emerson differentiates a poet from a mystic. After a painter has entered into the movement of children, he must come back to his creation in art.

A poet and a mystic share the concept of transparency and become absorbed in the external world by renouncing earthly division. However, the difference between them is that, while a mystic is absorbed into and indulges in an impression, a poet is initially absorbed and "thrilled," but does not permanently indulge in the impression. While a poet knows that absorption is a step toward a "clearer and grander" vision, and disengages himself from the particular experience, a mystic mistakes a specific experience for a universal one.

> The poet did not stop at the color or the form, but read their meaning; neither may he rest in this meaning, but he makes the same objects exponents of his new thought. Here is the difference betwixt the poet and the mystic, that the last nails a symbol to one sense, which was a true sense for a moment, but soon becomes old and false. For all symbols are fluxional, all language is vehicular and transitive, and is good, as ferries and horses are, for conveyance, not as farms and houses are, for homestead. Mysticism consists in the mistake of an accidental and individual symbol for an [sic] universal one. ("The Poet" *CW* 3: 20)

Exactly echoing Emerson's philosophy of flow and transition in circles, this passage in "The Poet" shows that what we define as an experience is a kaleidoscope, of which we are allowed to see only a single aspect at a time. To put it another way, an experience is a revolving "parti-colored wheel" ("Experience" *CW* 3: 34), which looks white because of its incessant movement, but is in fact a unified vision of numerous colors. A painter might, from a particular angle, see a deep and beautiful color, but the tint will change and can never be "nailed" down to "one sense."

A mystic who nails down a single aspect of experience is infused with the present moment and intoxicated by it. This stage of the pseudo-transparent world of perception is probably shared by the poet. However, since the aim of a mystic is to be in an ecstatic state, he cannot disengage himself from the pit of single-mindedness in which he consumes his own experience—in this state, he mistakes an "accidental and individual" experience for a "universal" one, which Emerson calls "a jail" (*JMN* 9: 383), constructed from the particular faith the mystic seeks to affirm.

A poet, despite being infused with an experience, is not trapped in it permanently or obsessed with "*One Idea*" (*JMN* 5: 446); he accepts the various changing facets of experience, discerning, comparing and sorting them. He sees multiple aspects of an experience simultaneously and feels a wonderful ecstasy; at the same time, he can maintain a certain aloofness and sense of perspective that allows him to control it. Hence, to use the image of a circle, his trajectory of imagination becomes *cyclical* in relation to the self.

Emerson explains that the common man is "the victim of events" ("Aristocracy" *W* 10: 37) and that "Most men's minds do not grasp anything. All slip through their fingers like paltry brass grooves" ("Natural History of Intellect" *W* 12: 48). Nevertheless, Emerson's poet can discern the degrees of experience that "fatally" descend on us, commanding the whole cycle.

> Thoughtless people contradict as readily the statement of perceptions as of opinions, or rather much more readily; for they do not distinguish between perception and notion. They fancy that I choose to see this or that thing. But perception is not whimsical, but fatal. ("Self-Reliance" *CW* 2: 38)

Emerson strongly advises us to become absorbed in our impressions—an experience that is sometimes a dreadful self-forgetting and sometimes an exhilarating ecstasy—and yet, as shown in his aversion to the mystic who immerses himself in a single aspect of experience, he rejects the idea of complete fusion. The poet has the power to escape from himself; his consciousness is still somewhat detached—not at the mercy of sentiment. In his "Natural History of Intellect," Emerson calls the power of control "detachment":

> This is the first property of the Intellect I am to point out; the mind detaches. A man is intellectual in proportion as he can make an object of every sensation, perception and tuition; so long as he has no engagement looking at it as somewhat foreign. . . . The detachment consists in seeing it under a new order, not under a personal but a universal light . . . . (*W* 12: 38–39)

Emerson sees himself "as somewhat foreign" and separates himself from the thing he contemplates. He understands that there is a separation between his consciousness and the object: "I grieve, but am not a grief; I love, but am not a love" (*JMN* 7: 466). In other words, he advises us to sing a song and be thrilled and moved by its beautiful tender lyrics, while warning us *not to become the emotion itself* and wail loudly. He lets emotions pass *through* the body.

Emerson advises us to move out from ourselves, because "the field cannot be well seen from within the field" ("Circles" *CW* 2: 185). Free from prejudice and preconceptions, a man becomes a detached observer and detects subtle likenesses and differences. The power of separating a fact from all local and personal references is the first step toward a higher level of discernment. The detachment Emerson refers to is a way of "distance-ing" oneself from pre-established reference points. This way of seeing objects "as somewhat foreign" is more elaborately developed in his *Journal* entry of December 18, 1837:

> It implies the power to separate the fact from yourself, from all personality, & look at it as if it existed for itself alone. It is entirely void of all affection, and sees an object, a thought, as it stands there in the light of the mind quite cool & disengaged. (*JMN* 5: 446)

Emerson's self-reliance is not a solipsistic world of egotistical thought. Emerson warns of the danger of solipsism, which he calls "organic egotism" and promotes its "antidote": "The antidote against this organic egotism, are, the range and variety of attractions, as gained by acquaintance with the world, with man of merit, with classes of society . . ." ("Culture" *CW* 6: 73).

Typical Emersonian concepts incorporate a dialectic and dual nature, as in expansion and concentration, engagement and withdrawal, Reason and Understanding, silence and expression, one and the many, and similar opposing pairs (*The Letters of Ralph Waldo Emerson* 1: 412–13; *JMN* 5: 270–73). The point that we should not miss, when exploring these dialectic and seemingly contradictory concepts, is that these opposing notions are not parallel; they are neither juxtaposed nor contrapuntal concepts. In Emerson, seemingly contradictory concepts merge: from commitment, the poet conceives of a new idea; from ecstasy, he achieves detachment.

The first stage of absorption and ecstasy offers broader perception and leads on to the second stage of control and disengagement. Although it may seem paradoxical, the loss of preconceptions leads to new revelations for Emerson. In "The Sovereignty of Ethics," Emerson summarizes this paradoxical truth of revelation through loss: "by humility we rise, by obedience we command, by poverty we are rich, by dying we live" (*W* 10: 208). Not until we experience humility, obedience, and poverty can we know the true meaning of life, happiness, and wealth. Only those who renounce themselves can come to themselves and achieve a state of perfect self-awareness. Emerson provides a place where these contradictory concepts can merge and create a new harmony. Emerson's nature is the monistic world of experience within the dualistic structure of noumenal and phenomenal worlds. This paradoxical theme of "revelation through loss" has great significance for Emerson.

IV. Paradox Discussed from the Perspective of Contemporary Criticism

Ever since Edward Said, the forerunner of post-colonialism, pointed out in *Orientalism* (1978) that there was a distorted understanding of Orientalism in literature (290), and a "singular avoidance" (291) of the Orient, scholars have explored the "Oriental" aspects of Transcendentalism. Malini Shueller's *U.S. Orientalisms* (1998) sheds light on the similarities between Asian and American literature; Lawrence Buell's *Emerson* (2003) designates Emerson as "a global figure" for his extensive reading of Buddhist and Persian texts. In his insightful article on the relationship between Zen Buddhism and Transcendentalism, Palmer Rampell says that Thoreau represents an "Eastern way of thinking" (623). According to Rampell, Daisetsu Suzuki's "Zen Theory of Emerson" (1896) presents four insights from Transcendentalism: "spiritual truth is ineffable; spiritual truth is intuitive; purification must be achieved through meditation; and forgetfulness of self precedes the final revelation of spiritual truth" (630). Though Rampell does not specify a paradox peculiar to Emerson and Thoreau, his summary of Transcendental ideas has many points in common with critical theories.

First of all, a paradox, by distorting two opposite words, enriches the image and presents a complex impression and creates a powerful impact on sensitive people. As Emerson says, "The beautiful is never plentiful" (*JMN* 13: 267); because a paradox is unstable in its meaning, it can create countless effects. For example, the transparent eyeball passage, "I am nothing . . . . I am part or particle of God" (*Nature CW* 1: 10) contains a paradoxical expression that contrasts "nothing" with "part of God." Gay Wilson Allen in his book, *Waldo Emerson*, argues that this passage contains all religious experiences described by William James in his book, *The Varieties of Religious Experience*. According to Allen, the expression "nothing" which also means "part of God" shows the concentrating but paradoxically expanding ego (277). These spiritual experiences are "ineffable" (James 299); however, a paradox is an effective way of presenting abstract experience. As Rampell points out, James's religious experiences have many similarities to Zen Buddhism; their ineffability is characteristic of "satori" or the enlightenment stage (630; Buell, *Emerson* 196–97).

Secondly, an abstract concept is best illustrated by being placed in two different situations. When Emerson describes flow and transition, he frequently uses an image of rivers and waters. Emerson says, "To the attentive eye, each moment of the year has its own beauty, and in the same field, it beholds, every hour, a picture which was never seen before, and which shall never be seen again" (*Nature CW* 1: 14). Incessant flow in nature can best be presented as contrasting with static or concrete objects. Transcendentalism was called the "Saturnalia or excess of Faith" ("The Transcendentalist" *CW* 1: 206) and was characterized by abstract ideas: Emerson's essays contain abstract terms, such as "nature" and "self-reliance." By contrast, Thoreau's strategy involves the use of concrete place names, such as Walden and Cape Cod. *The Maine Woods* lists the flora and fauna with place and dates Thoreau observed in Maine (298–325). Thoreau's accurate "botanical identifications" (Buell 301) tempted Emerson to start a "Notebook Naturalist" (*The Topical Notebooks of Ralph Waldo Emerson* 1: 27–56). Emerson and Thoreau both successfully represent the complex world of ideas and places, using different tactics to achieve their goal.

Thirdly, paradox in literature, if transferred to art, becomes "asymmetry." Asymmetry does not present a completed product. It forces the viewer to create balance in his own mind. The effects of "asymmetry" are not fixed; as a result, they create large movements in the viewer. Charles Anderson says, in *The Magic Circle of Walden*, that Thoreau was not satisfied with mechanical design (18). In communicating ideas, Emerson and Thoreau both avoid explanation and teaching, preferring to present commonplace and banal things and to invite us to create our own views. The final form is simply suggested; whether a reader can perceive this suggested structure depends on the reader himself. As a result, readers try to discover in paradox what was excluded or overlooked in the process of induction and integration. As F. O. Matthiessen aptly and shrewdly mentions in *American Renaissance* (9–10), the reader has to explore Emerson's "last chamber": "The last chamber, the last closet, he must feel was never opened; there is always a residuum unknown, unanalyzable" ("Circles" *CW* 2: 182). Thoreau also points out the "unexplorable" in "Spring" in *Walden*:

> At the same time that we are earnest to explore and learn all things, we require that all things be mysterious and unexplorable, that land and sea be infinitely wild, unsurveyed and unfathomed by us because unfathomable. (*Walden* 317–18)

We have to discern the "mysterious and unexplorable," like asymmetry, by ourselves. Its meaning must be created by us.

Fourthly, the theme that a paradox functions as an asymmetrical form, its meaning defined by the reader, has great significance in Emerson and Thoreau. A paradox is not "non-sense" but what Edmund Husserl called "anti-sense" (Mizuno 42–57). For example, the quote, "I have always been regretting that I was not as wise as the day I was born" has a contradiction in meaning, but is not "non-sense." The meaning of "wise" does not directly convey the expression, nor directly connect with the signified words, "I was not as wise as the day I was born." Yet the meaning that the writer intends to convey through this sentence is solemn and powerful, creating a deep impact.

By combining two "contrary" "dictions" (a contradiction), Emerson and Thoreau aim to transcend the physical world and reach the spiritual. As Maurice Merleau-Ponty says in *Phenomenology in Perception* (1945), a poet, by using given words and signifiers, wants to transcend expression (Mizuno 48). Likewise, by using "para" (contrary or distinct from) and "dox" (opinion), Emerson aims to transcend a world of five senses; Thoreau reaches from microcosm to macrocosm and "Higher Laws" (*Walden* 210–22). The paradoxical theme that a poet uses words and yet is never permanently absorbed by them—never dragged forward by superficial logic—shows the resilience and tenacity of Emerson and Thoreau. Not until we realize the depth of unspoken words and are aware of the unanalyzable—paradoxically speaking, sense the "anti-sense"—do we attain the state of an enlightenment. In midst of the diversity of the 21st century, this delicate attitude to seek the depth of intellect and paradox will lead us to the universal truth of Emerson and Thoreau. Just as paradoxes create a greater impact on the reader than a simple expression would, so the writings of Emerson and Thoreau, who chose to entrust the significance and interpretation of their work to us, will continue to be studied from many different aspects.

Notes

1 This woodchopper is unnamed in *Walden*, but Thoreau's *Journal* identifies him as Alek Therien (Porte, "Double Consciousness" 46–50; Gura 370–71). Kazuto Ono in his *Ikite-iru Michi: Thoreau no Hi-nichijo Sekai to Uchuu* [*A Living Way: Through Thoreau's Unusual Places to the Universe*] points out that this woodchopper is similar to Elisha Dugan, who appears in the poem, "The Old Marlborough Road", which Thoreau wrote in his *Journal* on July 16, 1850 and later included in "Walking"

(Ono 28–29 and 39 fn.10).

2 This comes from a Japanese Rinzai Buddhist sect dialogue. "What is the sound of one hand clapping?" is a question from the koans of Zen masters (Rampell 625).

Works Cited

Allen, Gay Wilson. *Waldo Emerson*. New York: Viking. 1981. Print.

Anderson, Charles R. *The Magic Circle of Walden*. New York: Holt Rinehart, and Winston, 1968. Print.

Buell, Lawrence. *Literary Transcendentalism*. Ithaca: Cornell UP. 1973. Print.

——. *Emerson*. Cambridge: Harvard UP. 2003. Print.

Cavanaugh, Cynthia A. "The Aeolian Harp: Beauty and Unity in the Poetry and Prose of Ralph Waldo Emerson." *Rocky Mountain Review*. Spring 2002. 25–35. Print.

Emerson, Ralph Waldo. *The Journals and Miscellaneous Notebooks of Ralph Waldo Emerson*. Ed. William H. Gilman et al. 16 vols. Cambridge: Harvard UP. 1960–1982. Print.

——. *The Collected Works of Ralph Waldo Emerson*. Ed. Robert E. Spiller et al. 10 vols. Cambridge: Harvard UP. 1971–2013. Print.

——. *The Complete Works of Ralph Waldo Emerson*. Ed. Edward Waldo Emerson. 12 vols. Boston: Houghton Mifflin, 1903–04. Print.

——. *The Letters of Ralph Waldo Emerson*. Eds. Ralph L. Rusk and Eleanor M. Tilton. 10 vols. New York: Columbia UP. 1939–95. Print.

——. *The Topical Notebooks of Ralph Waldo Emerson*. In Three Volumes. Chief Editor Ralph H. Orth. Vol. 1. Ed. Susan Sutton Smith. Columbia: U of Missouri P. 1990–94. Print.

Gelpi, Albert J. *The Tenth Muse: The Psych of the American Poet*. Cambridge: Harvard UP. 1975. Print.

Gura, Philip F. "Thoreau's Maine Woods Indians: More Representative Men." *American Literature* 49 (1977): 366–84. Print.

James, William. *The Varieties of Religious Experience*. 1902. Rpt. New York: Collier Books. 1961. Print.

Matthiessen, F. O. *American Renaissance: Art and Expression in the Age of Emerson and Whitman*. New York: Oxford UP. 1941. Print.

Mizuno, Kazuhisa. "Gengo no Gyakusetsu-sei ni kansuru Gensho-gaku teki Kousatsu" ["Phenomenological Study of Paradox in Language"]. *Shiso* 694. Tokyo: Iwanami-shoten. 1982. 42–57. Print.

Ono, Kazuto. *Ikite-iru Michi: Thoreau no Hi-nichijo Sekai to Uchuu* [*A Living Way: Through Thoreau's Unusual Places to the Universe*]. Tokyo: Kinseido P. 2015. Print.

Porte, Joel. *Representative Man: Ralph Waldo Emerson in His Time*. New York: Oxford UP. 1979. Print.

——. "Emerson, Thoreau, and the Double Consciousness." *The New England Quarterly*. 41(1968): 40–50. Print.

Rampell, Palmer. "Laws That Refuse To Be Stated: The Post-Sectarian Spiritualities of Emerson, Thoreau, and D. T. Suzuki." *The New England Quarterly* 84:4 (2011).

621–54. Print.
Said, Edward. *Orientalism*. Penguin Modern Classics. 1978. Print.
Shueller, Malini. *U.S. Orientalisms: Race, Nation, and Gender in Literature, 1790–1889*. Ann Arbor: U of Michigan P. 1998. Print.
Sutton, Walter. "The New Criticism." *Modern American Criticism*. Princeton: Princeton UP. 1963. 98–151. Print.
Tanner, Tony. *Reign of Wonder: Naivety and Reality in American Literature*. London: Cambridge UP. 1965. Print.
Thoreau, Henry David. *Walden: The Writings of Henry D. Thoreau*. Princeton: Princeton UP. 1971. Print.
——. *The Maine Woods*. Princeton: Princeton UP. 1972. Print.
——. "Walking." *Excursions: The Writings of Henry D. Thoreau*. Princeton: Princeton UP. 2007. 185–222. Print.

This paper is a part of research project supported by the Grant-in-Aid for Scientific Research program (C), entitled "The Transformation of Religion from Enlightenment to American Intellectual Independence," Japan Society for the Promotion of Science (Grant No. 16K02506).

Thoreau and Muir:
A Glance at the Shifting American Sense of Nature

Yoshiko Fujita

One of the biggest problems in the twenty-first century is the deterioration of the global environment. David Lowenthal names mass extinction, global warming, chemical pollutants, and nuclear contaminants as current threats (Marsh, "Introduction" xxxii). Reflecting our fear, the Paris Conference on the Climate Change was opened just in November 2015, aiming at the prevention of further global warming. The danger of "alter[ing] nature in wide-ranging and catastrophic ways" (Walls 19) has become visible. On the one hand, we are still threatened by huge natural disasters, while on the other, nature, in the scope of human activities, appears fragile, limited, and irreparable.

Based on the sense of crisis, the twentieth-century new nature writing was created, especially by Aldo Leopold and Rachel Carson. Today that literature is called "environmental literature," following Lawrence Buell, whose use of the term covers a period that begins with Henry David Thoreau, includes Leopold and Carson, and extends to the present day.[1] It is acknowledged today that Thoreau and John Muir (1830–1914) after him are the pioneers of this new nature writing, and both of them brought the astonishingly new idea of sacredness into their considerations of wilderness. In fact, responding to Thoreau, George Perkins Marsh's *Man and Nature* was published as early as in 1864 as the first American appeal for the general conservation of nature. This essay will discuss both Thoreau and Muir as the early pioneering authors of the twentieth-century nature writing and of the present day's environmental literature. It will pay regard to the continuity in this new line of the American sense of nature as well as, to some extent, to the variations which are also found there. In the conclusion, the two authors' legacy to our century will be examined.

I

A short survey of the changing American view of nature will be necessary in order to know how Thoreau was new. In America, wilderness was originally what had to be conquered; the Puritan mission was to conquer wilderness, eliminate heresies, and build churches. Later, for colonists, wilderness existed only for a utilitarian purpose—to produce riches and comforts. So long as colonists had to struggle against wilderness day after day, it remained the object of hostility and fear. In the early nineteenth century, European Romanticism with its idea of "the sublime," came and made the Americans see their great nature with new eyes. Concern for their native landscape joined the then-growing quest for national literature. As a result, the grandeur of American wilderness was looked for in the context of romanticism, and its uniqueness in the context of national literature. On the one hand, instinctive hostility and fear against wilderness was never eliminated completely, as Roderick Nash says (66), while on the other, wilderness was gaining acceptance according as the American sensibility changed. Wilderness worked as a refuge from, or a temporary alternative to, over-developed civilization. However, it had never been described as holy, sacred, or spiritual. In that climate, Ralph Waldo Emerson in 1836 presented nature as a means through which man achieves a mystical union with God. According to Emerson, "the noblest ministry of nature is to stand as the apparition of God. It is the great organ through which the universal spirit speaks to the individual" (*The Collected Works of Ralph Waldo Emerson* I: 37; hereafter abbreviated as *CW*). Thus nature acquired a radically new function and quality.

Thoreau started with the same philosophy of nature. At the same time, he maintained deep interest in and love for every natural object and so wrote new nature essays that were not simply philosophic or descriptive. "Wilderness" is one of the keywords in the twentieth-century nature writing, at the origin of which Thoreau stands. Therefore one thing must be explained here concerning the usage of the word. Since Emerson lived in the mild Concord area, he rarely used the word "wilderness" in his writings. And yet, Emerson was a central figure in the "Philosophers' Camp" held in the wilderness of the Adirondacks, and he also declares his love and sympathy with wilderness rather than with streets or villages (*CW* I: 10). We should think, therefore, that "wilderness" was not eliminated from his whole design but connoted in his "nature." The same thing is true with Thoreau. So far as at least *Walden* is concerned, Thoreau mostly uses the word "nature," but Walden Woods itself was such a place as two young late anglers were lost on their way home and wandered until the daybreak (*Walden*, "Village"). In those days "nature" was understood either as a "garden" or as "wilderness"; then, their "nature" definitely belonged to the latter.

Though Thoreau does not write of "seeing God's face" or "hearing God's words" in nature, he clearly expresses his consciousness of God in nature in his *Journal*: "My profession is to be always alert to find God in nature, to know his lurking places, to attend all the oratorios, the operas, in nature" (II: 472). The holiness of nature, God's lurking place, is symbolized in the pure Walden Pond, which is "God's Drop," and the water of which is mixed with the sacred water of the Ganges. In his essay on "Walking," Thoreau presents himself as a "Saunterer," or a holy pilgrim (*Collected Essays and Poems* 225; hereafter abbreviated as *CEP*), walking "to the Holy Land" (223). In other words, Walden Pond and Concord are holy places, and walking in them is such serious work that he should go as a saunterer "in the spirit of undying adventure, never to return" (226). This holy nature is not merely a material environment but it guides and supports man with its moral principles and sympathy and love. In *Walden*, only once Thoreau is disturbed by the thought that the near neighborhood of man might be essential to a serene and healthy life, and then:

> . . . I was suddenly sensible of such sweet and beneficent society in Nature, in the very pattering of the drops, and in every sound and sight around my house, an infinite and unaccountable friendliness all at once like an atmosphere sustaining me, as made the fancied advantages of human neighborhood insignificant. . . . (89)

Nature is a place for spiritual growth and purification from the evils of civilization. For this purpose Thoreau practices daily ritual bathing, meditation, and working in the fields under the heavenly influence of nature. Thoreau's confidence in nature is proved by the very fact that he lived in the woods for two years and that while teaching at school for a short period, he put a greater importance on field studies than any other subject.

Wildness is the unique Thoreauvian factor in his design for man's spiritual growth. "We need the tonic of wildness" (*Walden* 211), Thoreau declares. Wildness is radical energy which is beyond the standard of good and evil; it is not found only in the far distant wild places but also around us when domestic animals occasionally show the evidence of "their original wild habits and vigor"

(*CEP* 246). In this context ancient myths or ungrammatical languages of uncivilized people also are praised. "Walking" is best understood as an essay on wildness not on wilderness or on the protection of wilderness. Thoreau in this essay most clearly explains man's spiritual relation to wildness. "My spirits infallibly rise in proportion to the outward dreariness" (242), says Thoreau. And again:

> . . . there is something in the mountain-air that feeds the spirit and inspires. . . . I trust that we shall be more imaginative, that our thoughts will be clearer, fresher, and more ethereal, as our sky,—our understanding more comprehensive and broader, like our plains,—our intellect generally on a grander scale, like our thunder and lightning, our rivers and mountains and forests,—and our hearts shall even correspond in breadth and depth and grandeur to our inland seas. (238)

Man's spiritual growth and enlargement will be vitalized through the incentive of such primitive energy. Thus, wildness in nature is endowed with spiritual value for the first time in the American thought. Thoreau's vision of rebirth in nature is more clarified by the introducing of the idea of wildness.

Love and respect for nonhuman beings is another characteristic of the twentieth-century nature writing. It was originated in Thoreau. We are impressed by Thoreau when he sees purity and wisdom even in the eyes of such a small creature as a young partridge (*Walden* 152). *Walden* is rich in friendliness to a fox, a squirrel, a loon to mention only a few. They are all brute "neighbors." Here is another example:

> Ah, the pickerel of Walden! . . . I am always surprised by their rare beauty. . . . they have, to my eyes, if possible, yet rarer colors, like flowers and precious stones, as if they were the pearls, the animalized *nuclei* or crystals of the Walden water. . . . Easily, with a few convulsive quirks, they give up their watery ghosts, like a mortal translated before his time to the thin air of heaven. (189–90)

This is not the writing of a fisherman or a scientist. Thoreau feels love and a kind of respect for a fish, which is a far different entity from a human being. It is true that Thoreau was gradually shaping ecological thought especially on forest trees, but this feeling comes not from the ecological idea of interrelatedness in nature, but from personal love for the present living creature. Buell calls this, "deeply personal love and respect" (137). In addition, a recent study gives a linguistic consideration to Thoreau's animal passages. Michelle C. Neely cites the following from the "Higher Laws" chapter: "No humane being, past the thoughtless age of boyhood, will wantonly murder any creature, which holds its life by the same tenure that he does" (142). Neely notices the usage of the three words: "murder" instead of "kill," "creature" instead of "animal," and "tenure," which is a legal term used for humans. Thoreau has transferred words that are common to the human realm to the animal realm. In doing so, he blurs the boundaries between the human and the nonhuman and surpasses the limitations of nineteenth-century anthropocentrism.[2]

II

John Muir inherited Thoreau's sense of nature's holiness. Muir's *My First Summer in the Sierra* (1911) is overflowing with his delight at the beauty and holiness of the Sierra. Nature is described especially through the image of light. "The young river sings and shines like a happy living creature" (35), and "the new needles of the pines and firs are nearly full grown and shine gloriously" (65). Near the end of his trip, Muir gives the high mountains of the Sierra a new name, "the Range of Light" to take the place of "the Snowy Range" (236). Muir can write this way because he believes that nature is a "vast display of God's power" (132). Muir listens to God's sermons in rocks and sees His face on flowers. According as Muir moves higher, leading his sheep, however, the landscape changes less mild. One day, Muir climbs to the summit of Mount Hoffman, eleven thousand feet high. Having long aimed to make this climb, Muir recognizes the summit as "barren and desolate-looking . . . wasted by ages of gnawing storms" (150). But he is not discouraged. "*Looking at the surface in detail*," he writes, "one finds it covered by thousands and millions of charming plants with leaves and flowers so small . . ." (150–51; emphasis added). This reaction of Muir's proves his unwavering confidence in nature.

Wildness itself is a source of delight for Muir, this "wandering wilderness-lover" (254). In one passage from "A Perilous Night on Shasta's Summit," Muir is assaulted by a blizzard as he begins his descent and is forced to camp without any equipment. Frozen, famished, benumbed, he suffers. "Still," Muir says, "the pain was not always of that bitter, intense kind that precludes thought and takes away all capacity for *enjoyment*" (*Mountaineering Essays* 85; emphasis added; hereafter abbreviated as *ME*). Muir's longing for wildness brings about also this surprising experience. While engaged on a survey in the Sierra, Muir suspects an approaching fierce storm and hurries to the heights, where he can watch the tree-tops swirling "in wild ecstasy." When the storm reaches its height, Muir climbs up to the top of a Douglas spruce, one hundred feet high, and deliriously waves with the bough so that he is "free to take the wind into my [his] pulses" (*Nature Writings* 470; hereafter abbreviated as *NW*).

Muir's first reaction to holy nature is to want to know it. This wish is repeatedly expressed in a prayer like "Would I could understand them!" (*Summer* 21) For Muir to know means not to analyze or interpret but to observe the object humbly and intently, or, as in the case of that fierce storm, to try to assimilate with it. With this purpose in mind, Muir always carried a notebook when he walked, which he filled with sketches and observations. It is a well-known fact that his minute recordings of the traces of glaciers on the rocks later led to his theory of the Yosemite being formed by glaciers. At the same time, Muir wants to know also another side of nature. On the fourth day of the Sierra camp Muir is impressed by the beautiful forms of trees, which he saw as "definite symbols, divine hieroglyphics written with sunbeams" (21), and wishes to understand them someday. Throughout *Summer* Muir is delighted at the glorious beauty of nature, and is also "hopeful of some day knowing more, learning the meaning of these divine symbols crowded together on this wondrous page" (149). Like Thoreau, Muir maintains a subtle balance between the physical and spiritual sides of nature, though Muir seems to want to tell more of the latter to the reader.

"Exposure" is the keyword to denote Muir's ideal mode of seeing. Also the words, "immersion," "to be bathed," "to be absorbed" are used, signifying the same manner. One must forget one's own self and expose oneself to the influence of nature or be absorbed in it. One gradually blends with the landscape. "We are now in the mountains and they are in us" (*Summer* 15–16), Muir writes in one place; in another, "The trees wave and flowers bloom in our bodies as well as our souls" (*ME* 99). This mode of acceptance is reinforced by a metaphor of a photographic plate, as John C. Elder notices (377–78):

> One day's exposure to mountains is better than cartloads of books. See how willingly Nature poses herself upon photographers' plates. No earthly chemicals are so sensitive as those of the human soul. All that is required is exposure, and purity of material. (*ME* 103–04)

A romantic might oppose this comparison of human soul to inorganic material, but Muir's insistence on man's passive acceptance comes straight through this metaphor. As we expose ourselves to the light of nature, "harmony, joy, and, most importantly, [God's] love" (Williams 203) are developed in us. Spiritual rebirth is the expected result. It was Muir's purpose in writing *Summer* in his later years to invite the reader to this spiritual experience in nature. In *Summer*, Muir climbs up higher, led by the mountain voice calling, "Come higher." At every ascending a new world awaits him; on the summit of Mount Hoffman Muir sees "new plants, new animals, new crystals, and multitudes of new mountains far higher than Hoffman" (149). Thus, the subject of rebirth is reflected in Muir's mountain climbing itself, in the structure of his literary work. Although he rarely speaks personally of such a subtle experience, in his one mountaineering essay, Muir symbolizes his own rebirth process by using the archetypal pattern of a fall, fainting, and awakening with "the last of the town fog" "shaken from both head and feet" (*ME* 57–58).

Muir has also bequeathed love for nonhuman beings to the twentieth-century nature writing, as Thoreau did. This love is different from the protecting and sympathetic feeling sometimes found in Victorian England. This feeling is the same as what Joseph Wood Krutch calls, in regard of Thoreau, a sensibility "to find . . . a little fishy friend in Walden Pond" (54). Its especially telling example is found in *Summer*. One day Muir goes out of a camp for sketching without carrying a gun, and suddenly comes upon a huge mountain bear. Fearful staring at each other persists, until the bear at last slowly turns back to go home. In the evening that dreadful bear has already settled in Muir's mind as a dear mountain friend. Muir sends a cordial greeting to that bear, and also to a fly and a grasshopper he saw that day:

> Sundown, and I must to camp. Good-night, friends three,—brown bear, rugged boulder of energy in groves and gardens fair as Eden; restless, fussy fly with gauzy wings stirring the air around all the world; and grass-hopper, crisp, electric spark of joy enlivening the massy sublimity of the mountains like the laugh of a child. Thank you, thank you all three for your quickening company. Heaven guide every wing and leg. Good-night friends three, good-night. (141–42)

Muir's ecological thought serves as the philosophical background to this comradeship. Muir says, "The best gains of this trip were the lessons of unity and interrelation of all the features of the landscape" (240). This lesson is not limited to the landscape, as he writes: "When we try to pick out anything by itself, we find it hitched to everything else in the universe" (157); and finally, "We feel ourselves part of wild Nature, kin to everything" (243). Interrelationship in the universe is thus clearly known by Muir. In fact, this recognition sometimes gains a religious connotation as when Muir says that "everything kept in joyful rhythmic motion in the pulses of Nature's big heart" (73). As "Nature" with a capital "N" sometimes means in Muir "the Creator," this religious sensibility seems to somewhat distance Muir's recognition from twentieth-century ecology. And yet, Muir's ecological thinking strengthens his comradeship especially in facing small creatures. Small ants, flies, and mosquitoes are indispensable parts of the universe, and Muir feels happy at finding that they "seem to enjoy this fine climate" (169) of the Sierra in July.

In light of the first and second sections of this essay, we can now conclude that both Thoreau and Muir claimed nature as the place for spiritual rebirth, never as an object of exploitation nor as a dump.

III

"Compared with Thoreau," Nash says, "Muir was wild indeed" (127). Thoreau was not. The difference in their times must be considered first. Though Thoreau was ahead of his time in appealing for natural preservation, nineteenth-century eyes generally did not see the danger of "alter[ing] nature in wide-ranging and catastrophic ways" (Walls 19). On the other hand, the last decades of the nineteenth century and the first decades of the twentieth century saw the fiercest destruction of the wild nature. The Tuolumne Valley, Muir's sacred place, had been threatened with being covered by water, due to dam construction, and this danger confirmed Muir's belief that wildness itself was holy. The dam construction was finally permitted the year before Muir's death of 1914.

Thoreau believed that wildness was indispensable for spiritual growth and for preservation of the world. Actually in *The Maine Woods* he fears accelerating deforestation and calls for preserving the wilderness. However, he felt differently at the radical wildness near the summit of Mt. Ktaadn.[3] Thoreau confronts the wilderness which has no concern for man nor for his spiritual growth. Nature is here "something savage and awful" (70); he feels even its hostility to man. But here we must notice that Thoreau never loses his sense of awe: he says on the dreary summit that "it is a slight insult to the gods to climb and pry into their secrets" (65). Thoreau respects wildness as always, but finally he regards the ideal to be a combination of wildness and cultural refinement. The vigor must remain uninjured but the savagery must be softened. In "Walking" this idea is expressed as a balance of day and night, sunlight and moonlight.

Thoreau was not wild in the way that Muir was. The principal reason seems to lie in his ethical view of man. Thoreau says: "I found in myself, and still find, an instinct toward a higher, or, as it is named, spiritual life . . . and another toward a primitive rank and savage one, and I reverence them both" (*Walden* 140). This latter instinct is what he calls in *Journal* "the primitive vigor of Nature in us" (IX: 43), and it parallels the wildness in nature. However, in his serious mood Thoreau defines this duality of man as "the divine allied to beasts" (*Walden* 147). It never happens in the natural world, but inside man the distinction between wildness and the unclean beast is blurred; wildness acquires ambiguity because of Thoreau's severe view of man. Here we find the depth and complexity of Thoreau's thought. The outside wildness can vitalize and inspire human spirit, but at the same time it could work on and activate the inner wildness. In *The Maine Woods* Thoreau says: "I already and for weeks afterward felt my nature the coarser for this part of my woodland experience" (120). At a certain point in his life Thoreau renounced fishing and hunting, but he admits this: "If I were to live in a wilderness I should again be tempted to become a fisher and hunter in earnest" (*Walden* 143). The latter statement does not refer to the necessity of capturing food but to the insensitivity to killing. On Mt. Ktaadn, it is now remembered, confused Thoreau cried: "I stand in awe of my body" (71). The Body, independent of the spirit, will be allied to the outside wildness and might revolt inside man.

Both Thoreau's and Muir's writings appealed to contemporary but still more to later generations. That was through the power of literature and its core was the style. A Japanese environmental literature, Michiko Ishimure's *Kugaijodo* [*Heaven in the Sea of Sorrows*] (1969) is especially moving when people speak of their sorrows and sufferings in their native Kumamoto dialect. This is a surpassing example of literary style on the level of language—diction and phrasing. By contrast, the literary style of Thoreau and Muir is connected with their own way of seeing.

First, Muir must be examined again. "Exposure" is the keyword in his seeing the landscape. As Branch reminds us, Muir's roots are in romanticism and transcendentalism (100); Muir does present himself as religious, enthusiastic, and wild. And yet he believes that the only way of knowing nature is to extinguish the self and immerse oneself in nature. Just seeing and absorbing is more important than the seer's imagination or speculation. One good example of Muir's impersonal style is found in "A Near View of the High Sierra." Muir is climbing, heading for the summit of Mt. Ritter. After spending a severe night in the bitter cold, he welcomes glorious sunrise:

> How glorious a greeting the sun gives the mountains! . . . The highest peaks burned like islands in a sea of liquid shade. Then the lower peaks and spires caught the glow, and long lances of light, streaming through many a notch and pass, fell thick on the frozen meadows. The majestic form of Ritter was full in sight. (*ME* 36)

Immediately after praising the sunlight, the narrator retires from the scene and lets the landscape speak. Mountains themselves play the drama of light and the subject has been "referred from the self to the landscape itself" (Branch 108). Muir is absorbed in the spectacle and then starts walking, but the walking figure is only a tiny spot, fused into the landscape. A comparison of the two following passages will tell that Muir's effacing of the self comes through his conscious effort. Muir's famous sketch, "Yosemite Valley in Flood," describes the roaring and overflowing river after the two-days storm. The sketch ends thus:

> So sings Yosemite, with her hundred fellow-falls, to the trembling bushes, and solemn-waving pines, and winds, and clouds, and living, pulsing rocks—one stupendous unit of mountain power—one harmonious storm of mountain love. (*NW* 590)

Nature is joyously exercising its highest energy, obeying to its own laws. However, as Michael P. Cohen found, the first manuscript was different (137). Muir's *Journal* shows that he was going to describe the falls as "infuriate waters" which roared, screamed, and hissed like "a perfect hell of conflicting demons," but then Muir realized that this is nothing but a reflection of his own fixed ideas and that there is no fury among all the songs and gestures of these living waters.

Thoreau's landscape is quite differently presented:

> . . . it is itself unchanged, the same water which my youthful eyes fell on; all the change is in me. It has not acquired one permanent wrinkle after all its ripples. It is perennially young, and I may stand and see a swallow dip apparently to pick an insect from its surface as of yore. It struck me again to-night, as if I had not seen it almost daily for more than twenty years,—Why, here is Walden, the same woodland lake that I discovered so many years ago . . . the same thought is welling up to its surface that was then. . . . (*Walden* 130)

The focus is not on the lake of that evening but on Thoreau's consciousness of his own changes and on his remembrances, evoked by the lake tonight. Affected by Thoreau's consciousness, the landscape itself appears sad. Thoreau wrote, standing on the camp of romantics, in which the seer's self is most important in the act of seeing; his thought is tested, his morality is judged, and finally a new recognition is expected. In the passage quoted above the reader knows more of Thoreau's mind and less of the lake itself. Also in Thoreau's first book, *A Week on the Concord and Merrimack Rivers*, the author's mind does not stay on the riverside landscape but, inspired by it, expands in time and place to create a huge cultural history in spite of the fact that this work was originally intended as a travelogue. *Cape Cod*, another account of a journey, actually ends as a record of Thoreau's acquisition of a new, naturalistic view of nature.

The romantic self is what Muir tried to efface and Thoreau maintained. This is Thoreau's mode of seeing: "Wherever I sat, there I might live, and *the landscape radiated from me accordingly*" (*Walden* 55; emphasis added). Thoreau's self is centered and the landscape exists through his subjectivity. The existence of Thoreau's self in his writing produces social criticism, political opinions, or personal remembrances. The most important, in connection with the way of seeing, however, are the author's sense of ethical responsibility and his global imagination. Just seeing and absorbing nature is not enough for Thoreau. Thoreau says: "If they should feel the influence of the spring of springs arousing them, they would of necessity rise to a higher and more ethereal life" (*Walden* 28). In responding to the ethereal influence, man must rise. The repeatedly expressed idea of "conscious endeavor" supports this understanding. Inhabitants near the Walden woods, Therien, Flint, and Field, all live in the beautiful landscape and daily spend more hours in nature than Thoreau himself. Especially Field dwells in an adjunct of the Baker Farm, the beauty of which once almost enticed Thoreau into dwelling there. However, just receiving spiritual influence from nature, unaccompanied by conscious effort, is not enough for their growth. Thoreau's criticism of these and other farmers tells of his belief that just seeing isn't enough; the seer must couple observation with ethical responsibility.

Thoreau lived in narrow New England, but his landscape expands over geographical limits through his global imagination. Thoreau sits at the door of his tiny cabin:

> Though the view from my door was still more contracted, I did not feel crowded or confined in the least. There was pasture enough for my imagination. The low shrub-oak plateau to which the opposite shore arose, stretched away toward the prairies of the West and the steppes of Tartary. . . .
>
> Both place and time were changed, and I dwelt nearer to those parts of the universe and to those eras in history which had most attracted me. (59)

Thoreau's landscape expands even to the steppes of Tartary and to far remote eras. Thoreau's dwelling place is even imagined to be among the stars: "If it were worth the while to settle in those parts near to the Pleiades or the Hyades, to Aldebaran or Altair, then I was really there" (59). Not only the landscape but the whole text of *Walden* tends to expand in time and place. When preparing wood for house-warming, Thoreau thinks that "the New Englander and the New Hollander, the Parisian and the Celt . . . in most parts of the world the prince and the peasant, the scholar and the savage, equally require still a few sticks from the forest to warm them" (167–68). In like manner, a distant anonymous visitor at first seems as a true Homeric or Paphlagonian man (97) and Thoreau's hoeing against weeds as a long war of Greeks with Trojans (108). Thoreau's global imagination not only expands the text in time and place, but even changes the object seen. The cedar wood beyond Flint's Pond becomes a forest fit to stand before Valhalla Hall in Norse mythology (135), and the Old Marlborough Road in Concord changes to a road to go round the world ("Walking" 233). The present object does not disappear as in *A Week* but changes in front of Thoreau, reaching to the wide world. A dramatic transfiguration works on the tranquil Walden water as follows. After reading Bhagvat-Geeta for a while, Thoreau goes down to the lake for water, and feels as if he saw a servant of the Bramin there:

> The pure Walden water is mingled with the sacred water of the Ganges.

> With favoring winds it is wafted past the site of the fabulous islands of Atlantis and the Hesperides, makes the periplus of Hanno, and, floating by Ternate and Tidore and the mouth of the Persian Gulf, melts in the tropic gales of the Indian seas, and is landed in ports of which Alexander only heard the names. (199)

At the appearance of an imaginary servant, Walden water changes. It streams half-way round the globe past imaginary islands and real islands for the ports of India. The ice-export business of Walden might be suggested as its background, but that passage looks beyond such social, economic matters to Walden water's vigorous power to purify all the world. This instant transfiguration in Thoreau's works could be called, to borrow Henry Golemba's term for his extravagances and paradoxes, "Thoreau's wild rhetoric."[4]

Today man's limitless desire for riches and power has licked up almost every corner of the natural world. During this one century, destruction and pollution have been accelerated such that even the continuation of the earth seems to have been threatened. Speaking of the cruelty to nonhuman beings, repeated nuclear tests have destroyed numberless small creatures, the fact of which is seldom noticed. A fatal lack of awe is suspected at the base of human activity. Thoreau and Muir looked to nature for the sake of man and spirit; they saw nature with love and reverence. Voicing the same spirit, a Native American sang, "My brother the fox . . ." (*Poetry* 285). We must sometimes recall their sense of nature. It might be too late, and their views might seem out of date. However, we still retain some potential to respond to them if Nash is right in saying that though wilderness is neither moral nor immoral at present, "it might still, of course, be sacred in the sense of inspiring reverence and providing meaning" (269).

As importantly, Thoreau's mode of seeing can also guide us. Ethical responsibility that arises before nature originally implied the seer's own spiritual growth. Today the goal can be expanded to political and social spheres, though the seer's morality lies at the base of every act. Speaking of the social sphere, it must be added here that Thoreau and Muir actually worked for the preservation of wild nature. Global imagination, another Thoreauvian characteristic in seeing, invites us to connect every local landscape to the wide world. We know that our local water pollution will invade the vast ocean, and we can even visualize a tsunami that hits our country reaching the coasts of a faraway country.

Notes

1 In this essay, the term "environmental literature" is used more restrictively, rather as a synonym for "the twentieth-century new nature writing." The reason is that the idea of "environment" at present seems to me different from that in Thoreau's day.
2 This passage refers to Michelle C. Neely's "Reading Thoreau's Animals."
3 It must be added here that the first part, "Ktaadn" of *The Main Woods* was actually written in 1848.
4 This term is borrowed from Henry Golemba's *Thoreau's Wild Rhetoric*. But Golemba's concern is on the usage of language, not on the way of seeing.

Works Cited

Branch, Michael P. "Telling Nature's Story: John Muir and the Decentering of the Romantic Self." *John Muir in Historical Perspective*. Ed. Sally M. Miller. New York: Peter Lang, 1999. 99–122. Print.

Buell, Lawrence. *The Environmental Imagination*. Cambridge: The Belknap P of Harvard UP, 1995. Print.

Cohen, Michael P. *The Pathless Way: John Muir and American Wilderness*. Madison: U of Wisconsin P, 1984. Print.

Cronyn, George W. ed. *American Indian Poetry: An Anthology of Songs and Chants*. New York: Fawcett Columbine, 1962. Print.

Elder, John C. "John Muir and the Literature of Wilderness." *Massachusetts Review* 22.2 (1981): 375–86. Print.

Emerson, Ralph Waldo. *The Collected Works of Ralph Waldo Emerson I: Nature, Addresses, and Lectures*. Ed. Robert E. Spiller. Cambridge: The Belknap P of Harvard UP, 1971. Print.

Golemba, Henry. *Thoreau's Wild Rhetoric*. New York: New York UP, 1990. Print.

Krutch, J. W. ed. *Great American Nature Writing*. New York: William Sloane Associates, 1950. Print.

Marsh, George Perkins. *Man and Nature*. Ed. David Lowenthal. Seatle: U of Washington, 2003. Print.

Muir, John. *Mountaineering Essays*. Ed. Richard F. Fleck. Salt Lake City: U of Utah P, 1997. Print.

——. *My First Summer in the Sierra*. New York: Penguin, 1997. Print.

——. *Nature Writings*. Ed. William Cronon. New York: Library of America, 1997. Print.

Nash, Roderick Frazier. *Wilderness and the American Mind*. 4th ed. New Haven: Yale UP, 2001. Print.

Neely, Michelle C. "Reading Thoreau's Animals." *Concord Saunterer: A Journal of Thoreau Studies* 22 (2014): 126–35. Print.

Thoreau, Henry David. *Collected Essays and Poems*. Ed. Elizabeth Hall Witherell. New York: The Library of America, 2001. Print.

——. *The Journal of Henry David Thoreau: In Fourteen Volumes Bound as Two*. Ed. Bradford Torrey & Francis H. Allen. New York: Dover, 1962. Print.

——. *The Maine Woods*. Ed. Joseph Moldenhauer. Princeton: Princeton UP, 1972. Print.
——. *Walden and Resistance to Civil Government*. 2nd ed. Ed. William Rossi. New York: Norton, 1992. Print.
Walls, Laura Dassow. "Wilderness and Wildness in Thoreauvian Science." *Thoreau's Sense of Place: Essays in American Environmental Writing*. Ed. Richard J. Schneider. Iowa City: U of Iowa P, 2000. 15–27. Print.
Williams, Dennis C. *God's Wilds: John Muir's Vision of Nature*. College Station: Texas A & M UP, 2002. Print.

Ralph Waldo Emerson and Daisetsu Suzuki:
A Comparative Investigation on their Views of Nature, Mind, and Language

Yoshio Takanashi

Introduction

Daisetsu Teitarō Suzuki（鈴木大拙 1870–1966）is a world-famous Japanese Zen Buddhist teacher and scholar. During the middle decades of the twentieth century, he made a significant contribution to Western philosophical thought by bringing the teachings of modern Zen Buddhism to the attention of the Western world through his numerous books and lectures. In the year of 2016, 50 years after his death, Suzuki has again got into the spotlight in Japan.

In his college days when he began to develop his own Zen ideas, Suzuki turned to reading Ralph Waldo Emerson's essays, and the first essay he wrote was "Emerson no zengaku ron [Zen theory of Emerson]" printed in *Zen shū* [The Zen sect] in 1896. In this essay, he deeply sympathized with Emerson's thought, exclaiming, "Now it is becoming much clearer that Emerson preached on the cultivation of the mind in the same way Zen does!"[1] In his book *Zen and Japanese Culture* published in 1959, Suzuki pointed out the similarity of Emersonian Transcendentalism with the Zen concept of "emptiness"（*kū / kon* 空）in the following:

> Emerson's allusion to "sky-void idealism" is interesting. Apparently he means the Buddhist theory of *śūnyātā* ("emptiness" or "void"). Although it is doubtful how deeply he entered into the spirit of this theory, which is the basic principle of the Buddhist thought and from which Zen starts on its mystic appreciation of Nature, it is really wonderful to see the American mind, as represented by the exponents of Transcendentalism, even trying to probe into the abysmal darkness of the Oriental fantasy. I am now beginning to understand the meaning of the deep impressions made upon me while reading Emerson in my college days. I was not then studying the

> American philosopher but digging into the recesses of my own thought, which had been there ever since the awakening of Oriental consciousness. That was the reason why I had felt so familiar with him—I was, indeed, making acquaintance with myself then. (343–44)

After about 50 years at the age of 77, Suzuki recollected his first experience of reading Emerson's essay "Self-Reliance" in his younger days:

> I was deeply moved when I first read this essay. This is self-reliance! This is true freedom! This is true independence! We don't need to feel mean only because we are little. We can express anything we have regardless of our great or little ability. This is sincerity! In this way, I was deeply impressed. (*Tōyō teki na mikata* 277)

As shown in the above quotations, Suzuki, finding the remarkable affinity of the Zen spirit and American Transcendentalism, had a feeling of great intimacy with Emerson throughout his life. Suzuki was undoubtedly the principal figure driving the popularization of Zen in the West. Some of Japanese and American scholars, greatly influenced by Suzuki, have tended to assume that Zen Buddhism served as the primary medium through which Japanese intellectuals enthusiastically accepted Emerson during the late nineteenth and early twentieth centuries (See also Ames 67–69). In this article, comparative and critical investigations will be made on the essential differences as well as on the noticeable affinities between Suzuki's Zen and Emerson's Transcendentalist thought.[2]

1. Suzuki's *Jinen* and Emerson's Nature

Firstly, a comparative consideration to Suzuki's and Emerson's views on nature will be given. Suzuki explains about the Zen view of nature（自然）as follows:

> What is the most specific characteristic of Zen asceticism in connection with the Japanese love of Nature? It consists in paying Nature the fullest respect it deserves. By this it is meant that we may treat Nature not as an object to conquer and turn wantonly to our human service, but as a friend, as a fellow being, who is destined like ourselves for Buddhahood. Zen wants us to meet Nature as a friendly, well-meaning agent whose inner

> being is thoroughly like our own, always ready to work in accord with our legitimate aspirations. . . . Zen proposes to respect Nature, to love Nature, to live its own life; . . . . (*Zen and Japanese Culture* 351)

Emerson also expresses his view of nature similar to Suzuki's. The essential point of Emerson's thought can be recognized in its placing importance on the unity of man and nature, as he writes in his book *Nature*: "Embosomed for a season in nature, whose floods of life stream around and through us" (*The Collected Works of Ralph Waldo Emerson* 1: 7; hereafter abbreviated as *CW*); and he furthermore writes:

> In the presence of nature, a wild delight runs through the man, in spite of real sorrows. . . . The greatest delight which the fields and woods minister, is the suggestion of an occult relation between man and the vegetable. I am not alone and unacknowledged. . . . Yet it is certain that the power to produce this delight, does not reside in nature, but in man, or a harmony of both. (9–10)

Moreover, just as Suzuki writes: "Zen asceticism is not at all in sympathy with the materialistic trends so much in evidence all over the world, in science, industrialism, commercialism, and many other movements of thought" (*Zen and Japanese Culture* 351), Emerson was strongly against the materialistic and mechanical view of nature, which was a principle of the emerging industrial society and technological civilization, that man and nature are utterly separated and irreconcilable. He offers an organic view of nature, in which spontaneous powers of vitality inhere in all natural things and man and nature can be harmoniously united.

Suzuki gives a historical outline of the development of Mahāyāna Buddhism after it spread from India via Central Asia to China in the first century and of how Zen Buddhism was produced and enjoyed its great popularity during the periods of the Tang (唐 618–907) and the Song (宋 960–1279). First he explains how the Indian mind varies from the Chinese one in his book *Zen Buddhism*: "Roughly, then, the Chinese are above all a most practical people, while the Indians are visionary and highly speculative" (48). And it was this Chinese sense of practicalness and its love for the everyday facts of life, he stresses, that produced Zen Buddhism:

> The Chinese have no aptitude like the Indians for hiding themselves in the clouds of mystery and supernaturalism. . . . The Chinese are thoroughly practical. They must have their own way of interpreting the doctrine of Enlightenment as applied to their daily life, and they could not help creating Zen as an expression of their inmost spiritual experience. (56)

This practical aptitude of the Chinese, he points out, transformed the supernatural and abstract Mahāyāna Buddhist doctrines of *śūnyatā* into the natural and concrete Zen ideas, from which the Zen doctrine of non-duality（不二）came to be developed between the infinite and supernatural world and the finite and actual one.

Suzuki, moreover, explains about the doctrine of non-duality:

> Salvation must be sought in the finite itself, there is nothing infinite apart from finite things; if you seek something transcendental, that will cut you off from this world of relativity, which is the same thing as the annihilation of yourself. You do not want salvation at the cost of your own existence. If so, drink and eat, and find your way of freedom in this drinking and eating. . . . Therefore the finite is the infinite, and *vice versa*. These are not two separate things, though we are compelled to conceive them so, intellectually. (17–18)

Just as Suzuki preaches, "The ordinary mind is the Way"（平常心是道）, for Emerson, everyday life and ordinary moments held the greatest value, as he writes in the following quotations:

> I embrace the common, I explore and sit at the feet of the familiar, the low. (*CW* 1: 67)

> But the soul that ascends to worship the great God, is plain and true; has no rose-color, or no fine friends, no chivalry, no adventures; does not want admiration; dwells in the hour that now is, in the earnest experience of the common day,—by reason of the present moment and the mere trifle having become porous to thought, and bibulous of the sea of light. (*CW* 2: 171–72)

> As I went to Church I thought how seldom the present hour is seized upon a new moment. To a soul alive to God every moment is a new world. (*The*

Journals and Miscellaneous Notebooks of Ralph Waldo Emerson 4: 266; hereafter abbreviated as *JMN*)

Suzuki, moreover, states that the Zen doctrine of non-duality was profoundly influenced by the Daoist doctrine of non-being (*mu / wu* 無). Taking notice of the general Western use of the word "nature" to mean the material world and its phenomena existing independently of human activities, he stresses that in East Asia nature (自然) might be better called *jinen*, which means "suchness," or "things-as-they-are" beyond form, time, and human intellect and will. He says that *jinen* is the same as Laozi[3]'s concept of nature, as is written in the *Laozi or Dao De Jing* (*The Classic of the Way and Its Virtue*), "Dao models itself after Nature" (*A Source Book of Chinese Philosophy* 153; hereafter abbreviated as *SCP*), and as Tathātā (真如), "thusness" or "suchness," a central Buddhist concept, especially in Chinese Buddhism (*Tōyō teki na mikata* 219). This is also closely akin to the original meaning of the word nature, which is "what is innately endowed," and to *physis* in ancient Greek, signifying "to be spontaneously born and generate." Suzuki expresses his feeling of intimacy with Daoism, and says that the Daoist word *myō* (subtlety 妙) best shows the meaning of *jinen* and the Oriental spirit (100–02), quoting the first chapter of the *Laozi*: "The Nameless is the origin of Heaven and Earth; The Name is the mother of all things. Therefore let there always be non-being so we may see their subtlety, and let there always be being so we may see their outcome. The two are the same, but after they are produced, they have different names. They both may be called 'deep and profound' (玄). Deeper and more profound, the door of subtleties!" (*SCP* 139). In his lecture "Zen to nihonjin no kishitsu [Zen and the Japanese spirit]," Suzuki furthermore points out that the word *soku* (conformity 即) as well as *myō* is grounded in the Oriental way of viewing nature, stating that loving nature is not unifying with nature but conforming to nature (*Suzuki Daisetsu zenshū*, vol. 16: 101–06).

Zen's doctrine of non-duality was also greatly influenced by Zhuangzi[4]'s Daoism. Suzuki quoted the *Zhuangzi* in his lecture and tried translating some passages into English (105–06). Zhuangzi advanced beyond Laozi and presented the doctrine of the equality of all things (万物斉同) in the *Zhuangzi*: "Only the intelligent knows how to identify all things as one. Therefore he does not use his own judgment but abides in the common principle. The common means the useful and the useful means identification. Identification means being at ease with oneself. When one is at ease with himself, one is near

Dao. This is to let Nature take its own course" (*SCP* 184).

Suzuki goes on explaining about what Zen's attitude toward nature is. Zen, having a most penetrating insight into reality or the very depths of all existence and the heart of life, sees nature not in stationary but in dynamic and living state: "Nature is always in motion, never at a standstill; if Nature is to be loved, it must be caught while moving and in this way its aesthetic value must be appraised. To seek tranquility is to kill nature, to stop its pulsation, and to embrace the dead corpse that is left behind" (*Zen and Japanese Culture* 361).

The similar way of viewing nature in its spontaneity and motion can be recognized in Emerson as well. In his essay "Self-Reliance," he sees into the unfolding of a new world whereby things exist in the state of spontaneity or natural purity as they originally are: "These roses under my window make no reference to former roses or to better ones; they are for what they are; they exist with God to-day. There is no time to them. There is simply the rose; it is perfect in every moment of its existence. . . . Its nature is satisfied, and it satisfied nature, in all moments alike" (*CW* 2: 38–39). Emerson, moreover, expresses his Transcendentalist idea that all things in nature are ceaselessly changing and flowing at every moment in his essay "Circles": "There are no fixtures in nature. The universe is fluid and volatile. Permanence is but a word of degrees. Our globe seen by God, is a transparent law, not a mass of facts. The law dissolves the fact and holds it fluid" (179).

The affinities between Suzuki's and Emerson's view of nature have been closely examined thus far. The differences between the two as well will have to be considered. Emerson, while telling about his mystical experience of the unity of man and nature, contrary to Suzuki's recognition of non-duality or no distinction between nature and humans, defines nature as "Not Me," an objective matter against "Me," the subjective self of human beings, in the introduction of *Nature*:

> Philosophically considered, the universe is composed of Nature and the Soul. Strictly speaking, therefore, all that is separate from us, all which philosophy distinguishes as the Not Me, that is, both nature and art, all other men and my own body, must be ranked under this name. (*CW* 1: 8)

He moreover states in his essay "Fate": "Everything is pusher or pushed: and matter and mind are in perpetual tilt and balance, so" (*CW* 6: 23). Thus his view of nature is based on the conception of "polarity" (*CW* 2: 57). In his polarity, the two poles, subject and object, and the human mind and nature, while dualistically opposing each other, tend toward a higher state, and eventually achieve unity and harmony by overcoming their opposition through "metamorphosis" (*CW* 3: 15).

As has been shown in the above quotations, in spite of Suzuki's pointing out the affinities between his and Emerson's nature, Emerson's conception of nature is based on the dualistic polarity, in which the human mind and nature tend toward unity and harmony while contradicting and opposing each other. This isn't necessarily based on the dualism peculiar to the Western philosophy that spirit and matter are completely distinct and separate, but is clearly different from Suzuki's Zen view of "nature" that there can be recognized no distinction between humans and nature. As Suzuki writes, "Satori is not a higher unity in which two contradictory terms are synthesized. When a staff is not a staff and yet it is a staff, satori obtains" (*Living by Zen* 87), it is true that Suzuki's "non-duality" resembles Emerson's "unity," but these two are essentially different.

2. Suzuki's No-Mind and Emerson's Dual Mind

Secondly, Suzuki's and Emerson's views of the human mind will be examined. According to Suzuki, "satori," the sudden flashing into consciousness of a new truth, consists in acquiring a new viewpoint for penetrating deep into the essence of the nature of the human mind and things:

> Satori is seeing into one's own nature; and this "nature" is not an entity belonging to oneself as distinguished from others; and in the "seeing" there is no seer, there is nothing seen; . . . Satori is "mindlessness," "one absolute thought," "the absolute present," "originally pure," "emptiness," "suchness," and many other things. (74)

Emerson writes, just as Suzuki does, about his experience, in which the subject and the object are united into one in his essay "The Over-Soul":

> We live in succession, in division, in parts, in particles. Meantime within man is the soul of the whole; the wise silence; the universal beauty, to which every part and particle is equally related; the eternal One. And this deep power in which we exist, and whose beatitude is all accessible to us, is not only self-sufficing and perfect in every hour, but the act of seeing and the thing seen, the seer and the spectacle, the subject and the object,

are one." (*CW* 2: 160)

The above-quoted passages from Suzuki's and Emerson's writings might induce us to suppose that both of them present the same kind of view of the nature of the self, because they place emphasis on the original pure state of the human mind before the appearance of the dualistic division and opposition between the subject and the object. Suzuki's writings offer expressions such as the following that are comparable to Emerson's "God-within" and "Self-reliance": "If you wish to seek the Buddha, you ought to see into your own Nature; for this Nature is the Buddha himself" (*Essays in Zen Buddhism* 233). Both Suzuki's Zen and Emerson's Transcendentalism center on a spirit of truth-seeking, and specifically of seeking the spring of truth within, rather than in any outer traditional authority, institution, or form.

Yet a significant difference must be observed between Suzuki's "original self" and Emerson's "inner self." As Shōei Andō pointed out: "To recognize two selves in man and to seek *reality* by penetrating into inmost self,—this attitude toward truth-seeking is also found in Zen, but in point of the connotation of the concept of two selves in man there is a remarkable difference between Zen and Transcendentalism" (138–39). The original self of Zen Buddhism is revealed when a person utterly surrenders all attachments. As long as one clings to anything, one cannot enjoy the absolute freedom. In contrast, Emerson's thought entails a concept of double-consciousness, an awareness of both an outer and an inner self. Human beings can be in touch with the "eternal One" or the universal soul at the center of their inner selves, but only by overcoming the outer self through self-purification and self-denial. Though Emerson, breaking away from orthodox Christian doctrines, draws no definite distinction between God as the Creator and all things as his creatures, the separation in his thought of the two selves ultimately resolves into dualistic opposition and struggle in the inner human mind. Whereas Suzuki's self dissolves into oneness with nature, abandoning its personality, Emerson's self thus transcends its individuality to unite with the super-personal Over-soul.[5]

Suzuki's view is based on the Mahāyāna Buddhist doctrine of "emptiness" that all things in the phenomenal world, existing only in the relation to other things, have no immutable substance of their own (無自性). He, also denying the real existence of the human soul, explains about "no-mind" by quoting the sayings of the Zen master Huángbo Xiyùn[6]: "The Mind means 'no-mind-ness,' to attain which is the ultimate end of the Buddhist life. . . . This Mind has no beginning, was never born, and will never pass away" (*The Zen Doctrine of No-Mind* 129).[7] Emerson, in contrast, while telling about his mystical experience of the unity of the subject and the object, insists on the dual nature of the self. In his sermon "The Genuine Man" (*The Complete Sermons of Ralph Waldo Emerson* 4: 409–16), he preaches that "the essential man" dwells in the innermost soul, and that this indwelling essential self is a higher self, God's image, and Reason. Developing this idea, he states that a genuine man always listens to "the Spirit of God in us all" as well as to universal reason. Thus he expounded a "double consciousness" of the self explicitly in his sermon "Religion and Society": "I recognize the distinction of the outer and the inner self,—of the double consciousness" (215). A distinction of the inner and the outer thus delineates two aspects of the self, and he here identifies a consciousness of this duality as a central concept in his philosophy. According to Emerson, the supernatural inner self and the natural outer self are distinct. In seeking the inner, essential, and universal self, the Over-soul, the seeker must not merely confront but overcome entirely the outer, superficial, and selfish self. Though he draws no definite distinction between God as the Creator and all things in the universe as his creatures, the separation of the two selves in the inner human mind resolves into dualistic opposition and struggle (Takanashi, *Emerson and Neo-Confucianism* 145–46).

Suzuki, furthermore, points out the difference in meaning between *jiyū*（自由）and "freedom" or "liberty":

> Freedom and liberty do not have the meaning of *jiyū* but of freeing from bondage or restraint. This is negative in meaning, and greatly differs from the meaning of *jiyū* in the Orient. *Ji* (itself) is at the center of the word *jiyū*, and there is no oppression and restraint. It means to come into being by itself, spontaneously. (*Tōyō teki na mikata* 64–65)

The meaning of *jiyū* is also closely tied with that of *jinen*. For Suzuki, the purpose of Zen lies in being awakened to the highest truth by looking into the nature of all things and clinging to nothing in the absolutely emancipated state of the mind. He states that "a pure man who transcends and is no longer attached to any class of Buddhas or sentient beings"（一無位眞人）(209; *SCP* 445) is the awakened master who has realized the highest state of *jiyū*, that is, absolute enlightenment. Suzuki tells that perfect freedom can only be attained in the unconditional, formless, and empty state of the mind. Emerson likewise expresses the state of the mind analogous to the awakening of Zen in his essay "Spiritual Laws": "If in the hours of clear reason we should speak the severest truth, we should say, that we had never made a sacrifice. In these hours the mind seems so great, that nothing can be taken from us that seems much. All loss, all pain is particular: the universe remains to the heart unhurt. . . . For it is only the finite that has wrought and suffered; the infinite lies stretched in smiling repose" (*CW* 2: 77).

Emerson, on the other hand, confronted the problem of freedom and fate throughout his life (See also Whicher). Freedom for him is based on the concept of individual free will bestowed by God on human being. Although Emerson repudiated orthodox Unitarian Christianity, he continued to view freedom of will as essential to the significance of human existence. He thus argues, "God offers to every mind its choice between truth and repose. Take which you please,—you can never have both. Between these, as a pendulum, man oscillates" (202). For Emerson, each human mind, as "a selecting principle" (84), is duty-bound to aspire to moral perfection, unceasingly challenged by "its choice and between truth and repose." Emerson renounced the doctrine of the Last Judgment, but in his thought human beings are at every moment judged by "God-within." As he declared: "Thus of their own volition, souls proceed into heaven, into hell" (*CW* 1: 78).

Emerson views free will and fate as opposed to each other in his essay "Fate." While he acknowledges the dreadful power of nature, and hence, fate, he regards the mind in its "antagonism" (*CW* 6: 12) to nature to be unregulated by the natural order, and to have the power of will seek freedom. According to Emerson, human beings have the power to confront natural fate, which continually restricts their conditions, by virtue of another fate: their endowment of the abilities of free will, thinking, and moral sentiment. As he writes: "For, if Fate is so prevailing, man also is part of it, and can confront fate with fate" (13). In this understanding, one neither blindly submits as a "victim of fate" nor seeks without limits for freedom, but rather willingly accepts one's fate, as a human being, of "necessitated freedom" through submission and "build[ing] alters to the Beautiful Necessity" (26).

As we have seen, Suzuki's freedom of the self, accomplished through "satori," that is, seeing into one's own nature and having insight into the truth, connotes the meaning of "mindlessness" or "purposelessness." This can be made a distinction from Emerson's dualistic notion of freedom of the self, which only an individual, entirely self-reliant and independent, can pursue and enjoy.

3. Suzuki's Non-Verbal Truth and Emerson's Language of Nature

Thirdly, a comparative examination on how Suzuki and Emerson think about the nature of language will be made. Suzuki regards "the transmission of spiritual awakening without depending upon words and scriptures" (不立文字) as one of the most characteristic features of Zen. He, furthermore, asserting that the highest truth and spiritual enlightenment cannot be attained by adhering to the common-sense way of looking at things and "logical" interpretation, emphasizes the irrational and illogical methods of Zen instruction:

> Zen wants us to acquire an entirely new point of view whereby to look into the mysteries of life and the secrets of nature. This is because Zen has come to the definite conclusion that the ordinary logical process of reasoning is powerless to give final satisfaction to our deepest spiritual needs.
>
> We generally think that "A is A" is absolute, and that the proposition "A is not-A" or "A is B" is unthinkable. We have never been able to break through these conditions of the understanding; they have been too imposing. But now Zen declares that words are words and no more. . . .
>
> "The flower is not red, the willow is not green." This is regarded by Zen devotees as most refreshingly satisfying. So long as we think logic final we are chained, we have no freedom of spirit, and real facts of life are lost sight of. (*An Introduction to Zen Buddhism* 29–30)

Here it must be noted, however, that Suzuki doesn't necessarily make little of the effective use of words, as is shown by the introduction of the *koan* exercise, paradoxical questions for meditation, as a means of clearing off the intellectual obstruction and coming into the truth of Zen. Suzuki writes: "Words are only an index to this state; through them we are enabled to get into its signification, but do not look to words for absolute guidance" (24).

Emerson, just as Suzuki, thinks that words, lowering to a level of analytical or technical expression, are no longer pictures of the original state of nature but of merely social conventions. He also says that books, if not read in a right way, don't help to penetrate deep into the very nature of things and grasp directly the living truth of life: "Books are the best of things, well used; abused, among the worst. . . . They are for nothing but to inspire. . . . When he can read God directly, the hour is too precious to be wasted in other men's transcripts of their readings" (*CW* 1: 56–57). Emerson adopted the term "Reason" from the writings of Coleridge, who employed it in the sense of Kantian concept of *Vernunft* (Reason) to signify a cognitive faculty higher than "understanding," or the faculty of conceptualizing perceiving phenomena. Under Coleridge's influence, Emerson developed his concept of Reason in this sense as a central one in his early Transcendentalist thought. He regards Reason synonymous as eternal truth and universal soul, which cannot be attained by understanding, and sees awaking to Reason as the purpose of human life.

Emerson, in contrast to Suzuki's Zen doctrine of nonverbal truth, while recognizing the limits of logical reasoning, argues in *Nature* that the human race in the primeval stage of history spoke the "language of nature" (See also Gura 41–42), which was intimately connected with the universal origin to speech: "As we go back in history, language becomes more picturesque, until its infancy, when it is all poetry; or, all spiritual facts are represented by natural symbols. The same symbols are found to make the original elements of all languages" (*CW* 1: 19). For Emerson, nature is a map for penetrating into the spiritual world, and natural law corresponds to moral law. He thus developed his theory that correspondence between the human mind and nature can be achieved through the intervention of symbolic language. Hence the role of the human is to see through the symbolic language hidden in visible things and to unite language with these things, as he writes: "But wise men pierce this rotten diction and fasten words again to visible things; so that picturesque language is at once a commanding certificate that he who employs it, is a man in alliance with truth and God" (20). According to Emerson, through the act of transforming manifest and outer language into acoustic and inner language, created words into creative words, the human can liberate things and transforms them into higher organic forms and recover the unity of human thought and the essence of things. Here words can be considered to be identified with the indwelling essence of the human mind and natural things. The fundamental principle of his Transcendentalist thought can be concluded to lie in achieving the ultimate unity of natural law and moral law. The human, therefore, is required to be awakened to Reason and to strive for the unification with the universal law ruling over all things in the universe (*Emerson and Neo-Confucianism* 91–98).

As we have made a comparative examination, Suzuki rejects any conceptual discrimination and symbolic nature of language, while Emerson, thinking of nature as the symbol of the mind, interposes the concept of law. We may be led to a recognition that Suzuki's view that words have no relation to any indwelling essence of the human mind and things and his emphasis on absolute freedom from all conceptual restraints can be considered to be clearly opposed to Emerson's view that Nature is divine manifestation and symbolic language and that law is at the heart of human moral integrity.

Conclusion

Greatly influenced by Suzuki's writings, some of Japanese and American scholars have assumed that American Transcendentalism has much affinity with Zen Buddhism. It is true that Suzuki's Zen and Emerson's thought are grounded in their mystical experiences of the unity of the self and nature by seeking the spring of universal spirituality within the inner soul. However, Suzuki failed to observe that the Zen concept of emptiness—though it has a transcendent, metaphysical, and supersensible aspect—cannot be understood as supernatural in the sense of Emerson's conception of law, Reason, and "Over-soul." From the comparative investigations, therefore, we have made hitherto on Emerson's and Suzuki's philosophies, specifically in terms of their views of nature, the human mind, and language, we could be led to the conclusion: although some noticeable similarities exist between Suzuki's Zen and Emerson's thought, Suzuki's Zen, based on the Buddhist and Daoist concept of emptiness and "no-mind," is essentially different from Emersonian thought grounded in monistic dualism.

The view of Emerson's thought almost identical to Zen Buddhism, one of the characteristics recognizable since the late nineteenth century among some Japanese intellectuals, may have hindered their recognition of the supernatural, complex, and many-sided casts of American Transcendentalism. Some Western scholars also have supposed that Zen Buddhism is chiefly responsible for Japanese interest in Emersonianism. This seems to be closely related to the difficulty we have even in the present day in understanding the diversity and complexity of both Eastern and Western philosophies and religions. In the twenty-first century, when the cultural and economic interrelation across the Pacific is much more than before in the ascendant, we are required to step beyond Suzuki's framework of seeking the affinity between Eastern and Western thoughts and religions merely from the viewpoint of mystical experience and intuitive insight.

Notes

1 Suzuki, *Zen shū* 14, separate vol. 1 of *Suzuki Daisetsu zenshū*, 23. The translation is mine; hereafter the translations are mine, except as noted.
2 For Emerson and Zen Buddhism, see Rudy, Morris, Hakutani, Andō, Ames, and Detweiler. And for Emerson and Suzuki, see Hodder, Rampell, and Buell.
3 Laozi（老子 c.600 BC–c.501 BC）was the founder of philosophical Daoism and a religious figure in Zhou-dynasty China.
4 Zhuangzi（荘子 c.369 BC–c.286 BC）was a Chinese Daoist philosopher and the author of the *Zhuangzi*, who is supposed to have lived during the Warring States period.
5 For the differences between Emerson's thought and Zen Buddhism, see also Hakutani, 447, and Detweiler, 426–27.
6 Huángbò Xīyùn（黄檗希運 ?–850）was an influential Chinese master of Zen Buddhism during the Tang-dynasty China. He was the teacher of Linji Yixuan（臨済義玄 ?–866）, who founded the Linji school of Zen Buddhism.
7 Suzuki's notion of emptiness can be considered somewhat different from the Indian Mahāyāna Buddhist idea of emptiness, especially developed by Nāgārjuna, the founder of the Madhyamaka school.

Works Cited

Ames, Van Meter. *Zen and American Thought*. Honolulu: University of Hawaii Press, 1962. Print.

Andō, Shōei. *Zen and American Transcendentalism: An Investigation of One's Self*. Tokyo: Hokuseidō, 1970. Print.

Buell, Lawrence. *Emerson*. Cambridge, Mass.: Belknap Press of Harvard University, 2003. Print.

Chan, Wing-tsit, trans. and comp. *A Source Book in Chinese Philosophy*. Princeton: Princeton University Press, 1963. Print.

Detweiler, Robert. "Emerson and Zen." *American Quarterly* 14. 3 (1962): 422–38. Print.

Emerson, Ralph Waldo. *The Complete Sermons of Ralph Waldo Emerson*. Eds. Albert J. von Frank et al. 4 vols. Columbia: University of Missouri Press, 1989–92. Concerning the titles of Emerson's sermons, the author follows "A List of the Sermons" in *Young Emerson Speaks: Unpublished Discourses on Many Subjects* by Ralph Waldo Emerson. Ed. Arthur C. McGiffert, Jr. Boston: Houghton Mifflin, 1938, 263–71. Print.

——. *The Collected Works of Ralph Waldo Emerson*. Eds. Alfred R. Ferguson, Joseph Slater, Douglas Emory Wilson et al. 10 vols. Cambridge, Mass: Harvard University Press. 1971– 2013. Print.

——. *The Journals and Miscellaneous Notebooks of Ralph Waldo Emerson*. Eds. William H. Gilman, Ralph H. Orth et al. 16 vols. Cambridge, Mass.: Harvard University Press, 1960–82. Print.

Gura, Philip F. *American Transcendentalism: A History*. New York: Hill and Wang,

2007. Print.
Hakutani, Yoshinobu. "Emerson, Whitman, and Zen Buddhism," *Midwest Quarterly* 31, summer 1990: 433–48. Print.
Hodder, Alan. "Asia in Emerson and Emerson in Asia." Ed. Jean McClure Mudge. *Mr. Emerson's Revolution*. Open Book Publishers, 2015: 373–405. Print.
Morris, Stephen. "Beyond Christianity: Transcendentalism and Zen." *The Eastern Buddhist* 24 (2), autumn 1991: 33–68. Print.
Rampell, Palmer "Laws That Refuse To Be Stated: The Post-Sectarian Spiritualities of Emerson, Thoreau, and D. T. Suzuki." *New England Quarterly* 84.4 (2011): 621–54. Print.
Rudy, John G. *Emerson and Zen Buddhism*. Lewiston: Edwin Mellen Press, 2001. Print.
Suzuki, Daisetsu. T. *An Introduction to Zen Buddhism*. New York: Grove Press, 1964. Print.
——. *Essays in Zen Buddhism: First Series*. Ed. Christmas Humphreys. London: Rider, 1970. Print.
——. *Living by Zen*. Ed. Christmas Humphreys. New Delhi: Munshiram Manoharlal, 2011. Print.
——. *Suzuki Daisetsu zenshū* [*The Complete Works of Daisetsu Suzuki*]. 32 vols. Tokyo: Iwanami-shoten, 1968–70. Print.
——. *The Zen Doctrine of No-Mind: The Significance of the Sūtra of Hui-neng (Wei-lang)*. Ed. Christmas Humphreys. San Francisco and Newburyport: Weiser Books, 1972. Print.
——. *Tōyō teki na mikata* [*Oriental points of view*]. Ed. Shizuteru Ueda. Tokyo: Iwanami-shoten, 1997. Print.
——. *Zen and Japanese Culture*. Princeton, N. J.: Princeton University Press, 1959. Print.
——. *Zen Buddhism: Selected Writings of D. T. Suzuki*. Ed. William Barrett. New York: Three Leaves Press, 2006. Print.
Takanashi, Yoshio. *Emerson and Neo-Confucianism: Crossing Paths over the Pacific*. New York: Palgrave Macmillan, 2014. Print.
——. "The Reception of Ralph Waldo Emerson and Henry David Thoreau in Meiji to Taishō Japan." *Oxford Research Encyclopedia of Literature*. Oxford University Press. Web. Mar. 2017.
Whicher, Stephen E. *Freedom and Fate: An Inner Life of Ralph Waldo Emerson*. Philadelphia: University of Pennsylvania Press, 1953. Print.

The outline of this article was presented at the 27th Annual Meeting of the American Literature Association (San Francisco, May 27, 2016). This research is also supported by the Japan Society for the Promotion of Science, Grant No.15K02373.

Uses of the Early Emerson in the Present Age

Masaki Horiuchi

What can Ralph Waldo Emerson contribute in the light of thought in the twenty-first century? Where does the contemporary significance of Emerson lie after 9/11, in the era of terror, war refugees, and the disastrous gaps of the global capitalism? I would like to focus on the thought of the early Emerson as a whole, as found in his works from *Nature* to *Essays: Second Series*, and to make suggestions about what seem to be his most productive possibilities. In doing so, I will take him out of the context of the political situation of the United States and onto the plane of our contemporary world (including Japan); in other words, by taking the word "American" out of "The American Scholar," I want to offer what we can learn from the Emersonian "Scholar" in the twenty-first century.

My premise in doing so is to acknowledge that the central point of Emerson's argument about "self" lies in that he thoroughly nullifies the sense of the individualistic subject, contrary to the typical Western emphasis on the Cartesian concept of the *Ego*. In modern times when all religious institutions seem to be precariously unreliable, Emerson tries to induce readers to train themselves, as it were, into the state of *nothing* ("I am nothing; I see all" [*Nature* 10]). This is a way of handling the self. Whereas, facing obstacles caused by the egoism of others, one needs strong self-reliance, everyone in solitude should rely on nature, something common, and be determined to be passive and receptive to the composite of the true, the good, and the beautiful. This non-ego type of the self is a form of subjectivity based on the acknowledgement of the interaction between the body and the world, in opposition to the consideration of one's private gain in comparison with others. Emerson keeps the individual as a half-open junction of the self and the universal for the sake of anti-individualism.

Bodily Experience and Religiosity without Religion

What is regarded as "religious" is clearly apparent in Emerson. His texts often take on a mystical character, which, it seems, has repelled many academic researchers both in the United States and Japan. A few of the exceptions are such scholars as George Kateb, Lawrence Buell, and David M. Robinson. Kateb's highly acclaimed *Emerson and Self-Reliance* has one chapter titled "The Questions of Religiousness" (61–95). Buell provided one chapter in *Emerson* for the topics of religion, with the title of "Religious Radicalism" (156–98). Robinson edited an anthology of Emerson's essays concerning "spiritual" subject and, in "Introduction," deals with his religious side as "a spiritual guide" (1–20). I do not feel any institutionalized religion to be congenial, but I consider what can be called "religiosity" is highly important to our human world. The so-called religious or mystical side of Emerson should not be avoided but rather faced and evaluated in its most significant quality. What I want to argue regarding this point is Emerson's way to open up human subjectivity. The problem of religiosity, and not of religion, holds an essential place there.

First we have to be careful not to think of mysticism as something abstract or supersensual, because it is based on *experience*. For example, F. C. Happold, who edited the book, *Mysticism: A Study and Anthology*, and wrote a long essay on mysticism entitled "The Study," says, "Experience is . . . the primary thing" in thinking about mysticism (Happold 25); the features of the knowledge on mystical religion both in the East and West—what he calls "the Perennial Philosophy" (20)—can well be applied to many essays of the early Emerson. We can also take as an example the famous Japanese thinker, Toshi-hiko Izutsu, who points out in *Shinpi Tetsugaku* [*Mystical Philosophy*], written in his early period: "Platonic idealism is an undeniable fact of experience, not merely a philo-sophical standpoint" (Izutsu 235; my translation). On the tradition of mystical thought from the Pre-Socratics to Plotinus, he writes, "the emergence of the recognition of the universe is none other than the fact of experience, and, as experience itself, we have no other choice than to say it is the ultimate situation, completely undeniable" (216; my translation). According to Izutsu, to think of Platonism or Neoplatonism without considering the experiential dimension would be a fallacy. Above all things, Emerson detests any religious dogma expressing in fixed language which had originally appeared as a result of a human experience; what he thinks is real is the individual's vision originating from private experience. The most radical aspect of the stance of the early Emerson is to encourage readers to separate themselves from every kind of collective institution and to start everything anew from an individual standpoint, in viewing the world, the ethics of life, and participation in society.

Every experience is essentially singular and is received through each person's body. Religion gives it form in each culture and makes it into an immovable "Truth" beyond individual experience. That act, according to Emerson, is necessarily arrogant and full of errors. Every individual, without being affected by any outer authority, can feel something that could be categorized as "religious." What is to be found in the center of the experience is the *opening* in the dimension of the bodily sense. That problem, therefore, which seems to be one of religion at first, in fact turns out to be of the body. It is called "ecstasy" (127), in the meaning of "out of oneself," in "The Method of Nature," and is said to be taken in the condition of "entire possession" in "The Over-Soul" (396). In the latter, Emerson describes it, using the Christian term "Revelation," as "an influx of the Divine mind into our mind" (392). Yet, when he goes on to describe it as "A thrill passes through all men at the reception of new truth" (392), there is no doubt that this refers to a bodily sensation not limited to Christians only. The expression of the axiom, "The faith should blend with the light of rising and of setting suns, with the flying cloud, the singing bird, and the breath of flowers" (84), in "The Divinity School Address," implies that the standard of "faith" is the body, diversified in sight, hearing, and smell. In "Love" Emerson says:

> Behold there in the wood the fine madman! He is a palace of sweet sounds and sights; he dilates; he is twice a man; he walks with arms akimbo; he soliloquizes; he accosts the grass and the trees; he feels the blood of the violet, the clover, and the lily in his veins; and he talks with the brook that wets his foot. (331)

This is quite an Emersonian expression of the state of subjectivity, open through the whole body in nature. In "Nature" in *The Second Series*, Emerson, after enumerating examples of natural sounds and sights, calls them "the music and pictures of the most ancient religion." Just after this, he describes rowing out on a river with his friend in this way: "We penetrate bodily this incredible beauty; we dip our hands in this painted element: our eyes are bathed in these lights and forms" (543). In this context, his personal experience shows what lies at the core of "the most ancient religion." The interaction between the body and the world in Emerson is not the subject-object relation, but can be properly approached by Merleau-Ponty's concepts of "flesh" and "chiasm" (Merleau-Ponty 130–55). Such bodily experiences underpin Emersonian religiosity.

It was impossible for Emerson, living in the nineteenth century, to take the body as a concept superior to "spirit." Admitting this, if we seriously try to think about Emerson's contemporary significance, we should deliberately *invert* his Platonism. In the following passage from "The Divinity School Address," his priority surely seems to be placed on the ideal, universal "laws": "The perception of this law of laws awakens in the mind a sentiment which we call the religious sentiment, and which makes our highest happiness" (78). However, from our standpoint, the sequence should rather be reversed, even against Emerson's preference. When we focus on the real procedure of the individual's appreciation of the universal laws, first comes the bodily reception of "the religious sentiment," then occurs the verbalization of "laws" as an act of naming. In "Nature," outer nature is claimed to be the form spirit takes, but what should we read in the following passage?—"Nature is the incarnation of a thought, and turns to a thought again, as ice becomes water and gas. The world is mind precipitated, and the volatile essence is forever escaping again into the state of free thought" (555). Even though Emerson prefers "thought" or "spirit," we can judge that, in actuality, outer stimuli and inner thoughts are always changing into one another, and, from that point of view, it is useless to decide which comes first. In other words, when we argue about Emerson's thought, it is theoretically permissible to assume that the physical world exists first and the individuals in it experience its effects through the channels of sense. Emerson declares, in the "Idealism" chapter of *Nature*: "all men are capable of being raised by piety or by passion, into their region. . . . Like a new soul, they renew the body. We become physically nimble and lightsome" (37). Here the "soul" and "body" are inseparable, one with each other, and to claim hierarchy has no point.

The nimble movement of the "soul," the unity of the body and mind, is the thing Emerson esteems most. However, this is not the exclusive characteristic of the people endowed with a special constitution, as in shamanism. According to "The Over-Soul," "A certain tendency to insanity has always attended the opening of the religious sense in men," but just before this remark he notes:

> The character and duration of this enthusiasm varies with the state of the individual, from an ecstasy and trance and prophetic inspiration,—which

> is its rare appearance,—to the faintest glow of virtuous emotion, in which form it warms, like our household fires, all the families and associations of men, and makes society possible. (392)

Unlike genuine mysticism, Emerson supposes a scale of degrees in such enthusiasm that can be called "religious." The sense seems to him to take on a moral character that he deems to be the ties that bind society; moral sentiment held by the ordinary people is also regarded as part of the movement. Emerson stresses the commonality of the feeling in "The Poet" as follows: "The inwardness, and mystery, of this attachment, drives men of every class to the use of emblems. . . . The people fancy they hate poetry, and they are all poets and mystics!" (454) This is not only the problem of religion ("mystics") but also that of art ("poets"), and these problems are interchangeable. This in itself is a radical critique of institutional religions. The reason why the vision is viewed as moral is that, unless we affirm as good the fact that this world exists and all the organisms coexist in it, we cannot escape nihilism.

Emerson criticizes mysticism as an "ism" in "The Poet," because mystics fix "an accidental and individual symbol for an universal one" (463–64): an individual should not tread on the boundaries to impose his or her private sense on other people. The sense of mystique (not mysticism) should remain as a fragment to the end. The demand to "Insist on yourself; never imitate" (278) is necessary because, in order to synchronize oneself peacefully with the world, every coercion from above becomes an obstacle. We can detect a severe critique of religion with dogma taught in a fixed state, viewing it as too excessive, in a passage in "Circles": "We can never see Christianity from the catechism:—from the pastures, from a boat in the pond, from amidst the songs of wood-birds, we possibly may. . . . the instinct of man . . . gladly arms itself against the dogmatism of bigots . . ." (409).

Emerson intends to separate the individual from all institutions without rendering him or her an egoist. Emerson's religiosity runs counter to the Christian church by denying the personal God and obedience to any other person, and persuades each reader to decide all by oneself. Thus he warns, in "Circles," "Do not set the least value on what I do" (412), careful not to make his own words authoritative. *Religiosity without religion* is needed as an opening of the individual's subjectivity, so that the individual, as a fragment, can take a suitable position for participation in something common beyond one's personal desires.

Power as the Reality of the World

The sense of mystique felt inside the body by an individual refuses to be correctly verbalized, but once consciousness appears from there to grasp the world in concrete terms, the world, in Emerson's formulation, comes to be imaged as something that is becoming and in flux. A famous passage in "Self-Reliance" suggests:

> Life only avails, not the having lived. Power ceases in the instant of repose; it resides in the moment of transition from a past to a new state, in the shooting of the gulf, in the darting to an aim. This one fact the world hates, that the soul *becomes*; . . . . (271)

Taking the world as something always becoming and changing, Emerson regards the flowing aspect of power as the real state of the world, escaping the grid of language eternally. It is the hinge, the crossing point, of the thought of Emerson and the concept of power found in Nietzsche, of course.

We could find the same kind of aspect of the world almost everywhere in the early Emerson. For a typical example, I cite from "Circles": "There are no fixtures in nature. The universe is fluid and volatile. Permanence is but a word of degrees" (403). A more concrete image can be found in "The Method of Nature":

> The method of nature: who could ever analyze it? That rushing stream will not stop to be observed. We can never surprise nature in a corner; never find the end of a thread; never tell where to set the first stone. The bird hastens to lay her egg: the egg hastens to be a bird. The wholeness we admire in the order of the world, is the result of infinite distribution. Its smoothness is the smoothness of the pitch of the cataract. (119)

The image of the surface of the rushing water of a cataract shows a world with no fixture. Although often delineated in such a motion by velocity, the harmonic form of the real world, in essence, resembles, let us say, the paintings of water lilies or cathedrals by Claude Monet or the landscape of a red morning sky seen by myopic eyes. If we take the example of the image of velocity, the whiteness in "Experience" may be the most effective candidate in which the phenomenal white color displays the real aspect of the world: "The parti-colored wheel must revolve very fast to appear white" (477). Those glimpses reveal the world usually latent in the virtual dimension. When Emerson writes in "The Poet," "We stand before the secret of the world, there where Being passes into Appearance, and Unity into Variety" (453), his terms "Being" and "Unity" refer to the world in virtuality. The world is made into a *figure*, as compared with the *ground* in the Gestalt psychology and is segmented by language into "Appearance" or "Variety": it becomes actualized. That is the reason he says, in "Experience," "Life will be imaged, but cannot be divided nor doubled" (488).

Paraphrasing this in line with nature, Emerson tries to name it in "Nature" as "*natura naturans*," using traditional philosophical terminology. More important than the naming is the manner in which he presents the image of nature:

> . . . let us not longer omit our homage to the Efficient Nature, *natura naturans*, the quick cause, before which all forms flee as the driven snows, itself secret, its works driven before it in flocks and multitudes . . . . A little heat, that is, a little motion, is all that differences the bald, dazzling white, and deadly cold poles of the earth from the prolific tropical climates. All changes pass without violence, ... (546)

What produces extreme opposites is in fact a very trifling, small thing, and this claim of Emerson is clearly a radical critique of violence. In the next paragraph he writes, "The whirling bubble on the surface of a brook, admits us to the secret of the mechanics of the sky. Every shell on the beach is a key to it. A little water made to rotate in a cup explains the formation of the simpler shells; . . ." (547). As this metaphor suggests, Emerson's sensibility is apparent in that the secret of the becoming world is condensed into subtle differences of minute things. His examples of "the method of nature" which are other than the web of the human-made schema of conceptualization are small living things: "The squirrel hoards nuts, and the bee gathers honey, without knowing what they do, and they are thus provided for without selfishness or disgrace" ("The Transcendentalist" 198). The squirrel is a typical example in Emerson to show how life naturally manifests itself, and, in "Art," he also refers to it in the following way: "A squirrel leaping from bough to bough, and making the wood but one wide tree for his pleasure, fills the eye not less than a lion,—is beautiful, self-sufficing, and stands then and there for nature" (433). What is important in passages like these is not only smallness but also velocity because speed has the ability to impact and shake the usual image of the world, which has been made excessively stagnant and motionless by the limiting meshes of human recognition.

The essence of "Power," its real nature, which nimble small beings show, runs counter to the state of power in everyday life and in the social, political space, as a famous passage of "Experience" has it state: "Like a bird which alights nowhere, but hops perpetually from bough to bough, is the Power which abides in no man and in no woman, but for a moment speaks from this one, and for another moment from that one" (477). Power badly actualized in political situations should be, according to Emerson, rejected as something which a particular person holds like property and uses to manipulate others—something reactionary that will produce resentment. Power as power, Emerson claims, has no quality of staying in one place for a long time, and, when coming forth, without becoming property-like, shifts its place of appearance unexpectedly all the time. The way to symbolize it is by using a light, small being like a titmouse, a hummingbird, or a bumblebee—these are quintessentially Emersonian. This "power" is always circulating throughout the world, as he says in "The American Scholar": "There is never a beginning, there is never an end, to the inexplicable continuity of this web of God, but always circular power returning into itself" (55). Thus, "Power keeps quite another road than the turnpikes of choice and will, namely, the subterranean and invisible tunnels and channels of life" ("Experience" 482). This is the reason why a person becomes powerful "obliquely, and not by the direct stroke" ("Experience" 483). Such an argument is taken as real only when grounded on the sense of the bodily reception, as expounded in the previous section. Otherwise, it would be misunderstood as a mere myth or a fable.

This image of the world as power functions as a means of criticism on the so-called real world. Everywhere around him Emerson saw the crushing of the weak by power, property, and money. He says in "The American Scholar": "Men such as they are, very naturally seek money or power; and power because it is as good as money . . ." (66). He holds that we should convert this tendency of individuals by "revolution," through "the gradual domestication of the idea of Culture" (67). We are tempted to judge Emerson's politics as naïve when we read him say in "Lecture on the Times": "[The Reformers] do not rely on precisely that strength which wins me to their cause; not on love, not on a principle, but on men, on multitudes, on circumstances, on money, on party; that is, on fear, on wrath, and pride" (162). But at the same time, I myself cannot help asking: can we say yes to a world run by fear, wrath, and pride? Maybe I am naïve too, feeling disgust when others brag that, of course, we can. When Emerson deploringly says, "The Americans have no faith. They rely on power of a dollar" ("Man the Reformer" 146), the "faith" he alludes to is not that of institutionalized religions, but the thought that an individual should refine and practice, each in his or her own way. This thought entertains both relativization of the concept of possession and critique of the rule of government, which he attacks in "Self-Reliance": "the reliance on Property, including the reliance on governments which protect it, is the want of self-reliance" (281). Although he is aware, as "the order of nature," that "there will always be a government of force, where men are selfish" ("Politics" 570), what Emerson places in opposition to that government is "a purely moral force" (569). Therefore, it is a problem of self-government, not of government. Emerson is devoted, through and through, to the task of how to govern oneself, which allows us to have a strong foothold to criticize society.

How the Universal is Housed in the Individual

The idea of the universal takes a central place in Emerson's thought, and I conceive that it is tantamount to the concept of law, especially moral law. The cornerstone of the renewal of Emerson's thought in the twenty-first century depends on activating this point. In other words, it is the task of finding commonality of all in the global world of ours and making it afresh into a function of thought. The first step we should take is the concept of "life." In this respect the comment of Branka Arsić gets at the kernel:

> . . . I take him literally when he identifies the soul with life, claiming that it *is* (is real and actual). The soul or being is a life (indefinite, nonparticular, impersonal) shared and embodied by everything that is formed and so individualized, not only by human persons. (Arsić 93)

In "Self-Reliance" Emerson writes, "We first share the life by which things exist, and afterwards see them as appearances in nature, and forget that we have shared their cause" (269). Each person's life is as if borrowed for a while, a portion of that which everybody originally shares. I dare to redefine this commonality of life as that of the brain and of the body. Brain science tells us that human brains exactly take the same form, regardless of the differences of race, gender, and culture. The commonality of the structure of the body and the brain in humans supports the concept of the universal in Emerson as a clear fact.

We can go further to say that, in Emerson's text, the universal exists as an *effect* on the body. He correctly describes the process of the surfacing of the sense of the universal:

> Who looks upon a river in a meditative hour, and is not reminded of the flux of all things? Throw a stone into the stream, and the circles that propagate themselves are the beautiful type of all influence. Man is conscious of a universal soul within or behind his individual life, ... (*Nature* 21)

The same kind of sensory movement from the body toward the universal can be seen in a passage where he describes of his experience of seeing the spectacle of the morning in *Nature*: "I seem to partake its rapid transformations: the active enchantment reaches my dust, and I dilate and conspire with the morning wind" (15). The problem of the moral law can be considered as an extension of this argument. In the description of the moral law, in "Compensation," Emerson expresses the process of "a moral sentiment" shifting into the human realization of "law": "Thus is the universe alive. All things are moral. That soul, which within us is a sentiment, outside of us is a law" (289). The law beyond the individual can be felt as real only with the help of the bodily senses. Otherwise, it would be merely cerebral and could not be trusted.

Starting from inner sentiment, the individual reaches the universal. Emerson tries to grasp the process as a route *from the private to the public* as "The American Scholar" shows:

> He learns that he who has mastered any law in his private thoughts, is master to that extent of all men whose language he speaks, and of all into whose language his own can be translated. . . . the deeper he dives into his privatest, secretest presentiment, to his wonder he finds, this is the most acceptable, most public, and universally true. (64)

Only through "my sense of the sacredness of private integrity" ("Lecture on the Time" 163) is achieved the trust in the common public; this is Emerson's logic, which means that we cannot erase the individual. Without individual beings, the universal goodness cannot be actualized in the world. Therefore, he says, "I would have the island of a man inviolate" ("Manners" 522). The way from the individual to the universal opens of its own accord. "The fact that I am here certainly shows me that the soul had need of an organ here" ("Spiritual Laws" 321); the "I" is applicable to everyone and, insofar as one has the same structure as others, using the first person singular, everyone can bear the universal. Thus, Emerson writes, "The universal does not attract us until housed in an individual" ("The Method of Nature" 122).

But in what manner is the universal housed in an individual? Emerson focuses on the excessive sense of life that oversteps the bounds of the usual consciousness of the individual, that is, "ecstasy." He claims there is "one superincumbent tendency" in nature and "the whole . . . obeys that redundancy or excess of life which in conscious being we call *ecstasy*" ("The Method of Nature" 121). Jonathan Levin rightly points out that "*Ecstasy* and *tendency* call to mind the active processes that encompass (and constitute) individuals. Emerson figures nature as one magnificent *tendency*, a vast ongoing process that suffuses everything" (Levin 35). According to Emerson, "This ecstatical state seems to direct a regard to the whole and not to the parts; to the cause and not to the ends; to the tendency, and not to the act" ("The Method of Nature" 125). The "tendency" here is modelled after life, of which humans are one kind, and it can sometimes take the form of a small bumblebee, as in the poem "The Humble-Bee." The individual, therefore, cannot theoretically *know* what the "whole" is, to which its own tendency points. Rather, the individual exists as a kind of index to that which is common to all organisms: "Every man is not so much a workman in the world, as he is a suggestion of that he should be" ("Circles" 405). The tendency toward something good of the public is affirmed, but any particular *form* of the public should always remain temporary.

But does not this thinking lead to negate that every individual is unique and that diverse and conflicting individuals coexist in the world? The key Emerson offers to solve this question is the concept of "character," which works as a hinge to ensure the multiplicity of human beings. It is a concept that shows that, although all indices selfishly seem to point in varied directions, each bears his or her share of the whole. So Emerson claims:

> Each man has his own vocation. . . . There is one direction in which all space is open to him. . . . He is like a ship in a river; he runs against obstructions on every side but one; on that side all obstruction is taken away, and he sweeps serenely over a deepening channel into an infinite sea. ("Spiritual Laws" 310)

In this case, the ship does not know its destination but knows that it will surely reach some good place and that is enough. The route of the ship leaves a line or trace of its own and the line shows its character. It can only be known retroactively, by the others outside, after each one has finished its voyage, so that self-consciousness should carefully be avoided.

This image of a line, in Emerson's conception, although it looks straight because of its shortness, is a fragment supposed to be a part of the extraordinarily large arc, as he writes in "Nominalist and Realist":

> The least hint sets us on the pursuit of a character, which no man realizes. We have such exorbitant eyes, that on seeing the smallest arc, we complete the curve, and when the curtain is lifted from the diagram which it seemed to veil, we are vexed to find that no more was drawn, than just that fragment of an arc which we first beheld. (575)

Though this is a negative remark on real political associations—his realization of the actual situations with regard to the ideal—let us dare to take it positively as a suggestion of the relation of the individual to the whole. Each person lives to actualize his or her character (the ship's route), but the degree of its achievement respectively varies. The line itself remains fragmentary to the end, and it seems to be an index suggesting a possible periphery, so that we naturally imagine the circle supposed to be virtually existent. It is not simply a matter of the shortness of a lifetime. The individual, according to Emerson, always misses the mark, because of its overabundance:

> Nature sends no creature, no man into the world, without adding a small excess of his proper quality. . . . to every creature nature added a little violence of direction in its proper path, a shove to put it on its way; . . . . without this violence of direction, which men and women have, without a spice of bigot and fanatic, no excitement, no efficiency. We aim above the mark, to hit the mark. ("Nature" 549)

Each one's realized character cannot be the ideal piece that fits the arc. The individual must tame the excess, the violence added to the direction of the index, and, without lapsing into being a "bigot" or "fanatic," must embrace it. The individual is a fragment aiming at an ideal arc that is nonexistent in the real world. To conceive of the individual as a possible fragment, so that if we could gather all of them, we could constitute the largest circle imaginable, is required here as an act of ethics. "All" cannot be realizable, existing only as a mark glimpsed in the imagination for a short while. Thus, in the early Emerson, what seems to be a conflict among individuals is dissolved into an imaginary limitless arc; this is an Emersonian way of showing how to *use* idealism in the real world, no matter how impossible it may seem to verify it. "All persons exist to society by some shining trait of beauty or utility, which they have. We borrow the proportions of the man from that one fine feature, and finish the portrait symmetrically; which is false" ("Nominalist and Realist" 576); the ideal human portrait remains undrawn, and, contrary to the general view of him, Emerson *affirms* it. "Let us go for universals; for the magnetism, not for the needles. Human life and its persons are poor empirical pretensions" ("Nominalist and Realist" 577): "All promise outruns the performance" ("Nature" 552). This is the point of what Stanley Cavell calls "Emersonian perfectionism" (13). There is no thought to glue individuals into a seamless whole, yet every individual can head toward it as a fragmentary index. It is in that process when the largest arc *actually* works, holding an imaginary position intact.

Emerson succeeded in producing concepts of the body, power, and the universal in his own aesthetic style. Those, after all, concern an individual's mental attitude, the thought affirming the individual without using the standard of *doing* or achieving things, and the way to affirm the weak and the small even if they cannot do anything, even if they are branded as the defeated. Though he did surely commit himself to political movements such as abolitionism, the essential aspect of Emerson is not political, and I do not view it negatively. Rather, it is the thought of waking individuals to move toward a life of which politics is only a part. In doing so, education or culture is of the highest value he claims for every community. It is an endlessly ongoing process of transforming "power" into the "unattained but attainable self" ("History" 239). According to Emerson, "We are by nature observers, and thereby learners. That is our permanent state" ("Love" 337), that is, "scholars." The process of that learning is, however, the process of undoing what one has hoarded in knowledge, as he says: "Let us unlearn our wisdom of the world" ("Spiritual Laws" 320). If human growth of survival by the "wisdom of the world" is itself a quite natural process, Emerson's learning as unlearning can be seen as *anti-nature*: his "nature" is unnatural in this respect. However, because of it, education in anti-nature has an inexhaustible possibility. It is the thing we should promote for the sake of using his inventive thought.

Works Cited

Arsić, Branka. *On Leaving: A Reading in Emerson*. Cambridge, Massachusetts: Harvard UP, 2010. Print.

Buell, Lawrence. *Emerson*. Cambridge, Massachusetts: The Belknap P of Harvard UP, 2003. Print.

Cavell, Stanley. *Conditions Handsome and Unhandsome: The Constitution of Emersonian Perfectionism*. Chicago: The U of Chicago P, 1990. Print.

Emerson, Ralph Waldo. *Essays and Lectures*. New York: The Library of America, 1983. Print.

Happold, F. C. *Mysticism: A Study and Anthology*. London: Penguin Books, 1963. Print.

Izutsu, Toshihiko. *Izutsu Toshihiko Chosakushu 1: Shinpi Tetsugaku* [*Mystic Philosophy: The Works of Izutsu Toshihiko Vol. 1*]. Tokyo: Chuokoronsha, 1991. Print.

Kateb, George. *Emerson and Self-Reliance: New Edition*. Lanham: Rowan & Littlefield Publishers, INC., 2002. Print.

Levin, Jonathan. *The Poetics of Transition: Emerson, Pragmatism, & American Literary Modernism*. Durham: Duke UP, 1999. Print.

Merleau-Ponty, Maurice. *The Visible and the Invisible*. Tr. Alphonso Lingis. Evanston: Northwestern UP, 1968. Print.

Robinson, David M. "Introduction: Emerson's Spiritual Principles." *The Spiritual Emerson: Essential Writings*. Ed. David M. Robinson. Boston: Beacon Press, 2003. 1–20. Print.

This paper is a revised version of part of my paper published in Japanese. ("Jiko no Bigaku to Shinntai / Chikara / Huhen."["Aesthetics of Self and Body / Power / Universality"]. *Bulletin of the Graduate Division of Letters, Arts and Sciences of Waseda University*. 61: II (2016): 5–19.) It is also supported by Japan Society for the Promotion of Science (Grant No. 15K02373).

Contributors

YOSHIKO FUJITA is Professor Emeritus at Nara Women's University. She is the author of *Amerikan Runessansu no Shosou* (*Exploring Imagination in American Renaissance*, 1998) and has published multiple essays on Emerson, Thoreau, Melville, Fuller and others. She is a joint translator of *Emason-Shisen* (*Selected Poems of Ralph Waldo Emerson*, 2016).

MASAKI HORIUCHI is Professor of American Literature at Waseda University. He is the co-author of *Melville and the Wall of the Modern Age* (2010) and *Sorō to Amerika Seishin—Beibungaku no Genryu wo Motomete* (*Henry David Thoreau and the American Spirit—In Search of the Origin of American Literature*, 2012). He wrote numerous essays on American literature and comparative literature.

SHOKO ITOH is Professor Emeritus at Hiroshima University. She is the author of *Dismal Swamp and American Renaissance* (Tokyo, 2018), *Thoreau for the Beginners* (NHK, 2017), *Yomigaeru Sorō* (*Reviving Thoreau*, 1998, Satake Publishing Prize), *Arunhaim heno Michi* (*The Road to Arnheim*, Tokyo, 1986), and many other books. She has published multiple essays on Thoreau, Poe, Hawthorne, T. T. Williams, Rebecca Solnit and others. Her articles have also appeared in numerous journals, including *The Concord Saunterer* 12/13 (2004/2005).

JUNKO KANAZAWA teaches English and American Literature at Waseda University. She is the co-author of *Emiri Dikinsun no Shi no Sekai* (*The World of Emily Dickinson's Poetry*, 2011) and *Dokusha Nettowāku no Kakudai to Bungakukankyo no Henka—19 seikiiko ni Miru Eibei Shuppanjijou* (*The Expanding Networks of Readers and the Transition of Literary Environment: British and American Publication since Nineteenth-Century*, 2017), and she has also published articles on Elizabeth Bishop, Herman Melville, and others. She is a joint translator of *Ramona* by Helen Hunt Jackson (2007).

ASAKO MOTOOKA, associate professor of American Literature at Hiroshima University of Economics, has published several articles on Louisa May Alcott and is the co-author of *Ekkyou Suru Onna—19-seiki Amerika Josei Sakka no Chōsen* (*Women Transgressing Boarders: The Challenges by 19th Century American Women Writers*, 2014).

ATSUKO ODA is Professor of American Literature at Mie University. She has written essays on Melville, Hawthorne and Emerson, and edited *Emason-Shisen* (*Selected Poems of Ralph Waldo Emerson*, 2016).

IZUMI OGURA is Professor of English, Department of Political Science, Faculty of Law at Daito Bunka University. She published *John Cotton and Puritanism* (2004) and edited *Sorō to Amerika Seishin—Beibungaku no Genryu wo Motomete* (*Henry David Thoreau and the American Spirit—In Search of the Origin of American Literature*, 2012).

KAZUTO ONO is a Professor Emeritus at Kyushu University. He is the author of *Sorō to Raisīamu* (*Thoreau in Lyceum*, 1997) and *Ikiteiru Michi: Sorō no Hi-nichijou Kūkan to Uchū* (*A Living Way: Through Thoreau's Unusual Places to the Universe*, 2015) . Also he is the translator of *The Maine Woods* (1992) and *The Moon* (2008) by Thoreau.

MICHIKO ONO obtained her PhD in American literature from Tohoku University and her MA in TESOL from Columbia University. She is the author of *Henry D. Thoreau: His Educational Philosophy and Observation of Nature* (2013) and the translator of *Little Masterpieces of Kenji Miyazawa, Vols. I & II* (2002). She has published many papers on Thoreau, and three are included in the academic works published by the Thoreau Society of Japan in 1999, 2004 and 2012.

NAMIE OZAWA is Professor of English and American Literature and Culture at Rissho University. She is the author of *Amerikan Runessansu to Senjumin* (*American Renaissance and Native Americans*, 2005) and has contributed numerous articles on William Apess, Pequot writer, as well as mainstream ones such as Thoreau, Poe, Hawthorne, and others to various journals.

MAKI SADAHIRO is Associate Professor of American Literature at Meijigakuin University. Her recent publications include "The Transatlantic Melville Revival and the Construction of the American Past" (*Sky-Hawk*, 2014) and "Anthological Form of Unity: Herman Melville's Battle-Pieces" (*Studies in English: Regional Branches Combined Issue*, 2014).

MIKAYO SAKUMA is Professor of English at Wayo Women's University. Her essays appeared recently in the *Japanese Journal of American Studies* (2011), *the Pacific Coastal Philology* (2015), and *A Passion for Getting It Right: Essays and Appreciation in Honor of Michael J. Colacurcio's 50 Years of Teaching* (2016).

AYAKO TAKAHASHI is Associate Professor of Nagaoka University of Technology. She is co-translator of *Gendai Amerika Jyosei Shishu* (*Anthology of Contemporary American Women Poets: Anne Waldman, Diane di Prima, Joanne Kyger and Jane Hirshfield*, Shichosha, 2012) and her articles have also appeared in numerous journals, including *Comparative Literature Studies* (PENN STATE PRESS).

YOSHIO TAKANASHI is Professor of English and American Literature and Culture at Nagano Prefectural College, Japan. He is the author of *Emerson and Neo-Confucianism: Crossing Paths over the Pacific* (2014). His articles have also appeared in *ESQ: A Journal of American Renaissance, Oxford Research Encyclopedia of Literature* (online), and *The Japanese Journal of American Studies*.

FUMIKO TAKENO is Lecturer of English at Nagoya Gakuin University. Her works include "The Marble Faun and the Problem of Regeneration" in *Chubu American Literature* in 2014, "Nasanieru Hōsōn no Bungaku Sekai no Kouchiku" ("Nathaniel Hawthorne and a Construction of Literary World—'The Virtuoso's Collection' as a Museum") in *The American Review* in 2013.

MIKAKO TAKEUCHI is Professor of English at Keio University. She has most recently authored "Foregrounding Otherness: Ralph Ellison's Interpretation of Melville's Works" in *Sky-Hawk: The Journal of the Melville Society of Japan* (2015). Her writings have also appeared in journals such as *Studies in Henry David Thoreau* and *Studies in American Literature*.

MIKA TAKIGUCHI is Assistant Professor at Rissho University. She is one of the contributors to *Hikaku Bunka Ronsou: Ibunka no Kakehashi* (*Collected Essays on Comparative Studies: Bridges to Different Cultures*, 2017) and has written multiple essays on Irving, Longfellow, Thoreau and others.

TAKAO YAMAGUCHI is Assistant Professor of American Literature at Tokyo University of Social Welfare. He is the co-author of *Sorō to Amerika Seishin—Beibungaku no Genryu wo Motomete* (*Henry David Thoreau and the American Spirit—In Search of the Origin of American Literature*, 2012). His articles include "Sorō no Niwa to Sen-i-suru Konkōdo no Mori" ("Thoreau's Garden and the Succession of Concord's Forest") and "Shizen no Dezain: Shamporion no Hierogurifu Kaidoku to Sorō no Wōruden" ("The Designs on "Nature": Champollion's Decipherment of Hieroglyphs and Thoreau's *Walden*").

YOHEI YAMAMOTO is Senior Assistant Professor of General and Cultural Studies at Meiji University. He is the co-editor of the two-volume collection on Environmental Humanities, *Kankyō-jinbungaku I & II* (Bensei, 2017). He wrote several essays on Thoreau and Melville from an ecocritical perspective.

Index

Thoreau in the 21st Century: Perspectives from Japan

2017年10月31日　初版第1刷発行

発　　行　日本ソロー学会
代　　表　高橋　勤（会長）
編　　集　堀内 正規

日本ソロー学会事務局
〒819–0395　福岡県福岡市西区元岡744　九州大学言語文化研究院
電話：092–802–5751
E-mail: tsutomu@fle.kyushu-u.ac.jp

発 行 者　福岡 正人
発 行 所　株式会社　金星堂
〒101–0051　東京都千代田区神田神保町3–21
電話：03–3263–3828　Fax.: 03–3263–0716
http://www.kinsei-do.co.jp　E-mail: text@kinsei-do.co.jp

組版／ほんのしろ　　装丁デザイン／岡田知正
印刷／モリモト印刷　製本／牧製本
ISBN978–4–7647–1173–0 C1098

©2017 日本ソロー学会